AN OAKWOOD VALLEY NOVEL

Meet Me in the Vines

GINSA MICHELLE

To the victims and survivors of domestic abuse, this story is for you. If you're on the other side, you're not alone. If you're still in the trenches, you're not alone.

If you or someone you know is in an unsafe situation, please call 800-799-SAFE.
You no longer need to suffer in silence. Your story is worth telling.

Content Warning

Please be advised, *Meet Me in the Vines* contains some difficult topics that could be triggering to some readers.

Topics that take place on the page are: vulgar language; sexually explicit content; sexual, physical and mental abuse; gun violence; loss of family members and grief.

Topics that are referenced but do not take place on the page are: alcoholism, fatal car accident due to drunk driving, physical and mental abuse of a minor.

Your mental health matters. Please only consume content you are able to handle.

With love,
Ginsa

Chapter One

AUDREY

10 YEARS AGO

"Donovan James King."

The entire auditorium erupts in a rip-roaring cheer. Oakwood Valley's golden boy struts down the stage with his winning grin, flashing his charm and confidence all over the place. The entire soccer team is pumping their fists as they chant his name. The administrative staff applaud with endearing respect—I swear I even saw a tear or two shed by the PTA moms. There's no use in holding back my smile. The boy is contagious. That's what the Donovan King effect does to you.

Donovan strides over to Mr. Frommling, earning a beam of pride from Oakwood Valley's notoriously tough-nut principal with a firm handshake.

Stop thinking about what else those hands can do, Audrey.

My heart races as I watch him take his diploma and pump his fist over his head, exposing his perfectly sinewy forearm. Instinctively, I lick my lips.

"I love you, Mom!" he yells into the crowd of families, causing a wave of laughs and sighs of adoration. I turn around to see my grandparents sitting near Donovan's family. We lock eyes and I give an enthusiastic wave in their direction. The smile in their eyes says it all. My heart instantly warms at the glow on their faces as they blow me a kiss. I blow a kiss in return, turning around in my seat to face the stage.

A swarm of butterflies takes flight in my stomach as I observe Donovan warmly hugging his teachers and sharing high-fives with our peers on his way off the stage.

He shuffles his way through a row of classmates to get back to his seat, beaming a smile that has my heart going a mile a minute.

My attention draws to Jess Taylor and Rosie Teak sitting in front of me, whispering salaciously to each other.

"Are you gonna hook up with Donovan at his grad party tonight?" Rosie smirks at Jess. Jess has the attention of every boy in this town. Her silky blonde locks cascade down her slender shoulders, stopping past her massive tits—like DDs since the seventh grade. Icy blue eyes frame the feminine features on her face: a perfectly slant nose and full lips. It's so annoying how hot she is. Not only does she have the beauty, she's got the brains too. Oh, and money. Lots of it.

Her family owns the largest vineyard operation in Oakwood Valley, sitting pretty on a whopping two hundred and fifty acres. Although we live in a small town, wine country competition is a real thing. Donovan's family has the second largest vineyard, automatically crowning them the Napa County Prince and Princess. Gag. Officially, they never dated—but the rumor mill would have you believe otherwise.

"Oh my god, Rosie, have some class," Jess says sarcastically, giggling under her breath. "But yes," she whispers with a hair toss, "I am totally gonna go all the way with him tonight."

I roll my eyes and feel a sudden wave of sadness—and a bit of jealousy. I never get invited to parties; I didn't even know the Kings were throwing one. And that says a lot, considering how small our town is. I only have myself to blame for not trying hard enough to put myself out there these past four years. It wasn't like Gran and Pop were keeping me from socializing or anything. I just preferred the company of characters in books and getting lost in whatever world I was imagining versus my reality. I truly only had one real friend, and she moved to Texas our sophomore year. She was the only one who could get me out of my books. Well, her…and a certain blue-eyed boy who holds the entire town in the palm of his hand.

Donovan King has been every girl's crush since elementary school. Including mine. Still is. There's no way to avoid his effortless charm—how it naturally drapes around him like a superhero cape—or his stunning smile that makes the world rotate on its axis. The best part about him? Zero god complex. Not an ounce of conceit in his gorgeous body, even if it looks like it's been sculpted by Zeus himself. Anytime he's in my vicinity, on a scale of one to can't function? I'm at can't fucking function.

I fidget with the ends of my academic cord wrapped around my neck, my eyes fixed on Donovan in the distance as he laughs with the classmates near him. I'd love to make him laugh one day. Those dimples he sports would be the death of me. I've always loved those dimples.

The first time I saw them, I was sitting on the balcony outside my room reading a book when I heard footsteps approaching below. I glanced up for a moment to see the sweetest matching dimples smiling at my pop. My first glimpse of Donovan King. And lucky me, I got to steal plenty of looks at Donovan, both at school and when he'd come to our estate to work with his dad. My family's winery uses the King's grapes for production and has for generations.

Although we ran in different circles, our interactions were subtle, yet memorable. At least for me. It'd be brief exchanges of kind smiles or a simple *"hey"* in the classes we shared. Every time it made my heart flutter.

My shoulders jump as the announcer lists off the Ws, directing us to stand from our chairs and head towards the stage. "You can do this, Audrey," I whisper to myself. I chose a low, chunky heel this morning to prevent myself from eating shit on stage. I summon all the confidence within me, proud of my achievement of graduating Summa Cum Laude at the top of our class.

"Isabel Nicole Whitt." Shit. I'm next.

Feet don't fail me now.

I take a deep breath, roll my shoulders back, and steel my spine. I scan the crowd to find my grandparents. As my eyes wander, a beautiful set of blue eyes finds mine. Donovan is smiling at me. That irresistible, impossible-not-to-faint smile. Time stands still. He's clapping, our gazes locked onto one another. The beauty of this boy is so unfair. God truly has his favorites. The sound in the gym dampens as Donovan and I hold each other in an intense stare. My mouth falls open as I bite my lower lip, utterly captivated by his deep, blue gaze. His hand motions forward while he mouths, "Go!"

"Ahem...Audrey Wren Winthrop."

I snap out of my trance and awkwardly hustle along the stage, stumbling when I get to Mr. Frommling. Kill me now. The principal catches my arm and stabilizes me, giving me a concerned smile. I don't make eye contact out of embarrassment, ignoring the raucous sound of my classmates' laughter. I shake his hand with haste, grab my diploma, and get the fuck off stage. I slink back to my seat, cheeks burning with humiliation.

I see Jess and Rosie whisper something to each other, look back at me, then laugh again. An unexpected wave of rage surfaces.

"Something funny?" I ask.

They turn back, shocked that I'm talking to them.

"Excuse me? Are you talking to us?" Jess asks with her eyebrows nearly up to her hairline.

No shit, Sherlock. I'm talking to you.

"Uh, yeah. Clearly? Did you find something amusing?" I snap. Jess Taylor made sure I stayed in her shadow ever since our freshman year. I'm not sure why, considering I didn't see myself as a threat to her. It would be so little as an eye roll as I passed her down the hallway or a light snicker while I ate my lunch. What did I ever do to her? Now that I've walked the stage and I'm one step closer to leaving this town, it's clear that the courage from this confrontation stems from simply not giving a fuck anymore.

Jess thins her lips, and Rosie gives her a look, their eyes darting back to me.

"Nope. Nothing amusing at all," Jess mutters, flipping her blonde locks in my face as she whips back around.

That's what I thought.

I cross my arms and legs, gripping into the flesh of my arms, leaving little half moon imprints from my fingernails. I take a deep breath and count backward from five—something my gran taught me when I was little.

It's almost over, Audrey.

The last of our classmates grab their diplomas, shuffling back to their seats. Mr. Frommling gives the closing ceremony speech as my chest bubbles with excitement. The anticipation builds throughout the room, an undeniable energy vibrating off everyone in a cap and gown. Our school song plays over the intercom as everyone sings loudly at the top of their lungs, knowing it's the last time we will be in this auditorium as students. We link pinkies and sway, chanting the final words of the song.

Oakwood Valley proud! Oakwood Valley bred! Oakwood Valley through and through, forever blue and red!

"Ladies and gentlemen, I present to you the Oakwood Valley High School Class of 2014!"

Roars fill the gymnasium. Caps fly into the air. Only seventy-seven of us are graduating, but it sounds like a stadium of thousands. A wave of relief washes over me as I smile at the ceiling–I did it.

I side-hug a couple of classmates around me and look to the ground to find my cap. As I bend down, a sudden spark ignites in my fingertips as a large, strong hand skims mine, deftly lifting my cap.

"Hey, Audrey," he says brightly.

I struggle to catch my breath. Glimmers of gold sparkle near his irises, framed by tendrils of chocolate-brown hair that peek out from under his graduation cap. As he beams, his sturdy jawline flexes, giving way to the irresistible charm of his dimples.

"H-hh-i Donovan," I stutter. He smiles at me softly, handing me my cap.

"I'm having a grad party tonight at my place, and I wanted to see if you'd like to come?" he asks, catching me off guard. My eyes get wide, swallowing the hard lump in my throat.

Holy shit!

"U-uh, I mean yeah. Yes. Of course. I'd love to come to your party," I reply a little too enthusiastically, like I forgot how to talk properly. Did he just find me in the crowd to invite me to his party? My stomach does somersaults, flipping and twisting my insides. I bite the inside of my cheek to keep from showing an embarrassing giddy smile.

"That's great," he beams, putting his hand on my shoulder. His touch alone erupts goosebumps down the length of my arms. "I can't wait to see you. And hey, congratulations on NYU. It's a bit far though, don't you think?" he asks.

His question throws me a little, but I can feel his genuine curiosity. Most of our class is staying in California for college, but I didn't want to. I need to get out of this small town.

"NYU has an amazing hospitality program. My dream is to open my own bed-and-breakfast one day," I reply.

I don't know why I am sharing this with Donovan in the middle of the chaos, but he's easy to be around. And that scares me. Is it always this easy around him? Or is this just his Donovan King magic that works on all the girls?

He gives me a smile that's ear to ear. When Donovan smiles, his eyes do too.

"That's amazing, Audrey. I'm so happy for you. You're going to crush it in New York. Don't forget about us when you're out there in the big city," he gushes.

I could never forget you, Donovan King.

My cheeks flush at his compliment.

"I'll see you tonight! Seven o'clock! Promise me you'll be there!" he shouts while walking backward, his voice getting further away.

"I promise!" I shout back. He gives me a wink and waves me off as he disappears into the arms of his soccer team.

I look down and smile at the thought that Donovan King is excited to see *me* tonight at *his* party.

Take that, Jess Taylor.

"Audrey, honey!" My grandparents push through the crowd as I run towards them.

"Gran! Pop!"

"Oh honey, congratulations! We are so proud of you," Gran beams, oozing with pride. She hugs me tight while Pop rests his hand on my shoulder and waits for his turn.

"She's right, kid. We are so proud of you. How about we get home and dig into your favorite cake to celebrate?" Pop asks, knowing cake is my weakness. Any dessert, really. My gran is the best baker. I'd give my kidney for her chocolate cake.

My eyes light up, and I hold them both tight, my arms around their waists as we head toward the gym exit. "That sounds amazing. But after, I may have plans..." I mumble.

Pop tilts his head to the side at my words and lifts one of his eyebrows. "Plans, huh?" I look up at him, smiling.

"Mhmm."

Gran gives me a mischievous grin. "Does this plan include a boy?" she teases. Gran and Pop raised me for as long as I can remember. My mother died giving birth to me, so Gran has always been the motherly figure in my life. She'd lend an ear when I'd talk about boys or have questions about love. She always knows the right things to say.

"Maybe," I sing, smiling at them both. "Donovan King invited me to his grad party. I think I'm going to go."

We pause at their car. "I never get to go to parties, and he invited me...personally." I look down, smiling, thinking back to the moment he found me in the crowd.

My grandparents give each other a look and nod. "Well, kid, you're eighteen after all, and it is your graduation. As long as you don't drink and drive, you should go have fun with your classmates and celebrate," Pop says with a smirk. He always inserts the safety quip, but it makes me love him more for it.

I give them both a kiss on the cheek and squeeze them tight. "Thank you. I'll meet you both back at the house for cake," I chirp. We wave each other off, and I grab my keys and head towards my car.

My phone vibrates in the pocket of my dress, and I grab it, thankful for the saint who decided women deserve pockets too. I flash a huge smile as I answer the phone. "Heyyy Tia!" I beam. My best friend screeches happily into the phone, causing me to flinch at the piercing decibel of her voice. Ever since she moved, it's been the hardest two years without her.

"Congrats on graduating, bitch!" she shouts, grunting like a linebacker at the word bitch. I laugh, shaking my head at her crassness, but honestly? I love her special way of showing affection. "Well, this *bitch* got invited to the hottest party in town," I say proudly, like it's the biggest accomplishment outside of my 4.0 GPA.

"Would it happen to be Donovan King's party?" she croons. I can hear Tia's smile on the other end of the line. *How the hell did she know about the party?* She continues, as if reading my mind. "It's all over social media, Audrey. If I lived closer, I'd totally be there! It sounds like the entire town is going."

I feel a small pang in my chest when she says that. Like my personal invite isn't special anymore because apparently the whole town is going to be there.

I sigh. "Oh, well, you know I don't do social media, so I wouldn't have known." Trying not to sound hurt. Ever since my dad made headlines in the paper when I was thirteen, I made the choice to stay off social media once I got older. The kids at school were already whispering around me, gossiping about my family and the drama behind it all. I didn't need to read it on the internet either. Tia knows that.

"Look, I love you and just wanted to congratulate you on finishing high school. I wish I were there to celebrate with you. I miss you so much, Auds." My heart sinks.

I fumble with my keys and slide into the driver's seat.

"I miss you too, bitch."

We both laugh and sigh at the same time, which makes us laugh even harder. "I wish you were here too, T. Thank you for calling. It means the world. I have to head back to eat cake with my grandparents, but I'll Skype you tomorrow, okay?"

"I can't wait. And get some dick tonight at the King's!"

She really knows how to get to the point.

"Aye aye, Captain," I huff out a laugh, turning on the ignition.

"Love you, Auds, talk to you later."

"Bye, T. Love you more."

I pull out of the parking lot as the call ends and watch the grape-laden hills rise and fall outside my window as I drive back to the family winery.

It looks like a tornado went through my room. There are clothes everywhere, and it's already 7:00 p.m., which means I am late.

"Ugh, nothing looks good on me!" I cry out in frustration and toss another not-quite-right top on the floor.

There's a faint knock at the door. "Audrey, sweetheart, may I come in?" Gran asks sweetly.

I sigh and plop myself down on my bed, tossing on a baggy sleep t-shirt.

"Yes, Gran, come in."

She softly opens the door and peeks in, ensuring I'm decent. Her eyes fill with concern at the sight of me lying on my back with tears pooling in the corners of my eyes.

"Oh honey, what's the matter? Can't find a thing to wear tonight?" Gran's forehead creases, softly shifting the stray hairs out of my face. I close my eyes as she brushes my hair through her fingers, so soft and delicate. She would do this for me after a bad day, instantly calming my nerves or negative feelings. My gran is special. Her aura glows like a rainbow, so full of life and color. It's hard to stay upset with an angel like her in my life.

"It's my first party, Gran. High school was supposed to be about making memories. I've been pretty terrible at that." I let out with a sigh, "And I have nothing to wear."

Gran gives me a soft smile and helps me sit up on the bed. She tucks a loose strand of hair behind my ear and holds my hands. "I remember when I was your age, I was feeling quite the same as you are now when your grandfather and I were about to go on our first date."

I sit up taller, loving when she tells me stories.

"I wanted everything to go perfectly, and my mother came into my room and held my hands, just like I am yours." She rubs her thumbs along the top of my hands. "She told me, 'Violet, if that man doesn't love how you look in a burlap sack, he's not the one for you.'"

I let out a giggle, and she leans in and kisses my temple. "All that means is, what's in here," she points to my heart, "matters more than anything on the outside. Be present and live life for today. The older you get like me, the more you'll understand. Can you try and do that for me, sweetheart?"

I wipe a single tear from my eye and hug her close. I bask in her scent of lavender and chamomile tea.

"Yes, Gran, I'll do that. Thank you."

She smiles and gives me a pat on my knee. "Great, now put on that burlap sack and have fun at your party that you are now—" She checks her watch. "Ten minutes late for." She heads for the door when I feel a quiver of insecurity rise from my stomach.

"Wait, Gran?"

"What is it, honey?"

"What if I show up and he pays no attention to me? I mean, Donovan is literally the most loved boy in this town. Have you seen Mrs. Dickson practically maul him every time we are at the diner?! Even the old ladies can't resist him!"

Gran puts her hands on her hips. "Hey now, I may be Mrs. Dickson's age, but I am not old," she teases.

"You know I didn't mean that *you* are old, Gran," I drawl playfully. "But what's so special about me? I'm not Jess Taylor or any of those other popular girls. I'm just..." I run my hands up and down my body before I slap them dramatically on my lap. "I'm just me." I sigh, running a defeated hand through my hair.

She hums, giving a pregnant pause. "Well, that's just it, honey. You're just you. And that's more than enough for Donovan King. Don't you think?" I feel a tug in the corners of my mouth. My grandmother always knows how to cheer me up when I am feeling small.

"And don't think I didn't miss him practically running to you after the ceremony today. A boy with a look in his eyes like that can only mean one thing." She has my full attention now and my eyebrows raise in anticipation of what I hope she will say.

"And what's that?" Butterflies start to form.

"That you will be the center of his night. Trust me on this, sweetheart." She gives me a wink and blows me a kiss, but before she shuts my door, I hear her voice trail off. "I've always liked that boy...." The door quietly clicks closed with Gran's footsteps receding, and I give myself a moment to digest her words, gripping the bed beneath me.

"You will be the center of his night."

Her words echo through my mind.

He invited me to his party, after all. It didn't feel like a pity invite either. It felt...genuine. Slowly, the insecurity and doubt that was rearing its ugly face earlier is fading. I puff my chest, lulling my head side to side before standing to my feet.

I feel a lot better after my pep talk with Gran, and she's right—he came to find *me* in the crowd. If Gran thinks I'm enough, then I can believe it, too. Now let's give Donovan King something to look at.

I sit down at my vanity and reapply some mascara, blush, and tinted strawberry gloss. I look in the mirror and spot an ivory sundress in my reflection that Gran gifted me last summer.

I turn around, my eyes smiling. It's flowy with thin straps crisscrossing the back. It's not too long, perfect to show a bit of leg. Tia tells me I've got great legs, so if there's anytime to show them off, it's tonight. It's a bit low cut, but fuck it. Not that my boobs are huge, but I can fill out a dress. I definitely can't wear a bra with this.

Maybe he'll enjoy that. I shake my head at the thought of anything happening with Donovan tonight. *Yeah right, Audrey.*

But I slip on a pair of white lace panties...just in case.

I decide to wear my hair down in loose waves and put on a pair of strappy wedges to give me some height. With the whole look together, I turn side to side in the mirror for final inspection. Not bad.

"Be the center of his night. Quit being a little bitch."

My pep talks to myself aren't as wise as Gran's, but it's enough for me to get my ass out the door.

Chapter Two

DONOVAN

The soft warm hue of the string lights above me cast a glow over the bustling party. Every direction I look, it's a classmate, a friend, folks from Oakwood Valley. A true sight to be seen. As I watch my friends dance with their hands swaying freely in the air, I exhale the most relieving of breaths. High school is over, and this summer is for me.

I pace slowly on the outskirts of the commotion, chuckling under my breath at my soccer teammates jumping up and down to an upbeat song with their arms around each other, howling into the night. Absolute barbarians. I love it.

My eyes shift to a table nearby that houses every school photo of me since kindergarten. Definitely my mother's doing. I pick up the picture of a five-year-old me, all gap-toothed and cheesing so hard my eyes are nearly closed. I laugh, my heart warming at how much I look like my little brothers in these younger photos. As if on cue, the little hellions appear in my periphery, swiping bits of my graduation cake with their mischievous grins—no doubt hiding from my parents.

I sneak my way over, light on my toes like a ninja ready to strike. I bite my lip to stifle a laugh as I reach my hands forward, gripping their shoulders with force. "Boo!"

"Ahhh!" they shout in unison. Their faces turn as white as the frosting on their fingers. Their shoulders relax when they realize their apprehender is me and a hearty laugh breaks out between us. I pull them in for a group hug, kissing the tops of their heads.

"You're lucky I'm the one who caught you eating my cake before Mom or Dad," I scold playfully, squeezing them both tight to me. They beam their wide, brace-faced smiles as I lean forward and swipe my finger through the cake, stealing a taste just as they did.

"Now, if you boys get in trouble, we all will. But Mom can't be mad at the graduate," I tease, ruffling their hair in my hands. My eyes flit back and forth between them, my best buds, my little brothers. Wyatt, the middle child, looks to me like I've hung the moon. Although he's fourteen, I still see him as the little kid who followed me everywhere. Then there's Kerry, the baby of the family. Our sunshine boy, always full of light and mischief. At eleven, he's a talented artist, always doodling and taking pictures on the digital camera my parents got him for Christmas last year.

Damn, I'm really gonna miss them when I leave at the end of the summer. I lean down once more, kissing their cheeks. "Go on, get out of here. I'll see you two in a bit. Love you boys."

"Love you boys," Wyatt beams.

"Love you boys," Kerry follows.

Love you boys.

Those words seal our brotherly bond.

Warmth spreads throughout my heart as I watch my little brothers disappear into the party. A small smile tugs at the corner of my lips. I'll take care of those two for as long as I breathe. I promised *him* I would. My chest squeezes as the memories of my big brother overtake me. Before I can sit in the moment, a firm clap on my shoulder makes me wince.

"Donovan! Congratulations on graduating, son." Frank Bozer has a deep, boisterous voice that you can hear from a mile away. Frank is the wine tasting manager at Audrey's family winery. Matter of fact, where is she? I glance over Frank's shoulder briefly to see if I can spot a beautiful head of strawberry hair. Frank clears his throat.

I bring my gaze back to him, wrapping my arms around his broad shoulders for a giant bear hug. "Thank you, Mr. Bozer. It's greatly appreciated." His collar smells of sweet grapes and rich soil. Just like home.

"Now, I have known you since you were just a spring chicken," Frank boasts. "I hope you're proud of your accomplishments leading up to this day, my boy. Your father told me you got All-State and MVP for OV High. Is that right?" I get embarrassed when my father brags about me, but I suppose it's his way of showing affection—if he even knows the meaning.

I clear my throat before I respond, putting my hands in my pockets and rocking back and forth from my heels to my toes. "Yes, sir. I was proud to help lead our team to state this year," I say.

"And *win*. Can't forget that detail, my boy," Frank adds. He winks and slaps my shoulder. My eyes beam with pride, remembering the sweet memory of the entire team holding up the state trophy, pouring Gatorade all over each other.

"You deserve that full ride to UC Davis, son. You make us all proud here in Oakwood Valley. I hope you know that," he gushes.

"I do, Mr. Bozer. I won't let you down." Frank shines his big smile and pulls me in again for a hug. Amazing how this man has shown me more affection in two minutes than my dad has in eighteen years. My father is charismatic and personable to everyone around him, apart from his own son.

Frank releases me as my father approaches.

"You know Frank, we knew this boy was talented in the sport since he was in diapers. But he's gotta keep at least a 3.7 GPA to keep playing soccer in college. He's got a big future here at the vineyard that he has to focus on," my dad says as the tension in my shoulders heighten. "That's more important than kicking a ball around. Isn't that right, Donovan?" My dad clamps a firm hand on my shoulder, revealing his showman smile to Frank. Leave it to Caleb King to rain on my parade.

"Well, Caleb, you've got a remarkable boy here. I'm sure he'll do just fine. Lighten up, will ya? Let the boy enjoy his night," he says with a soft smile. Frank always knows how to get my dad to chill out. "Let's get a beer then, Frank. Son, enjoy your party," my dad says flatly. Frank puts his arm around my father and whisks him away to the bar. Thank god.

My parents went all out. You'd think it was a wedding with all the catering, wait staff, and live music. They've got a knack for entertaining. I'll give them that. I grew up with my house being the main place of gathering for extravagant parties.

The music, the lights, the energy of this party? It's all absorbing into my skin, getting me amped up to ask out the perfect girl. My ultimate dream girl. If she shows, that is. It's already half past seven and I've yet to see Audrey.

My patience for socializing is running low. There are only so many monotonous conversations I can have when I only want to talk to her. Did I tell her what time to come tonight? I swear I did. I replay our interaction from earlier in my head, sifting through our conversation. God, she's pretty.

Focus, Donovan.

Surely I told her the party started at seven? What is wrong with me? I scan the space, searching for a glimmer of her sunset hair in the crowd. Everyone from school seems to be here. But no sign of Audrey. I sigh, pacing around the backyard, constantly glancing over at the gate.

I've waited years to get a chance with Audrey Winthrop. The quiet beauty lost in her books. My closest friends have known about my crush since middle school, but I never had the guts to do anything about it. Until today. She's the only girl who makes me nervous—like shaking in my bones nervous. But if she walks through that gate tonight, there's no going back. Senior year is over and I want this summer to be one I'll never forget.

"Hey, Donovan! What a turnout tonight, huh?" Rosie chirps in my face, obstructing my view of the gate. "Uh, hey Rosie. And yeah, everyone showed up tonight." Except the one girl I asked to be here. I crane my head around hers, and I'm hit with a sting of tequila as Rosie breathes in my face.

"You know, Jess has been looking for you since you kind of blew her off when she got here. I know that..." Her voice trails off when I notice a flash of movement at the entrance gate. My eyes immediately lock on as it slowly swings open.

Please be her. Please be her.

I don't have to daydream about Audrey anymore. She's really here. Holy shit, she actually showed up.

"Okay Rosie, see you later," I say mindlessly as I brush past her. My focus is on one girl and one girl only.

She glides in and bites her bottom lip.

Let me bite that lip.

Her silky strawberry-blonde hair shines under the string of lights. Her fair skin looks soft and supple. My mouth runs dry as I try unsuccessfully to coat the inside with saliva. I could fall to my knees at the sight of her. Even in her graduation gown earlier, she took my breath away. But seeing her like this? Wandering in like a fragile fawn, oblivious to her own beauty? It has me completely and utterly done for. I want to reach out and touch her. What's it like in that gorgeous head of hers? Would she let me in?

I watch her as she walks slowly through the crowd, returning the stares with a nervous smile. In front of me is no longer the girl with the awkward limbs. She's a woman. A goddamn goddess.

Fuck, I'm so screwed.

Audrey Winthrop is the most beautiful being I've ever laid eyes on.

My smile fills my face. One thought echoes through my head.

I have to talk to her.

The band kicks off the intro to "Make It With You" by Bread. This is my mom's request, no doubt. When I was little, I'd sit on our staircase and watch Mom and Dad dance in the living room to oldies music when I was supposed to be asleep.

Couples pair off, swaying slowly to the music, and drunk giggles fill the surrounding space. I can't get to her fast enough. My heart beats through my ears. How many more paces between us?

Our eyes meet and I sink into the pools of green that shine brightly at me. She walks towards me and smiles shyly, making my stomach flip.

We are face to face. I decide to be bold, grabbing her hands in mine. She gasps, but doesn't let go.

"Hey," I whisper, unable to hold back my smile

"Hey," she whispers back, her smile mirroring mine.

I walk backward, keeping her hands in mine, and lead her to the middle of the dance floor.

"Donovan…I-I just got here. What are you doing?" Her eyes flicker around the room. She's so fucking cute when she's nervous.

"I've been waiting for you. Dance with me?" I ask, praying I don't trip on my feet.

I pull her close to me, completely disarming her as my hands wrap gently around her waist. Her hands wrap around my neck in response and we sway to the melody. She looks down at her feet and bites her lip. A smile creeps on my lips and I tip her chin up to look at me.

"I'm not a good dancer. Everyone is staring at me," she murmurs.

"Audrey, they're staring because you look beautiful."

She rolls her eyes and I laugh at the gesture. "You're quite the charmer, aren't you?" she teases. One of her eyebrows lifts as she tilts her head.

"I mean it. You are stunning. And I am really glad you came," I confide softly. "What do you think of all of…this?" I ask, swirling my finger in the air, motioning to the whole setup.

"It's definitely up to the King standard. It's gorgeous. I'm pretty sure the entire senior class is here," she replies, glancing around the party. She's not wrong. People would've shown up, invited or not.

"You looked super cute at graduation," I tease, admiring the charming specks of freckles sprinkled like stars across the bridge of her nose.

Her cheeks light up with a sudden blush as she groans and rolls her eyes again, a dance of frustration and humor playing on her face.

"Oh my god, that was the most embarrassing moment of my life," she grumbles, burying her face in my chest.

"Did you not hear your name being called? He said it like three times!" I jest. I can't help but laugh. I love teasing her. I guess they're right in elementary school about boys teasing the girls they like.

"You didn't hear him because you just couldn't stop looking at me, huh?" I say playfully, biting my lip to stifle a laugh.

"You're not that cute, Donovan King," she retorts. I can tell she's lying since she breaks eye contact.

"Cute enough to make you trip and cute enough that now you're here at my house, dancing with me tonight," I whisper huskily in her ear.

I waggle my eyebrows, earning a playful hit to the chest with one of her delicate hands.

"Okay, okay, I'm sorry. I'll stop teasing you," I say.

I lift my hands in surrender, give her a grin, and grab her by the waist again, pulling her close to me. Damn, her pink lips look kissable.

"Okay, maybe you're a little cute," she chuckles, laying her head on my chest as we sway together.

I press my lips to her head, breathing her in. She smells like a field of fresh flowers and strawberries. We sway together, no words exchanged, just hearts beating.

A flash tears my attention from Audrey as I look toward the source. My friend Isabel holds a camera, her eyes fixed on the preview screen. "Wow, you guys are too cute. Let me take another. Smile!" she beams, pointing the camera at Audrey and me. Audrey chuckles into my chest as I lean my cheek on top of her head, flashing Isabel my best grin. Another bright flash. "Enjoy the night, you cuties," she sings, winking as she saunters off.

I look down at Audrey, whose face is bashful and coy. I open my mouth to speak, but before I can form the words, a bubbly voice cuts in. "Hey Donovan, you promised me a dance earlier. I've been waiting." I'm met by Jess' impatient gaze and signature hair flip. She's fixated on me, completely ignoring the girl who was in my arms only seconds ago. Audrey looks uncomfortable and puts her hands by her side. I immediately miss her touch.

"Jess, I was in the middle of dancing with Audrey," I grit, hoping she hears the annoyance in my tone and backs off. She doesn't.

"Oh, I'm so sorry, Audrey, you don't mind if I cut in to dance with Donovan, right?" Jess asks, giving Audrey the fakest of smiles.

"Go ahead. I'm gonna grab a drink. You two have a nice night," she replies curtly. As she moves to walk away, my hand instinctively reaches for hers. She looks up, her eyes widening in surprise, a delicate smile forming on her lips.

"I'll come with you. I'm thirsty anyway." I'm not planning on leaving her side tonight. I didn't wait all these years for my chance with Audrey to be stunted by Jess. No freaking way. I'm done being chicken shit. I let everyone else in my life dictate my decisions, especially my dad. He didn't want me dating or staying out too late. He had me hyper-focused on school, sports, and the family business. With Audrey in my grasp, there's only one thing I want this summer. And that's the girl in my hold with the forest green eyes I can't get enough of. For once, I'm going after what I truly want.

"It's okay, Donovan. You have a lot of guests here to talk to. Go make your rounds. I'll be here." She squeezes my hand and flashes me a reassuring smile.

I lean close and whisper, "Don't go too far. I'll come back to find you."

She bites her bottom lip and nods. I can't resist watching her beautiful backside as she saunters away. She is *definitely* wearing the hell out of that dress.

It takes all my willpower not to follow her right then and there. Jess stands firm in front of me with her arms crossed, pushing up her massive boobs. If I could roll my eyes further into the back of my head, they'd fall out.

Sure, Jess is an attractive girl. And yes, she's popular. Hell, most of my teammates would fantasize about being in my position right now. But I fantasize about one girl, and she's not the one standing in front of me.

"Are you going to make me wait any longer, or are you going to dance with me?" Her hands snake around my waist as the band picks up the energy with an upbeat pop song. I keep my hands to my side.

"Why are you wasting your time with Audrey Winthrop, Donovan? She's not one of us," she scoffs. Jess moves her body sensually to the beat, wrapping her arms around my neck. Discomfort overtakes me. Jess's touch feels nothing like Audrey's.

"One of us? What the hell does that even mean, Jess?" I ask in frustration.

"You know what I mean, Donovan. How are you going to deny our feelings for each other? Don't tell me you forgot about our amazing night after the state game. That meant something to you, didn't it?" she croons as she moves in closer, her hips bucking against mine. I take her wrists from behind my neck and peel her off of me. It was a drunken mistake to hook up with Jess. Impulsive and stupid.

I sigh, locking my eyes on hers. "Jess, that night didn't mean what you think it did. We were drunk. It never should've happened. I'm really sorry." I can see the hurt in her expression, like my words are a sharp dagger to her heart. A pang of guilt rises in my stomach. I don't want Jess, but I'm not a complete douchebag. And what I did to her was pretty douchey.

"Well, it meant something to me, Donovan. I want you..." She trails off, reaching for the collar of my shirt, pulling me in. Her lips graze mine, and I'm quick to shove her off of me.

"Jesus, Jess, that's enough!"

My voice booms enough to capture unwanted attention, causing heads to turn. "Look, I'm really sorry. Okay? I need to go find Audrey. Enjoy the party," I say dryly and walk away, refusing to look back at her.

I hear her scoff and shout at me as I leave her in my path.

"You're such a fucking dick, Donavan!"

Yeah, well, so be it, Jess.

"Dude, this party is the shit. Rosie Teak has been on me all night. Can I borrow your quad and take her down past the sunset house? I think we are totally gonna hook up tonight, man."

A laugh escapes me as I stare into my best friend's ardent eyes. Logan has been trying to get in Rosie's pants since sophomore year. He will probably revoke my bro card if I deny him. I shake my head, clasping his shoulder with a thud.

"Glad you're enjoying yourself, bud. Keys are already in the ignition. Stay on the path or Jeff is gonna kill you. Don't make me regret this." I say sarcastically in my dad voice. Our vineyard manager would shit a brick if he saw any unwanted quad marks on the soil.

Logan rams into my chest for a hug. We've known each other since birth. Our moms met in a yoga birthing class, convinced it would make their labor easier. Joke was on them. They bonded over mocktails and the kismet fact that their due dates were on the same day. I always give Logan shit for me coming out first, four days before him. We've celebrated every birthday together since we were one. He leaves for college in Texas at the end of the summer—our first birthday apart. Deep down, I wish he wasn't going so far away. But according to Logan, Austin is home to the most beautiful girls in the world. He'll need to show me where he cites that source because I'll have to disagree with him on that one. The most beautiful girl in the world is somewhere in this backyard, and I'm aching to get back to her.

"Thanks, man. I love ya. Go get your girl. She looks pretty lonely sitting there all by herself." Logan nods his head over behind me where Audrey is sitting by the fire pit holding a drink, gazing up at the sky.

"And looking fine as hell, might I add," he quips, waggling his brows. He lands a kiss on my head as I playfully shove him off, attempting to kick him in the nuts. He flips me off with both of his middle fingers as he shuffles backwards, shouting at Rosie to follow him. I shake my head and laugh, making my way to the fire pit with my hands nervously twitching in my pockets.

Audrey keeps her eyes on the sky, and I stand there, unable to stop myself from staring. She must feel my eyes on her, prompting her to turn her head toward me. Our eyes meet just as they did during graduation, and my stomach clenches at the sight of her. I move toward her, instantly pulled by her gravity. The moment I sit beside her, that bright white smiles melts my insides. I'm so gone for this girl.

"You came back for me."

"I told you I would. Having fun?" I watch the embers dance in her green irises as she stares into the flames.

"I am. I never get invited to parties, so I guess it's easy to keep me entertained," she says, her eyes finding mine. "Thank you again for inviting me. It seems I didn't do a great job making memories in high school. So this is...nice."

There's a sadness in her tone. I scoot myself closer to her and take the drink out of her hand, placing it on a side table. I grab both her hands and look down at her dainty fingers, gently caressing her knuckles.

"Donovan..." Her voice is barely above a whisper. "What are we doing?"

Don't be a chickenshit.

I take a deep inhale through my nose and breathe out slowly. I squeeze her hands and look up at her. "Audrey, I've known you my whole life. I know we didn't run in the same circles growing up, but that doesn't mean I never noticed you. I've wanted to ask you this for a long time and...now that we've graduated and have our futures ahead of us, I want to feel free this summer." I swallow. "I want to spend it with you."

I try to decode her expression, but her pinched brow unsettles me. She looks back at the flames, and I wonder if I've said something wrong.

"But...why? Why now? We barely know each other," she whispers as her eyes settle on our hands linked with one another. She studies them as if they're an ancient artifact, curious to how they fit so perfectly together.

I peek up at her gaze. "I know you got into NYU early admission and that you're one of the smartest girls in our school? I know your favorite author is Jane Austen because your nose is always in one of her books."

Her eyes widen at the Jane Austen comment. She starts to say something, but I need to say more, afraid she'll reject me.

"All I'm saying is, I may not *know you* know you, but I want the chance to. You're beautiful, smart, kind. I'm drawn to you, and I think I'll go crazy if I don't ask you," I stammer, kicking myself internally on why I sound like a trembling mess of nerves.

Get it together, man.

"So, Audrey…will you go on a date with me tomorrow night?"

I'm known for being a smooth talker, but this girl has me sweating through my shirt. Her hands squeeze mine as she scoots closer to me. With her cheeks adorably flushed, the corners of her delectable lips curve up in the most tantalizing way.

"Donovan, I'd love to."

Holy shit, she said yes.

Her lips are inches from mine. Strawberries and firewood engulf my senses, putting me in a dreamy haze that's all Audrey. I lean in, my nose touching hers. This is it.

A loud cough alerts me to my father on the other side of the fire pit, standing with his hands on his hips. Audrey jerks away quickly. An audible sigh escapes me.

"Hey, Dad…uh, you remember Audrey Winthrop?" I stand and straighten myself up while Audrey does the same.

My father doesn't move an inch.

"Hello, Ms. Winthrop. Donovan, a word, son?"

"Yes, sir." I turn to Audrey. "I'll be right back. Don't go anywhere," I whisper and tuck a loose strand of her hair behind her ear.

I walk past my dad, refusing to make eye contact. He puts a firm hand on my shoulder, spinning me around to face him.

"Son, what are you doing?" He looks at me with stern concern, which makes me entirely confused.

"What do you mean? I was talking to Audrey and enjoying the

graduation party that *you* threw for me." Would have been more enjoyable if he hadn't interrupted a kiss with the girl of my dreams.

"I don't appreciate the sarcasm, son. Look, I'm glad you're enjoying the party, but don't get involved with that girl. I don't want you getting tangled up with her family."

I take a step back from him and scoff. "Her family? The Winthrops have been nothing but amazing to us. I don't get where this is coming from, Dad." Now I'm pissed. "You don't even know her. Just let me enjoy my summer, please," I plead, on the edge of losing my temper.

I begin to walk away, but he holds me firmly in place by the wrist. "Son, I'm trying to help. You never met her father. That man is a dangerous drunk. Don't forget about what happened to your brother."

The tips of my ears flame with heat. I face him with annoyance and square up my shoulders, huffing an exasperated breath.

"You think I care what people say about her dad? It doesn't matter. She's nothing like you think she is," I mutter, keeping my tone stern and even. "And using James's death to dictate my dating life?" I scoff. "Low blow, Dad. Even for you." I try to keep my voice restrained once I notice I'm getting unwanted eyes and ears around me.

"I've done what you've asked. I graduated with honors. I was MVP and helped lead the team to state. I didn't date. I was always home on time." My frustration bubbles inside my chest. "The last thing you want is to push me away before I leave for school. Let me live my life. I'm *not* gonna stop seeing Audrey." His expression is hard like stone, but I can tell I've hit a nerve. I didn't expect to go toe to toe with my dad tonight, but here we are.

"Boys, everything okay here?"

Mom to the rescue. Grace King is a saint. My mom has a mythical way of calming the waters around her. Her ultimate super power. Since my big brother James passed two years ago, she's really been the one to hold us all together. The literal glue of our broken family. It was a drunk driver that killed James on impact, fresh off a debaucherous and deadly day of winery hopping. Grief hasn't been kind to my dad, and I've taken the brunt end of that. My brother was his golden child, his legacy—and my best friend. If he were here, he'd be slapping us both on the back of the head, wondering why we're always at each other's throats. James was always the voice of reason. The heartbeat of this family. He and my mom have that in common.

I stare at my dad, giving him the look of *"Don't you dare ruin this night for her."*

He reads my expression and puts his arm around her waist.

"Everything is fine, dear. Just telling Donovan here that we are very proud of him," he says with a hefty breath.

I smile at my mom and kiss her on the cheek. "Thanks for the party, Mom. I'm gonna head back to my friends. Love you." I reach out and give her hand a squeeze.

"Have fun, sweetheart. Let's get back to our guests, Caleb. Duke Taylor is looking for you. He says he has a proposal."

I roll my eyes at the thought of Jess's father trying to snake his way to do business with my dad. The apple doesn't fall far from the tree. Duke has been hounding my father for years, trying to get our grapes in his production line—but we've got a strict agreement with the Winthrops, regardless of my dad's personal hangups with Audrey.

"Okay, honey. Let's see what he has to say. Donovan." My dad gives me a nod.

"Sir."

I walk past him, my eyes dead set on a mission.

Make Audrey my girl.

Audrey's eyes widen as I stride with purpose toward her, my lips curling as I close in on the distance between us. "Donovan, what—"

Feeling a sudden rush of daring, I grab her hand, and together we run. With her hand laced in mine, we dodge bodies on the dance floor as the music thumps to the same rhythm as my heartbeat. Wild and free. Audrey's excited squeals set lightning to my feet as I bring us closer to escaping through the gate that leads out to the vineyard.

"Donovan! I'm wearing heels!" she giggles, catching her breath.

I stop in my tracks and stand in front of her. Her eyes twinkle under the stars, full of wonder and intrigue. I reach out and tuck a strand of hair behind her ear. Her cheeks flush with the prettiest shade of pink, matching her lips that I ache to kiss.

"Hop on my back then. I need to show you something," I murmur, grinning as she nervously averts her gaze. I lightly grip her chin to bring her gaze back to me, brushing my thumb along the bottom of her pillowy pout.

Her breath hitches at the touch. My hand rests on her delicate cheek, the other reaching out to hold her hand.

"What has gotten into you?" she whispers, her smile piercing straight through my soul.

This girl is going to be the death of me. I swear it.

"Come on, Audrey. Do you trust me?" I breathe out.

Our chests rise and fall together, feeling the surge of adrenaline and electricity forming between us. Without hesitation, she responds.

"I trust you."

Chapter Three

AUDREY

I've never been the spontaneous girl. The girl that lets the wind fly through her hair and leaves all her worries behind. But tonight, in this moment, I feel free for the first time in my life. My arms hold tightly to Donovan's neck and my legs wrap around his waist as we run wildly through the vineyard.

Our loud laughter fills the air, and I cling to his back, praying I don't fall off. My dress is flying up in the wind, feeling a little more exposed than I'm usually comfortable with, but with Donovan, I don't care.

I lean my head forward and nuzzle my face into the crook of his shoulder. I take a deep inhale, trying to memorize his scent. His sweat smells sweet, mixed with teak and firewood—probably from earlier.

I wish I could bottle up this smell and keep it forever.

"Donovan! Where are you taking me?!"

I shriek with delight as he picks up speed. My god, this boy is fit.

"Almost there. Hold on tight!"

Playfulness stretches across his face, the summer breeze rippling through his thick, brown locks. I hear the steady thump of his feet hitting the ground beneath us, mirroring my heart. His unfettered presence makes me feel awake for the first time in years, filling the deep cracks in my soul with his laughter alone.

His pace is slowing, bringing me back down to earth. If I weren't holding on so tight, I'd float up to the stars and take Donovan with me. I look past his shoulder and see a white gazebo ahead, adorned with the beam of the moon. A faint echo of music from the party lingers in the air. I realize it's just us two. Alone.

"We're here. You like it?" he asks as he gently puts me down and takes my hand, barely needing to catch his breath.

It's a simple wooden gazebo nestled within the vineyard. Some of the wood is weathered, and looking closely, I spy white strokes of paint from what looks like a stiff-bristled brush. But despite this simplicity, it's magical. Like a buoy in the middle of a vast sea of rolling grapevines. If planks of wood could talk, I'd want to know their story.

"It's breathtaking," I whisper softly.

I take my time moving up the steps, memorizing every divot and ridge along the rails as I drag my fingers across. I sense Donovan's eyes on me as he stands at the bottom of the steps, watching my every move. I feel an etch beneath my touch and tilt my head to read an inscription carved into the railing.

"*Meet Me in the Vines.*" My voice is just above a whisper.

My eyes stay on the inscription as I hear Donovan slowly walk up the steps, caging me in from behind, resting his hand on top of mine.

"The story goes that my great grandmother would sneak out late at night to meet my great grandfather here." His gravelly voice vibrates against my ear, spiking gooseflesh down my neck. "He proposed to her in this very spot."

His fingers trace up and down my arms, his lips gently graze the side of my neck. I lean back against him, letting myself melt into his touch.

"He sounds like a romantic," I croon, turning my head slightly and catch his profile. The perfect slant of his nose, the fullness of his bottom lip, the thick dark lashes that enhance the navy blue in his eyes. He wraps his arms tighter around me, smiling against my neck. He gently presses a kiss into my pulse, trailing down to my shoulder.

Could this be the rest of my summer? Sneaking away late at night, being held in the arms of a boy who unlocks every part of my heart? Would it be holding hands down Main? Stealing kisses in a gazebo?

I close my eyes, letting the doubt that forms in my stomach dissipate with his touch. I thought what I wanted was to leave, start a new life. So why is it that now, in this moment, I'm content to put that on hold? The Donovan King effect should really be studied by scientists.

Donovan turns me to face him, hands wrapping around my waist. His thumbs stroke the small of my back. He leans forward and presses his forehead to mine, our breaths matching one another. I snake my arms around his nape, eager to feel the electricity of his skin beneath my fingers, and draw our noses together to touch.

"I think I want to kiss you," he whispers. His eyes flit back and forth from my eyes to my lips.

Can he hear how loud my heart is beating? The thump in my ears is heavy. I hold my breath, anticipating our lips to touch.

"I think I want you to," I breathe out.

The corners of his lips tug up slightly as his lips finally meet mine. I melt into his kiss, like putty in his arms, letting out a soft whimper when he pulls me in against his hips. It's hot sparks and fire, and I let my mouth open slightly to invite his tongue. We explore each other, tasting the desire, learning each other. My hands tangle in his hair as our kiss intensifies, and in one swift movement, he lifts me off the ground.

My legs wrap around him, and he leads us onto a built-in bench. I settle on his lap, straddling him as the arousal in my core builds. This kiss is filled with years of wondering, full of *what ifs*. We grasp each other with need, like this kiss is the only thing keeping us alive. The temperature around us spikes, feeling more like the heat of a sweltering desert summer than a cool, brisk night.

I take notice of the throbbing ache between my legs, the euphoric sensations pricking along my skin with every touch from Donovan. He swallows each moan that escapes my throat, our desire tipping us closer and closer to the edge of losing my innocence.

Our lips part, giving us a moment to catch our breath. His eyes study my face, drinking in every detail. Heat floods my cheeks as his look intensifies, suddenly making me feel vulnerable. He reaches out and traces the freckles over my nose with his index, then down my cheek. His thumb rubs over my bottom lip, swollen with our kiss.

He leans in and smiles against my lips, peppering them with tiny kisses that lead down to the column of my throat. I tilt my head back and let out a moan that comes from the deepest desires of my body, melting away the vulnerability I felt just a moment ago.

"I could kiss you all night if you'd let me," he whispers. His voice is low and full of rasp, heat pooling between my legs at the sound.

"I'll let you," I reply. My words are breathless. The effect he has on me makes my vision blur and my brain go foggy. I'm dancing in a wild storm named Donovan, and I don't care that I'm in the middle of it.

"But first..." I bite my bottom lip, stifling a smirk that's creeping on the corner of my mouth.

I slide off of his lap and take one step back, still close enough where he can reach out and touch me.

"But first what?" he asks, one brow cocking up. His expression is full of intrigue. He leans back against the bench and crosses his arms over his hard chest. His eyes hang heavy from our intoxicating kiss as he runs a hand through the hair I tousled with hungry desperation. He looks good enough to eat.

"First, we play a game," I tease, flashing him a mischievous grin. A sudden bravery wraps around me like armor as I bend down and take off my heels, throwing them to the side. His hands rest behind his head, and that grin I can't resist forms on his lips.

"A game? Okay. I love games. For the record, I win at *everything*," he says the last part lazily, his legs spread wide apart in a confident stance. Even just the way he sits makes me want to jump on his lap and let him do unspeakable things to me.

I like this cocky side of him.

"Okay, Mr. MVP," I laugh. "But you've never played against me."

I lean forward, putting my hands on his thighs, dangerously close to his length. He looks down and groans.

"I think I like this game already," he growls, a smirk forms on his lips.

He runs his hands up the outside of my legs, trailing to my thighs. I push off him, and he scrubs a hand over his face in frustration. I like seeing him all worked up.

I could get used to this.

"The game is cat and mouse."

"Like tag?" he asks, curious where this is going.

"Yeah, exactly like tag. You're cat and I'm mouse. I get a ten-second head start, and the gazebo is home base. Close your eyes while you count, though."

He flashes me a smile and stands to his feet.

"Okay, fair enough. So, I get to kiss you all night if I win?"

He walks towards me, and instead of stepping back, I wrap my arms around his middle. I look up at his towering frame and lean in, my lips barely touching his.

"*If* you win," I whisper, pressing my lips into the corner of his mouth.

I gently push him back, daring him to take a dive with me into the unknown. Tonight, we play. Tonight, we explore the possibility of an unforgettable summer together. I'm willing to take the leap if he is.

"Are you ready?" I ask, adrenaline spiking through my veins.

"I was born ready, baby," a low growl rumbling from the depth of his chest.

He slips off his shoes and socks, leaving him barefoot on the planks. He gives me a wink, puts his hands over his eyes, and starts at ten.

Ten…nine…

My bare feet thud on the soft grass beneath me, inhaling fresh soil and crisp summer air as I leave my laugh trailing behind my steps.

Eight...seven...

Donovan's voice fades the further I run, already wishing I could turn back to be near him.

Six...five...

I lick my lips. His taste lingers like my favorite dessert, sweet and delicious. I instantly want his mouth back on mine to satisfy my craving.

Four...three...

Maybe I'd let him catch me.

Two...one...

Maybe not.

"You can't hide from me forever!" Donovan's voice cuts through the night. I see him walking a couple of rows away from me as I tiptoe in the same direction he moves.

"Yes I can," I say in a sing-songy voice, his head whipping toward me, catching a peek of me through the vines.

The moon is high in the sky, its beams reflecting off the top of his chocolate hair. We mirror each other in step, our eyes lock through the stems. My upper lip curls under my teeth, trying to hold back the smile that's taking over my face. I see a sheen of thin sweat over his brow and just below his collarbone, feeding a hungry desire in me to end the game now and reach out to touch him. I didn't think sweat could turn me on.

His eyes rake me up and down as we stare at each other through an opening in the vines. He scrubs his hand over his jaw and clenches.

"You in that dress..." he moans, shooting an arousal through my heat.

"You like this dress?" I tease, pulling the hem of my dress up to flash him a peek of my white lace panties.

His mouth gapes open and a low growl rumbles in his throat. His tongue swipes at his bottom lip as he takes a step toward me.

I take a step back, keeping the hem of my dress up. My eyes lock onto his. The navy hue turns black with desire, hungry like a wolf who hasn't had a meal in days. He's on the verge of feral behavior, and I'm savoring every moment.

He takes another step, like he is waiting for my next move. I take another step back, this time slipping the strap from my dress down my shoulder.

Just as he gets close enough to touch me, I take off running and leave him in my dust. I halt a couple rows over, expecting to find him on my heels, but he hasn't moved. He stands with his hands on his hips, flashing that beautiful grin.

"Don't you want me to kiss you all night, Mouse?" he yells out.

I bite my lip to keep me from laughing. Mouse. I like that.

Hell yes, I want you to kiss me all night.

"Come and get me!" I yell back, and he darts in my direction. I shriek and make a run for the gazebo. A hearty laugh bubbles from my chest as I hear his footsteps gaining. The gazebo steps are just ten strides away. My breathing is erratic, laced with uncontrollable giggles.

Just as I'm about to reach the steps, I stop in my tracks.

Donovan's momentum carries him forward as he lunges toward me, hooking his strong arms around my waist. His face buries into the crook of my neck, his hard chest pressed against my back.

I turn to face him, and he lifts me up, cupping his hands beneath my thighs. We both breathe hard in unison, smiling at each other. He licks his lips—my eyes follow.

"I win," he says in a husky tone.

My eyes stay on his lips, my hands wrap around his neck.

"You win."

I could've stepped on the gazebo steps and ended our night right then and there. Thanks for a great kiss. Goodnight. But we both know that this night isn't the end. It's just the beginning.

"So, do I get my prize now?" he teases, knowing full well he gets to kiss me as much as he wants. But I don't want just the kiss. I want more.

"Take me into the gazebo," I say with full confidence, knowing exactly what *I* want for once.

He crashes his lips into mine, our tongues grappling. Is it too soon to crave the way he tastes? I want it every second of every day.

He carries me up the steps with his mouth sealed on mine, his hands gripping my bare skin with the force of a hurricane. Wild and untamed.

I break the kiss and find his hooded gaze, happy to drown in his ocean blues. He slowly lowers me, every curve of my body pressing hard against him. My bare feet find the wooden planks beneath me, my hips glued to his.

I feel his steely length press against me, sending desire tingling through my entire body.

"Donovan…I want you."

I breathe out, clinging onto him like my life depends on it. My hands slip under his shirt and trail up his back, lightly scratching the length of his spine. The heat radiating off of his skin lights a burning fire inside me—I need to explore every inch of him. I feel his skin prick up in goosebumps, and he lets out a deep moan.

"Are you sure, Audrey? I want you to know that I didn't bring you all the way out here for that."

He brings his hands up to frame my jaw, face full of concern, as he shifts the loose strands of my hair aside.

His eyes search mine for hesitation, but he won't find it. I want this to happen. I *need* this to happen.

"I've never been more sure of anything. I want you to be my first. Please," I beg, desperate for him to touch me. I kiss him hard with need.

His hands grasp the hem of my dress, gathering the ivory fabric by the fistful. I lift my arms and close my eyes, letting the dress come up over me, bearing everything to him.

His eyes widen slightly, surprised to find my bare breasts under my dress. Here I am, in my most vulnerable state, standing in nothing but my panties. My body pulses with heat as he reaches back behind him to pull his shirt off over his head.

Holy shit, he's gorgeous.

The center of his night.

"You are the most stunning girl I have ever laid eyes on," he says breathlessly.

His hands explore my body, tracing the curve of my breast, trailing up my ribcage and down over my shoulder. It sends a shiver down my spine, turning me to jello.

He grips the soft flesh on my hips and pulls me close, his fingers toying with the band of my panties. My hands sweep over his chest, down to his washboard abs. His skin is hot to the touch, lighting my fingertips with every trace.

He bends down to kiss my shoulder and snakes his tongue up to my neck. I lull my head to the side and hum in pleasure, letting him take his time kissing and licking my skin.

My hands grip the button of his jeans, pausing as I reach for his zipper.

"Do you have protection?"

He nods and reaches into his back pocket, pulling out a condom. I give him a teasing smile. "Didn't think this would happen tonight, huh?"

He smiles and kisses me deeply, his tongue moving languid against mine. Our mouths cling together as I pull down his zipper and let his jeans drop, pooling at his ankles. He breaks the kiss, kicking them away, and I trace the outline of his bulge against his briefs with my eyes.

We stand nearly naked—breathing, shaking, nervous as hell. He grabs my hands, pulling me close. Our foreheads press against each other, eyes closed, and fingers linked.

I'd always imagined what it might be like to lose my virginity one day, but I never thought it would feel like this. It feels safe. And I'm ready.

"Audrey, I just want you to know that I've never done this before. This is my first time, so I'm sorry if I'm not very good…or…if I don't last very long…" He holds my hands and presses my knuckles to his lips, shaking.

His first time, too?

I'm surprised at how nervous he is. Donovan King is never nervous, but here he is in front of me—trembling.

I open my hand to his cheek, and he kisses the inside of my palm.

"It's okay, I'm nervous too. I trust you," I whisper.

I give him a reassuring smile, tracing my thumb along the length of his jaw.

"I trust you too," he replies, leaning down to plant kisses along my collarbone and on my chest.

With my hands in his, he gently lowers us onto the floor, laying me down beneath him. His hand grazes over my mound, radiating my heat and arousal in the palm of his hand. I shudder at his touch, tilting my hips up toward him to take off my panties.

He hooks his thumbs in the bands and slowly slides them down my thighs, his eyes drinking in every inch of me. He licks his lips, and I'm about ready to combust.

I prop myself up on my elbows, pointing with my eyes at his briefs.

"Oh, shit," he mutters under his breath. A small giggle escapes my throat as he frantically pulls down his briefs. My eyes stretch open at his size. Was he sculpted by Zeus himself? *Wow.*

He grabs the condom and rips off the foil, his hands trembling as he tries to coax it out of its package.

"Fuck," he stammers, his fingers fumbling with the opening of the latex. I notice his growing frustration, so I lean forward and wrap my hands around his, stilling his movement. He looks at me and lets out a deep breath.

"Donovan, it's okay. Let me do it."

I smile softly and take the condom. My free hand presses against his arousal. His eyes close and he quivers against my touch. My hands should shake, but they stay steady, keeping calm under the pressure. A small smile tugs at my lips, seeing Donovan nervous.

I make him nervous.

I slide the rubber down his length and thank Ms. Harrison in my head for the health class demonstration junior year that day with the bananas.

I lay back as he settles between me, adjusting himself.

Now I'm nervous.

This is it. He kisses me gently, and I feel him at my entrance. My arms wrap around his nape, pulling his face close to me. Our chests touch, our heartbeats thud in unison.

"Are you ready?" he asks, voice shaking, and I nod my head quickly, biting my bottom lip so hard it leaves a stinging indention.

And just like that, I give Donovan my whole self. Every part of me belongs to him.

This night will always belong to us.

Chapter Four

AUDREY

The room is pitch black. I wake up slowly, my brain moving faster than my body. The piercing sound of my alarm jolts me out of my hazy slumber. I feel around me, moving my hands across the satin sheets. Kellan is gone—must have been an early morning in the office.

I turn over, hitting stop on my alarm. My hand shuffles around the top of my bedside table, hunting for the remote that opens my blinds.

"Damn it."

I hear it drop on the floor.

I grunt in frustration, hanging half of my body off the bed precariously like the floor beneath me is a dozen stories down. After several unsuccessful flailing attempts, the remote is finally in my grasp. I sit up, gripping it tightly in response to last night's gnawing migraine returning with a fresh lash of pain.

Well, I'm in a fucking mood.

I push the top button, prompting the thick velvet blackout curtains to open. As the morning sun peeks in, I squint my eyes and let out a loud yawn. Rolling over, I swipe my phone from the night-stand and check my notifications.

KELLAN

Good morning. Be at the office by 8:30 am. I need you to sort out some files that came in late last night.

I swing my legs over the side of the bed and do some quick stretches, bending my neck from side to side, taking in the city skyline.

This view never gets old. You'd think six years of the same view might lose some magic, but it's the glint on the Chrysler Building that gets me out of bed most days. That's the New York I dreamed about as a girl in Oakwood Valley. I'm just not sure it really exists anymore.

Kellan owns the entire top floor of this penthouse, giving us three hundred and sixty degree views, forty floors up above the city. It's the buildings outside of these walls that make this penthouse to die for—I certainly don't feel at home inside of them.

Once upon a time, I *had* felt it was my home, I suppose. It was my sophomore year when Kellan laid his charm and devilishly handsome looks on me. I was nineteen, my heart still wounded and vulnerable from the events of the previous summer. Kellan was an adjunct at just twenty-two, commanding a lecture hall on hospitality with his quick wit and unfailing confidence. How could I not be smitten?

He strode with confidence toward me after the keynote, instantly flushing my cheeks with heat. I was drawn to the attractive curve of his lips as he spoke, his voice smooth like aged whiskey. I lapped up every delicious word he'd say, hypnotized by him. Consumed by him.

His wealth and power were mesmerizing; I couldn't fathom the level of importance his family held within New York's elite. He was next in line to take over after his hotel-magnate father and stood to inherit a wealth unlike anything I've ever seen. Coming from wine country, I thought I knew rich—but not this level of rich. This was like, never ever worry about your life ever again rich.

I wondered then if I could ever form my own legacy. My dream of opening my bed-and-breakfast shrank with every year passed, working the mundane role of Kellan's personal assistant. Scheduling, emails, meetings. More meetings. More work that smothered the fire of my dream, now a distant memory.

A deep exhale escapes me as I walk into the shower, letting the hot water pelt my body. I wince when it hits my shoulder and gaze down to see a deep bruise. My fingers brush across the lesion softly, as they've done numerous times. I survey the rest of my body wherever my eyes can land, noticing trails of dark blues and purples along my shoulders, neck, and arms.

The first time it happened, the shock overtook my entire body, paralyzing my senses. The sharp sting of a strong hand across my face. I immediately reach up and brush my cheek in response to the memory. Feel that sting enough times, you learn to comply. You learn to be obedient—no matter how hard you shake the iron bars you're trapped behind, wailing for help.

A single tear slips from the corner of my eye, merging with the water as I let the stream of the showerhead rain over my face. Flashes of Kellan gripping my shoulder with force boom behind my eyelids, shoving me against the wall for being defiant.

"When I say get me off, I mean now. Not when you decide, but when I do."

It isn't until I'm gasping for air that I realize I've water-boarded myself beneath the showerhead, forcing me to escape the flashback from the other night.

I pant with fervor as the emotions build within my chest. To calm myself, I pump a generous amount of teak-scented soap into a loofah and lather myself in small, circular motions. My eyes close, and I allow the familiar scent to send me back in time, escaping to a much warmer memory. Ocean-blue eyes appear, and I feel safe to drown in them.

My face is buried in the nape of his neck. We run into the night, moonbeams glowing off his glorious skin. I breathe him in, instantly high off his smell. My hair is wild, my spirit is free. My smile is so big they pinch the apples of my cheeks. His laugh weaves in and out of my ears, the soundtrack to my life. His touch ignites a burning flame within me, and his kiss only stokes it further. I feel him all around me.

"Almost there. Hold on tight!"

I'm trying to hold on. I really am.

My phone vibrates on the bathroom counter, startling my eyes open. I let the remaining tears fall, quietly slipping away from my revery. I steel myself for another day ahead.

Don't make him angry today, Audrey.

I step out and dry myself off, wrapping the towel around my body. My wet hair sticks to my shoulders as I look in the mirror, not recognizing the girl staring back.

Her strawberry blonde hair is now covered with semi-permanent brown hair dye because that's what he wants. Her green eyes are sunken and dark, no longer bright and beaming. Bruises pepper her skin from a man who claims to love her. She's lost her spirit, her strength. She's lost herself.

"How the fuck are you going to get out of this, Audrey?" I whisper to her in the mirror, my eyes red on the edges.

I stare down at my phone with Kellan's name lit up on the screen. It taunts me, posing as a daily reminder of how fucked up everything is. Yet, I pick up the phone anyway, opening the text thread with Kellan.

KELLAN

Are you awake? I'm missing you this morning.
Please don't stay mad at me.

I sigh, running a hand through my wet hair. Anger brews from the pit of my stomach, almost to the point of nausea. My thumbs tremble, furiously tapping into the keyboard, unable to stop the emotions spilling onto the screen.

AUDREY

I'm fucking angry with you. You hurt me! Why? Why do you do this to me?

I pause as my breaths grow more tattered, my jaw ticking like a fuse running quickly to ignite an explosion. The anger suddenly turns to pleas, aching for something so tantalizingly out of my reach. *Love.*

AUDREY

> Why Kellan? What did I do to deserve it? Why can't you just fucking love me?

An unbidden tear splatters on the screen. I wipe my eyes quickly and take the end of the towel wrapped around me to wipe it off my phone. I stare at the words I've typed, my lip quivering as my thumb hangs over the send button.

delete

AUDREY

> I just got out of the shower. I'll be on my way shortly.

I turn on the lights to the massive walk-in closet that Kellan had custom made. A wave of leather and cedar enters my nostrils. A stark black marble island sits in the middle, filled with jewelry and watches that are worth more than the penthouse itself. Floor-to-ceiling shelving houses Kellan's expensive dress shirts, carefully pressed and ironed—not a wrinkle in sight. His suit collection oscillates between midnight black to ocean navy, reminding me of a certain pair of eyes I just can't shake.

My work clothes fill a whole wall. Or, more accurately, the clothes Kellan picked out for me fill a whole wall. It's all muted, neutral tones. Chiffon and silk blouses and skin-tight pencil skirts. Below my somber wardrobe is a row of wooden drawers with gold accented knobs that showcase an array of lingerie. Kellan says lingerie is part of the uniform, in case he wants to have his way with me in his office. Which happens more often than not.

I slip on a black lacy thing to put underneath my outfit for the day, which is basically scraps of material that do a horrible job of covering anything. Kellan will like it, though.

I opt for a high-neck blouse to cover the bruises. I slip on a form-fitting pencil skirt and sheer black thigh highs with a seam running up the back. I find a pair of black pumps and a black blazer to finish the look. My prison uniform. Hopefully, this is enough for Kellan today. I don't have the energy to put up a fight.

I sit at my vanity and put on my makeup the way Kellan likes. Dark, smoky eyeshadow, thick mascara, and a dark red lip. A low bun, tiny gold hoops, a spritz of Chanel No. 5 and I'm the perfect imitation of a powerful woman.

I flick the light off as I make my way into the open-concept living room. Kellan designed this place with the starkness of a modern art museum. The room is slate gray and expansive, punctuated by a black leather sectional exactly in the center and authenticated art acquired at private auctions adorning the walls. Perhaps the most garish is the chandelier gleaming above the sofa, making this apartment feel more like a billionaire's lair than a home. Because that's exactly what this is—this is Kellan's place, not mine.

"Darling, I have taste. You don't have to worry about any of the design. I'll have my people to take care of everything."

At the time, I thought he was spoiling me, not wanting me to lift a finger. I found it endearing, as if he knew what I would like because he had me in mind when building our—*his*—home. Now I know it for what it really was: control. Control over every decision when it came to us. When it came to me.

"Eat this, Audrey. It's good for you." "Wear this, Audrey. It suits you." "Do it like this, Audrey. You know it drives me wild for you."

He wore manipulation like a mask, infiltrating every crevice of my soul. I fell in line, unable to resist his pull. I didn't realize until I was far, far deep in the hole, that I was no longer myself.

I grab a banana from the counter and shove it in my purse, my heels clacking against the black marble floor with every step I take. This apartment is cold. Lifeless.

I clutch my purse and head toward the elevator. There's a soft ding one floor down as my momentum slows and the door opens to a familiar face with a wispy handlebar mustache.

My neighbor gives me a bright smile and a polite nod as he enters the elevator.

"Morning, Ms. Winthrop. Busy day today?" he bellows. The heavy hand he had with his cologne this morning wafts in the enclosed space, making me lightheaded the second it engulfs my nostrils.

Richard Hammond is kind enough on our morning elevator rides. He's a lot like Pop—friendly and wise with a warm buttery voice that wraps you like a comforting hug. Today is not a day I feel like making small talk. But I do it anyway.

"Good morning, Mr. Hammond," I say in the friendliest manner I can muster. "Busy as always," I chirp with the fakest of smiles on my face.

More like busy contemplating my life choices.

Mr. Hammond's gaze drifts to my wrist, and my own eyes follow, spotting a bruise subtly emerging from beneath the cuff of my blazer. I immediately shove my sleeve down over it, giving Mr. Hammond a nervous smile.

"Are you alright, honey?" His voice carries a warm concern, mirrored by the worry creasing his forehead.

"Oh, that's nothing," I chuckle with false bravado. "I'm so clumsy. Always bumping into things."

I've never been a good liar. I couldn't get away with it growing up either. My grandfather could always read it all over my face. He knew I wasn't okay that summer before I left, ignoring my insistent claims of *"I'm fine"* and *"Nothing happened."* I think that's why he didn't argue when I asked to leave for New York two months early. We didn't talk about it, but he seemed to understand that I needed to leave and put the pieces back together.

The man standing before me now, still looking at my covered bruise, has the same intuition. It must be a grandfather thing. I know he doesn't believe me, but he doesn't probe any further.

"Alright, well, you know that if you ever need anything, you let me know. Okay, sweet pea? I mean it."

Don't cry. Don't cry.

"Thank you."

I need to get the hell out of this elevator.

To my relief, we finally reach the ground floor, and he gestures for me to exit first. I nod and walk into the lobby toward the gold carousel doors.

"Have a great day, Audrey. Good seeing you."

"You too, Mr. Hammond."

We wave goodbye, and I walk toward the town car waiting for me outside. I tug at my collar, wishing it wasn't so high up my neck. It's warm out today, with summer approaching quickly in the city.

My bodyguard stands at the car door.

"Morning, Ms. Winthrop. Everything alright?" His voice is low and gravelly, but warm.

"Morning, Briggs. I'm fine, thanks. I'm set for breakfast today, so no need to stop. Straight for the office, please."

Kellan hired Briggs as my personal security when I moved into the penthouse. We'd become unlikely friends. Allies, really. He doesn't hover, but his build alone can intimidate anyone who breathes on me. His protective nature makes me feel safe. A lot safer than I feel in that penthouse.

Sure, he has tattoos lining his enormous arms and his tailored black suits make him look like a CIA agent. But inside, he's a big ol' softy.

"Yes, ma'am."

He opens the car door for me, and I struggle to slide in, feeling the confinement of this goddamn skirt. As the car slides forward, my phone buzzes with a text.

KELLAN

Great. Let me make it up to you, little bird. Stop by my office when you get here.

I roll my eyes and toss my phone in my purse. *Little bird.* My skin crawls when he calls me that. He sees me like a fragile little bird, shivering in the palm of his hand—her wings clipped, unable to fly away.

I stare out the window, watching the hustle and bustle of the city, wondering what their lives are like compared to mine.

I hope they're happier than I am.

I reach up and touch the bruise on my shoulder and shudder at the pain.

Chapter Five

AUDREY

I knock on the door to Kellan's office.

"Come in."

He's sitting in a leather chair behind his massive desk, a rich brown oak that matches the ceiling-height bookshelf behind him. The windows are large and grand, showcasing the impressive New York architecture that surrounds the office. Sun flares reflect off the tile floor and his dirty blonde hair, slicked back with stiff pomade. His tall, lean frame is draped in a fitted gray suit. His Rolex glints in my direction, catching the light from his office and reflecting straight into my eye.

He flashes a grin in my direction, his dark brown eyes gleaming as he pulls out a bouquet of red roses from underneath his desk.

"Hey, little bird. Come here," he says softly. He rolls his chair back, motioning me to sit in his lap. I shut the door, and he points to the lock. I oblige and click the lock into place.

"These are for you."

He hands me the roses and pulls me down onto him, my back pressed against his chest. I bury my nose in the petals to inhale morning dew and fresh-cut stems.

"Thank you, Kellan. They're lovely," I whisper. If I had a nickel for every rose he's given me after his outbursts, I'd be richer than him.

It's moments like this when he is soft and disarming that have kept me in his hold for so long. Kellan knows how to lift me so high that I swear he would never hurt me again, only to drop me so low that I can't see a possibility of surviving this.

"Let me show you how sorry I am for the other night," he murmurs into my ear. Leather and spice sting my nose as he scrubs his rough stubble over my cheek. I flinch at the texture, and he grips my chin, forcing me to meet his gaze.

"Kellan, you hurt me. Why do you do that?" I say with a break in my voice. I know why. It's because this is who he is. He needs control over everything and everyone in his life. Especially me. Isn't being an heir to an international hotel empire enough? Isn't loving me enough?

His eyes soften as he loosens his grip on my chin. That's the look. The look that has me coming back, over and over. It says, *"I won't hurt you again." "I promise, I'll do better." "I love you."*

"Little bird, I already told you I was sorry," he whispers huskily. The pad of his thumb rubs against a bruise on my neck. I shudder at his touch, squeezing my eyes shut to keep the tears from slipping.

My heart is in a tug of war with anger and forgiveness. The ache is too much to bear—I melt into his touch, craving the love I desperately want. He smirks, feeling my submission.

"See, I knew you'd forgive me," he growls, his voice suddenly dark and ominous, sending chills down my spine. In the blink of an eye, gone is all the tenderness, the soft Kellan I try so desperately to reach. He trails kisses down my neck, sucking and biting my flesh. I tense my body at the pressure he holds on my hips as he grinds himself underneath me. My breath quickens as his touch becomes harsher, his desire searing through me as it burns my skin.

He cups his hands around my breasts, squeezing my nipples through my blouse.

"Take this blazer off."

He lets out a grunt, stripping the sleeves off my arms and tossing the blazer on the floor. My vision blurs through the dam of tears I refuse to let loose.

His large hands spread my legs apart, his fingers graze over my panties. Not an ounce of arousal is in me. I'm just a body built for his pleasure, and I hate myself for it. He calls it love, but I call it punishment.

Punishment for allowing myself to sink deeper into Kellan's hooks and being too weak to do anything about it. Punishment for letting my father put those same evil hooks into me for my entire childhood.

A vision of my father adds to the sting in my eyes. I smell his whiskey breath. His strong hand strikes my face. I hear him screaming at me. *"It's your fault your mother died."*

Kellan brings me back to reality as his hand comes out from under my skirt and grabs my neck, nearly choking me. This is an angry grab, not an aroused one. Sadly, I know the difference.

"Why aren't you wet for me?" he growls out. I freeze and hold my breath. Like if I breathe, it will start this chain of violence that I so desperately want to escape. The way he touches me should turn me on, but it doesn't. There's no warmth. No play. No intimacy. It's cold and fueled with revenge. It's laced with an anger I can't explain. Of course it doesn't get me wet.

"I'm sorry, let me help with that," I breathe out. More lies. More deceit. I have to survive, and if that means giving my body to Kellan, then so be it.

With my back still pressed against his chest, I slightly turn my torso and put my fingers in his mouth, taking him by surprise. His eyes suddenly go dark and desire fills his face as his erection hardens underneath me.

He stands me up and grabs my wrist, guiding it under my skirt to touch myself. He takes my neck and pushes me down on his desk, slamming my face on its side. I feel a sting of pain and hear a slight ringing in my ear. His spicy cologne floods my senses, making me nauseous.

I hear him frantically taking off his belt and pushing down his suit pants and briefs. And with one painful thrust, he enters me with no warning. I wince at the lack of wetness. He thrusts again, forcing me to adjust to his size. He keeps one hand on my neck, pinning me to his desk, and the other on the small of my back. He grunts and speaks filthy words to me, but all I do is stare into nothingness. No love, no pleasure. A tear falls across the bridge of my nose as he thrusts faster, finding his release inside me.

As soon as he finishes, the pressure of his hands lets up, and I stand, wiping the tears quickly before he sees. I smooth out my skirt, and he turns me to face him, kissing me hard. His tongue invades my mouth like an unwanted visitor, but I let him in anyway. He breaks the kiss and looks into my eyes.

"I love you, little bird."

I used to believe him. I used to love him. Or whatever I thought love was. But this—this is not love. This is delusion.

"I love you too."

Another lie.

The workday is a blur. Most days are. After my morning with Kellan in his office, I excused myself to a private restroom on our floor and scrubbed my intimate parts raw with soap and water while I cried. I hate that he was inside me, and I hate myself more for tolerating it.

Back at my desk, I gather myself and do what Kellan tasked me to do, filing paperwork for prospect hotel locations and setting appointments on his calendar. I notice he has a business trip coming up next weekend and pray that I don't have to come with. The thought of being without him for a weekend gives me more joy than I've had in years.

I fantasize about this glimpse of freedom, losing myself to the possibilities. Maybe try out a new recipe to bake. Eat gelato on the Met steps. Go to the public library and get lost in a sea of books.

The vibration of my phone interrupts my daydreams. I see my grandfather's picture light up on the screen, and my heart drops. I haven't called in months. Hell, I haven't seen them in nine years. I'm running from home, and everyone knows it. The guilt gnaws at me from the inside out.

The last time I saw them was at the San Francisco airport waving goodbye after a short visit home for Christmas during my freshman year at NYU. Kellan came into my life the following semester, and well, I got swept up.

The longer I stayed away, the longer I *needed* to stay away. I couldn't tell them the truth about my relationship, my facade of a life. So I don't tell them anything at all.

I hesitate to pick up, bracing myself for the voice on the other line.

"Hey, Pop. Look, I'm really sorry I haven't called. I've been so busy here and—" I stop when I hear stifled sobs on the other end. The uneasy feeling in my stomach grows, and I hope that whatever comes out of his mouth next will extinguish it.

I stay quiet until he speaks.

"Audrey, I'm sorry to let you know that Gran passed away early this morning. She died peacefully in her sleep, hon, and she loved you very much."

My hands lose feeling, and my phone drops to the floor, my knees following quickly behind. I grasp at my chest with a hand, feeling nauseous, like my insides are about to fall out. Pop's muffled voice calls out to me, the sound trudging through mud. I bury my face in my hands and sob.

Gran is dead. And I wasn't there.

Guilt and bile rises from the depths of my stomach, and I heave into the trash can under my desk. I wipe my mouth with my sleeve and grab the phone off the floor, shakily pressing it into my ear.

"Audrey, honey? Are you there?"

I take a deep breath, my legs crossed beneath me on the floor.

"Yeah, I'm here, Pop." Quiet sobs take over me, shaking my shoulders up and down.

"Audrey, sweetheart, you listen to me now," my grandfather croons gently. "Don't put this on yourself. It was her time to go. She knows how much you loved her. She lived a full life with no regrets. It's okay, honey."

I can hear the heartbreak in my grandfather's voice. She was the love of his life. They had been together since they were eighteen years old. Sixty years of love. And here he is, comforting me when it should be the other way around.

"Pop, I need to come home." The reality of returning to an Oakwood Valley without Gran hits me with another wave of sickness.

Take a deep breath, count backward from five.

"I'll book a flight right away." My voice cracks, unable to shake the sudden grief that sinks into my body.

"I would love that." Pop pauses to collect himself. "Just...come home, kid." His voice breaks, shattering my heart into a million tiny shards all over my office floor.

"Of course, Pop. I'll look at flights now and text you when I book."

Is it truly home without Gran? How can I think about setting foot in Oakwood Valley when a huge piece of my heart is gone? But that's my fault. I never came back to see her. I dug myself a hole so deep that it took her dying for me to find the strength to climb out.

"Sounds good, honey," his voice falters. "And Audrey...I'm so sorry."

I shake my head. "No, Pop, I'm sorry. Talk to you soon. I love you."

"I love you too, sweetheart."

I stay seated on the floor for minutes after the line goes dead, held down by the weight of the news. I didn't think this day could get any worse. One phone call quickly proved otherwise.

Kellan strides into the room and finds me on the floor. I look up at him, mascara streaking down my cheeks.

"What happened?" he asks dryly.

I scoff in my head. No, "are you alright?" No hugs. No tenderness.

"My grandmother passed away this morning. I just got the call," I say in a curt, emotionless tone.

"Oh, well, I'm sorry to hear that. I'm wrapping up, and then we can head home," he says, plowing right ahead. "I was thinking we could pick up dinner from that new Thai place on St. Mark's Place?"

I shake my head and push myself up to stand.

"I'm booking a flight to go home for a few days. I need to be with my grandfather." We speak as if we're in a business meeting.

His eyes remain fixed on his phone, typing up something that I'm sure can wait, showing zero empathy. This is supposed to be the man who loves me. Gran just died, and here he stands, emotionless—assuming I'm just void as he is.

"Fine." His body tenses. "When?" he asks with a slight annoyance in his tone. I shrug it off, not able to deal with it right now.

"Whenever I can, Kellan. It just happened. I don't know. But I have to go," I sigh.

"Okay. I'll send Briggs with you," he clips.

It doesn't surprise me in the slightest that Kellan didn't offer to accompany me. Of course he would have Briggs be a stand in, as if my grief is nothing but an inconvenience to him and his schedule.

I furrow my brows in frustration. "No. I don't need Briggs. Please, I'm going home to grieve. Let me have this. Alone." I sound defeated, but there's no emotion left in my body after today.

He never brings his eyes up to me. They just stay on that goddamn phone. I put both hands on my desk to brace myself, suddenly feeling light-headed.

Take a deep breath, count backward from five.

"Alright then. No Briggs. Let's go home. I'm starved."

He leaves my office and a tidal wave of relief washes over me. It's rare for him to agree with me, but when he does, I don't dare draw any attention to myself for fear that he may change his mind. I'm relieved to escape from him, even just for a weekend.

Back at home, we sit silently across from each other, eating our takeout. I glance up at Kellan while he sends off email after email, scooping yellow curry into his mouth.

I used to find his mouth so sexy, the way his bottom lip forms a pout, the slight curl in his top lip to form what I used to think was a dashing smirk. Now, all I see is rage.

He catches me staring and cocks up his eyebrow. "Like what you see, little bird?"

I give him the fakest of smiles.

Yes, Kellan. Of course, Kellan. Whatever you want to hear that will get me on this flight and away from you.

"You know I do." Another performance. "I booked my flight for next Thursday. Briggs will drop me off at the airport, and I'll be back the following Monday night."

I get the information out as quickly as possible, praying he doesn't linger too long on the fact that I'll be out of his reach for five full days. So I play the game—stalking over to him, spreading his knees apart, perching myself on his lap. I dig my fingernails into his nape, earning a low groan from the base of his throat.

"Oh? Is this what I have to look forward to when you come home?" he drawls, raking his hands down my backside, squeezing me hungrily in his palms.

Mission successful. I feel his length harden beneath me as he gives me a devious smile. He lifts me and puts me down on the dining table, stripping me naked.

I let him have his way with me until he has no more left to give. He's breathless, his forehead resting on my bare chest. I feel the warm liquid drip between my thighs, but on the inside, I'm drowning in my own screams.

Chapter Six

AUDREY

One week after the worst phone call of my life, the wheels finally touch down in San Francisco after an anxious six-hour flight from JFK. I was thankful that Kellan had already left for the office when I woke up this morning, so I didn't have to say a physical goodbye. Thank god. I take my phone off airplane mode and a few texts come through.

KELLAN

Good morning, little bird. I will be on a red eye to Chicago tonight through the weekend. Don't stay away too long. I don't like having you far away from me.

I roll my eyes and reply.

AUDREY

I just landed. I'll be back Monday night. Have a nice trip.

Of course, he doesn't care that I'm going home to spread my gran's ashes. All he cares about is making sure my ass is back in New York when he says. I feel lucky to have this much time away from him. A tiny ball of hope forms in the center of my body, brimming with the brightness of being out of Kellan's shadow. I look back at my phone and message my pop.

POP

hi honey. let me know when you land. can't wait to see you, have a safe flight

AUDREY

hey Pop, i just touched down. i'm getting a rental and will be there in about 2 hours. love you.

POP

very excited to give you a hug. welcome home.

Home. My chest tightens at the thought of a bear hug from my grandfather and seeing Oakwood Valley again. During the entire flight, I was a mess of nerves. Would everything look the same? Is Mrs. Dickson still hitting on younger guys at the diner? Are the teenagers still hooking up at Sunset Valley Point?

Is *he* still around?

I close my eyes and whisper his name for the first time in ten years.

"Donovan."

It's strange having his name leave my lips. I cursed his name a thousand times before I left for New York all those years ago and then I promised myself I would never say his name again. But I just did. Truthfully, I thought about him the entire flight. I thought about him nearly every day for the last ten years. Donovan.

We were just kids all those years ago, but he took something from me I could never get back. He took my body and my heart, then crushed it to dust.

The memory of me sitting on my front porch, waiting for him to show up in his dusty blue pickup, is a painful one. I sat in a wooden Adirondack chair, checking my phone every two minutes, hoping he would text or call. My heart dropped with every minute that passed, doing everything I could to hold back the tears that were stinging my eyes. Forty-five minutes, an hour, then two. The sun set selfishly behind the lush green of the valley, driving the stake further into my heart—he never came for me.

I felt so foolish for letting him in the way I did, thinking the night we spent together actually meant something more than just a one-night stand.

He used me, then tossed me away. I was so naïve to take his words at face value. I believed the tremble in his words as he shook like a leaf before asking me on the date that never happened that night around the firepit. The promise of a summer together, his sweet musings about how amazing our night together had been. It was all just words. Nothing but bullshit. Words to get my clothes off and claim me as another one of his trophies. I believed him with my whole heart when he said it was his first time, too. I learned to never believe him ever again. No call. No texts. No word from Donovan King for ten years.

I shake off the memory and grab my carry-on from the overhead bin. I don't want to think about the possibility of seeing Donovan again. I'm here for one thing and one thing only. To spread my favorite person in the world's ashes and say my final goodbye to her. My gran.

I almost forgot how stunning the drive into Oakwood Valley is. The beautiful peaks and valleys of the wine country landscape nearly take my breath away. I've been surrounded by traffic and skyscrapers for too long. For the first time in a long time, a bubble of hope brews inside me. Hope for a better outcome in my life. Hope that I'll escape the nightmare waiting for me on the other side of the country. But for now, I'm taking Gran's advice to live for today.

The closer I get to Oakwood Valley, the stronger I feel. I can't avoid the pull, no matter how hard I tried to stay away.

This town and all the amazing people in it. I chose to leave. I chose to forget. And now, I hoped it would choose me back and welcome me with open arms.

I pass the charming wooden sign on the side of the road that reads, "Welcome to Oakwood Valley." A mixture of excitement and nerves swirls inside my stomach. As I approach Main Street, I roll my windows down to take in the scene and the smells. It's like going back in a time machine. Nothing has changed. The Golden Grape Diner, with the best burgers and fries in town, flashes its open sign. Vintage Blossom Flowers has a row of beautiful bouquets outside their storefront—I see lilies, Gran's favorite. My favorite coffee shop, Sip & Savor, has its door invitingly open, spilling out the smell of freshly ground coffee beans and sugar in the air.

As if on cue, my stomach grumbles for a sweet pastry and a caramel macchiato. I take an empty parking spot in front of the shop and put the car in park. I walk in and see a young barista drying some mugs while two people sit in the cafe with headphones and laptops in front of them. She greets me with a friendly smile.

"Hi! Welcome to Sip & Savor. What can I get ya?" I can't help but smile back at her inviting and warm energy. She has a slight lisp and big brown eyes. A little thrill runs through me as I admire her icy blonde hair, painted with pink streaks. Kellan would hate it, so I love it. I look at her name tag, decorated with an Oakwood Valley High School and guitar pin.

"Josie, is it?" She gives me a friendly nod. "I'll have a caramel macchiato, upside down, non-fat to go, please."

"You got it…?" Her words hang in the air like she's waiting for a pin to drop until I realize she's asking for my name.

"Oh, my god, I'm so sorry. It's Audrey," I let out with a nervous chuckle.

I have to remember how to socialize with small-town folk. Everyone here is so outwardly friendly that they want to know your name and invite you to dinner that night.

She lets out a giggle.

"No worries. It's nice to meet you, Audrey. So, are you visiting Oakwood Valley? I've never seen you here before." She talks and makes my drink order at the same time, her eyes darting back and forth between me and the coffee bar.

"I guess I'm visiting. I'm actually from here, but it's been a long time since I've been home. I'm here because my grandmother passed away last week."

I realize I may be oversharing, but since I've stepped foot on home soil, I feel like a different person. It's like the small town safety bubble wraps around me, something I don't get with Kellan in the city.

Josie stops and puts down the to-go cup she was about to pour my coffee into. Her eyes widen as she stares directly at me.

"Oh my gosh, are you Violet Winthrop's granddaughter?"

I shouldn't be surprised at this. My grandparents are well-loved in this town; I'm sure her passing has touched many people here.

"Yeah, I am," I answer, giving her a sympathetic smile. Her mouth opens wide as her hand goes straight to her chest.

"I am so sorry for your loss. Violet was the best. She and Noah would come here every Sunday morning to grab cinnamon rolls and hot chocolates together."

I smile at the thought of my grandparents walking hand in hand down Main on their favorite Sunday morning tradition. I feel tears stinging my eyes, but I try to keep them at bay. I'm not trying to cry the first five minutes I get into town.

"Yup," I say, popping the P. "That's my gran and pop." Pride swells in my chest, knowing everyone loved them together.

Josie pours the rest of my coffee into the cup and shuts it with a lid. She hands me a napkin and grabs a cinnamon roll from the display case.

"Here, Audrey. It's on me."

"Oh, no, Josie, that's okay. Let me pay—"

"For Violet."

That's all she has to say, and I shut my mouth, giving her an appreciative smile as I raise the contents in my hand as a thank you.

I turn to leave when a sign on the bar catches my eye.

Winthrop Wine Special Happy Hour. Friday 7:00–10:00 p.m. That's tomorrow night.

"Hey Josie, where can I put down these cases?"

A raspy, masculine voice cuts through the air. I turn around to drink in a tall man sliding through the doorway. His face is blocked by the wine cases he's holding, corded forearms straining from the weight. I scan his tanned arms down to his rugged hands — they grip the boxes as if they weigh nothing at all. My eyes trail down to a pair of faded blue jeans that hug his strong thighs, squeezing in all the right places. *My god.* I crane my head at an angle to try and get a good look at his face, but all I can glimpse is a peek of chocolate brown hair from behind the boxes.

"You can go straight to the back and put them on the wine shelf! I organized it all for you earlier," Josie replies, raising her voice above the whir of the espresso machine.

He angles himself in the opposite direction, not letting me get a look. Jesus, his body is built like a god.

"You got it. Thanks, Jojo." There he goes again with that sexy voice.

Who is this guy? He walks past me, his face hidden on the other side of the cases. His back muscles press against his white cotton tee, a trail of sweat beading down his spine. He's been working hard today. Can the back of someone's head turn you on? Because the back of his head is *definitely* a turn-on. His ass fills out the back of his jeans, flexing with each step he takes. His masculine scent lingers as he kicks open the door to the back room, filling the air around me with musk, teak, and sandalwood. I didn't even see his face, but I want to bottle up his smell and bathe in it.

So this is how it feels to be horny. It's been a long time.

With the sexy mystery man out of range, I come back down to earth and return to my conversation with Josie, who thankfully missed my peep show on the man with the perfect ass.

"Josie, what's this Winthrop Happy Hour about?" I ask, setting down my coffee on the bar and leaning forward to rest on my forearms.

"Oh, duh," she laughs. "You're literally a Winthrop. Noah made a Cabernet Sauvignon dedicated to your grandmother before she passed. Violet's Vintage, Noah called it. Then once the news hit, we decided to hold a happy hour in honor of her. And of course, we had to stock lots of Violet's Vintage," she beams with a megawatt smile.

"Huh. I'm sure I'll hear all about it from my grandfather when I get home. Violet's Vintage…I love it." I take a swig of macchiato. "Will you be there?" I ask.

"Yup! I'll be playing some live music. Too young to drink, though," she jests. We both laugh, and she turns around, wiping the equipment with a wet towel.

"Is that why you have the guitar pin? You're a musician?" I point to her pins on her apron. Her face lights with pride. "Sure am. I'm a singer/songwriter, play guitar and piano, and I also teach lessons around town."

"And you go to Oak Valley High?" I ask.

"I just graduated. I'm going to Berkeley College of Music in the fall. Just working this summer to save up."

I already admire this chick. She's driven, hardworking, independent. Everything I wanted to be at her age. Hell, everything I want to be right now.

"Wow. Congratulations. Getting out of Oakwood Valley is a big deal. And for music? I can't wait to come to one of your sold-out shows one day," I gush.

"Thanks, Audrey. That's the plan!" Her dreams are so big they fill the entire room. Maybe, if I bask in her optimism long enough, my dreams will grow big and bold like hers.

The swinging of the back door steals my focus.

Mystery man emerges, sans boxes. His tousled hair covers his eyes as he gazes down at his boots. One glorious hand reaches up to his face, pushing away thick locks of hair. His eyes flit to meet mine.

Oh. My. God.

Those deep ocean blues are the ones that haunt my dreams. My body freezes in place, my feet root into the ground. I can't take a breath—the oxygen is gone. Non-existent.

He takes a moment to register who I am as he slows his pace, coming to a full halt when it hits him. You could cut the tension with a knife, electricity buzzing in the ten feet between us. My heart beats in my ears, my chest tightens, and I feel suddenly lightheaded.

"Audrey?" he utters softly, like if he were to speak any louder, I'd vanish into thin air.

I open my mouth, but no sound comes out. There's a tornado of anger, confusion, hurt, and happiness swirling inside of me. He takes a step closer, and I take a step back, the edges of my eyes brimming with tears. The tension in my shoulders shakes, the oxygen in my lungs leave all too quickly.

Facing him? Impossible. It's like staring down a storm. I swivel and flee the shop, my feet barely touching the ground. I race to my car with the singular thought of escaping that beautiful disaster behind me.

Chapter Seven

DONOVAN

My heart beats wildly out of my chest. I didn't expect to see her right here, right now. There's so much I want to say, but I can't utter the words. I whisper her name, like a ghost from my past, convincing myself that this moment is real.

I almost didn't recognize her with light brown hair. Had she dyed it? Or had it been ten years of time naturally changing it? Her makeup is heavier than I remembered. Are the tiny freckles that I love still underneath?

But man, those eyes. Those forest green eyes still take my breath away.

"Audrey, wait!" I shout, stumbling out after her. I need to be close to her. I need to explain myself. *I need to*—I stop my train of thought before I get carried away, imagining that maybe we could start again.

She ignores me completely, rightfully so. She forcefully pulls open her car door and slides in the driver's seat in record time. The door slams shut as soon as I approach her window. My palms slap the glass, desperate for her attention.

"Audrey, please! Wait!"

I see Josie in my peripheral vision, holding Audrey's coffee and a paper bag on the curb. My eyes refocus on Audrey as she fumbles with her keys, struggling to put it in the ignition.

"Shit," I stammer, swiping the coffee from Josie. I hear the engine rip alive and sprint back to the driver's seat window as she whips her car in reverse.

"Audrey! Your coffee! Damn it," I yell out. She peels out of the parking spot, her tires squealing as she furiously turns the wheel and speeds down Main.

"Fuck," I mutter. I pull my keys out of my pocket, sprinting to my truck parked a few spots down.

"Donovan! The cinnamon roll!" Josie shouts from the curb. I wave my hand in the air as I approach my driver's seat.

"Leave it, Jojo! Gotta go!" I shout back, shoving Audrey's coffee into the cupholder.

"Ow, fucking shit!" I cry out, splashing hot coffee on my wrist. The engine roars, and I speed out on Main, desperate to catch up with Audrey.

My mind is going a million miles an hour. What would I say? Would she give me the chance to explain? Seeing her is like seeing a rare comet burning through the sky with only one chance to catch it. This is my chance.

I take the familiar turns toward the winery. I lean on the gas, tearing down the winding driveway as oak trees blur past on either side, the Winthrop Estate in view just ahead. A ball of dust covers my windshield, kicked up by her tires.

One conversation, Audrey. Just give me one conversation.

I add frantic pressure to the pedal, gaining precious ground. Suddenly, her brake lights flash red.

"Jesus Christ!" I shout, slamming hard on my brakes.

Her car door flies open, and out comes an angry, gorgeous Audrey.

I throw my car in park and fling open the door. Her long legs stride toward me, and she slams my door shut before I can get out.

"Why are you following me? I need you to leave. Now!" she shouts angrily.

The swell of her breasts moves up and down with her erratic breathing, and I can see her nipples pebbled beneath her skin-tight, olive green tank top. Her leggings cling to every curve as if sculpted out of marble. Her pink lips part in a tantalizing pout, instantly making my mouth dry. My dick twitches at the sight of her, and I shake away the thought, realizing it's not the time to fantasize about her.

She takes the cardigan she's wearing and wraps it across her chest, her arms crossing over her breasts like an extra layer of protection from me. I roll the window down and put my hands up in surrender. She glares at me with daggers, ready to puncture any hope I have of explaining myself.

"I'm sorry. I wasn't trying to follow you," I say softly.

She scoffs and tears her gaze away from me, looking towards her house.

"Donovan, I don't want you here. Turn around and get the fuck off my driveway," she demands, her words frothing with hate and frustration. I take it all because I fucking deserve it.

But god, hearing her say my name, even in spite, restarts my heart.

I grab her coffee from the cupholder and hang it out of the window, gesturing for her to take it. "You left this. Take it." I say, arching my eyebrows.

She crosses her arms. Her stare is cold like stone. I give her a playful grin and swirl her coffee in her view, trying to ease the tension. Does she know how incredibly sorry I am for fucking up and that if I could go back and change it all, I would? No, she doesn't know. I've never told her—and that's my fault.

She rolls her eyes and yanks the coffee out of my hand, spilling some right at the tops of her breasts. I bite my lip and try to stifle a laugh.

"Fucking great," she groans with a frustrated sigh, wiping away the errant coffee with her free hand.

Damn, I wish those were my hands instead.

"Oh shit, I'm sorry. Here, let me get you a napkin," I say apologetically.

Her scowl burns a hole through my soul, but it won't stop me from trying. Before I can grab a napkin from my truck, she's stomping back to her SUV.

Nuh-uh, get back here.

I jump out of my truck so fast that she can't even process I'm closing in on her. She hears me gaining on her heels and angrily turns to face me after placing her coffee on the roof of her car. Our noses are just a few inches from each other. Memories of her flood my senses.

She still smells like strawberries and fresh-cut flowers. Her skin looks soft and supple, her dainty fingers so delicate I want to kiss each one. Her hands suddenly reach up and touch my chest, like she is holding me back from coming closer.

Boom. Lightning strikes. Does she feel the electricity between us when her hands are on me? I hope she can feel my heart thumping through my shirt, beating only for her.

Her eyes dart quickly back and forth on her hands, and she shoves me away with force, causing me to step back as my heel drags on the path below.

"No! Don't come any closer to me," she cries out. Her brow furrows and her lip quivers. Frustration vibrates her body, showing me every ounce of her anger. I did this to her.

My hands open at my sides and I shrug my shoulders up, then down. "Audrey, please let me explain. I—"

Another shove to my chest. I stumble back, surprised at her reaction.

"You don't need to explain anything to me. I want you *gone*. Why are you even here, Donovan? Just leave!" she screams. Her voice is shrill and tears fill her eyes. If she'd let me, I'd wipe every single one away.

"Okay, you want me gone? Fine. I deserve that. I just...you're here. In the flesh. I thought I'd never see you again," I sigh out, my heart sinking deeper with every tear slipping down her face.

My feet stride towards her, and I'm powerless to stop them. If I were a better man, I'd do what she asks and leave. But I know if let her out of my sight this time, there won't be a next time. I'm powered by a single thought:

Get. Closer. To. Audrey.

Surprisingly, she doesn't retreat. I move closer, inch by inch, drawn by those rings of emerald green. I know these eyes, but there's a brokenness in them I don't recognize. The protector in me wants to kill anyone who had a part in breaking her.

Is that someone me?

A tear falls, running down her cheekbone. I reach up and catch it, wiping it away with my thumb. She closes her eyes as another tear falls from the opposite eye. I catch it with my other thumb, my hands now cupping her face.

I'm searching for Audrey in there, but I can't find her. I'm desperate to see a glimmer of her spirit, the one that captivated my heart that unforgettable night.

"Hey, talk to me?" I say with a gentleness, and when her eyes open, I catch a glimpse of that glimmer.

There's my girl.

She reaches up and gently takes my hands away from her face, and I immediately miss her warmth under my touch.

"Talk, huh? You did always talk a big game, Donovan King."

There's a spark in her eyes. Her tone is almost playful, flirtatious even.

Holy fuck. Is she flirting with me right now?

She stares at my mouth as she licks her delicious, pouty lips. Her hands snake up my chest, sending me straight to heaven. I feel like I'm about to pass out.

"I, uh, I—" I stutter. She has me tongue-tied, my mouth bobbing open like a fish out of water. I swallow hard, my breath hitching as she pins me in place with her siren eyes.

What the fuck is she doing to me?

Her gaze fixates on my lips like she wants to devour me, her hands hold steady on my chest.

"I have a boyfriend, you know. You shouldn't be following me."

Her tone is still playful as she grips my shirt and pulls me closer, her lips just inches from mine.

So it's true? She has a boyfriend. It should sting, but it doesn't. Not even a little. Probably because her hands are on my body and she's licking her lips like she's wondering how I taste after all these years.

"I. Don't. Care," I growl, keeping my voice low, barely above a whisper. I reach out and grip her waist, my hands buzzing from the contact. Our faces are so close, just one tilt forward and my lips will be on hers.

A blur of movement. A searing pulse of sudden pain. Can't. Breathe. No air.

Fucking hell.

Audrey Winthrop kneed me right in the balls. I double over, letting out a loud groan and a strained laugh. My hands cup my balls through my jeans, pleading for the ache to stop.

There's my minx.

"Think again. Now leave," she fumes, turning on her heel.

I let out a pained laugh as the nausea from her knee to my nuts subsides and fight to stand upright as she walks away. I probably shouldn't do this, but...

"It's really good to see you, Mouse," I tease, grinning playfully.

She freezes with one hand on the door handle. Her head turns, putting the dainty profile of her face directly in my line of sight. Her chest rises and falls in big, deep breaths. Her jaw clenches for a moment, then softens. I can hear her exhale while she swipes her coffee from the roof of her car. She slips into the driver's seat, slamming the door shut.

Just as I think she's about to drive off, our eyes meet in her side-view mirror. A subtle upward curl forms on her lips, and in that fleeting moment, I'm back in the game.

Audrey is home, and this time, I'm not stopping until I win back her heart.

Chapter Eight

AUDREY

My hands grip the steering wheel so hard I'm afraid it will crumble beneath me. I rest my forehead on the top of the wheel and let out a breath. *Mouse*. The audacity to call me that nickname with that stupid, beautiful grin on his gorgeous face.

The worst part is it made me smile. I'm almost sure he saw it, too. Damn him. I guess I started it by flirting with him. I couldn't help myself. Kellan and I never joke or play. It's always rough sex and business. It's different with Donovan, and it terrifies me.

My breath hitched when he touched my face and wiped my tears. I had forgotten what it was like to be touched so gently, so delicately, like I might break beneath his hands.

And he just *had* to age like fine wine. Couldn't he have gotten a beer gut and stained teeth? Instead, he had grown out of his baby face and right into a chiseled jaw covered with irresistible stubble—not yet a full beard, but a little more than a shadow. His muscles were more formed, firmer, bigger. I felt it when my hands touched his rock-hard chest. Heat floods between my legs just thinking about it.

That sexy, dimple-forming grin still makes me buckle at the knees. I remember making him smile that night, tracing my tongue up and down his sun-kissed olive skin.

"Audrey, stop it," I grit to myself, looking in the rear-view mirror.

"He humped and dumped you and made you out to be a fucking fool. Get. It. Together." There's my sad attempt at a pep talk. I sigh. "I'm so fucked."

But then a playful smirk appears on my lips when I think about my knee to his balls. He deserved it.

I sit up straight and look out to the wrap-around front porch at the house I grew up in. I've been so consumed with Donovan that it hasn't hit me until now.

I'm finally home.

Three pine green Adirondack chairs sit, facing the view—one for Pop, one for Gran, and one for me. Sweet memories flood my brain of the three of us sitting together, drinking tea and telling stories. Mostly Gran telling the stories. She was the best storyteller. Pop and I would sit here, listening to her all night like she hung the moon.

Home has a rustic wine-country visage with aged vines snaking up the earth-toned stones on the facade—a touch of nature to make this massive estate approachable.

I especially love the Juliet balcony off to the side, where I used to sit and read books until the moon was my only company.

This house was far too large for just Gran and Pop, but they had plans to fill it with lots of children and grandchildren. Sadly, my gran went through a tough journey of infertility and lost more babies than anyone should in their lifetime. My chest gets heavy with the thought of Gran's miracle baby, my father, who turned out to be an utter disappointment. I wonder if he even knows Gran died.

I step out of the car and grab my carry-on from the trunk. The scent of eucalyptus and olive trees overtakes my nostrils. Rolling green hills as far as the eyes can see paint the background of my childhood. The front door opening shakes me from my nostalgic revery, flooding me with warmth and sunshine.

I drop everything and run up the front porch steps like when I was five years old, crashing straight into my grandfather's arms.

"Oof! Well, hey there, kid. Oh, I missed you so much," he murmurs. His Carhart jacket smells like cinnamon and Earl Grey tea.

I'm unable to hold in the tears that stream down my face. I hold on to him like I'll die if I don't.

"Hey, Pop. God, I missed you so much. I love you so much."

We squeeze each other tighter, and I notice he is more frail than before. My pop is getting older, and I missed so many years being away. He holds onto me and moves his hands to cup my face. He kisses my forehead and pulls me in for another bear hug.

"I love you too, sweetheart," he hums.

We hold each other for what feels like hours until I finally let go, turning down the steps to grab my belongings from the ground.

"Come on, Audrey. I got an early dinner for us."

I walk inside and take a deep breath in. It still smells like Gran. I do a full turn, taking in all the pictures on the walls and the warm tones of this house. Even though this house holds painful memories, it's also where I spent the most time with my grandparents. They raised me, protected me, nurtured me.

"What do you think?" Pop puts his hands on his hips, following my eyes as I look around me.

"It's the same. Nothing has changed. I missed it so much," I coo, running my fingers along a framed picture of Gran at the entryway table. This house is a stark contrast to Kellan's New York penthouse. My grandparents made this a real home for me.

I survey the entry way, drinking in every detail I took for granted back then. The grand staircase with the charming wood finishes. The crown molding that adds a sense of character. The enormous wood beams that adorn the vaulted ceiling, filling my adolescent mind with wonder. But most precious of all are the paintings by Gran and my mother that scatter along the walls.

My mother was a gifted artist. I remember being a little kid, pretending that I was in a museum of my mom's work, admiring everything she made like I was a famous art collector.

My eyes land on a picture resting on the fireplace. *Mom.* She's pregnant with me, her hands making a heart on my belly as she looks down and smiles. I touch the edges of the frame, wondering if she'd be disappointed at how my life had turned out.

"She was a beauty, wasn't she?" he interjects. Bringing my gaze to his. "You are the spitting image of your mother," he says softly.

I flinch at his words. They carry a painful weight behind them. There isn't a single picture of my father in this house, my grandfather's only son.

My grandparents always raved about how lucky my father was to find my mother. They loved her fiercely, as if she were their own daughter. My father loved her with every fiber of his being. A sharp pang of envy rips through me, wondering why I was never enough to deserve the love I craved from my father. Gran and Pop did their best to mend what was lost with their son when my mother died. The day she died, my father died with her. I suppose a part of me did too. And the start of his alcohol abuse became a heavy weight on my grandparents' shoulders for years to come.

His grief drove him mad as his drunken tirades escalated from verbal lashings to attempted arson. My father sealed his own fate the night he drunkenly decided to set the King Family Vineyard on fire. Why? I guess that's a secret between him and the case of whiskey he drank that night. But I've always thought he figured if his life was already burned to the ground, he might as well burn everything else, too. The Kings didn't deserve the trauma my father put them through. He was unhinged in his drunken stupor, targeting Donovan's family for contributing to our winery. A place that reminded him so much of my mother, a place where they had built a life together.

And just like everything Ted Winthrop touches, his attempt to burn down their vineyard failed, too. Pop caught him just as the first vine started to catch and called the authorities. But the real damage was done. Pop cut him off and exiled him right then and there. The night Ted left was the best night of my life.

My father used to tell me I was the spitting image of my mother and that he hated me for it. I can still smell the whiskey and wine on his breath as he pinned me down, bruising my wrists and screaming in my face. Kellan's rage smells more like cognac. Same anger, different flavor.

My grandfather notices my discomfort with his words—unintentional, of course—but he changes the subject, anyway.

"Let's eat and catch up, kiddo. Come on."

He gestures me into the large, open kitchen and pulls out a barstool from the island. My eyes devour the delicious spread of sandwiches. I pause on the bottle of Violet's Vintage, taking in every inch of the label.

"So the town gets to try this wine tomorrow at Sip & Savor?" I point at the bottle in front of me.

"Oh! You must've stopped by earlier. It's great, isn't it?" Pop beams. "A pre-celebration for Gran. This town has been so supportive. I wish she were here to see it," he whispers, sadness flashes in his eyes.

"I do too," I reply empathetically. "It's amazing, Pop. Truly. It'll be great," I say softly, my smile reaching my eyes, thinking about everyone coming together for my gran tomorrow.

The smallest of flutters bubble in my stomach at the thought of seeing Donovan again, but I push them back down as fast as they come.

My stomach grumbles, and Pop's eyes widen at the sound.

"I've been talking your ear off, kid. Dig in! So, tell me, how's New York?" he asks, placing a sandwich on his plate.

I grab a turkey avocado sandwich and grab the open bottle of wine. Knowing Pop, this has been breathing for half an hour. Just perfect. I point it in his direction, and he quickly nods as I pour us a glass.

"New York is fine. Kellan is fine," I say flatly, because I am an awful liar and he knows it. I don't want to talk about Kellan while I'm here. My pop can get anything out of me and I know he'll ask, so this is my attempt to shut it down. I don't have the mental capacity to have Gran, Kellan, *and* Donovan on my mind right now.

He cocks up an eyebrow. "Just fine? Do you want to talk about it?" he asks.

"Nope."

He puts his hands up in surrender and doesn't probe further.

I swirl the deep red wine in my glass and stick my nose halfway down, taking a generous sniff. There's a gleam in Pop's eye, ready for my review of a wine that he and Gran worked so hard on. A wine that represents her life, her legacy, their love. God, was I lucky enough to witness their love.

"On the nose, I'm getting ripe blackberries, dark cherry, and a hint of plum." I take another sniff. "Mmm, I'm also getting some undertones of tobacco and slate. Like a wet rock?" His laugh is hearty, full of life.

"You've got a great nose, kid." Pop smiles at me.

I give it one more swirl and take a sip. "Okay, wow, this is absolutely perfect, Pop."

"Isn't it? Your Gran loved it. She said it was our very best."

My heart breaks at the thought that Gran isn't sitting here tasting wine and eating sandwiches with us. She'd give me her notes on the wine, and we'd compare flavor profiles. She'd urge me to keep eating, *"Put some meat on your bones!"* Her laugh would echo throughout this kitchen, probably at some corny joke from Pop. She loved his corny jokes. She and I have that in common.

"Why 2018? What's so special about that year?" I say while chewing, not my best manners. I hold the bottle and observe the label. Right above the date is a sketching of Gran's beloved cottage.

Gran had always wanted a place to escape to, to paint, read books, and journal. So, Pop remodeled the old cottage that had been sitting vacant on the property since the 1950s. It was old then, an original building on our forty-acre plot back when the winery was established in 1910 by my great grandfather. The cottage was a twenty-fifth anniversary gift to Gran. She always said it was the sweetest thing he'd ever done.

"2018 was the year we returned to business with the Kings."

I stop chewing and swallow the rest of my sandwich, gulping it down. Since when did my family stop working with the Kings? Was I really so out of touch that I didn't care to know this about my family? I take a sip of wine and keep my eyes steady on the glass.

"I-I didn't know that, Pop. I'm sorry," I whisper.

Regret takes over my body. I'm overcome with a sadness that I can't shake away. I thought I was protecting them by keeping my distance, shielding them from my pain. Now I can see the pain that I've caused by being absent. I know nothing about my home, my family.

I should've known that my grandfather and Donovan's family went back into business. It makes sense now why Donovan was carrying Winthrop Wine cases earlier. Why didn't I know this? Because I didn't care enough to ask or call enough to care. The shittiest granddaughter award goes to me.

He waves me off and shakes his head. "You've been busy with your life in New York," Pop says with a soft smile, but I don't miss the veiled worry in his eye. "It's not your fault."

"Who were the Kings working with before then?" I query, arching my eyebrow. Pop takes a deep breath before taking another swig of wine.

"The Taylor Family."

My eyes get wide as I blow out a strained breath. My heart feels like it's sitting deep within my stomach.

The Taylors? What the fuck?

I notice my mouth agape, and I shut it closed before probing Pop for more information.

"What happened with the Taylors?" I ask, at a loss. Clearly, I have no pulse with news in Oakwood Valley or the wine world. Between Kellan's short leash and my social media aversion, if something happens back home, I'm the last to know about it.

Pop takes another sip before speaking.

"Turns out Duke Taylor had substantial investments in various sectors outside the wine business. He got arrested for insider trading and tipping. The man was found guilty on all charges when it went to court. He's been in prison since…well, since we bottled this wine from the barrel," he says matter-of-factly, raising his glass to the light to admire its color.

My mouth drops at this news. If Duke Taylor is in prison, what happened to Jess? We never liked each other, but I wouldn't wish this on my worst enemy. I know all too well what having a destructive dad is like.

"As part of the legal proceedings, the court ordered a seizure of Duke's assets, including the Taylor Winery and Vineyard."

My hand flies to my mouth as I gasp out loud. "Oh my god!"

"Their vineyard went to auction after his prison sentence. Twenty years. The list of charges was endless and a lot of money was involved. That's all I know."

I'm shaken to my core. This is massive news. My mind races as I take in this information. Duke Taylor is in jail. Jess is who knows where. Donovan is carrying crates of our wine. And why the hell did Caleb King cut ties with my family in the first place?

"I have so many questions, but first, who took the vineyard?" I ask.

"Once it went to auction, it took several years to get everything in order because of how large the case was. A wealthy wine family from Holly Hill put a bid on it during the pandemic and won."

This is so much information. I'm trying to eat, drink, and process at the same time, but it's overwhelming. My mind keeps flickering back to Jess and her whereabouts, like a game of *Where in the World is Carmen Sandiego.*

"What happened to Jess Taylor?"

Pop shrugs his shoulders and purses his lips.

"No idea, kid. Last I heard, Jess and her mother fled California after Duke's sentencing," he replies, cutting the crust off his sandwich. Just like Gran used to do for him.

Wow, that's not how I imagined her life going. I guess others could say the same for me, too. I was living a lie, and no one knew. Jess and I aren't all that different in the end.

This still doesn't add up with Caleb, though. I can't help but wonder, what does Donovan think of all this? And more than that, why do I care about what Donovan thinks?

Focus, Audrey.

"Pop, I don't understand why Caleb cut ties in the first place. Did he ever explain outside of wanting to shift directions?" I prod, burning for answers.

None of this makes sense. My brain can't put the pieces together, like the synapses aren't synapsing. I rub my temples and take another sip of wine. Yeah, more wine should do it. Bottoms up.

"Caleb and I have always had respect for each other. It was a business decision, and I respected it. The winery was doing okay after we parted with the Kings," he reassures me, taking a sip before moving on. "We got to work with other great vineyards in neighboring towns and made good wine in those years," he beams, clearly proud of the work he puts in as a winemaker. He's trying to make light of this for me, but it all feels too heavy for me to carry.

"I'm sorry, Pop. I didn't mean for the Spanish Inquisition. I've been gone for so long. I feel guilty for not being here to help you and Gran. And now she's gone, and I never got to say goodbye." My voice cracks as my eyes well up, staring into my wine glass—the only piece of Gran I have left. Pop scoots closer to me, draping his arm around my shoulder.

"Your Gran and I were fine. We knew you had dreams to chase in New York. Sure, you could've called more, but we could've too. It's on us too."

His eyes look sorry, and I pull him in for another hug because I need it.

"Well, I'm here now for you. And Gran." I raise my glass for a toast. Pop does the same, our glasses clinking together.

"I know you are," he sniffs, wiping a tear from the corner of his eye. "Now, I have something for you. Wait here."

I give him a quizzical look as I take another bite of my sandwich. I swivel in my barstool, watching him enter another room and come out with his hands behind his back.

"What you got there, Pop? No gifts." I wipe the corner of my mouth with a napkin and place my hands on my lap.

"Your Gran wanted you to have this." He reaches for my hand and opens my palm, placing a silver key with a lavender silk ribbon tied to it. I lift it up, examining it to see if I recognize it, but I don't.

"A key? A key for what?"

And then it hits me. My eyes widen as I bring my hand to my chest, cradling the key to my heart.

"Wait, Gran's cottage?"

He nods, a tear slipping from the corner of his eye. "She wanted you to have it. If you want, you can stay there while you're here and make it your own. And if you ever decide to move back home, the cottage is all yours," he says with a wink.

My heart is bursting at the seams. My own escape. Gran gifted me her most favorite place in the world. My eyes shimmer with wetness as I press the key to my chest, squeezing it tight.

"Thank you, Pop. This is the best gift. Thank you, Gran," I say, looking up to the sky.

"You can drive up in your rental car. We added on a garage a couple years ago," he says, planting a kiss on my forehead.

I'm so happy I could float. I've always loved Gran's cottage. She used to take me there when I was sad and let me paint with her and bake cookies. God, I miss her.

Pop and I talk over a bottle of wine and sandwiches, losing track of time. We laugh and cry over stories about gran; it feels so good to be in his presence.

I can feel Gran here too, smiling down on us and watching over us. Pop tells me that Gran wanted her ashes spread at Beleza Point, an hour and a half north of the valley. She grew up camping there as a kid, he explains. I remember camping there too. It must've meant a lot to her, being able to share her favorite places with us.

"So we spread her ashes on Sunday?" I ask while tidying up the kitchen.

Pop answers with a simple hum as he corks the bottle of wine we didn't finish. A small smile tugs at my lips, and I walk straight into his arms. I rest my head on his chest and close my eyes—I see my Gran.

He leans down and kisses the top of my head. "Night, kid. I'm so glad you're home."

I rise to my tiptoes and kiss his cheek. "Me too, Pop."

I grab the key from the counter, buzzing with excitement. *Alright Gran, let's see your place.* A quick wave to Pop and I'm out the door with my suitcase in hand.

Back at the car, I toss my luggage into the trunk. I'm about to slip into the driver's seat when I spy a note on the windshield. I grab it, unfolding it along the edge.

> *Mouse,*
> *Here's your napkin for your spilled coffee.*
> *-D*

"Oh, for fuck's sake," I whisper, shaking my head and laughing. I go to crumple the napkin and toss it in the backseat when my hands stop me. I stare at the words written, running my fingers across them. My gaze softens as I think about Donovan scribbling this note with a mischievous grin. Instead, I neatly fold the napkin and slip it into the pocket of my leggings.

My eyes trail to the now cold macchiato sitting in the cup holder. I bite my lip, thinking about the way Donovan stared at my tits where the spilled coffee dripped. He's not so slick. I clocked him right away.

Oakwood Valley is a small town, and I'm here for five days. The chances of me avoiding Donovan are slim to none. For the last ten years, I've been building my wall brick by brick to shut out any residual feelings for the boy who broke my heart. But now here he is, effortlessly dismantling what I've worked so hard to build until I have nowhere left to hide.

I'm not sure how much longer I can hold up. One more look from those ocean blues and I am completely *done for*.

Chapter Nine

DONOVAN

"Are you okay, bro?"

My little brother Wyatt gives me a concerned stare, no doubt wondering why I'm zoned out, staring into nothingness. His voice shakes me out of my funk. I blink my eyes hard, willing myself to refocus on my task. These cases won't pack themselves with wine. T-minus eight hours until I see Audrey again at the happy hour tonight.

"Yeah, sorry, I was just zoning out." He can tell I'm lying, and since he loves being all up in my business, he doesn't stop probing.

"You're such a liar. Audrey Winthrop comes into town and she has you so fucked up. What's it been? Nine years since you've seen her?" he smirks.

"Ten," I reply dryly.

All night, I thought about her green eyes. She kneed me in the balls, and weirdly enough, I liked it. Don't get me wrong, it hurt like hell. But it showed me that the feisty, playful, free-spirited girl I knew was still in there. She can try to hide it with hair dye and heavy makeup. But I see her.

That was us in the driveway. Just two kids who never got the chance to love each other to the fullest. And god, I want that chance again.

"Damn. Does Dad know?"

Wyatt knows everything that went down between my dad and me on graduation night. He demanded I tell him what was going on when I started avoiding all family functions and hardly ever came home. I lived with Logan until I left for summer soccer training at UC Davis.

It took some time, but I finally realized that my distance wasn't just a punishment for my dad—it hurt everyone impacted by the shrapnel of our blowout. I had promised Wyatt and Kerry a summer of brotherly bonding, and when I fell short, Wyatt was the one who held me accountable. So, I made a pact with my brothers that no matter what was happening between my dad and me, it wouldn't take away from our time together. I started coming home from university once a month just to have our brother bonding time.

I wanted to live up to James and what an amazing big brother he was to us. I owed it to Wyatt and Kerry.

"Yeah, he knows. I mean, he's not stupid. Violet just died, so I'm sure he can piece together that Audrey would come home for Noah," I state very matter-of-fact. He nods, helping me load supplies for tonight in my truck.

"He's trying, you know. He's changed, Donovan. Give him a chance."

Wyatt may be right, but my father and I have never seen eye to eye. Our relationship, although better than before, is still strained.

"I just need time, Wy," I grumble, wanting this conversation to be over.

My brother stops loading the truck and turns to face me, crossing his arms over his chest. I sigh and give him my attention.

"You've had time, D. Don't pull away. Not after James. He needs you."

I remain stoic, clenching my jaw.

"All Dad did my whole life was compare me to James in everything. Sports, grades, manners, you name it," I mutter, the frustration building in my tone. "Nothing I did was good enough for him, and after James died, he shut me out then fucked me over," I huff out, breathing harder than I intended.

Wyatt props himself up on the tailgate of my truck and pats his hand on the space next to him. I remain standing and he rolls his eyes.

"You're fucking stubborn, just like him. It's called grief, D. And yes, I agree, what he made you do was fucked up. But Audrey is here now," he says softly, making me wonder where my grumpy little brother went. "Time heals our grief, but that doesn't mean we forget. I fucking miss him, too. I know he was your best friend…" His voice trails, not able to find the words.

He sits quietly, his eyes fixed on a stray cork on the ground. I slide into the space next to him and sling my arm over his shoulder. *"You're* my best friend, Wy," I say while pointing to his heart. He gives me a weak smile.

"I just don't want our family to drift further apart. Please, Donovan. Make it right? Talk to Dad?"

When I look into his eyes, I see that little kid who looked at me like I'd hung the moon.

"Okay. For you." I elbow him in the rib and kiss the top of his head.

"He's hurting about Violet too, Donovan. We all are."

He balls his hand into a fist and bops my knee, sliding off the tailgate to continue loading the truck. I look down at my work boots and ride out the wave of grief that hits me.

Violet's death impacted our small town. She was the heartbeat, spreading goodness and joy to everyone who knew her. She and Noah were there for me when everything came crashing down with Audrey —and never once did they spite me for it.

I found out that Audrey left for New York two weeks after our night together, and every time I'd come home I'd visit Violet and Noah almost every day. I never told them what happened, but it didn't matter to them. They gave me grace when I needed it. Being with them made me feel closer to her. I know when she left for New York as soon as she did, it was my doing.

During the five years my father was in business with Duke Taylor, I wanted nothing to do with it. So, when I graduated from school with a degree in viticulture and enology, I decided to work directly with Noah as his assistant winemaker at the Winthrop Family Winery. My father was disappointed, but he had no right to be upset.

The following year, shit hit the fan with Duke after his arrest. My dad pleaded with Noah to work together again and begged for his forgiveness. Noah said that there was nothing to forgive, because that's the man Noah Winthrop is. He's the most respectable person I know—steadfast and humble—and he brought my family back into his life with open arms.

I slide off the tailgate to help Wyatt with the final cases to load. We work in silence, and I glance up once in a while to look at my brother with admiration.

The best thing about this job is hands down working side by side with Wyatt. Tonight will be a testament to our hard work and the love that Noah and Violet literally poured into this wine. I'm honored that Wyatt and I had a part in it.

We harvested a fucking great batch of grapes in 2018, and now the town gets to have a taste of Violet's Vintage. A wine that represents resilience, love, and family. A wine that I'm proud of. A wine for the angel and saint that she is: Violet Winthrop.

"What do you think, Jojo? You want it facing this way or on the other side?" Wyatt and I hold up the banner.

Winthrop Wine Happy Hour: In Loving Memory of Violet Winthrop
1945–2024

Josie holds her finger to her mouth like she is putting a lot of thought into this. We want it to look perfect for when Noah arrives—and Audrey, too…selfishly.

Wyatt's arms extend way above his head. He huffs out in annoyance, "Josie, come on, you've had us holding this sign forever. Just pick a damn spot."

She completely ignores him, earning a snicker from me.

"Hmm," she murmurs. "Put it on the other side across the bar, next to the stage. That should be good." She glares at my brother and sticks her tongue out at him. He mimics her, earning an eye roll from Josie before she returns to setting up her instruments for the performance later.

"Hey Josie, if you sing off-key tonight, I'll boo," Wyatt teases.

"Bite me, Wyatt." Josie gives him the finger.

"You wish." He puckers his lips, and I slap the back of his head.

"Stop fucking messing with her and help me finish this, dickhead." We laugh while trying to nut check each other, acting like we did when we were boys.

We pin up the sign and admire our work. My heart squeezes reading Violet's name with an end date on her life. Death is weird. The same pain that wrenches for Violet hits again as I think about James. Duller, but still achey.

He was my big bear, and I was his little bear—nicknames that stuck since we were kids when we'd play pretend animals, and I'd claim myself as the little version of whatever he was. The times I'd visit James's grave, I'd stare deep into the date of death on his headstone. How is it that one day, you're laughing, dreaming about the future? And the next, you're six feet under with an expiration date to your life.

Wyatt puts his arm around me, reading my mind.

"I know she's up there with James. He'd be really proud of you."

My arm crosses over my chest, and I rest my hand on his, smiling. "Yeah, I sure hope so."

The door swings open and my youngest brother Kerry walks in with two bags in tow. Josie gives him a wave as he makes his way toward us.

"Hey fuckers, look what I got!" he smirks in classic Kerry fashion, thrusting the bags out for us to examine.

"Disposable cameras?" Wyatt asks with his eyebrow arched.

"Dude, yes! I bought like twenty. I thought it would be cool if we left a couple at each table for everyone to take their own pictures tonight." He walks back out the door and returns momentarily with a wooden box. "Then when they're done, they drop it off in here and I can develop them tomorrow morning. Cool, right?"

I grin at my youngest brother, admiring his creativity. He's a talented photographer with a great eye. Our dad wanted him to go to school for business or marketing to help with the vineyard, but he got a full ride to UCLA after winning a national photography contest. Seeing him walk the stage at graduation, art degree in hand, is one of the proudest moments of my life.

I grip his shoulder and say, "Very cool, kid. You can put them on the tables. Wy and I already set them up earlier."

"Thanks, big bro. Love you," he replies, smiling from ear to ear.

Kerry is our sunshine boy. He's always happy, the glass always half full. Wyatt, on the other hand, is a grumpy motherfucker, but fiercely loyal with a sensitive heart. He skipped out on college to stay behind with Dad and help with the vineyard, training under Jeff, our longtime vineyard manager, who finally retired after thirty years. Wyatt spends most of his days outside in the dirt, maintaining the entire property. His job is vital to the success of the family business, and he played a large part in helping with the harvest that cultivated Violet's Vintage.

I finish setting up while Wyatt and Kerry sit at the bar chatting with Jackson, Kerry's best friend. He bartends down the street at Siren's Flask, the only bar in town. He came to help with the wine tasting tonight because he loved Violet, too. Everyone did.

"Hey boys, I'm gonna change in my car. Guests are arriving soon, so make sure every group gets a flight of three reds and three whites. More wine is stacked in the back if you need, Jack," I shout behind me as I make my way out the door. Jackson gives me a salute, and my brothers nod in my direction.

The sun dips lower into the sky and a crisp breeze blows gently as I walk through the back parking lot. I unlock the driver's seat door of my trusty blue Ford truck. It's a 1994 Ford F-150, my baby through thick and thin. I bought it with my own cash at sixteen and fixed her up with spare parts from a junkyard. It's an old truck, but I take good care of it, and I can't seem to let it go.

I slip the shirt off my back to change for the party and spot the duffle bag I brought on the passenger seat floor. As I round the corner of my tailgate, I notice Audrey standing at her car a few feet away, eyes fixated on my bare chest.

I know an eye fuck when I see one.

She's frozen in space, arms and legs crossed, as if binding her limbs tightly together might hold in her expression. But her smirk gives her away. She *definitely* likes what she sees. I puff out my chest and flex my abs subtly, plastering a grin on my face. My hands slip into the front pockets of my jeans and I jut my chin out toward her.

"Like what you see, Mouse?" I tease, intending to rile her up. I can't help myself.

"Spend all night icing your balls, Donovan?" she quips. Her eyebrow raises at me, and she walks toward the coffee shop with sass and fire. I hate to watch her walk away, but damn, her body looks delectable in her tight jeans and knee-high boots.

She's wearing her hair down and straight tonight, and it ribbons through the air as she saunters off. I catch a whiff of her strawberry scent in the breeze. I chuckle and grab my duffle bag to put on a fitting black polo before I rush over to catch up with her.

"Audrey, wait up!" I shout.

She keeps walking, her pace not slowing for me. I jog next to her and match her stride.

"Where's Noah?" I ask. She gives me the side-eye like she's annoyed I'm invading her space. I mean, I kind of am, but that's beside the point.

"He's riding with Frank Bozer. They should be here any minute." She throws her hair behind one shoulder. "Can you, like, not walk so close to me?" she says curtly while holding her palm up to put space between us.

I make a big show of moving my feet half an inch away, punctuating the gesture with a smile and a cocked eyebrow. I'll try anything to hear her laugh again.

God, I dream about her laugh.

She scoffs and shakes her head, moving further away from me, keeping her eyes forward. I'll take what I can get.

"So, how long are you in town for? Or...are you home for good now?" I ask.

Please say the latter.

"Pop and I are spreading Gran's ashes on Sunday, then back home to New York the next day."

Damn, my heart drops at her calling New York her home.

"You are home, Mou—Audrey," I correct myself, not wanting to annoy her more than I already have. She keeps her head down at my comment. If she's only going to be here for a few more days, then I need to man the fuck up.

I step in front of her and block her from rounding the corner to Sip & Savor. She stops in her tracks and crosses her arms, looking drop-dead gorgeous as she tilts her head and slightly pouts her lips.

"What are you doing, Donovan?" she sighs, running her fingers through her hair.

I hold out my hands for her to grab. She looks down, hesitant, but keeps her arms crossed. Stoic as ever.

"I want you to be surprised when we get to the front of the shop. Close your eyes. Please?" I beg softly. I give her my best puppy dog eyes, and a tiny smile forms on her lips.

She's so fucking pretty.

She rolls her eyes before closing them, putting her hands in mine. A jolt of electricity zaps when we touch, fully charged. Her hands mold into mine like they were created for each other. A perfect fit.

I walk backward slowly, making sure I don't eat shit and mess up this moment. She takes a wobbly step forward and laughs, biting her lip. I breathe out a chuckle with a beaming grin on my face. I'm glad her eyes are closed so she doesn't see how stupid I look. Her laugh is the best sound in the world.

We get to the front of the shop and I stand behind her, adjusting her shoulders to face forward.

"Donovan, I know you're dragging this out. Can I open my eyes now?" she asks impatiently. She sucks in a deep inhale through her nose and exhales while lulling her neck from side to side.

My arms snake around her waist from behind, and her breath hitches. I expect her to throw me off, but she doesn't. I lean my chin on her shoulder and breathe in her sweet, floral skin.

"I hope you like what we did in there. You know, for Violet," I murmur softly in her ear.

With her eyes still closed, she rests her hands on mine and lets me hold her, melting into my touch.

Let me just stay here a while longer.

"Open your eyes," I whisper.

Her eyes flutter open and land on a framed black-and-white picture of Violet holding a glass of wine that rests on an easel by the door. She turns her head to face me with teary eyes, and I squeeze her tighter.

"Kerry took that picture of her one night at Siren's Flask. He's a photographer now. Violet loved happy hour with the boys," I chuckle, basking in the good times we had when Violet and Mrs. Dickson would crash our boys' nights at the bar. Her gaze stays fixed on the picture as she leans her head back on my chest. It takes everything in me to stop myself from kissing her.

"I love it. Thank you, Donovan."

Anything for you, Mouse.

"You're welcome."

Chapter Ten

AUDREY

My hand rests over my heart as I walk into Sip & Savor, Donovan trailing behind me. There are high-top tables spread throughout the shop with violet-colored cloths that drape to the floor. Very fitting. Lillies stand in crystal vases that scatter throughout the shop. Pictures of my gran in dainty gold frames hang on the walls, her smile adding a warmth to every corner of this place.

The space is large, enough to fit at least fifty people. In high school, mornings here would buzz with teenagers drinking coffee before class, hurriedly copying each other's homework. I'd watch Donovan and his soccer teammates laughing down Main from my study table by the window. Sometimes they'd be accompanied by a bunch of girls—that made my insides twist with jealousy. He always had this town in the palm of his hand. The Prince of The Valley, Oakwood's very own hometown hero.

And now he stands behind me. Not in my dreams, but in real life. It's beautiful what they did. What *he* did. It's beautiful how this town came together to celebrate my gran.

I turn to face him and smile softly. "It's beautiful. She would've loved this. You did all of this?" I spin around and take in the atmosphere.

"Yeah. I mean me, my brothers, and Josie."

Donovan bites back a smile, but a dimpled grin slips, and I turn away quickly before he can see the burn on my cheeks.

I see Wyatt and Kerry sitting at the bar, their eyes darting back and forth between Donovan and I, smirking. Wow, they've really grown up. They all have the same olive skin and chocolate brown hair, but slightly different builds.

I approach them and they both stand up to greet me. "Wow, Wyatt and Kerry King. You boys are no longer boys, huh?"

They smile and Kerry lifts me up in a hug, catching me by surprise. I catch Donovan scowling in my peripheral.

"Audrey! Welcome home. I hope you love the picture of Violet. I'm sorry for your loss," Kerry says with a soft smile. He's always been so sweet, even as a kid. It's easy to feel at ease around him. He slowly puts me down as I pat his chest.

"Thank you, Kerry. The picture is beautiful. You're so talented, truly," I beam. His chest puffs with pride in response. He gazes over to Donovan, whose scowl has disappeared, replaced by the kind eyes of a proud big brother.

"Audrey, hey. I'm also sorry for your loss," Wyatt says quietly, giving me a sympathetic look and a gentle touch on the elbow—not as affectionate as Kerry, but still appreciated.

"Thanks, Wyatt. And thank you guys so much for all of this," my hands lift, gesturing to the whole shop. "It's amazing."

Donovan steps in and waves his brothers off. I'm assuming it's sibling telepathy for *"fuck off now."*

"Kerry put disposable cameras out for the guests. We'll get the photos developed before you leave so you can always keep a piece of home with you."

I can't hide my smile. It's all so thoughtful—it almost feels like my life isn't a giant mess right now. "That's a great idea. God, thank you so much. Kerry is the sweetest."

Donovan fakes a pain in his chest. "No, no, no, you got it all wrong. I'm the sweet one, remember?"

A flash of my eighteen-year-old self, crying on the front porch steps, appears behind my eyes. A naive girl, waiting for an empty promise. I tear my gaze from Donovan before he can see the emotions stirring in me and see Josie on the stage, setting up a mic stand.

"I'm gonna say hi to Josie. If you'll excuse me."

I brush past him, our shoulders grazing. I can't deny the electricity between us every time we touch, but no. He's not the sweet one.

I keep reminding myself of the way he used me, the way he changed everything in one selfish evening. So why the hell is it so hard to stay mad at him? I'm stuck between my head and my heart. My head is screaming, *"stay away,"* but my heart…Donovan King did always know the way to my heart. But I'm not ready to forgive him yet. Not until I give him a piece of my mind. Tonight, it's about Gran.

Josie and I mingle as people flood in the door. So many people are here—many I recognize, like my high school principal, Mr. Frommling, and Mrs. Dickson from the diner. I've never hugged more people in the span of ten minutes. Jackson pours wine tasting flights at the bar while Donovan and his brothers set them up on tables. Pop and Frank walk in and everyone claps, a gesture that melts my heart. Pop just smiles and waves as Frank's arm wraps around him, showing him off like a prized bass.

I excuse myself from Josie and walk straight into Pop's warm embrace. Why did I ever want to leave? Twenty-four hours here and my heart feels like it's slowly piecing itself back together, even if Donovan makes me crazy. Apparently, I've got a thing for crazy.

Pop kisses the top of my head and slings his arm around my shoulder, turning us to face everyone in the room.

"Thank you all for joining us this evening to celebrate the most wonderful person I've…*we've*," he looks down at me. "—ever known. Violet Winthrop was a force of nature and a gentle soul." Pop's eyes shift down towards Kerry's picture of Gran, a tear streaming down his face. "She was the love of my life, and I am so proud to share this wine with you all tonight. And to make the night even better, my beautiful granddaughter is finally home." I wipe the tears with my sleeve and kiss his cheek, his arm squeezing me tighter as everyone claps and cheers.

The night is lively and people are definitely getting tipsy—myself included. Every table has a variety flight with three of Gran's favorite reds and whites. I'm two flights deep, avoiding Donovan like the plague. My goal with every glass of wine I consume tonight is to keep me away from that beautiful man who has my heart in a chokehold. My jaw ticks every time I see a new woman flirting and laughing with him, caressing his arm.

Hello, jealousy. Nice to meet you.

He's friendly and smiles back, but he always excuses himself and leaves them hanging. He stares at me, his sexy, strong arms crossed over his chest while he leans against the bar.

Now whose eye fucking who?

I look away, because if I stare any longer, I will combust on the spot. He got me all worked up when he caught me staring in the parking lot with his shirt off. Yeah, I eye fucked the shit out of him. And by the looks of that ridiculous muscle-flexing routine of his, he knows it too. He doesn't even need to try hard. It's annoying how hot he is. I haven't felt this turned on in a *very long time.*

I do my best to move throughout the room and catch up with everyone. High school classmates who have moved back home and started their own families give me their condolences. They ask how my life is in New York and I'm curt at best. *"It's great." "I'm so busy all the time." "I love the city."* If they only knew the truth.

"It's awful." "I'm going nowhere career wise." "My boyfriend hurts me."

I feel a tap on my shoulder and spin around to face Donovan's parents.

"Audrey, honey, welcome back," Grace beams at me. "You're just as beautiful as ever." She pulls me in for a deep hug. It takes a second for my arms to reciprocate. I can't tell if it's because of the wine or because when she hugs me, it's a comfort I've been craving my entire life. A mother's warm embrace. She has the same chocolate brown hair as Donovan and the same beautiful ocean-blue eyes. I've always known her to be incredibly kind, gorgeous, and charming.

Just like Donovan.

"Thank you. It's nice to be back."

I look over her shoulder. Caleb looks uncomfortable. He wasn't exactly warm and fuzzy the last time I remember. His hand extends my way. "I'm sorry for your loss, Audrey. Violet was an amazing woman." I shake his hand awkwardly.

Okay, not super cold, but not the warmest. I'll take it.

"Thank you, Mr. and Mrs. King. Thanks for taking care of my Pop."

Caleb's eyes break from mine, but Grace keeps her sympathetic gaze toward me and gives me another hug before walking away.

After playing a few songs, Josie slides up to the mic for an announcement. "Okay, ladies and gents. We have a special guest coming to the stage to perform for you all."

My eyes get wide, looking around to see who this special guest is. Everyone else is doing the same.

"Oakwood Valley folks, please welcome Donovan King to the stage!"

My mouth drops to the floor. He strides past me, his hand grazing the small of my back as he confidently struts on stage. Josie passes him a guitar, and he slings it over his shoulder and sits on the stool next to her. Kerry and Wyatt make whistle noises at him. Jesus, he is so gorgeous. I sip the rest of the wine in my glass and motion Jackson for another. He juts his chin toward me as his eyes say, *"I got you, girl."*

Good man.

"Uh, good evening, everyone. Josie here has been giving me lessons for the past year. I want to dedicate this song to Violet and Noah."

I sit on a barstool and see my pop across the room at a table with Caleb and Grace. Pop's eyes glimmer as soon as Donovan strums the first note. Josie follows, strumming alongside Donovan.

I know this song. I know this melody. I look down at my feet, trying to remember where I know it from. My chest squeezes the moment I realize. I look up and Donovan is staring straight into my eyes. *Make It With You.* The song we danced to the night at his graduation party. The night that changed my life.

It's too many emotions at once. It's anger, it's heartbreak, it's overwhelming happiness. My eyes fixate on him as he stares intently at his guitar strings. The moment he looks up, he finds me. His lips subtly curl at the corners as his eyes fill with longing. Before I can look away to catch my breath, he sings. My hands grip the edge of the bar, turning my fingers white. It takes everything in me not to faint.

He isn't singing to everyone. He is singing to me.

The center of his night.

My eyes well with conflicting emotion as he strums his guitar, searing his deep blue gaze into my broken heart. I'm glued to the bar stool as his voice holds me against my will, pinning me down in this torturous moment. The words that escape his lips talk about making it work with someone and going the distance. A chance we never got.

The overwhelming sense of loss crashes through me as I squeeze my eyes shut, trying everything in my power to forget the pain that courses violently through my veins. My head spins, dizzying me into a dark shadow of my mind where Donovan left me. He abandoned me. He hurt me and broke my heart in half. I can't recover fast enough as I feel myself slipping, my breaths becoming erratic. I can't keep looking at what could've been. His voice taunts me with every beautiful word that leaves him. I can't sit through this anymore.

I need to get the hell out of here.

I chug the rest of my wine and rush out toward the back door, stumbling into a couple of shoulders as I frantically shove my way toward the exit.

The moon shines bright above me. Cool air hits my face as I wipe my tears away. I lean my back against the wall with my hands on my knees.

Take a deep breath, count backward from five.

Heavy sobs assault my throat. I couldn't stop it if I tried. I sit on the pavement with my head between my knees, grieving for so many things. My gran, Donovan, my whole fucking life. I think about

Kellan and how terrified I am of going back to New York. But I have to go back. I can't stay here. The hole I've dug myself is too deep.

Oakwood Valley is a fantasy that is too far out of my reach. I don't belong here anymore.

I hear muted clapping and cheers, when suddenly the back door swings open and Donovan is there. He hesitates by the door, observing my mascara-streaked face with sad eyes. I gaze down between my legs, letting silent tears fall. I hear his footsteps softly as he slowly walks towards me, stopping when the front of his boots touch mine. He bends down in front of me and reaches for my face, gently lifting my chin with his finger.

"Mouse," he whispers.

I silently nod and cry harder. His hands tuck under my arms and he lifts me to my feet, pulling me into an embrace. *Heaven.* I let my sobs soak his shirt, and we hold on to each other like if we let go, we'd fall through the earth and never come back. He kisses my hair and squeezes me tighter, his hands rubbing along my spine. He cups my face between his large hands, wiping my tears with the pads of his thumbs.

"Was I really that shitty of a singer?"

And for the first time in years, I let out the loudest belly laugh. I mean, really loud and not at all cute. There's nothing I can do to control the fit of laughter taking over my body. This laugh is coming straight from my soul, and damn, it feels so fucking good.

Donovan holds me up as we both lose ourselves in a frenzy of uncontrollable hysterics. I throw my head back, but no sound leaves me. When I look through teary eyes, Donovan doubles over as he clutches his stomach, silently crying. We collapse to the ground, holding onto each other as if it's second nature.

When we finally catch our breath, he pulls me into his lap as he leans back against the wall. I turn to straddle him, taking him by surprise. His hands rest on the small of my back while his thumbs stroke up and down. I love being touched by him.

"I don't think I've ever laughed that hard in my life," I breathe, smiling at him as my fingers lace around his neck.

He softens his gaze with the most knee-buckling smirk on his lips. "I think I remember a time where you did." I bite my lip in response, a crimson blush appearing on my cheeks.

"If I died this second, and that was the last thing I heard before I go, I'd die a happy man." He presses his forehead to mine. We sit as if in meditation, breathing each other in, holding on to this version of reality. It feels so natural with Donovan. The fire between us clearly has never gone out, and right now, I don't care that what I'm doing is wrong.

"I'm a little drunk," I hiccup and let out a giggle. He laughs and strokes my hair. "And you made me cry," I whisper. His face turns sad, and he searches my eyes for answers. "Your song...our song. You did that on purpose," I say quietly, lightly scratching his nape with my fingernails.

"Audrey, I was trying to express to you how sorry I am. How fucking sorry I am for everything. I...I just—" I put my finger to his lips.

"No, not now. I'm too drunk for this. And you are too sexy right now for me to have this conversation." My head spins as I stare at his delicious lips.

"You still find me sexy, Mouse?" His voice is low. His hands lightly scratch the outside of my arms, giving me goosebumps. I lean my head back and moan before I can stop myself.

"Donovan..." I whimper. I feel his hard cock through his jeans as I straddle him. My hips grind slowly along his length, and his hands go down to my ass, helping me along. "More," I growl, not giving a fuck about anything else but him. Us. Right now.

He lifts me up in one swift movement, his strong arms whisking me into position, legs wrapped around his torso. He's running through the parking lot, and I throw my head back, laughing into the night. This feels familiar.

He unlocks the tailgate with one swipe of his hand and sets me down on the edge. His arms clamp down on either side of me, caging me in. My hands snake up the back of his shirt, needing to feel his skin beneath my touch.

"Audrey, you're playing a very dangerous game," he growls. I smirk and wrap my legs tight around him, using my heels to drag his bulge straight into my heat.

"Last I remember, you liked games. Don't you?" I buck my hips into him, feeling how hard he is for me.

"God damn," he groans. My hands find their way along his chiseled abs, feeling the V-cut that leads down past the waist of his jeans.

"I knew you were in there somewhere, Mouse. Tell me, what do you want?"

His voice is raspy and full of desire. His lips are inches away and I can smell his masculine cologne mixed with red wine and musk. I've never wanted him more than I do right now. "Kiss me. Now," I demand, my hands coming out from under his shirt and grabbing his collar.

"Fuck it," he growls out. His lips crash into mine and the years of heartache, loss, and anger quickly melt away. His tongue swipes my bottom lip, and I open my mouth to invite him in. He tastes so good. I dreamed of kissing him every night, what it would be like to drink him in again.

His hands cup my face and he grinds his cock into me. I let out a moan while he groans into my mouth, devouring me and kissing away the pain between us.

I rake my fingers through his thick locks, something I've done over and over in my dreams. His hands move down to my breasts, squeezing them with need as our bodies move against one another. We fall into a rhythm, as if we memorized each other's bodies after all this time.

After what feels like hours, he breaks the kiss and I whimper, not wanting him to stop. His forehead presses against mine as he works to catch his breath.

"Audrey, I've been dreaming about this kiss every day for the last ten years. I dreamed of the day when I could taste you again, feel your body against mine."

I bring him closer to me and nip his bottom lip, my hand dragging down to his zipper. He grabs my wrist and stops me. Hurt flashes across my eyes.

"What are you doing? Why are you stopping? Don't you want me?" I whimper, slightly offended.

There's pain in his eyes and he lets out a groan, taking a half step back to put some space between us. Well, fuck that, I don't want space. I take my heels and drag him into me again, making him laugh. I smile at his beautiful face and those irresistible dimples.

"I've never wanted you more. You're so fucking beautiful. I missed these lips so much." His thumb swipes my bottom lip, and he tips my chin up to meet his gaze. "Tonight, we will have this kiss. You're drunk, and I don't want to take advantage of you." Oh, now he wants to be a gentleman? Take the high road?

Fuck that. I'm pissed now.

"Donovan, I'm begging you to fuck me and now you're trying to be the good guy and not *take advantage of me?*" I say the last part sarcastically with air quotes. Rage floods my senses. I let the word vomit flow before I can stop myself. "You know, you fucked me before and got what you wanted. At least this time, if you never speak to me again, I won't be so fucked up about it. I *expect* it," I seethe. I know it's mean, but I'm mad and drunk and Donovan King won't give me an orgasm.

"Audrey, you're angry with me and I deserve that. But please, let me take you home where you can sleep it off. I'll explain everything tomorrow, if you'll let me?"

I scoff and push him off of me, sliding off the tailgate of his truck.

"I don't believe a word you say, Donovan. You're a liar and a fake. You missed your chance to get in my pants and that's the last opportunity you'll *ever* get." I'm walking in a not-so-straight line back toward the coffee shop when he grabs my wrist, gentle but firm.

"Mouse—"

I grunt in frustration and push him in the chest.

"Ugh! Don't fucking call me that anymore! You *hurt* me, Donovan. You took away my virginity, and you fucking *left* me there thinking that night meant something more to you!" He opens his mouth to say something, but I hold my hand up to his face. "No! I'm talking. You used me and then never spoke to me again. I waited for you and you didn't even have the decency to call or text or, god forbid, break it off in person! You told me you wanted me. You wanted the summer together. You said all of those things. And you FUCKED up!" I'm yelling and crying, letting the wine fill me with liquid courage as I empty the anger I've had towards him for the last decade.

"What was it, Donovan? Huh? Was I just one of your trophies to brag to your friends? Did someone dare you to fuck me? Did you lie about your virginity too?" My thoughts are like a fast-moving train, obliterating anything in the way, no brakes.

I can see him grind his molars as his jaw flexes. His eyes shimmer under the reflection of the streetlight above us.

"It wasn't just a quick high school fuck for me, Donovan. That night changed my life. You *took* my innocence. And you were too much of a pussy to man the fuck up and tell me the truth."

He just stands there, hands on his hips, taking every word I spit at him like a knife to the heart.

"So, no. You will not get the opportunity to explain because you're ten years too fucking late. I'm done, Donovan. Stay away from me, I mean it." I stand there, crying, trying to catch my breath after unleashing this swirling whirlwind of rage I've kept locked inside me for too long.

His silence is so loud. I thought I'd feel relieved, but I feel worse than before. When his eyes lock onto mine, a single tear falls down his cheek, shattering my heart into tiny fragments all over the parking lot. He trudges to his truck, the gravel crunching under his boots, ignites the engine and pulls away.

I'm nothing but a reflection in his rearview mirror, crumbling to the ground as sobs rack my entire body.

Chapter Eleven

DONOVAN

I stand in a lonely corner of the Winthrop estate, my eyes scanning around the vast living room filled with people in mourning. A testament to how loved Violet was. Or is. It's jarring to see everyone dressed in black, only driving the stake further into my heart that Violet is truly gone. The funeral was exactly what she would've wanted. Short, sweet, and to the point. There was no bullshitting with Violet, and I loved her for it.

"Can I get you something to drink, D?" Wyatt asks, squeezing my shoulder with a soft smile. The corner of my lip turns up slightly before I reply, "Sure, Wy. I'll take a glass of the Pinot. Thanks." He nods and walks past me. I keep my eyes fixed on Audrey as she stands at the front of the house, giving hugs to all the guests, offering their condolences. She avoided me for the entire funeral, rightfully so. She's avoiding me now.

"I'm done, Donovan. Stay away from me, I mean it."

I take a deep inhale as her words from last night ring in my ears. Every piece of my heart shattered the moment I drove away from her. I deserved her anger. I deserved her reaction. I didn't think I could stop myself the moment we kissed. The way her body fit against mine like she's the missing piece to the broken puzzle of my soul. She told me to stay away, but I need to explain myself. I need her to know how sorry I am. I feel a dull thud in my temples, frustration building inside of me. The gravity between Audrey and me is too strong. I can't avoid it if I tried. I feel myself being pulled into her orbit, one foot trailing in front of the other.

Wyatt steps in front of me, offering my glass of wine with a swirl. I grasp it, immediately missing Audrey's pull. He glances over his shoulder, his eyes locking on Audrey before bringing them back to mine. "So, what's going on between you two?" he probes, lifting his eyebrow as he sips his wine. I shake my head and take a generous sip. "I fucked up. Again." My chest clenches at the sight of Audrey over Wyatt's shoulder. Her smile is one of grief, the kind that you put on when you feel numb inside. I know the feeling. God, I just wanna hold her, tell her everything is going to be okay.

Even with swollen eyes from crying, I'm in awe of her beauty. My gaze snaps back to Wyatt, who is about to say something when our father approaches us. Wyatt flits his eyes between Dad and me. "Um, I'm gonna make sure Kerry isn't eating all the deviled eggs," he says awkwardly before walking away. My eyes roll slightly at his exit, leaving us alone to make awkward conversation.

"Hi, Son. How are you holding up?" my father asks, his hands buried in his pockets while he uncomfortably sways back and forth on his heels. I sigh. "I'm fine, Dad." He shifts his gaze slightly toward Audrey, deep in conversation with Mrs. Dickson. He clears his throat before bringing his attention back to me.

"I, uh… I noticed that you've been avoiding Audrey. Is…everything okay?" he drawls. Jesus, why does he have to make this so awkward? Since when does he care about Audrey? Since when does he care about whether I talk to her? My jaw ticks at his probing, heat flaring under a dress shirt that's too starchy and uncomfortable as it is.

I chug the rest of my wine, swirling it in my mouth before I swallow. "Yeah, well, she won't talk to me," I clip. "And you made fucking sure of that, didn't you?"

My dad gives me a pained look, like I'd just snapped his olive branch in half. When I look at him, all I see is anger and hurt for what he did to me. What he did to *Audrey and me*. I recall my conversation with Wyatt yesterday morning, briefly tearing my gaze away from my dad.

"I just don't want our family to drift further apart. Please, Donovan. Make it right? Talk to Dad?"

How can I make it right when he has everything to do with the last ten years of pain and heartache? I glimpse at Audrey, trailing her with my eyes as she slips out the side door.

"Excuse me," I grumble curtly as I push past my dad, clipping his shoulder. I place my empty wineglass on a table nearby and make a beeline toward the door. My hand freezes as I grip the knob, taking a deep breath before I turn it.

Audrey stands with her back to me, her long black dress draped perfectly on her body, shifting in the wind. Her head turns to the side when she hears me approaching, her eyes quickly retreating toward the rolling green hills that show off in front of us.

I stop a few feet behind her to give her space. Her arms cross over her chest as she looks into the distance. I've never heard silence this loud. The energy between us is deafening, begging to be disturbed and shaken. Every ounce of control I have threatens to leave me as my body is screaming to reach out for her. She looks to the side again, hiding her face from me.

"What do you want, Donovan?" she asks. Her voice is small. Hurt. I take a hesitant step and fill the space next to her. Her eyes shift back toward the valley, glimmering in the sun. She's been crying —I wonder if any of those tears fell today because of me.

I pause, my gaze locked on her beautiful face. "I want to explain what happened between us, Audrey. I want to apologize," I say in a hushed tone.

Please look at me?

Audrey sighs, closing her eyes before turning to face me. I swear the air leaves my lungs the second her eyes meet mine. God, I can't fuck this up again.

"It was a long time ago, Donovan. Look," she says, keeping her arms over her chest. "I'm sorry for what I said last night. I was very drunk, and it was a mistake. I shouldn't have asked you to kiss me. I'm sorry."

"I'm not," I reply gently. "I'm not sorry that I kissed you. But I am sorry for the last ten years. I—"

"Donovan, please," she interrupts, putting her hand up to keep me from talking. She averts her gaze, tears welling up in her eyes. I want to reach out to brush them away, but I don't. "I don't need your apology, okay? We were just kids. It didn't mean anything."

"Audrey, it meant everything to me. Let me just—"

"Donovan, no." She cuts me off, a tear slipping down her cheek. "I just lost my gran," she chokes. "There's nothing anyone can do to change the past. So please, can we stop trying?" Her eyes are full of sorrow. The grief of Violet, the grief of *us*. Guilt coils in my chest, knowing I'm causing her more heartache than she deserves. Today of all days. She takes a deep inhale, uncrossing her arms to wipe the tears that I so desperately want to wipe for her.

"It's fine, Donovan. Okay? We can move on."

"Well, what if I don't want to move on?" I interject. The words rush out before I can contain them.

Damn it, Donovan. She told you to stop.

She scoffs, her fingers threading through her hair.

"You can't tell me that there still isn't something between us. The second we saw each other, you knew it wasn't over." Her lip quivers as she puts her hands by her side. I'm stupid enough to reach out and grab her hand, lacing her fingers through mine, placing it over my heart. I'll take the risk. She chokes out a cry as I take a step closer, squeezing her hand tightly against my chest.

"Tell me, Audrey. Are you happy in New York? Are you happy with him?" I ask breathlessly. "Because I see you. I see it in your eyes. They're so beautiful, but broken." I swallow the hard lump in my throat.

She clenches her jaw, failing to stifle the soft sobs that escape her. I cup my hands around her face, swiping the tears with my thumbs. Her hands rest on my chest, my heart beating beneath her palms.

"Stay. Please stay with me. Don't go back," I whisper, resting my forehead on hers. My insides flutter at the thought of Audrey staying. We'd have another chance, another go at this. A real shot. I look into her eyes and witness a battle in them. They flit back and forth between mine, her brows knitted with worry and doubt.

Please say yes. Stay with me.

"I can't," she murmurs, closing her eyes as thick droplets cascade down her cheekbone. "I have to go back. I need to go back." She gently grips my wrists, pulling them away from her face. She takes a step back and turns around, her hand covering her forehead. I crave her warmth, my body turning frigid the second she walks away.

She turns to face me with distance between us now, her hands on her waist. "It's too late, Donovan. I have to go back."

"You really want to go back to him? After last night, you really—"

"Yes, Donovan! I'm going back to him!" she cries, raising her voice which booms through my chest. My heart drops into my stomach, feeling the distance between us stretch for miles and miles—I can no longer reach her.

"I'm not doing this with you again. I already told you, last night was a mistake. I need to go," she sobs, turning on her heel, leaving me standing alone in the backyard. I watch her disappear inside, tears streaking down her face. I clutch my chest, pacing the backyard as I try to catch my breath. I'm hit with a violent storm of grief, bringing me to my knees.

Flashes of me sitting in my dad's office the morning after graduation play in my mind. The betrayal, the hurt, the anger I felt. His words haunt me, taunting me, slow and torturous.

"Donovan, you must end it. If you don't, your future will be ruined."

My hands fall to the grass below me as my vision blurs, unwanted tears welling in the brims of my eyes. I grip the soft blades in my fingers and squeeze, willing the painful memory to leave me.

I hear a door shut and whip my head up to see my dad standing in the doorway. I quickly stand to my feet, my breaths ragged. The hurt is too much, swelling my heart into a painful ache that I can't escape. My dad slowly walks toward me, looking ironically like a father who cares about his son. He's the last person I want to see right now. And he's about to get caught in the middle of my storm.

"This is all *your* fault," I grit, quickly approaching him. "She left because of *you*. You did this!" I shout, pressing my index into his chest. The rage boils in my blood, pumping through me and pulsing in every vein. My dad lifts his hands in surrender, slowly backing away. "Son, let's calm down and talk."

"Don't tell me to calm down," I seethe, my face just inches from his. I breathe like a bull through my nose, huffing hard, as if I'm ready to charge straight through him. Wyatt and Kerry slip through the door with hurried steps, rushing toward my dad and me in a standoff. Wyatt places a gentle hand on my shoulder, but my eyes stay fixed on my dad. I don't miss the hurt in his eyes. The sadness that dances in his irises.

"Hey, brother. Let's go inside. Come on," Wyatt pleads softly, tugging my arm back. Kerry stands by my dad, his hand placed on his shoulder. "Dad, give him some space," Kerry tells him. I shrug Wyatt off of me, storming my way out of the gate toward my truck. I need to get out of here.

"Donovan, wait!" Wyatt calls after me, nipping at my heels. I fix my gaze forward. Away from my dad. Away from Audrey. "Not now, Wy. I gotta get the fuck out of here," I clip, unlatching the gate, pushing my way through it. Wyatt's steps halt, and I trudge my feet back to my truck, wading through years of anger and resentment. The weight on my heart hangs heavier, knowing that Audrey is choosing a life in New York. With *him*.

I fumble with my keys in my pocket, hands trembling as I unlock the front door. As soon as I slam it shut, my head drops into my hands. "Fuck!" I yell at the top of my lungs, slamming my fists on the steering wheel. My head falls back against the headrest, tears spilling involuntarily.

I look toward the front porch of the Winthrop estate, seeing a ghost of my eighteen-year-old self sitting in a chair with Noah and Violet. The summer Audrey left for New York, I sat on that front porch as a broken kid every chance I got when I'd come home from college on the weekends. Violet would make me lemonade, and they'd sit and listen to me grieve for Audrey. The guilt consumed me, but never once did they judge me.

Violet would embrace me in her arms, stroking the back of my head. *"Oh, my sweet boy. Don't worry. It will pass,"* she'd say. The days I couldn't look my father in the eye, I'd come running to Noah and Violet.

I tear my eyes away from the porch, jolting me out of the memory. I start the truck, slowly making my way down the winding driveway. My jaw clenches as I hold back the tears, watching my future with Audrey once again fade away in my rearview mirror.

"Yes, Donovan! I'm going back to him!"

I flinch at her admission, sending a sharp pain in my gut. Of course she's choosing him. What have I done to prove to her I deserve her? All I've done was cause her pain. Pain I wish I could desperately take away.

Losing Audrey once nearly broke me. Losing her again might just finish the job.

Chapter Twelve

AUDREY

My pen moves fluid on the paper, the words flowing out of me as natural as water streaming down a steady river.

"No matter how hard I try, I can't escape you. And I don't think I ever want to..."

It's been a month since Gran's funeral. A month without speaking to Donovan after he came crashing back into my soul. The ache of missing him has become too much to bear. I've willed myself to deny the pull, to cut the invisible string that connects us. But I can't. I won't. How can I? I pour my heart onto the page as I scribble sweet nothings, a mixture of heartache and arousal swirling inside me.

"I miss your touch. Your taste. The way I feel when you hold me..."

I squeeze my legs tight under my desk as heat forms in the apex of my thighs. I chew on the tip of my pen, a small grin forming on my lips as I daydream about Donovan's intoxicating kiss. His large hands gripping me.

"Little bird, let's go," Kellan interrupts, opening the door to my office so suddenly I nearly jump out of my chair. He cocks his head to the side as warmth heats my cheeks. I carefully shift my purse in front of the letter, my feet wobbling slightly as I stand from my chair. "Yes, darling. Let me just grab my things," I say in a light tone, sliding the letter under my laptop as I place it stealthily in my bag.

Kellan's eyes study my body, and I do my best to lower my heart rate before approaching him. Thankfully, his phone buzzes, stealing his gaze from me. In that brief respite, I move quickly to make sure the letter is safely out of sight, deep within my bag. I have no intentions of sharing it with anyone, not even Donovan. Especially not Kellan. I'll probably burn it later.

I step behind Kellan with my bag slung over my shoulder. I remind myself to breathe normally since this letter could burn a hole through the leather with its heat and secrets. With Kellan's eyes fixated on his phone, I fight the smirk that wants to play on my lips as my mind once again wanders to Donovan.

Focus, Audrey.

Walking side by side with Kellan down the hall en route to this meeting, it's like I'm not even there. His hand grazes mine as we walk, but no sparks fly. No electricity buzzing between us. It's hollow and all business. Emptiness.

"We're meeting SuiteSync Systems today, a tech company from upstate," he says dryly, his eyes glued to his phone. "They're pitching for smart rooms for the East Coast launch next year. Take notes."

"Okay," I reply quietly. He pushes the door open to the conference room with the Empire State Building in full view out the window. It's buzzing with casual conversation and a lot of men in tailored suits. Expensive cologne and a waft of aftershave fill my senses. My eyes draw to a flash of long, blonde, silky hair. Jesus, her tits are massive. The swell of her breasts push up toward her collarbone, where the top button of her white dress shirt is undone. Well, that's one way to do business.

Kellan places his hand on the small of her back as I watch from a distance. She turns to face him, showing off her pearly white teeth and full lips. His eyes draw straight to her breasts, earning a tiny scoff from me.

I wait for the tinge of jealousy to settle in my stomach…crickets. Nothing. My boyfriend is practically taking a swim in a pair of massive tits, and I feel absolutely nothing. Not like the way I felt when I saw multiple women flirting with Donovan at the happy hour.

Caressing his arm, laughing at his jokes. Now that? That pissed me off. But it shouldn't, because Donovan's not mine.

Kellan grasps her hand, turning his charm up to max volume. With a subtle eye roll, I find my seat at the table, opening my laptop for yet another boring meeting that I have to endure. I'd rather be baking cinnamon rolls, hand-feeding them to Donovan.

Snap out of it, Audrey.

"Okay, everyone, let's take our seats. Mr. Vanguard is here, so let's get started," says Derek Franz, VP of marketing for Vanguard Hotels. The blonde stays standing as everyone settles in, and I quirk an eyebrow the longer I look at her face. Do I know her? She turns on the projector and holds a clicker in her hand, squaring her shoulders to the room with a million-dollar smile.

Oh my god. I *do* know her.

"Hello everyone. Thank you for being here. My name is Jessica Taylor, sales director here at SuiteSync Systems," she announces.

Jess freaking Taylor. Is here. This would happen to me. Of course, she would be the director of something. This is the queen of getting what she wants in life. Persuasive, beautiful, smart. The whole package. I slink down subtly in my chair, tucking my eyes behind my screen in hopes we don't make eye contact. I'm hard to avoid, considering we are the only two women in the room.

Kellan sits across from me, his eyes laser focused on Jess. Meanwhile, I'm not registering anything coming out of her mouth as I turn myself on autopilot to catch these notes.

I can feel Jess's eyes on me in my peripheral vision. I look up from my screen for a split second to see her expression slightly change from "I'm in control" to "Oh, fuck." Or, at least, that's what it seems like. I'm positive I'm mirroring her, my neck flushing with heat as I tug on my collar. Suddenly, I'm itchy everywhere and I need to get the hell out of this room.

"Any questions?" Jess asks, looking at everyone else in the room but me. Yup, nothing's changed since high school. Scattered applause erupts around the table as Jess nods and smiles, thanking everyone in a sweet tone. I can see why she's good at sales.

I quickly shut my laptop when Kellan knocks his knuckles against the table, garnering my attention. "Little bird, grab me a coffee? The one here tastes like shit. I want the place on 5th next to Magnolia's. You know my order," he demands. Jess walks by, stopping right by Kellan to steal our attention.

We stand from our seats as Kellan flashes her his best grin. She looks over at me, stoic and expressionless. A fake smile at best. "Mr. Vanguard, what did you think of the presentation?" she asks sweetly. If this were Donovan, I'd claw her eyes out over the table. I clutch my laptop close to my chest, as if I'm shielding myself from her, hoping she doesn't see me. Too late.

"It was very impressive, Ms. Taylor. We'll be in touch soon," Kellan replies. "Ms. Taylor, meet my assistant, Audrey Winthrop." He gestures me to come around the table.

Kill me now.

What's worse than embarrassment? Humiliation? That's it. My body might as well shrivel into a little ball and sink below the earth, hiding away from everyone in this room. I'm a pathetic assistant, going nowhere.

Jess smiles politely when I approach, extending a polite hand-shake. This is fucking weird. I grasp her hand in mine, giving a weak shake. "It's nice to meet you, Ms. Winthrop," she croons. Her bright blue eyes gleam in the sun's rays peeking through the window. She doesn't look like a girl who had her life torn up by her father's bad decisions. The eyes I see before me are bright and thriving. Envy creeps up my neck. I shake it away and smile back. "It's nice to meet you too, Ms. Taylor," I reply curtly.

"Audrey was just going to fetch a coffee. Did you want anything?" Kellan offers. The heat burns my cheeks, my palms damp and clammy. There's no way I'm fetching coffee like a dog for Jess Taylor too.

"Actually, I need some air. I can accompany you, Ms. Winthrop?" she beams.

Why is this happening to me?

"Uh, sure. It's just down the block," I mumble, earning a glare from Kellan like I'm a petulant child. "Alright. Get anything you want, Ms. Taylor. It's on me," he says politely. "I'll be in my office. Ladies." He dismisses himself to finish conversing with the remaining men in the room. Jess and I share an awkward glance as I gesture for her to exit the room first.

I watch her saunter in front of me, her high-waisted slacks hugging every curve like a second skin. I'm eighteen again, slinking in the shadow of Jess Taylor. Briggs sneakily paces behind us, as he usually does. I never know when he is lurking. Once Jess and I are walking in stride together, her eyes remain on our heels clacking the floor.

"Who's that burly man following us?" she asks, tilting her head slightly to catch a glimpse of Briggs. I smirk, sensing her discomfort.

"That's my bodyguard. He's harmless. That is, if no one touches me," I tease, my lame attempt to break the tension. She huffs out a chuckle, craning her neck all the way around to look at Briggs.

"Wow, a bodyguard? You must be important to have one of those," she retorts, quirking her eyebrow at me.

Something like that.

The line at Sweetners is annoyingly long today—heavy on the annoying because Jess Taylor won't stop staring at me like I have something in my teeth. I give her a cautious sideways glance, totally weirded out that she's standing next to me. Last I remember, Jess loathed me. This isn't exactly a wholesome high school reunion for me.

My eyes flicker back and forth between Jess and the lone barista, speeding to make everyone's coffee order. "Jess, why do you keep staring at me? Why are you even here?" My tone comes off harsh, but I'm not really sorry about it.

She pinches the bridge of her nose before responding. "Audrey, I'm sorry I acted like I didn't know you in there. I just...wasn't expecting to see you. It caught me off guard," she sighs, biting her bottom lip as we slowly shuffle up the line. "I wanna talk. Could we sit in a booth for a bit?" she asks, incessantly rubbing her palms up and down the sides of her pants.

"Okay, just stop fidgeting. You're making me nervous," I mutter. A grin tugs at the corner of her lips as she mouths, "sorry."

After what seems like hours, we finally get our coffee and quietly slip into a booth against a window. I settle in and see Briggs standing outside, pressing his back against the brick wall of the coffee shop.

"So, he really follows you everywhere?" she asks, hiking her thumb back.

"Yup." I pause. "So…what's up?" I ask impatiently. I'm not in the mood for small talk with an old high school mean girl. Her eyes get shiny, like she is on the verge of crying. I'm confused and uncomfortable.

"Jess, you wanted to talk? Are you okay?"

She lets out a breath and intertwines her fingers, resting them on the table. "I'm sure you heard about what happened with my father," she mutters. I gulp and quickly nod. "He wasn't a good person." She continues. "He was a liar and manipulated my mother and me our whole lives." It's all very matter of fact. I lean in closer, feeling a small spark of empathy because I know what it feels like to be manipulated and lied to.

"He deserved what he got, and I guess karma came for me as well." I act like I understand where she's going with this, but I have no fucking clue.

"I'm sorry about your father, but karma clearly avoided you. You're a successful career woman in New York City. That counts for something," I say empathetically. This isn't the same woman that was leading a sales pitch. She's slipping. Her fingers tremble around the handle of her coffee mug.

"Audrey, I never meant for any of this to happen. I didn't know that it would keep you away from him all these years. I was angry and jealous, and what I did was wrong. So, so wrong. I'm so sorry. I'm so sorry for everything," she utters frantically, her tone on the cusp of shrill.

Okay, now…what the fuck?

"Jess, what are you talking about? Who's him? Why are you apologizing to me? I'm sorry, but I'm not following," I reply, puzzled, furrowing my brow. Her eyes get wide and she leans closer over the table, like I've been living under a rock or something.

"Wait, you don't know?" she whispers.

Clearly fucking not.

I shake my head at her and shrug my shoulders. She looks down at her hands and takes a deep breath, then exhales slowly. Her big blue eyes meet mine, nervous and timid.

"My father forced me to get dirt on the King's. He wanted their vineyard, and he knew that Donovan's dad would never go for it as long as he was loyal to your grandfather," she explains, taking another deep inhale. The thumping of my heart picks up speed hearing Donovan's name in this.

"I was in love with Donovan. And when I saw him with you on graduation night, I got jealous. Like, really stupid, jealous. Donovan basically told me to fuck off after I interrupted your dance together, then ran off to find you," she mutters.

My mind flashes back to that night where we danced. The first time we held each other close. I stay silent and lean back against the leather booth, crossing my arms. The rapid thud of my heartbeat pulses hard against my chest. I take a deep breath to try and slow it down.

"I saw you two running out of the party, and it made me so angry. So, I followed you," she says quietly, her voice small.

My stomach drops. I barely maintain a grasp on the anger threatening to bubble up in my throat. I take a moment to choose my words before opening my mouth.

"You-you followed me? And Donovan?" I choke out. She nods, tears filling her eyes. I wish I could stop the involuntary tears building behind my eyes. The sting I hate so much taunting me, a feeling that's been more familiar than not.

"I saw you two laughing and kissing. I stayed hidden and all I thought at that moment was how I wanted you out of the picture to have Donovan to myself," she admits another confession. My breathing turns ragged as the liquid brimming my eyes puddle. "And then I saw you guys together. In the gazebo," she cries, wiping her fingers under her eyes. I shut my eyes, and the tears fall, knowing where this is going. Heat pricks the tops of my ears thinking about Jess seeing us in that private moment.

"I took out my phone, and I filmed you two having sex. There was my dirt, and there was my way of keeping you out of the picture," she breathes with a crack in her voice. Her confession is a direct stab in my heart. An instant kill. She wipes her tears quickly before they fall past her chin, looking out the window toward the busy street.

My chin trembles as I look at Jess, her eyes refusing to meet mine at this moment. I open my mouth, words struggling to form. This is why Donovan didn't come pick me up the next day. She held that sex tape over his head, and he carried that burden for *ten fucking years*. He carried it for me. I rest my elbows on the table, covering my face with my hands as I quietly cry into them. I cry for Donovan. I cry for our lost love. I turn my head to face the window, wondering how everything got so fucked. I count the yellow cabs that pass by, each one representing the missed opportunities Donovan and I had. Too many to count.

I finally muster enough strength to turn toward Jess. I study her expression—she seems lost in her own thoughts. Her lips purse tightly together, her bright blue eyes swim in sadness.

"So, you brought the footage to your father, and he blackmailed Caleb King with it," I say, putting the pieces together. She nods, shame and guilt mark her face. "And that's why Caleb cut ties with my grandfather," I add, another guilty nod from Jess. "And that's why Donovan never spoke to me again. To protect me." A final nod.

Damn.

Donovan was protecting me. All this time, he let me go to keep me safe. To save me from humiliation. My heart cracks wide open, imagining Donovan with this weight on his shoulders at just eighteen years old. We were kids. A victim to horrendous blackmail, and he took the fall for it to let me go.

"Audrey, I'm so sorry. It was stupid and petty, and clearly my family got what they deserved. I lost my dad, my home, and Donovan. Although, I never really had him. His heart always belonged to you," she sighs, a sad grin playing on her lips. "I just didn't want to see it," she whispers.

I wipe my tears with the pads of my fingers, meeting her gaze. Here we are, two women with broken pasts. Somehow intertwined with one another. A true collision of fate. All in the same city. Ten years of confusion, solved.

"Thank you for telling me. Thank you for apologizing," I murmur.

Maybe Jess and I aren't so different after all. I couldn't see it then, but sitting here together half a world away from home, we're just two girls who have been hurt. She doesn't need my anger—hell, I don't need it either. We're not spiteful kids. It's time to let it go.

She gives me a sad smile and reaches out for my hands. I place mine in hers and a huge weight lifts off my shoulders, like another ghost from my past freeing itself from me. I have answers. Even if it wasn't from Donovan, it was from the source. I know she was telling the hard truth. A truth that has me close to booking a ticket back to California to tell Donovan I love him.

"Audrey, I want you to know that the tape doesn't exist. It was destroyed with my father's assets. It never saw the light of day," she reassures me. Instant relief coats my heart with her sharing that detail with me. I don't particularly like the idea of me losing my virginity on tape in the ether.

"I hope you can forgive me. It was never Donovan's fault."

She's right. It wasn't Donovan's fault. The unsolved equation in my head finally found an answer that works. An answer that fits. But ten years of silence wasn't easy to endure. And although I have the answer, the hurt still lingers in every fiber of my being. Jess picks up on my doubt, like an intuition broken girls share. Her eyes soften and her hands squeeze mine before she places them back in her lap.

"Audrey, Donovan was terrified. You know, when he figured out I did it, he laid into me pretty fucking bad. He told me he would do anything to protect you and your future. He said that you were going to New York, and that I was a piece of shit for trying to mess with your life," she says, leaning closer on the table, propping on her elbows. "He was right. I was awful to put you in that position, even if you had no idea. His future was at risk too, and his father branded that into his brain."

"She left because of you. You did this!"

Donovan's voice booms through my mind. The realization hits me like a ton of bricks. Donovan hadn't noticed when I watched him go head to head with Caleb in the backyard during Gran's funeral reception. I heard a commotion when Wyatt and Kerry secretly slipped out the door. Caleb was the one who kept Donovan from telling me. Donovan blamed his father all these years for what happened between us. My chest clenches, aching for all that was lost.

"He may not have said it to you, but he loved you. He told me how he felt about you and that I would never compare," Jess huffs, a small laugh slips from her lips. My eyes flicker with hurt for her, but she waves me off. "Oh, Audrey. It's okay. He was totally right. I was a bitch." We share an unexpected chuckle at the truth of it all. She really was a bitch, but this woman in front of me is different. I suppose I am too.

I stand up from the booth with Jess mirroring me. We face one another, not quite friends, but no longer enemies. And after a moment, we embrace. It's not exactly warm, not exactly cold. Just a regular hug. But a hug, nonetheless. It's forgiveness.

"Thank you for giving me a chance. Now maybe you can give him his," she murmurs. She rubs the side of my arm and walks away, her blonde hair wafting vanilla and sugar in my face.

She pauses for a beat, turning back to me to say, "Oh, by the way —Kellan is a major dick." Her lip turns up as she turns back around, heading toward the exit.

Yeah, he sure is.

I slide back into the booth and let her words linger. She walks past the window, her gaze meeting mine one last time, and waves, disappearing into a sea of people on the busy sidewalk.

Briggs notices Jess walking out of the shop, then comes in to find me, sliding in the booth across from me.

"We should get back. Mr. Vanguard is expecting you," he mutters, lacing his fingers together on the table.

I stare out the window, squinting up at the skyscrapers surrounding me. I imagine them gone, with nothing but rolling vineyards for miles as far as the eye can see. The buzz of cars and people quiet themselves in my mind, and it's replaced with birds chirping, a cool breeze brushing my ear. I imagine a gentle graze from Donovan's hand on my cheek.

"What's on your mind, Ms. Winthrop?" Briggs asks.

Donovan. Always Donovan.

"Nothing. Let's go."

Chapter Thirteen

DONOVAN

Twenty-eight days. It's been twenty-eight days since I left the hope of Audrey in my rearview mirror. I deserved every word that she spewed onto me. Seeing her back in Oakwood Valley, I thought maybe we could start over, try again like the past never happened. I know how much I hurt her. Watching her push me away, the pain written all over her face as she told me she wouldn't stay…that's the worst I've felt in a long time. At least, in the ten years since I stood her up for our first date.

Noah clears his throat to bring me back to the task at hand. My mind is wandering so often these days. It's hard to focus on anything other than her radiant eyes and her strawberry scent. For now, the smell of fermented grapes will have to do as we pace through the vast wine cellar under the Winthrop property, taking inventory of various vintages from the last twenty years, tallying up shiny bottles of wine and towering oak barrels lining the walls.

"What's on your mind, son?" He always knows when something is up. Nothing gets past him.

"Audrey." No point in lying. He knows I've been fucked up over her since I was a teenager. He hums and matches my pace beside me with his hands behind his back. Even though he says nothing, I feel the need to say more.

"I messed up. Again." He just nods. He's really going to get it all out of me right now, isn't he? I let out a sigh and stop walking. Noah halts beside me.

"I kissed her, because she wanted me to. And…well, things were getting a little heated…" I look over at him, feeling awkward because that's her grandfather. He chuckles and shakes his head.

"Son, I was young once. You know, Vi and I were really adventurous when we were your age. One time, she and I were going at it in the back of—" I throw my hands over my ears and start yelling nonsense words to avoid hearing where this conversation is going. His laugh is hearty as he claps on my shoulder.

"You're trying, son. You've got a good heart, and I can see how much you care for Audrey. But you've got to understand the hurt runs deep. Growing up without her mother, dealing with the chaos her dad brought into her life, mourning her first big heartbreak." Noah gives me a soft smile that I feel I don't deserve. I broke her heart. I did. God, I want to fix it. "Well, that doesn't heal quick. Be patient. Give her time," he replies.

I absorb his words, averting my gaze to focus on a lone cork on the ground. I bend down to pick it up, prodding it with my fingernails. *Give her time.* Yeah, well, how's ten years' time for you? It hurts every part of me knowing that Audrey's life wasn't easy. It hurts even more knowing that I contributed to make it more difficult than it already was. Noah lets out a deep exhale, breaking me out of my daze.

"And now she's in a relationship with someone she doesn't even want to be with."

My eyes widen. "What do you mean? Did she say something to you?"

He sighs and rubs his face. "No. She hasn't said anything, but I know. I know my granddaughter." His voice chokes up slightly, and I put my hand on his shoulder.

"She's broken. When she came in through the door for the first time in nine years, I let out a breath I'd been holding. I looked into her eyes, and they were empty," he murmurs, his eyes fixed on me. I know what he means. I saw the emptiness and brokenness too. But then I'd watch her come back for a fleeting moment, gone as fast as it came.

"She wouldn't talk to me about New York, you know? About Kellan? So, I stopped pushing," he sighs, resting his hands on his hips as he looks out at a wall of barrels.

"Look, all I want is for Audrey to be happy. And I'm saying you've got a chance, kid. So get her back," he says, poking his index into my chest.

Get her back? As easy as that, huh? Audrey slipped right through my fingers when I'd begged for her to stay with me. She chose to stay with *him*. She chose her life in New York, making it crystal clear that there was no longer space for me in her life. Over the last month, I'd gotten used to the dull ache in my heart. An ache that yearned for her so desperately, no matter how hard I tried to let her go.

"Have you talked to her since she left?" he asks. I dig my thumb nail deep into the cork I picked up earlier, leaving a half-moon indent before stuffing it in my pocket. "No. By the way things ended last month, she doesn't want to hear from me again," I mutter, wiping the sweat from my brow with the back of my hand. Noah scoffs and tilts his head.

"Son, I was married for sixty years to the same woman I was in love with since I was eighteen years old. Quit being stupid. She wants to hear from you again. You just need to step up and fight."

I put my hands on my hips and look down at my boots.

"Noah, I did that—"

"So do it again," he clips, quirking his brow with a sly smirk on his lips.

"So what, I fly to New York and get her back?" It doesn't sound that crazy when I say it out loud. I wasted too many years on sulking and blaming everyone else. Jess, Duke, my dad, but never me. I did this. She doesn't even know why. If I have any chance of getting her to forgive me, I need her to know the truth. And I won't stop until she hears it from me.

"That's exactly what you do. You love her, don't you?" The question hits me hard. Do I love her? Do I think about her every second of every day? Do I live for her laugh, her smile, the way she says my name? Do I love the way she fits in my arms, and how we touch and play?

I love her. I love Audrey.

"I do, Noah. I really do." He smiles.

"Well, son, I think I got inventory covered for the next couple of days," he says casually as he makes marks on the clipboard he was holding, a subtle curl in his lips.

I stand there, my heart pumping blood through my ears. Am I really doing this? Noah puts his hand on my back and says, "Well, what are you standing here for? Don't you have a girl to win back?"

That's all it takes for me to take off running out of the cellar and straight to my cabin to arrange a flight.

Time to get my girl.

Chapter Fourteen

AUDREY

Cool air whooshes across my face as I open the door to the penthouse. It's silent and dark, with only the light of dusk seeping through the windows.

My heels echo through the empty kitchen, glancing around for any sign of life. "Hello? Kellan?" I call out, only hearing the faint sound of the air conditioning whirring. He must be working in his office.

I place the takeout I picked up for dinner on the dining room table, slipping my heels off in relief.

I wiggle my toes and stretch the arches of my feet while unpacking our dinner, pulling pad thai and spring rolls out of the plastic bag and arranging them at our place settings.

I call out for Kellan, letting him know dinner is ready. Silence. I sit down against the plush velvet chair and bring my leg across my knee, massaging the pads of my feet after walking in stilettos all day.

My mind takes me to Donovan, as it usually does. After talking to Jess, Donovan has taken up permanent residency in my thoughts these days. I wonder if he's out in the vineyard, his skin gleaming under the sun. Does he think about our kiss? Or the way our bodies melded into one another? Like they were made for each other?

I startle out of my thoughts when I hear Kellan's voice carry down the hallway. "Little bird, come to my office."

I take a deep breath and saunter down the hall. His door is slightly ajar, and I lean on the door frame to find him sitting on the leather couch.

"Hey. I picked up Thai. Your favorite," I say softly.

His eyes are dark, narrowing at me. A glass of cognac sits on a coaster in front of him. His legs spread open as he leans back on the couch, the top buttons of his dress shirt undone. His hair is unusually disheveled—a far cry from his typical uniform quiff, slicked to perfection. An uneasiness creeps over me, a heavy rock sitting in the pit of my stomach.

"Come here," he says huskily, beckoning me with his finger. I walk toward him, bracing myself on instinct. I lower myself onto the couch and Kellan's body moves swiftly on top of mine. He pins my arms above my head and bites my neck. Hard.

His lips are on mine before I can register the pain. "Open your mouth," he growls, and I comply.

What did you do, Audrey?

His tongue assaults my mouth. Swirling around with traces of cognac on my taste buds. Spicy cologne and alcohol sting my nostrils. He grips my wrists tighter above my head, grinding his hard length on top of me. I grunt and struggle as he puts his entire body weight over mine.

"What are you thinking about right now, little bird?" he growls.

Donovan's face flashes into my mind. Kellan looks at me with curiosity, and I try my best to lie.

"You. I'm thinking about you," I murmur, doing my best to sell him on my act.

His smile is sinister, making my insides twist in fear. Panic beats down the door to my chest. I try to keep my breathing as even as possible.

"Are you lying to me?" he asks deviously. I feel the heat spreading down my neck to my lungs. The pulse in my throat beats rapidly.

"No," I reply, looking straight into his whiskey eyes, praying he buys it.

Please, please don't hurt me.

His smile disappears and the face staring back at me is pure evil. It's an empty shell of a man who is no longer in there. All that's left is rage and revenge. It turns my blood ice cold.

"You're a *fucking* liar, aren't you?" he sneers, gripping my cheeks between his large, calloused hand. A low groan vibrates in his chest as he tightens his grip, biting down on my bottom lip as I wince.

Our kiss breaks, and I taste iron and metal.

"You sure you're not thinking about *Donovan*, little bird?" he hisses in my ear. My eyes widen in fear at the sound of Donovan's name coming out of Kellan's mouth.

Stay calm, Audrey.

I wrap my legs tighter around Kellan's waist and confidently look into his eyes.

"Donovan, who? He means nothing," I softly whisper.

Donovan who? Donovan King, my everything.

He applies unbearable pressure on my hips, giving me no control. The tip of his nose traces along my jaw, down to my neck. He trails his lips back up to my ear.

"Do you think I'm fucking stupid, Audrey?" he seethes, his teeth nipping my earlobe. I try to flinch away, but he squeezes my wrists harder, putting me in my place.

"Did you think you could hide that little love letter to your *precious* Donovan?"

Fuck.

He knew. He knew I was hiding something the minute he came into my office on the day I wrote it. My reaction to him barging in must have piqued his interest. Why didn't I burn that fucking letter like I had intended? Goddamn it.

"That meant nothing, Kellan. I'm yours. Take me, please," I plead, needing to do anything to get his mind off of Donovan. His pupils grow larger, his eyes almost black. He lifts his face up further from mine, tilting his head.

"You fucked him, didn't you?" he grins devilishly, striking an ungodly fear in the deepest parts of my soul.

"No!" I bark, squirming beneath him.

"I bet you're wet right now, huh? Thinking about Donovan. Let's see," he drawls, holding my wrists with one hand and sliding the other down toward my skirt.

I squeeze my eyes shut, trying to shut Donovan out of my mind. But all I see is his beautiful face. His charming grin. I hear his laugh. I feel his warmth. I taste his kiss.

God damn it, Donovan.

I twist my hips around, trying to keep Kellan's hands from getting underneath my skirt. I fail, and he succeeds.

He cocks his eyebrow up once his hand is beneath my legs. "You *are* wet for him. You little *slut*."

Fucking fight, Audrey. Fight back.

Tears are forming in the back of my eyes, the familiar sting balling up, ready to be released. Donovan's face refuses to leave me. He's begging me to not give up. Those pleading ocean eyes, telling me to fight like hell.

I stare daggers into Kellan's gaze, a rush of motivation flowing in my blood. I brace myself, turning my spine to steel as I flash him the same devilish grin he gave me earlier.

You want a fight, Kellan? I'll give you a fight.

"You will *never* make me wet the way he does. You will *never* make me feel the way he makes me feel," I seethe, my voice sharp like a double-edged sword. "And you will *never* fucking touch me ever again," I growl out, my voice unrecognizable.

Before Kellan can react, I spit in his face and jab my knee up into his balls, forcing him to release me.

Run, Audrey.

Adrenaline pumps through my blood as I slide off the couch, Kellan groaning behind me. As I get up to run, he grabs my ankle, dragging me back toward him.

"You fucking cunt, get over here!" he yells, fighting the pain in his groin. He yanks me by my ankle, dragging me on my back. I use my free leg to kick him in the chest, sending him stumbling.

I scramble to get back on my feet, making a beeline out of his office. His heavy footsteps are close behind me. I know I can't outrun him.

Think fast, Audrey.

A large vase sits on a display just within my reach. I outstretch my arm and grip the neck just as Kellan's fingers grapple with my top, trying to pull me back into his hold. The adrenaline charged in my body fuels my strength to heave the vase at his head, smashing apart into tiny fragments around us.

"Agh, fucking bitch!" he grunts angrily, grasping at the eyelid that's slashed with glass. Blood. I see blood.

Keep going.

I frantically stumble into the hall, picking my feet up as fast as they can take me. My heart thumps a thousand beats per minute. My entire body stings. I can't move fast enough. A rip of fabric, a firm hand twisting my hair, and the brute force of a man's power slams me facedown onto the cold, marble floor.

"I fucking gave you everything, Audrey! And this is how you repay me? Fucking another man?!" he screams out as I struggle to get back on my feet. Next thing I know, I'm being flung against the glass coffee table in the middle of the living room.

Sharp pain shoots through my body as the glass shatters around me. In me. Kellan grasps my nape and jerks me through the glass, lacerating my legs with every inch. Searing pain. I scream until my vocal cords fry. I can't get his hands off of me.

Don't give up. Keep fighting.

He tosses me on the cold floor and straddles my torso, hitting the side of my head so hard with his fist that my ears ring.

"I gave you this penthouse! I gave you lavish gifts! I gave you a fucking life here when you had nothing!" he roars in my face. His saliva sprays across my cheek. My head spins. I'm losing control.

Keep going, Audrey. Don't give up.

I open my palm and strike him hard against his cheek, but it barely makes a dent. I go in for another hit, using all the strength I have left. He catches my wrist mid-air, slamming it down.

"Fuck you, Kellan!"

My scream is guttural, casting out from the depths of my soul. Tears soak my face. I feel no pain, even though I'm bleeding from so many places. How much blood can a person lose before they die? I wish I knew the answer. I'm afraid I'll find out.

Kellan wraps his hands around my throat, immediately cutting off my oxygen. My eyes bulge, flitting back and forth between his pupils, the blood from his face dripping onto my clothes.

"I fucking love you, Audrey. Why do you do this to me?!" he grunts out. The edges of my vision darken. I'm losing air quickly.

Stay awake. Don't go.

"I love you. God, I love you, little bird," he sobs. His hands grip harder. Anger shakes his body. I lose my hearing. I'm fading. I can't hold on anymore.

In my last lucid moment, I see a shadow blurring in the corner of my eye, and Kellan's hands suddenly release my neck. I gasp and struggle for air, my throat on fire.

My vision is hazy, no matter how fervently I blink to bring the room back into focus. A scuffle happens in front of me, bodies moving. I can't tell what I am looking at. I float in and out of consciousness, struggling to stay awake.

I want to sleep. Let me rest my eyes now.

The struggle turns still. I feel strong arms wrap around me and lift me up. The noises around me muffle, dampened by the enormous pounding in my head. There's someone beside us, another blurry silhouette smudged like ink spilled on wet paper.

My eyelids shut.

I can't do it.

"I've got you, baby. It's okay. Mouse, I'm here. I've got you," he echoes.

Donovan?

Sleep takes me away as soon as I hear *Mouse*. Quiet, dark, still, and gone.

The first thing I smell is sterile air, almost too clean. A fifty-pound weight sits heavily on my chest as I try to get up. The pain is unbearable, like I've been dragged through a sea of glass. There's the sharp stabbing up and down my legs. The dull ache in my temples, thumping with every blink. The screaming ring in my ears. But I'm alive.

The fluorescent white lights above blind me and I blink rapidly to focus my vision. A faint beeping sound blips in my ear as I look over and see the neon green line on the monitor spike in a steady cadence.

I open my mouth to call out for help and a hot torch of scorching fire brands my vocal cords. I silently cry out, wincing at the pain. A hoarse breath escapes my throat. I run my fingers down the column of my throat. It's sensitive to the touch. I gently press my lymph nodes, puffy and swollen.

My head stops spinning for a moment to focus on the corner of the room where a body slumps in a chair. I squint my eyes only to see a sleeping, beautiful man. My man.

My Donovan.

His arms are crossed, chin tucked into himself. His shoulders rise and fall with every breath. I need to see his eyes.

He's here? He's in New York? How long? The dull ache in my temples persists as I try to piece together the last memories I have. I wince at the sharp stab that pierces the side of my head. What the fuck happened to me?

I shuffle in the hospital bed, tubes attached to my arms, constricting my range of motion. His head slowly rises and his eyes flicker open. And then he looks my way. The pull from his ocean blues searing into me is enough to take any pain I feel away in an instant. And for a moment, I feel nothing. No throbbing, no sharpness, no sting. As soon as his eyes meet mine, I know I'm going to be okay.

He scrubs a hand over his face and rushes to the side of my bed, dragging the chair with him along the floor. The instant our hands touch, the years of heartache, confusion, and anger fade to nothing. He's here.

"Hey, Mouse," he whispers sweetly. His smile is small, but it's enough to expose his sweet dimples—I'd reach out and touch them if I could. He opens up my hand and lays my palm on his cheek, kissing the inside. I try to respond, but he shushes me and laces his fingers through mine, pressing his lips against my knuckles.

You're here. I missed you. I love you.

"It's best you don't talk. Your throat needs to heal. There's a lot of bruising and your vocal cords are swollen. You also have a mild concussion, but with rest, you'll be okay," he softly whispers. My eyes search his for answers, and it's like he reads my mind.

"I booked a flight yesterday. Noah gave me your address. He wasn't completely sure if you still lived there, but I came anyway."

He gently kisses my fingers, taking a deep breath before he continues. "I landed and took a cab straight to your apartment. The doorman wouldn't let me in when I asked to see you. A guy walking in asked how I knew your name. He told me his name was Briggs." A small smile of relief appears on my lips. I knew Briggs was good people.

"I begged him to let me come up to see you. I came to fight for you, to explain everything and ask for your forgiveness," he murmurs. His gaze tears away from me for only a second, and my hand is on his cheek, gently moving him back to look in my direction. His jaw clenches, and his Adam's apple bobs up and down.

"He's a good guy. He let me in, and that's when we heard you screaming," he croaks out, his eyes watering. He clears his throat and pushes the tears away, squeezing my hand tighter.

"Briggs and I barged in just in time as Kellan was...choking you," he fumes, his eyes darkening as he replays the painful memory back in his head. The memory of Kellan's death grip around my neck suddenly becomes clear. Lack of air, scorching pain, everything fading to black. "I tackled him to get him off of you, and Briggs came in and knocked him out with the butt end of his handgun."

I close my eyes and take a second to absorb his words. It's a lot to take in. A heavy weight of guilt and shame form in my chest.

If I had never written that letter to Donovan, I wouldn't have made Kellan so angry. It's my fault that I'm lying here, beaten. Donovan shouldn't have to see me this way. The tears build up beneath my eyelids, but I'm too tired to push them away. I'm tired of lying. I'm tired of being weak.

My lip quivers, thinking about how sorry I am for this whole mess. When I look up at Donovan, the shadows under his eyes give weight to his expression: sad, hurt, and angry. I did this to him.

I mouth, "I'm sorry," and he shakes his head.

"No, Mouse. I'm sorry. I'm so sorry I wasn't there for you," his voice cracks. I can see the tears welling in his eyes. He is trying to be strong for me, but I need him to know how grateful I am. He came back for me.

I lift his chin to meet my gaze and point to his chest. I mouth the words *you…saved*, then point to my heart, *me*.

He leans over and wraps his arms gently behind my head, holding me and peppering gentle kisses all over my face and lips. My hands wrap around the back of his head, and I kiss him deeply, with so much longing and forgiveness. I taste the salt on his lips from his tears. The pain he must feel to have watched me in that state.

He pulls back, settling into the chair. His finger lightly traces the side of my head where Kellan hit me.

A faint knock thumps on the door. Briggs' burly frame slides in as he nods at Donovan and smiles softly in my direction.

"Hey, Ms. Winthrop. Good to see you awake," he utters, gravel voiced, standing beside my bed as he pats my shoulder. I reach out for him to take my hand, and he gently places it in his large palm. I squeeze my fingers with his, showing as much gratitude as I can.

"What's the update, Briggs?" Donovan asks, lightly tracing the pads of his fingers along my arm. His touch is keeping me calm. Grounded. A reminder that I've made it through the worst night of my life.

"It took some convincing, but the doctor agreed to release her tomorrow morning," he says, a weary sigh slips past his lips. "But Kellan is only being held for the night." Briggs and Donovan share a look of concern before they both turn back to me. Just for the night? *He tried to fucking kill me.* My breaths become short and ragged, stinging my chest as random spurts of pain shoot through me.

"Fuck," Donovan mutters. "Briggs, do you mind giving us a minute?" he asks, standing from his chair.

"Sure thing, Mr. King. I'll be right outside," Briggs replies, shaking Donovan's hand and grazing my elbow as he quietly leaves the room.

Donovan comes back and settles beside me, grasping my hands in his. "Listen to me, Mouse," he murmurs. I nod and urge him to go on. "With Kellan getting released tomorrow, I can't let you stay here a minute longer. I'll book us two tickets home for tomorrow morning —just say you'll have me," he whispers. If only my vocal cords weren't swollen, I'd tell him I'm ready to leave with him anywhere. The only way I know how is to show him. He opens his mouth to say something, and I muster all of my strength to kiss him.

I'll follow you anywhere. As long as I'm with you. Take me away.

He returns my kiss, gently cupping my cheek. I ache for more, but he pulls away, resting his forehead on mine. The overwhelming scent of musk and teak overpowers the sterile hospital air. I draw in another breath of his scent, grounding myself in the reality that he's here with me. He lifts his gaze to mine, taking a deep breath.

"Audrey, I want you to come home with me, but I have to tell you what happened that night," he murmurs. I press my finger to his lips, quietly shaking my head. I swallow a lump in my throat, feeling the burning sensation as my vocal cords uncomfortably rub together.

I need to tell him I know. I know everything. I work up enough strength to exhale just below a whisper, holding his face close so he can hear me.

"I know what happened," I breathe out. He places a soft kiss on the column of my throat. With every kiss, it holds the magic to heal me. The pain escapes with every touch. I let out a weak smile and stare into his eyes.

"You know? But how? Noah never knew..." His brow furrows while his eyes flicker between our hands.

"Jess." I hold my throat while searching for his gaze. "Jess," I whisper softly.

"Jess? She told you? But h—" I nod and kiss him lightly on the lips, holding him close while I nuzzle my nose in the crook of his neck. His hand wraps around my nape, kissing my hair. He moves my head back to face him again.

"I just need you to hear it from me, okay?" he begs softly. I mouth *okay* as he tucks a strand of my hair away from my face. This explanation is one that I've yearned to know the answer to for ten years. Hearing it from Jess is one thing, but hearing it from Donovan means *everything*. I realize now that it wasn't just my loss that summer, it was his. Ours. No matter what words leave his lips in this moment, I choose forgiveness. I choose us.

"I'm so sorry I didn't fight harder for us. I meant everything I said that night. Everything I felt, everything we did? It was all real for me," he murmurs, holding my hand against his cheek. His eyes shimmer and a slight grin appears on his gorgeous face. "You are the realest thing that has ever happened to me, Mouse. You changed my life that night. I never should have let you go," he whispers.

There are no more dull aches or stabbing pains shooting through me at this very moment. Donovan's words heal me from the inside out. Kellan's vicious mark is defeated by Donovan's overwhelming love.

"I won't let anyone hurt you again. I vow to protect you, to keep you safe. Please. Can you forgive me? Come home with me?" he asks with teary eyes.

"Yes and yes," I whisper hoarsely. Our lips meld into one another. Made for each other. Ten years of wondering, answered with a simple kiss.

Chapter Fifteen

DONOVAN

I prop myself up on my side, resting on my elbow as I stroke the delicate outline of her face while she sleeps. The early morning sun peeks through my window and lights up her locks with tinges of red and blonde. Her hair is lighter now since the last time she was home. The dye is fading with every wash, revealing more of the girl I fell in love with at eighteen.

We took an early flight out of New York after an exhausting night in the hospital. My blood boils thinking back to the moment I saw her body lifeless under Kellan's hold—her face blue, the color in her eyes drained.

I don't think about what would happen if I wasn't there. I won't let myself get in that headspace. The point is, I *was* there. Thank god Briggs let me up. And thank god we found her in time.

It's been two weeks since coming home to Oakwood Valley. I brought Audrey back to my cabin, nestled in a quiet corner of my family's vineyard, to spare Noah from seeing her in that battered state. He was thankful, as long as she was okay. He knew she was safe with me, and I held him while he cried into my shoulder.

I took time off work to take care of Audrey.

I cooked her my mom's homemade chicken soup and brewed her

mint tea with honey to soothe her throat. We'd sit on the front porch and watch the sunset, our fingers laced together. I'd spend all night holding her in my arms, thanking my lucky stars that she was home with me. I'd gently bathe her, softly lathering her with a sponge, and my stomach would drop when I'd see the cuts and bruises all over her body. I'd gently kiss them while we would lie in bed together, knowing they would fade, but hurting because the trauma behind the bruises would take longer to heal. And with every passing day, she gained back more of her strength.

I've seen her naked every day since she's come home with me, but I haven't acted on it. She was in a delicate and fragile state when she got here, but this morning is the first time I've seen her with color in her cheeks.

I lean forward and trace my index finger across her freckles, like I did that night at the gazebo. I remember reaching out and touching her, as if I were dipping my fingers into the most alluring constellation the universe had to offer. I couldn't resist her gorgeous face then, and I can't resist it now. I press my lips into her soft pout, unable to contain the need to taste her.

Her eyes flutter open like the most magnificent set of wings on a butterfly. That's what Audrey's eyes are. She's most beautiful like this, with her hair tousled from sleeping, her eyes half-lidded and dreamy. She's wearing nothing but my UC Davis soccer shirt that stops mid-thigh and a pair of black panties that make her ass look edible. My cock throbs under my briefs just looking at her.

"Morning," she smiles and snuggles into my chest. Her voice is getting stronger each day and every time I hear her speak, it makes my insides flip. It's got a little rasp to it, but it's still her.

"Morning, Mouse. You sleep okay?" I trace the light bruising on the column of her throat, and she grabs my hand and intertwines her fingers through it. I love us like this, the quiet moments in the morning where we can't keep our hands off each other.

Given the circumstances, we haven't touched outside of cuddling, kissing, and bathing. I didn't want her to get the wrong idea, and she needed time to rest.

"I slept amazing. Mmm, you smell good," she murmurs, burying her nose in my chest, pressing a light kiss between my pecs.

She sits up, stretching her arms high over her head like a cat in the morning. I sit up against my bed frame and watch her eyes close, her head leaning side to side, a look of contentment on her beautiful face. Her eyes slowly open and she huffs out a giggle, getting on all fours, and crawling over to kiss me.

"Are you hungry? I can make us breakfast?" I ask as she straddles my lap. I hear her stomach grumble and cock up an eyebrow.

"I assume that's a yes?"

"Eggs, bacon, and pancakes?" she chirps, and I can't hold back my laugh at her appetite. She's tiny but eats like a baby dinosaur. It's amazing.

"Anything for you, Mouse." I kiss her on the tip of her nose and she slides off of my lap, both of us stepping out of bed.

"I'm gonna hop in the shower," she says, slinking her way to the bathroom, hips swaying, blanket trailing behind her. Why is every single movement she does so sexy? A lump catches in my throat as I watch her grab the hem of her sleep shirt and pull it swiftly over her head.

My mouth gapes open as she saunters away slowly. Topless. Her round, perfect ass accentuated by her black panties.

Holy hell.

I am fully eye fucking her as she turns her head to the side, smiling before she disappears into the bathroom.

Should I follow her? Does she want me to follow her? No. She would've said something. I won't engage until she's ready. But damn, she's teasing the fuck out of me. I adjust my rock hard dick in my briefs and turn toward the kitchen, needing to make a buffet of a breakfast to distract myself.

I blare music through the bluetooth speaker in my kitchen, starting on the pancake batter. My eyes keep glancing at the bathroom door, thinking about Audrey showering, the warm water cascading over her supple tits and taut nipples. I want to wash her body with my hands, lathering soap in places that I dream of burying myself in. I whisk the batter faster, trying to get a hold of myself.

With my bedroom door open, I see Audrey walk out of the bathroom, her skin shiny and wet. Her towel wraps around her body, showing the swell of her breasts and putting her long legs on display. Her hair is damp, sticking to the middle of her back.

She carries a bottle of lotion and places it on the bed, shaking her hair out and stretching her elegant neck.

I keep my eyes on her, whisking the pancake batter slowly as I watch her lift a leg on the bed and lather lotion from her thigh down to her dainty ankles. The morning sun reflects through the windows of the room, casting a light on her that looks like it's from heaven itself. A glowing angel.

She lathers the other leg, slow and sensual, and I wonder if she knows I'm watching. She hasn't once looked out of the room to notice me, even though the door is wide open. Part of me feels like she's putting on a show, and I've got a front-row seat.

My throat suddenly runs dry as she drops her towel, my mouth agape as I take in her side profile. The perfect curve of her breast, the slope of her perky nipples, the dip in her hip, the delicious curve of her ass. I drop the whisk and bite my fist, leaning on the kitchen island as I watch her.

She pumps more lotion into her hand, rubbing it over her tits, down her flat stomach, and right over her pubic bone.

I look down and my cock is sticking out of my briefs, clearly entertained by Audrey's lotion show.

"Fuck," I grit, gripping the edge of the kitchen island like I'm about to break it off. The wild beast inside of me thrashes from within my ribcage, demanding to be released. I lick my lips as I think about burying my face between her legs. Damn, I wanna hear her scream my name.

She turns around, lathering more lotion on her ass, the small of her back, and over her shoulders. She turns her head to the side and smirks, slowly bending down, rubbing lotion on the backs of her thighs. My chin hits the counter at the sight, her pretty pink pussy glistening as she bends over.

Fuck pancakes, my breakfast is in the bedroom right now.

I keep the kitchen island between me and her, because if I don't, I'll cross a line I can't uncross.

Hold it together, man.

My cock is leaking, begging for Audrey. It's painful to watch her, but I can't get enough.

She turns around to face me, our eyes finally locking onto each other. She stalks in front of the bed, her eyes never leaving mine. I take my phone and turn off the music from the speaker.

Cock tease.

She lowers herself on the front of the bed, a sexy crease forming at her hips when she sits. Her arms rest behind her, palms flat on the mattress. My heart beats out of my chest, my length painfully straining.

Her grin is teasing, her teeth sinking into her bottom lip. Then she slowly spreads her legs, her wet slit on full display. She tilts her head, her tits heavy and full. Her nipples jut out, waiting for my mouth to devour each one.

She curls her index finger toward herself, beckoning me to come.

And that's all it takes.

I fucking *run*.

"You drive me fucking crazy. You know that?" I groan, staring down at her kitten eyes as I stand between her legs. Her hands reach out and touch my abs, lightly grazing her fingers down to the band of my briefs.

"Is this what you want?" I pant out, needing to hear her say yes.

"Yes. This is what I want, Donovan."

She grips the edge of my briefs and slowly pulls them down, my cock springing free. A bead of pre-cum drips down the tip. She licks her lips and takes in my size with her eyes. "Fuck, you're massive," she whispers huskily.

It's been a long time since anyone has touched my cock. I could blow my load right this second with her just staring at it.

She sits at the edge of the bed, inches away from my throbbing cock. She wastes no time and traces her tongue up and down my entire length. I hiss and grab a handful of her hair. Her lips wrap around the tip of my cock as she sucks.

"Audrey, slow down. Fuck." She's really going at it, and I don't want to start the morning with me blowing my load in thirty seconds. I lift her head off of my dick, fighting to keep my composure. She gazes up at me with puppy eyes and licks her lips.

"You taste so good. Why did you stop me? Am I bad at it?" she asks, her voice small. I lean down, kissing her hard.

"Don't you ever say that. You're so good that I was about to come in your mouth in about ten seconds." She grins, kissing me back, her tongue languid with mine. She moans into my mouth as I lean over her, breaking our kiss.

"If this is happening, I want you coming on my mouth first," I growl. She bites her lip and nods with no hesitation. "Scoot up for me, baby."

She does as I say, using her elbows to move further up the bed. I crawl toward her and prop myself on my knees as I drink her in. Her pussy is glistening with wetness and she slowly spreads her legs, presenting herself like an all-you-can-eat buffet.

"Fuck, Audrey. You're so perfect. Look at you." Her skin is glowing, burning on the inside for me. For us. I can feel it.

I hover over her, taking a handful of her tits in my hands as I brush her nipples with my thumbs. She whimpers and shakes, arching her back into my touch. I squeeze them together, claiming one nipple in my mouth. I suck and nip, going back and forth between her perfect, perky tits.

"You've been fucking teasing me all morning with these tits. These are *mine*," I groan, biting gently on her taut peaks.

"All yours," she pants, writhing beneath me. I kiss and lick down her canvas, leaving a trail of saliva down the peaks and valleys of her gorgeous body. I stop right at the top of her mound, kissing down the inside of her thighs, dangerously close to her heat.

My hands gently push her wider as I lick her lips, teasing her, playing with her.

"Donovan, please. I need more," she begs, her hands threading through my hair. I smile, swiping my finger through her slit. She gasps, her hips buck at the contact.

"You're so wet, baby," I rasp, my tongue slowly licking circles around her clit. She's panting, sexy mewling noises escape her lips.

"I'm only wet for you. All for you," she breathes out, her whimpers turn into moans as I suck and lick fervently.

All for you.

Her words mark me. This woman owns me. I watch her body squirm and buck as I bring her closer to the edge. Her pussy is the most pure and potent drug, and I'm fully addicted.

I swirl my tongue throughout her wetness, licking in her entrance.

"Oh my god, yes!" she yells out. I've never been more turned on by hearing her pleasure. I take my finger and drive it into her heat, her back arching on the bed. My free hand holds her down by her hip, pushing her inner thigh wider to give me more access.

"Holy fuck, Donovan. Please don't stop. Just like that," she moans, her legs flex wide for me. It's the sexiest thing I've ever seen. Her eyes lock hard on me, her mouth slightly parted as I drive a second digit into her. She throws her head back onto the bed and screams out, completely letting go of herself.

"That's it, baby. Get loud for me. I want the whole fucking town to hear you come," I groan into her pussy, licking and sucking her clit that's swelling in my mouth. I bring one hand up and tweak her hard nipple. My fingers pump into her harder, feeling her walls tightening.

"Fuck, Donovan. I'm coming! I'm—" Her breath hitches, and I feel her orgasm on my fingers as I pump into her harder, wanting to draw out every single bit of pleasure from her.

She screams my name as she explodes, her juices leaking on my face. I lap up every bit as I devour her pussy. She twitches and pulses, her toes curl.

I take out my fingers and kiss her clit as she comes down. I prop up on my knees, my cock dripping with pre-cum. I put my fingers in my mouth and groan, tasting all of her goodness.

"You taste so fucking good. I love watching you come apart for me. Please let me do that to you every morning for the rest of our lives." She laughs while trying to catch her breath, and I lean down and kiss her hard, letting her taste herself on my tongue.

She breaks the kiss and I cage her in between my arms, her hands grabbing my ass. "I want you to make me come like that every morning for the rest of our lives." Our voices are teasing, but my heart squeezes at the thought that she would want us forever. There's no way I'm fucking letting her go now that she's home.

"You're *mine* now, Mouse. *All mine*. Forever."

Her eyes shine for me, and a flutter storm rages through my stomach as I lose myself in the forests of her green irises. I've never felt so intense with anyone but Audrey.

In the past, I've had short-term girlfriends that lasted only a couple of months. This right here, the way she is looking at me and the overwhelming feeling of love, it's too good to let go.

"I want to make you feel good," she whispers huskily. I quirk up my eyebrow.

"You do make me feel good, Mouse. So fucking good." That playful grin I love so much appears on her lips. I feel her hand snake down the front side of my body and she grabs my cock, stroking it with her fingers. I moan and bury my face in her neck, licking and kissing her ear.

"You're going to be the death of me, woman," I say, growling in her ear. She giggles and flips me on my back to finish what she started earlier.

"My turn," she hums, stroking my thick cock.

Damn, I love when she takes control. It's the same flash I saw all those years ago—a woman with strength and spirit. She could choose anything, but she chose me. I run my fingers through her hair as she licks her way down my body. Mirroring what I did to her.

"Suck it, baby," I hiss out as her tongue licks the pre-cum off the tip.

She wraps her mouth around my cock and swirls her tongue around as her head bobs up and down over my shaft. My fingers grip her hair as I slowly guide her. She takes me in so fucking deep. My eyes roll to the back of my head.

"You take my cock so fucking good in your mouth," I groan. She hums in pleasure as she continues sucking and swirling her tongue. The vibrations from her moans bring me closer to my release.

I nearly shoot off the bed when she spits on the tip of my dick and starts jacking me off while sucking at the same time.

Oh my fucking god.

"Damn, you're my dirty girl, aren't you?"

"Mhmm," she says with her mouth so full of my cock. So fucking hot. Her eyes lock with mine and she winks while giving me the best blowjob I've ever had in my life. One pump, two pumps, and three.

White lights burst behind my eyes as I groan out her name and rip through my orgasm. I expect her to pull out, but she surprises me and takes every ounce of cum I unload down the back of her throat.

"Holy shit, Audrey. You like when I come in your mouth, baby?" I ride out the last pulses of my orgasm while her mouth still works over my length, sucking me clean. She kisses the tip and wipes her bottom lip with her thumb. I'll blow another load right now watching her do that.

"Did you like that?" she asks playfully as she lies on top of my chest, her forearms resting on my pecs.

"Did I *like* that? You are fucking magic, baby."

She kisses me, not caring that I taste myself on her lips. "I love the way you taste," she moans, licking her lips as she pushes my hair back with her hand.

"We're gonna have a lot of fun together now, aren't we, Mouse?" I sit up and straddle her on my lap, my hands resting on the small of her back. Her arms wrap around my neck and she brushes her nose against mine.

"Oh, you don't even know what's coming next, baby," she teases.

I lean back against the bedframe and rest my hands behind my head. Her eyes rake up and down my body. My dick likes the attention and hardens with just her eyes on me.

"You like what you see this time, Mouse?" I jest, teasing her for when she eye fucked me in the parking lot at Sip & Savor. I waggle my brows, my cock jutting straight out in front of her. She nods and lets out a giggle as I bury my face in her neck, nipping and sucking her flesh.

"Donovan! That tickles!" she yelps, trying to shield her body away from me. But I don't let her. I never want her to hide her body from me.

I love her laugh so fucking much. I fucking love us like this. "Nuh-uh, you're mine and I'm gonna make you come again," I growl. She squeals as I pin her on her back, my mouth finding one of her hard nipples.

"But pancakes?" she pants, throwing her head back as I devour her tits.

"Orgasm first. Pancakes later," I tease. When she laughs, it's like the call of a siren who lures sailors to the edges of their ships, only to drown them with lust.

Well, take me down with you, Audrey.

I want to go so far into the depths of the ocean with her until I can't breathe. It's all consuming, warped so deep into her I never want to escape. Let me drown in her then, if it means I get her for the rest of my life.

I worship every inch of her skin, leaving no place unkissed or untouched.

For the rest of the morning, I'm on my knees for this woman, making her scream my name over and over again.

Chapter Sixteen

AUDREY

I wipe the foggy mirror with my hand after I step out of the shower. I've spent the last three weeks in Donovan's cabin, healing and processing. Not to mention the endless orgasms. Since we willingly crossed that line last week, it's been nonstop between us. Absolutely insatiable. We hadn't had sex yet—he's waiting for me to be ready. But he's made me feel so good, better than I've ever felt.

It's not just the way he touches me, but the way he believes in me and lets me take things at my own pace. He's been waiting on me hand and foot from the second I came flying back into his life, and I have a good feeling that he's not letting me go this time.

I don't want him to.

I lean in closer to the mirror and tilt my head back to see that the bruising on my neck is nearly gone. As I rub along the column of my throat, the painful memory of Kellan choking me flashes in my mind. But this time, it's quickly overtaken by the memories of Donovan waking me up every morning with kisses, holding hands on the front porch, and nights spent laughing so hard we can hardly breathe.

I drop my towel down to see the bruising on my arms and shoulders have disappeared, replaced by ghosts of Donovan's kisses. I shake out my hair from the towel and rest my palms flat on the bathroom counter. The eyes that look back resemble my own, and my hair is back to its original color. I lean in closer and touch the freckles across my nose. The corners of my mouth turn up. I feel like I can *finally breathe.*

No more hiding, no more fear, no more anger. It's been a long time since I've seen this version of myself. I want her to stick around.

I hear the bathroom door creak open as Donovan walks in wearing only a pair of athletic shorts, glistening with sweat. He went for a run this morning and it shows. The veins on his arms bulge, his muscles swollen with the morning pump.

The hard line between his chest that traces down to his six—no, eight pack—is perfectly tan and smooth. I drool over the way his Adonis belt points a perfect V down past the band of his shorts, leaving my imagination rampant.

He sees me naked in front of the mirror and smiles, coming up behind me and wrapping his arms around my waist. He presses a soft kiss into my hair.

"Hey, Mouse. Sorry, I'm sweaty."

I don't care. I love feeling his warmth and the way our bodies seamlessly fit together. His chin rests on top of my shoulder as we stare at each other through the mirror.

"I think I'm gonna go see Pop today. I miss him, and I know he's been worried about me," I utter softly. His thumbs rub tiny circles right below my belly button. He breathes me in before responding.

"I think that's a great idea, if you're feeling up for it. There's no rush," he says with genuine care.

"Yes, I'm ready. I'm gonna go into town as well and run some errands." I shrug my shoulders and rest my head on his shoulder. He kisses my cheek and looks back in the mirror.

"I can come with you?" he sweetly offers. I smile and turn to kiss him on the mouth. He lifts me up onto the bathroom counter with ease, as if I weigh nothing. I break our kiss and lay my hands on his hard chest.

"It's okay. I'll go. You need to go back to work." Donovan has taken the last three weeks off to be with me. The three most *phenomenal* weeks.

Every day we went for quad rides around the property. We'd make out like teenagers in the woods. He'd play his guitar while I would read my favorite romance novels. He would even try all of my breakfast concoctions like berry strudels and truffle quiches. We kept each other fed in *every* way possible. It's the time I needed to get back on my feet. Now I can focus on myself and the dreams I had stowed away.

"I don't want to go back to work with you looking like this in front of me," he rasps, peppering kisses down my neck and over my chest, making me giggle as my legs wrap around his torso.

"You stink. Go take a shower," I counter.

The playful grin on his lips softens, his eyes follow suit. I tilt my head, observing him closely. The perfect dip of his Cupid's bow, the definition of his strong jawline. He lifts his hand to my cheek, gently caressing my skin. Gooseflesh pricks along where his fingers trail, lightly touching the column of my throat.

His eyes graze my entire body, savoring me. Warmth creeps into my cheeks as I timidly cross my arms over my breasts.

"Nuh-uh, don't hide from me, baby. Let me see you," he whispers huskily, gently uncrossing my arms. His hands grip into my hips, gently lifting me off the counter to stand. The pads of his fingers lightly trace over my pubic bone, around to the small of my back. He slowly turns me toward the mirror, our eyes meeting in the reflection.

"I want you to see what I see," he murmurs against my ear, sending shivers down my neck from his breath. He holds me from behind, melting into his chest.

"What do you see?" I croon. He presses his lips into my shoulder before responding.

"I see a woman who fought really hard to be here."

An intense flutter moves through me. I soak in his words and stare back into my reflection. "I see the most beautiful person I've ever known," he whispers, kissing my neck. "And I see us making it, Mouse. A real shot at this—nothing holding us back," he says intently in the mirror, his dimpled grin melting my insides.

I see it too.

Donovan and I drive down the winding roads through the vineyard on the way to the house I grew up in. It's weird to call it my house these days, because it doesn't really feel like *my* house since spending every night in Donovan's cabin. It's Gran and Pop's house. I know that the moment I step foot into that place, I have to tell Pop everything. My stomach is in knots just thinking about it.

Donovan's fingers intertwine with mine over the center console. He catches me staring and pulls my hand in to kiss it.

"You okay, Mouse?" he asks, concern growing on his face. I love that he knows when something is on my mind.

"I'm nervous to see Pop. I know I'm gonna have to unpack everything that happened with Kellan," I murmur. Saying his name seems foreign now but still tastes like battery acid as it rolls off my tongue. "But these last few weeks with you have been amazing. It's just hard to bring up the bad stuff when I've been in all the good with you," I sigh.

A subtle grin tugs his lips as he keeps his eyes on the road. I lean over, kissing him on the cheek. We really can't keep our hands off each other. I blame it on the ten years of separation.

"It's going to be hard, but you are the strongest woman I know. Noah loves you and he trusts that you're going to be alright. With or without me. You are enough on your own. You know that, right?"

I bring his hand to my cheek and kiss his fingers. My eyes well up with tears. I've never had anyone tell me I was enough. The way Donovan says it makes me truly believe that I can be strong on my own two feet, that I don't need to be controlled by fear or manipulation anymore.

"I'd rather be alright *with* you than without," I admit, smiling into his hand.

"Always, baby," he softly whispers.

"Do you love me?" I blurt out. The words come out faster than I could stop them.

What the hell, Audrey?

Donovan's mouth gapes open, his eyes flitting back and forth between me and the road. I cover my face in embarrassment.

"I don't know why I asked that. Don't answer that. I'm sorry," I mutter into my hands.

I feel the truck swerve to the side of the road and Donovan hits the brakes. I peek through my fingers as he puts the truck in park, the engine still running. He grabs both of my hands across the console and looks at me intensely with those navy eyes. He takes a deep breath and lightly kisses my knuckles.

"Audrey Wren Winthrop, I didn't know it then, but I have loved you since I was eighteen years old. I loved you from the moment I watched you walk through the gate in your white dress. I loved you from the moment I heard your laugh and kissed you in the gazebo. I loved you from the moment we made love for the first time, just two young kids not knowing what they were getting themselves into. I have loved you for the last ten years, and every moment since, and every moment forward."

The words are too much for my heart to handle. I lunge forward and wrap my arms around his neck, kissing him like it'd be my last. He slides me onto his lap to straddle him and he holds me, his chin resting on my shoulder. "So, to answer your question? Yeah. I love you, Mouse," he whispers.

I pull my head back and hold his face in my hands. "Say it again," I whisper back, smiling so big my cheeks hurt.

He peppers me with small kisses and smiles against my lips, over and over. "I love you. I love you. I love you. I love you," he murmurs, meaning every word. I throw my head back and laugh as he attacks my entire face with kisses. I catch my breath and lock in on those deep ocean blues.

"I, I—" I stutter, not being able to choke out the three words I want to say. The last time I said those words, I gave them to a man who didn't deserve it. Donovan places a finger on my lips and shakes his head.

"Shh, it's okay, Mouse. You don't have to say it back. Only when you're ready," he whispers sweetly, melting me into his touch.

He gives me one last peck and I slide back into the passenger seat, floating in bliss.

Donovan King loves me.

He flashes a playful wink before taking my hand in his.

"So, I have a winery tour at 2:00 p.m. and a private wine tasting party at 3:00. I also have a surprise for you in Noah's garage when you get there." There's a glint in his eye because he knows I loathe surprises.

"Donovan! *No surprises*. You know I can't handle them!" I laugh, covering my face with my hands.

"Baby, you'll love this. I promise. When you're done in town, come back to Noah's house. I'm taking you out tonight."

He waggles his brows, and I playfully hit his arm.

"Why do you do this to me?" I sigh out, and he kisses my hand.

"Because I love you," he retorts.

Well, I can't argue with that. He loves me and the teenage girl inside me is doing backflips.

I turn to face the passenger window and smile as I watch the lush green hills pass by in the background, thankful it's not sky scrapers and thick city air.

I roll the window down and stick my body halfway out, leaning back as my top flies up, exposing my stomach and white lace bra.

"You're beautiful, baby!" Donovan yells out to me, and I laugh without a care in the world.

The breeze blows my hair wild, and I close my eyes to appreciate this moment.

I'm free. Donovan loves me. And I'm *alive.*

He laughs and holds my hand as I yell out unabashedly at the top of my lungs in the wind. I extend my free arm over my head, letting the California sun kiss my freckles.

Chapter Seventeen

AUDREY

Donovan drops me off, leaving me standing in front of the garage at Pop's house. I lift the handle to slide the door up, and my chin nearly hits the floor.

It's my Jeep Wrangler, Jules. It felt right to name my first car when I was sixteen. She was old when I got her, now she's a bona fide antique. Still beautiful, though. I walk around and inspect her, seeing that nothing has changed. There are still little scuffs and tiny dents in the white paint, giving her a lived-in personality, like a fine patina. I open the hood and note the new engine. *Nice.* Walking around to the driver's side door, I glimpse a picture of me and Tia on the dash from the day I got my license.

The happiest memories flood my brain of Tia and me driving through the hills, singing at the top of our lungs. I smile at the thought and raise my phone up to take a selfie in front of the Jeep. I text the picture to Tia.

AUDREY

Look who is back in business, baby!

TIA

Holy shit! Is that Jules?! The O.G. Jules?! And wait, you're home?!

A pang of guilt hits my chest, realizing that I've kept Tia in the dark about me leaving New York. She knew about Kellan, but not the details. She knew I wasn't happy, and she insisted on me flying down to Austin to visit her, but I never did. I'd been a shit friend, but she always stood by my side all these years.

AUDREY

Yeah, I'm home. It's a lot to explain. I'll have to call later, but yes. It's Jules back to life.

TIA

As long as you're okay, babe. Take that baby out for a ride! She needs to spread her legs!

AUDREY

I don't think that's the saying lol. I miss you.

TIA

Bitch, I miss you more. Call me anytime. Love you.

AUDREY

Love you too.

I hover over Donovan's name to send him a text.

AUDREY

Donovan, did you do this?

DONOVAN

With Noah's permission. Surprise Mouse. Enjoy it. I love you.

AUDREY

Thank you. I love it baby.

DONOVAN

Check the center console.

I lean over the driver's seat to open the console, pulling out an aerosol can. I rotate it to examine the label. *Pepper Spray.* I chuckle, putting the spray back inside, tucking it away safely.

AUDREY

Let's hope I never have to use that.

DONOVAN

Let's hope you never do. But, if you do, use it.

The keys are in the ignition and I take them out and put them in my pocket, making my way to the front porch steps.

My heart is palpitating through my ears; I feel nauseous. We just lost Gran. I can hardly bear to load Pop's plate with more sadness. I imagine the look on his face when I tell him; will he be disappointed? Donovan told me all Pop wants is to see me safe—and I am safe. I'm no longer in the hands of an abuser. I am home, where my family is. Where Donovan is.

I take a deep breath and let myself in, yelling out for my grandfather in the foyer. "Pop? It's me! I'm home!" I smile at the word *home*, and Donovan's face comes to my mind. I walk into the large living room and see Pop peek out from the other side of the house.

"There's my girl! Oh, come here, kid," he bellows, his voice filled with the familiar warmth that wraps around me like my favorite blanket. I hurry my steps toward him and thud into his chest. His chuckles give way to an amused grunt on impact as he returns the hug, kissing my hair. "It's good to have you back, sweetheart. Man, I've missed ya."

I squeeze him tighter and inhale the scent of his signature Carhart jacket swirled with cinnamon and his favorite Earl Grey tea.

"Did you see your surprise in the garage?" he beams, looking down at me with his kind, brown eyes.

"Yes. It's amazing. I'd never thought she'd run again," I reply, his smile big and bright.

"Donovan did all the work. He just asked me to keep quiet." I break our embrace as I put my hands on my hips.

"Wait, so he did this after I left the weekend of Gran's funeral?"

"Mhmm. In case you came home," he says softly, shrugging his shoulders up and down.

I give myself a quiet moment, pacing back and forth in the living room. My eyes stay fixed on the scruff marks that are scored into the wood floors as I process the intense flood of emotion that comes over me.

"Honey, let's sit on the porch. It's a gorgeous day," he says softly, inadvertently knocking me out of my head. I smile sweetly and nod as he guides me out to the porch.

"You want something to drink? I've got a great Sauvignon Blanc that we just bottled a few weeks ago. It's featured on our tasting menu this summer," he beams.

"I'll have a glass if you're having one?"

He smiles and goes into the kitchen while I settle myself on a chair that looks out over the large oak trees and miles of rolling hills. The sun is high in the sky, and I sit back and close my eyes, letting peace wash over me for the first time in a long time.

My eyes shoot open when I hear Pop approaching with the clinking of two glasses and a chilled bottle of wine.

He pours us each a glass and sets it on the table that separates us as he takes a seat next to me. "Cheers, Pop. Love you," I say, tipping my glass toward him for a clink.

"Cheers, kid. So," he pauses, savoring the taste of the wine. "How are you?"

I take a sip and the crisp taste of alcohol and floral notes hit my tongue. Damn, that's good. I take a second to reply, swirling the wine in my glass.

"I'm better now. I'm sorry I haven't stopped by the last few weeks since I've been home. I'm sure Donovan had his reasons considering my...state." I try to choose my words carefully, because I don't want my grandfather to worry about me too much or even pity me.

He takes a sip and holds out his hand to me. I place my hand in his and feel the years of hard work on his calloused palm.

"He didn't tell me everything, but he told me you were gonna be okay. And that was enough for me. I know that boy loves you. He has for a long time," he confesses with a crinkle in his eye.

"I'm okay, Pop. I wasn't for a while, but today, I'm better than okay," I sigh with a smile on my lips.

His eyes get teary and he looks out into the distance.

"I'm sorry, Audrey. I should've been there for you when you were hurting. I…I had a feeling, but I didn't want to push you away," he whispers, looking down at his feet. "I can't help but feel that part of this is my fault." His voice trembles. My eyes grow wide at his words and I put my wineglass down. I walk over to my grandfather and kneel next to his chair, holding his hands in mine.

"Pop, what happened to me had nothing to do with you. You have always been there for me. You took care of me when my dad couldn't." My lip quivers as I look into the eyes of the man who always had my back, who loves me unconditionally. "You supported me through every endeavor I wanted to pursue, like dance team and chess club—and I sucked at both." He lets out a laugh and I do the same, a tear slipping from the corner of my eye. I take a deep breath, summoning every bit of courage in my body to share what I do next.

"He hurt me. Kellan hurt me. It didn't start that way. I thought I was in love, but over time, he broke me down," I murmur, taking a deep breath before continuing.

"It started with small things, like encouraging me to dye my hair because he preferred it to my natural color. I didn't see it, but he was grooming me." My voice breaks and I suck in a sharp inhale to keep going.

"He would say he needed me, that he couldn't bear for me to be away from him. He used emotional manipulation to keep me in the palm of his hand, and I let him," I mutter. I take another deep breath to spew out the hardest confession.

"The physical abuse started around five years ago."

He lifts a hand to squeeze his eyes shut and scrubs his fingers over his face in disbelief.

"Five years? Five years you endured that? I should've been there for you," he chokes out a sob, and I scoot closer to him, squeezing his hands tighter.

"Pop, it was my fault. I was so ashamed of the situation I got myself in. I didn't want you and Gran to see me that way. I couldn't leave him, no matter how hard I tried. He always had me coming back," I spoke softly. Each confession lifts another weight off my shoulders, even though it's painful to admit.

His eyes search for the sun, squinting as tears flow from his eyes.

"Hey, look at me, Pop," I whisper, craning my head to meet his gaze. "I'm okay now. Donovan...he saved my life," I choke out. It's a powerful thing to say out loud.

"Each day I feel stronger, Pop. I'm here for a new beginning. The dreams I tucked away to forget? I believe in them again. That's because of *you*, Pop. You always believed in me," I cry out, and he picks me up off my knees and pulls me in for an embrace. He breathes in my hair and stifles his sobs. I pull back and kiss him on the cheek, resting my head in his lap as he strokes my hair, just like he did when I was little.

"Tell me about your dreams, kid."

Taking Jules out to spread her legs, per Tia's advice, makes me feel sixteen again. I love this car. The windowless soft top invites the cool breeze, my hair flying wild as I zoom down the road. It's summer in Oakwood Valley, the best time of the year. The sun is high in the sky, not one cloud in sight. Cut grass and soil simmer in the air, plus the occasional waft of freshly baked bread and espresso as I make my way down Main.

I see a bachelorette group taking a selfie on the sidewalk in front of the hottest bar in town, Siren's Flask. Kerry's best friend, Jackson, owns the place. Gran loved it there. Donovan told me that Gran would crash their boys nights, taking shots and having endless conversations with them all night. God, I wish I was there for all of that.

But I'm here now and I need to get a new phone. I focused my attention these last few weeks on healing my body and letting Donovan heal my soul, but it's time to close the door on Kellan once and for all. Since Briggs let us know that Kellan was released the morning after the incident, an unsettling ache has sat in the pit of my stomach. A mere slap on the wrist for nearly killing me. I'll feel safer once I get a new phone and a new number. Fresh start.

Thankfully, Oakwood Valley has a T-Mobile store and I don't have to go further out of town to take care of my business. I pull into a parking spot as my phone vibrates in my purse.

DONOVAN

Hey baby. I need you to stop somewhere before you come back to Noah's house tonight.

AUDREY

Sure, what do you need?

DONOVAN

Stop by Lavender Lane Boutique after you get your new phone. It's right by T-Mobile. Go to the front desk and ask for Isabel. She'll have something waiting for you.

AUDREY

Another surprise? You're killing me. But okay, I'll deal with it for you.

DONOVAN

It's worth it, I promise. I love you.

I'm able to get all of my contacts transferred to my new phone, plus a brand new number. But if all my contacts were transferred that means...

Kellan's number is still here.

I type his name in the contact search, holding the wrist that holds my phone with my free hand to keep it from trembling.

My breathing tattered, I hover my thumb over the Delete Contact button. I wish I could press this button and it would delete the last nine years. From the moment he asked me to get coffee with that glint in his eye or when he asked me to move in with him. Or when he told me he loved me for the first time. I blink away the lone tear that slips from the corner of my eye and tap my thumb to the screen.

Delete.

I let out the breath that was lodged in my chest, releasing years of anger and anguish from my body. My fingers fist the roots of my hair as I stare blankly at the screen where Kellan's name used to live. Gone from my phone, gone from my heart, and gone from my life. Is this grief? This doesn't feel like when I lost Gran, or the grief of years missed with my mother. This...this is different. Kellan made promises to me he couldn't keep. He kept an open palm, a strong grip, and a closed fist instead of those promises. The promise to love me. To protect me.

No. This is anger.

I shove out the unwanted feeling of grief. He doesn't deserve my grief. He doesn't deserve *me.*

"Ma'am, everything okay?" The store employee's voice cuts through my thoughts as I snap my eyes to him. He gives me a soft smile, and I give him one in return. "Yeah, sorry. New phone is weird to get used to. Thanks," I stutter, waving my phone as I thin my lips.

I glance out the store window mindlessly and do a double-take when something catches my eye. I squint to focus, kitting my brows together.

Why is that guy staring at me?

No, that's not right. I'm in my head. I avert my gaze, staring at the blank screen of my phone, my eyes peeking up beneath my lashes to see a man dressed in a black jacket and jeans peering through the window. Sunglasses cover his eyes, and his face is hard to make out from the slight tint of the window. If he's a customer, he would've just walked in. *Why is he looking at me?* Panic quickly rises in my chest, but I push it back down with a huff of my breath. I flick my eyes back toward him, aggravated, and give him a hard stare.

Yeah, I see you.

My heart is racing and I feel my fingers tingle as he walks out of view. I take a second, but I move my feet and swing open the door to look in the direction he is walking. I see him turn a sharp corner and debate whether I should go after him.

Yup. I'm going after him.

Adrenaline surges through my veins as I quicken my pace to close the distance between us. Who does this guy think he is? I turn the corner that leads down an alley between the flower shop and the boutique. I see him get into a black SUV and drive off the back roads around Main.

"Fuck," I mutter. What the fuck? Am I paranoid? I put my hand over my chest and feel the heavy thump of my heart. This dark, sinking feeling sits in my stomach and I suddenly feel sick. I run into the alley to get out of view from bystanders and retch, but nothing comes out. A tear escapes my eye and suddenly I'm back in Kellan's emotional hold. This is what he's done to me. His parting gift.

He haunts my thoughts. I try to picture Donovan. All I see is my body lifeless and Kellan's hands around my neck. I shut my eyes and shake my head, begging for my brain to stop this spiral.

Take a deep breath, count backward from five.

A vision of Kellan's whiskey eyes and the curl of his lip pulse around me, taking over from the inside out like a filthy parasite I can't escape.

Don't fucking let him in. He doesn't control you anymore.

My fingers shake as I find Donovan's name and start a new text thread.

AUDREY

Hey baby. Here's my new number.

DONOVAN

Who is this? ;-)

I laugh under my breath and instantly feel better. He always knows how to make me smile.

AUDREY

It's the love of your life. On my way to Lavender Lane now.

DONOVAN

Can't wait to see you later, love of my life. This wine tasting group is wild btw. A bunch of old ladies drunk off one flight. Imagine eight Mrs. Dicksons. They've already asked me to take selfies with them. One of them touched my ass.

AUDREY

lol. What can I say? The ladies love you.

DONOVAN

Jealous, Mouse?

AUDREY

Very.

DONOVAN

Don't worry. There's only one woman for me.

The darkness that was sitting in my gut dissipates. I take a deep breath and walk the few feet to Lavender Lane Boutique, shaking off whatever the fuck just happened. I won't worry about it right now. I have a night with my man to look forward to.

The bell dings above the door as I walk into the cutest little boutique. This place wasn't here when I was growing up; it must have opened for business while I was away. The walls are lavender, hence the name, and dainty gold fixtures accent the space. The clothes are absolutely gorgeous, very Napa Valley chic. I hear shuffling underneath the one cash register. I stalk closer and spy a pair of adorable heels peeking out from behind the desk.

"Hello?" I ask.

"Oh, shit," she whispers. I let out a giggle. A beautiful brunette woman emerges from under the desk, and I take a second to make out her face. My eyes get wide when I realize who it is.

"Oh my god! I should've known when Donovan said Isabel!" Isabel Whitt, a friend from high school, comes out from behind the desk and gives me a tight squeeze. Her hair smells like lavender and citrus. I always envied her for being in Donovan's close group of friends. She was always kind to me, so it's nice to run into a friendly face.

"Audrey Winthrop, as I live and breathe. Wow, you are more stunning than I remember, babe." She takes hold of my hands and looks me up and down. "Are you home for good?" she asks, flipping her perfectly waved hair over her shoulder.

"Yup, I am," I reply, shrugging my shoulders. She smiles and goes back behind the desk.

"Welcome home, babe. You like the digs? I opened about six years ago when I moved back after college. You know I went to fashion school?" she beams, her big blue eyes twinkle beneath the chandelier above us.

"Yeah, I knew that! And look at you." I take in her outfit—a crocheted halter with a pair of high-waisted flares and strappy wedges. I envy that kind of confidence. "Look at this place! It's amazing. Congrats," I chirp. She flashes her perfect white teeth in a bright grin.

"Thanks, girl. Oh, by the way. I'm sorry to hear about your grandmother. She was one classy lady."

I give her a weak smile. "Aw, thanks Isabel. She really was," I say softly.

"I was bummed to miss out on her happy hour celebration while I was out of town, but I heard it was a real hit." I think back to my drunk self, throwing myself at Donovan, then yelling at him to go away forever. A grin tugs at the corner of my lips, thinking about where we are now compared to that night.

"Yeah, it was a lot of fun. She would've loved it," I beam at her, and she mirrors me.

"Okay, now to the goods," she squeals with excitement. She reaches down below the desk, pulling out a large white box with a silk lavender ribbon. I rest my hands on the counter and run my fingers along the silk.

"Let me just say I've never seen Donovan more smitten. He came in last week and I swear that man had literal hearts in his eyes. I knew you guys would get together eventually. Ugh. You two are so cute, I can't. Anyway, here's this too," she rambles, causing my cheeks to flame bright pink as she hands me an envelope. I turn it over and see *Mouse* written on the front. She notices my expression and gives me a soft smile.

"You should've seen the way he looked at you in high school, babe. It was adorable," she drawls, waggling her eyebrows.

"Really? I never noticed," I say softly, but curiosity gets a hold of me. "Did he ever say anything?" I feel like a giddy schoolgirl.

"Girl, you were all he ever talked about. We would sit at the lunch table and he would *literally* stare at you from across the room," she gushes, like we are in middle school talking about our crushes. "But look at you two now. He finally got his *dream girl*, as Donovan would say," she giggles, mocking Donovan's tone.

"He called me that?" I blush. Isabel furrows her brow playfully and crosses her arms.

"He's been saying it since we were freshman. I don't blame him, though. Look at you," she whistles, causing a fit of laughter between us.

"I'm gonna step in the back and do some inventory. Please come back and shop now that you live here. It was so great to see you, Audrey." She comes around the desk and gives me a tight squeeze before rushing into the back.

I slip the envelope under the box's silk ribbon and tuck the package under my arm for the walk back to my car. Settling into the driver's seat, I place the box to the side and gently pry the card from the envelope.

Mouse,
I saw this in the store and thought it should belong to you. I hope you like it. Love,
D

I let out a quiet squeal and pull the box in my lap, undoing the lavender silk ribbon around it. I open the top and remove the tissue paper, revealing the most beautiful dress.

"Oh my god," I whisper as I lift the dress by its straps, my mouth agape. It's almost identical to the dress I wore on graduation night. A beautiful ivory fabric with thin straps and a sweetheart neckline. The straps in the back crisscross, just like I remember. I hug it to my chest and let the sweet memory of that night flood my senses.

Is this man even real?

I put the dress back in the box and make my way back to Pop's house to get ready. I can't wait to see Donovan's face when he sees me in this. He picked this for me because it made him think of me. He didn't pick it to control me or tell me what to wear. He chose this dress because he saw *me* in it. It's a reminder of who the real me is. I'm beautiful. I'm spirited. I'm free.

He sees that in me, and in turn, I see it in myself.

Chapter Eighteen

DONOVAN

I've never been so nervous about going on a date. But this is not just *any* date. This is my redemption date. The date that should've happened that night after graduation. The date I promised her.

Tonight, I'll be taking Audrey for a picnic at Sunset Valley Point. I picked up burgers and fries from the Golden Grape Diner and got her a bouquet from Vintage Blossom.

I look at my phone. It's five forty-five. I push my hair back and decide it looks good enough. She'll probably mess it up later, anyway. She loves running her hands through my hair.

Hell, I hope she messes it up later.

"Ow, mother fu—!" I mutter to myself as I ram my knee into the bed post. A sharp stabbing pain shoots through my leg as I hobble around my room, trying to shake it off. This is nothing compared to Audrey kneeing me in the nuts, though.

Worth it.

I'm a nervous wreck. I want this night to be perfect. It's the night that I always envisioned happening.

Can't fuck it up, D.

I limp into the living room and triple check my list.

"Okay, guitar, flowers, sweater for Audrey, blanket, food, wallet, keys," I mumble. I'm frantically pacing around like a madman, rubbing my palms up and down the sides of my jeans like I can't get out a stubborn stain.

"Dude, chill the fuck out!" I grumble to myself, my fingers laced behind my neck. I look up at the ceiling and groan. My hands come down to my hips as I let out an exasperated sigh.

"Okay. It's gonna be perfect. She's gonna love it. You got this. Don't be a pussy," I rally, gathering everything by the door to load into my truck.

The air outside is crisp. The sun is low, but not yet set. The cool breeze instantly calms me and the nerves that were building up shift into pure excitement. I place the food in the back seat and toss everything else into the bed of my truck before hopping into the driver's seat.

DONOVAN

Mouse, I'm on my way. See you in 15.

AUDREY

I'll be waiting :)

This time, I'd show up. I wouldn't keep her waiting. I'd finally get the chance to give her everything.

Fuck, I love this woman.

I grip the steering wheel so tight that I'm vibrating in my seat. Last time I was this stoked, I was eleven. My dad took James and I see the midnight showing of *Star Wars: Episode III*. This date tops that by a landslide.

I see the winery just over the hill, the long, winding driveway in view. I wonder if I would've felt exactly like this ten years ago. Would I be nervous to take her on a first date after our night together? If things went well, would she have let me have her the entire summer? Those questions don't matter anymore because we have today.

Today and every day after, Audrey is mine.

The giant oak trees lining the driveway cast shadows on my truck in the late afternoon sun as I pull down the road. When the front porch comes into view, all the air empties from my lungs.

Wow.

She's leaning against a column on the porch, looking like an angel in that white dress. Or maybe more like a minx. The dress hugs every curve, accentuating her hips. I trail my eyes down her feminine legs, appreciating the invention of high heels. She tousles her loose waves over her shoulders, kissed by the sun from our days riding the quads outside. Her hair sparkles in the golden-hour glow. But nothing beats her bright smile. That smile is for me.

I'm inside a time capsule, suddenly eighteen again, picking up the girl of my dreams for a first date. She was beautiful then, and she is beautiful now.

That's my girl.

I pull up in front of the porch and park the truck, leaving the engine on. She stands poised, looking like a goddess, and my mouth runs drier than the Sahara. I come around the truck with the flowers and run up the porch steps, lifting her up and kissing her hard. I'd been aching for her kiss all day.

Our tongues fight one another and she softly moans into my mouth. My hands cup her backside as I try not to crush the flowers in my grip.

If I could take her right here, right now, I would. But it's not my call. It's hers. I'll wait as long as she needs me to.

She breaks the kiss, and I gently set her back down, our breathing heavy. She rests her forehead on mine and wraps her arms around my neck.

"Baby, you look… God, you look…" I stutter, her effect on me causing me to lose all function.

"You showed up this time," she hums, kissing me and smiling against my lips.

"I'm sorry I'm ten years late to our first date, Mouse," I whisper. I bury my face in her neck and breathe in her scent of freshly cut flowers and berries. Her eyes shimmer with wetness.

"It's okay. This time, you didn't keep me waiting," she murmurs, rubbing her nose against mine.

"These are for you." I unwrap my arms from her waist and give her the flowers I picked from the shop. It's a combination of lilies and tulips—her and Violet's favorites. She leans in and smells them, humming in pleasure.

"Donovan, they're so beautiful. Thank you," she breathes out. I hold her hand and help her down the steps, opening the passenger door for her. I get a flash of her ass as she climbs in and my dick twitches in my jeans.

Down, boy.

"Are you ready, Mouse?" I ask through her open window.

"I've been ready for a decade, baby," she teases. Her voice, light and airy. She leans over and kisses me before I jog around the front of the truck and slide into the driver's seat.

She grabs my hand and laces her fingers through mine as we head toward Sunset Valley Point.

Let the redemption date begin.

Sunset Valley Point overlooks all of Oakwood Valley. If you listen close enough, you can hear the rush of the Napa River lapping against the rocks as it flows through the rugged hills. Gallant mountains paint the background in the distance and evergreen forests stretch for miles. It's like living in the middle of a postcard, but this beauty doesn't hold a candle compared to the woman next to me.

This is a local spot, so there are usually no tourists on the trail. We don't need to hike far to find ourselves a quiet, secluded spot in the soft grass to spread out our blanket. The sky fades to an orange hue, highlighting the strands of red in Audrey's hair. I stare as she gets herself settled. She slips off her heels, showing off her pink painted toenails. *That's new.* Never thought painted toe nails could turn me on. She sits with her legs sideways, tucking them just beneath her. Her eyes glow with the sunlight, brightening every delicate feature of her face. It's surreal to be here with her after dreaming about what our first date would've been like in this very spot.

Damn, she's pretty.

"Are you gonna sit there gawking or what?" she teases, earning a chuckle from me.

"You just...you're the most beautiful woman I've ever seen. I mean, Jesus. Look at you," I boast, my eyes caressing her entire body.

Her cheeks flame in that pretty shade of pink that I love as she sinks her teeth into her bottom lip.

"Thank you for the dress," she coos. "I love it."

"You're welcome. It looks perfect on you." I shift my eyes down and smirk.

"What?" she asks as her eyes and hands skim her dress like she's spilled something on it.

I bring my gaze back to her and stare. I stare hard. I see her the way I did all those years ago. A love-struck kid who wondered what it was like to be with Audrey Winthrop. The quiet, mysterious girl stuck in a book, in another world.

"Nothing. It's just—" I scratch the back of my head. "I never thought I'd have another chance, you know? To do this," I say, lifting my hands up to gesture around me. Her gaze softens as she reaches for my hand.

"I'm never letting you go, Audrey. Never again," I whisper. Her bright eyes shimmer and a smile so wide forms on her lips, it knocks the air clear out of my lungs.

"Then don't."

She tugs my hand and pulls me toward her. Her arms wrap around my neck as we embrace. A long, peaceful embrace. She buries her face in the crook of my neck and holds me there. No words spoken, just a physical exchange of forgiveness and hope.

A loud grumble escapes her stomach as we pull back from our hug. "Let's eat," I chuckle under my breath.

"Ooh, what did you bring us?" she beams. I empty the contents of the picnic basket and lay out all the goods in front of her. Her eyes widen and she licks her lips. I eagerly lean forward, nipping at her sexy, pink, pouty lip.

"I brought us burgers and fries from Golden Grape, chocolate-covered strawberries from Sip & Savor—thanks to Josie—and a bottle of Pinot Noir, made by yours truly," I gloat, winking at her. I go to grab the wineglasses from the basket, but they aren't in there.

"Shit, I forgot the wine glasses," I stammer. She swipes the bottle from my hand, uncorks it, and takes a sip straight from the opening.

"Don't need 'em," she says playfully. I raise an eyebrow and smirk.

"I like your style, Mouse. Dig in." I place a box in front of her containing her burger and fries, and when she opens the box, she licks her lips again.

"Baby, if you keep licking those lips like that, I'm gonna give you something else to lick," I grumble, narrowing my eyes at her.

She bites her bottom lip and grabs the burger, taking a huge bite while rolling her eyes to the back of her head. That gets a hearty laugh out of me.

"So, Isabel had a lot to say about you when I stopped by earlier," she hums. Her eyebrow quirks up at me as she pops a fry into her mouth. Isabel could never keep her mouth quiet.

"Good things, I hope?" I ask. She finishes chewing and crosses her arms over her chest.

Uh oh.

"You used to stare at me in the cafeteria?" she teases.

Damn it, Isabel.

I scratch the back of my head and let out a defeated sigh. Heat floods my cheeks from embarrassment. She really had to out me like that.

"I would see your nose in a book, lost in your own world. I wondered what it would be like to take a peek into that beautiful head of yours. You always acted like no one else existed. I envied it a bit," I confess. Her expression stays neutral. Her eyes move to her hands, fidgeting with her fingers.

"Acting like no one existed didn't really do me any favors, since no one really talked to me in school and everyone thought I was an ice queen." A hollow laugh slips from her lips. "I *always* envied you. Everyone loved you. You could hold everyone's attention with just your smile. I admired your confidence. I didn't have that," she admits, her eyes glued on her hands. Her voice is barely above a whisper.

"I remember the Monday after you guys won state, everyone lined the halls cheering and chanting your name," she recalls as I flow back into that memory with her. Her gaze meets mine, giving me half a grin. "You weren't cocky or milking the attention. You were humble and kind...you still are," she whispers.

Can this woman make my heart explode anymore than she already has? It makes my stomach squeeze, knowing she still sees me that way.

"I didn't care for the attention." I shrug my shoulders. "I didn't even ask for it half of the time. When I'd see you in class or at your locker, I only ever wanted *your* attention." Another confession. Her face lights up, her eyes gleaming from the setting sun.

"Well, you have it now. All of it," she murmurs, sealing her admission with a kiss. I gently pull her bottom lip with the pad of my thumb.

Audrey's eyes twinkle as she readjusts her position. "So, I was thinking," she says with a tiny smirk. "The estate is too big for Pop. What if I converted it into a B&B? We could have people stay there while they visit the winery. We could offer different stay packages, exclusive tasting and tours?" she beams brightly, her cheeks flushed from the excitement. "You and Pop could still run the winery side, and I can do the hospitality side."

Pride radiates from my chest. Her voice comes alive, and I'm the lucky bastard who gets to hear it. She pours out her dreams like the wine we're drinking, smooth and full of body.

"I can also bake all the pastries to provide for the guests?" She's shining so brightly you would think it's morning and not sunset. "I can make all my favorite recipes and share it with everyone..." She bites her lip and quirks her brow. "I don't know. Is it too much? Too crazy?"

The happiness swelling in my chest is so much I could burst. With every idea, every thought she has, I see the cracks in her heart fill and heal. The smile plastered on my face could make a star explode with how bright it is.

"Baby, that's amazing. I love that idea. Noah would go for it. It's a smart business decision. Other wineries in the area don't have their own B&B. You could be the first to do it," I say. I love seeing this look of belief in her eyes.

The first time I saw her when she came back home, her eyes were empty. Broken. I'd prayed that I'd see her eyes shine brightly again. Now, as she sits across from me, sharing her dreams, listening to her passion, I've never admired her more.

She crawls into my lap and swings her legs on either side. I lean forward, resting my hands on her backside.

"Thank you for believing in me. It means the world," she murmurs. I tuck a loose strand of her hair behind her ear.

"Of course, Mouse. I'm so proud of you. You make me want to be a better man." It's true. I want to give her the world. Her hands come up to my face and her thumbs trace the edges of my jaw.

"Do you like being a winemaker?" she asks, her fingers drag through my hair.

"*Assistant* winemaker," I correct, teasing. "And yes. I love it. I went to school for it and learned a lot. I love learning from Noah, though. He's been an amazing mentor for me."

She smiles at my comment about her grandfather. He's the only family she has left, so I know it means a lot to her when people speak highly of him.

"Noah calls Oakwood Valley the 'Goldilocks Zone.' It's not too hot, not too cold, but *just right* to curate world-class wine. We want to take over the world," I say proudly. Audrey has a playful look on her face and she inches her lips closer to mine.

"What about me? Am I your Goldilocks?" she purrs. Her lips graze mine and I stare at her perfect pout as her lips slightly part.

"Yeah, Mouse. Just right. Perfect for me." I nip her bottom lip. "I have another surprise for you," I blurt out, earning an eye roll.

"Donovan, enough! I can't handle it!" she whines.

"Roll your eyes at me again and I'll take you over my knee," I grumble, squeezing her ass in my palms. She can't contain her laugh or the flush in her cheeks.

I gently slide her off of my lap and she crosses her arms and rubs them up and down. A cool breeze blows through, rustling the leaves of the tree above us. The last rays of the sun stretch as far as they can go, creating a perfect sunset sky with cotton candy clouds. I hand her my UC Davis crewneck sweater and she puts it on. She looks so sexy in my clothes I have to tame the boner rising in my jeans.

I adjust myself before grabbing my guitar and pulling it out of its case. Audrey grabs a chocolate-covered strawberry and sucks one in her mouth.

"You want a bite?" she coos.

Do I ever.

I open my mouth in invitation. She leans in to feed me and yanks the strawberry away before I can bite, replacing it with her luscious lips and giggling at her master scheme. She tastes like chocolate and sweetness. I slip my tongue into her mouth and groan as she opens for me wantonly. Fuck, she tastes so good. She breaks our kiss and places the strawberry in my mouth, eagerly licking chocolate off the corner of my lip as I enjoy her offering. I put the guitar between us to block any further advances. My dick is straining in these jeans.

She leans back on her hands, my sweater covering the hem of her dress. Her lips are swollen from my kiss with a tinge of red from the strawberries. She looks fucking delicious.

I strum a chord and adjust my capo.

"Are you about to serenade me, baby?" she murmurs coyly. I laugh and strum another chord.

"I heard this song playing over the speakers in the wine tasting room and thought of us. I learned the chords earlier when I had a ten-minute gap," I boast, proud that my lessons with Josie are paying off in my favor.

She heard me sing at the happy hour and ran away. This time, I want her to really listen to me, so I can express exactly how I feel about her. About us.

She raises an eyebrow and leans back, resting her palms on the blanket while crossing one lean leg over the other, wiggling those pretty painted toes at me.

"You heard a song that made you think of us and learned it in ten minutes to play for me tonight?" she croons.

I grin and nod my head. "Mhmm."

I lightly strum the melody and she tilts her head, leaning it on one shoulder, listening intently.

Her ears perk and eyes light up. "Oh my god. I love this song Donovan," she gasps. There's that smile of hers, setting off a flutter storm in my heart. I play the melody to *Heaven*, the Jason Aldean version, and she lightly sways her shoulders. I sing softly, lifting my gaze from the guitar strings to look at my girl.

The lyrics match our story exactly. How we were young, wild and free, and nothing would ever come between us. She's the only one I want in my arms when I fall asleep, and she's the first face I want to see when I wake up. She's once in a lifetime.

She's my heaven.

Her eyes well up and she sits closer to me, her chin resting on my shoulder while I sing and strum. I get a whiff of her strawberry shampoo; her skin smells warm, like cinnamon rolls fresh from the oven. Her hand finds its way under my shirt, the delicate pads of her fingers lightly trace along my abdomen. Gooseflesh erupts throughout my body with her touch.

She trails soft kisses along my jaw, and I turn my head to see her face, singing the words while she holds my gaze. I mean every single word. I want her to know that she's safe, that no one could ever take her away from me. I'm a simple man. I don't need much in this life.

All I need is *her*.

"I love you," she whispers.

My heart stops beating the second she utters those words. Those three words. They echo in my head over and over until I fall back hard into reality. This is real. I stop mid-song and move my guitar to the side, pulling her back into my lap. The sun sets behind us, giving her an angelic glow as I hold her face in my hands and look into her eyes.

"Say it again," I whisper back and grin. Her finger grazes over my dimple. She bites her lip to stifle a smile.

"I love you, Donovan King."

Audrey Winthrop loves me.

She kisses me deep and glides her fingers through my mane. My hands rest on her nape as she grinds herself slowly along my hard length. Our breathing gets more desperate as we devour each other's mouths. Her soft hands rest on my chest underneath my shirt. Her touch is like lightning, burning me from the inside out.

I move my hands up her dress, cupping her perfect ass. I break the kiss and my eyes widen when I realize she's not wearing panties.

Fuck. Me.

"Fuck, baby. Are you trying to kill me?" I pant, my arousal growing bigger as my palms explore her bare skin. So soft, like putty in my hands.

She smiles against my lips and grinds her bare heat along my strained cock. I squeeze her ass and guide her against my length, hungry and eager for more.

"Tell me what you want. Say it," I rasp into her mouth. She playfully bites my bottom lip, her hand slipping between us. She grabs my cock through my jeans and gives it a desperate stroke.

"I want you to take me home and make love to me," she breathes heavily, her voice thick with need.

"We better leave before I ravage you right here," I whisper huskily. She gives my cock one last tug before sliding her hand out and kissing me.

We frantically throw everything into the basket and gather our belongings. The sky is dark, but there is still enough light out to see the trail back to the truck. We fly down the path, Audrey squealing as I chase her.

She's running barefoot in front of me, her dress flying up in the wind, flashing me with glimpses of her bare ass. Our laughs cut through the twilight. We hurry back to the truck, tossing everything into the bed in a haste and racing into our seats.

I need to get my girl naked, like yesterday.

Chapter Nineteen

AUDREY

I'm ready. I'm ready to make love to Donovan. Again. This truly feels like the first time. It's the first time I'm in love with a man who worships me. He lets me be feminine, he protects me. And I know now, without a shadow of a doubt: I've never felt safer. I've never been more sure.

We stumble into his cabin, our mouths locked together in hunger. The delicious taste of strawberries and chocolate linger in his mouth as our tongues wrestle for attention.

He throws off his boots, and they fly into the air, knocking something with a crash. We don't care. I take off his shirt and fling it on the ground. He lifts the sweater over my head, leaving me in my dress. He hoists me up and hastily carries me into the bedroom. He groans into my mouth as he massages my ass in his hands. I feel his hardness beneath me.

He gently puts me down at the foot of the bed, and our kiss deepens and slows down. It's more sensual than desperate. I turn him around so his back faces the bed and push him to lie back. He props up on his elbows and watches me with dark eyes.

His delectable lips hang in a perfect pout, his hair disheveled from my hands. His corded forearms gleam in the moonlight streaming in from the window, casting a desirable light that highlights every hard crevice on his chest and washboard abs. I want to lick over every surface, appreciate his masculine body.

I slide a strap down from one shoulder and slip off the other. His hand grips his massive erection, and my body responds to his gesture, my core aching for him.

I slip my dress down past my perky tits, my nipples already hard and wanting. He groans and scrubs a hand over his stubble. He tries to get up to come closer, but I lift my foot and gently push him in the abdomen back on the bed. He laughs under his breath.

I'm in control.

My hands cup my breasts as I tweak my hard peaks for him. His eyes roll back and he leans on his elbows in sexual frustration. I love teasing him, getting him worked up like this.

"Eyes on me, baby," I purr in a siren-like voice, light and seductive. This man gives me confidence I didn't know I had. I can tease, play, be in control—and he meets me there. Every time.

"I love when you're like this, baby," he groans, his eyes waiting for my next move.

I pull down the rest of my dress, leaving me completely bare in front of him. I take one step toward him until I'm between his knees at the edge of the bed. He leans forward, kissing my stomach and the dip in my hips. His large hands cover my breasts, squeezing my nipples between his thumb and forefinger. A moan from deep within my arousal escapes my lips, my hands splayed throughout his thick hair.

He looks up at me with longing eyes. "You're perfect, Audrey," he whispers his sweet confession. My pussy throbs at his praise. I kneel between his knees and unbutton his jeans. I slowly move my finger down to unzip his zipper, and he lifts his hips up so I can pull down the rest. We move slowly, our eyes glued to each other. Savoring every moment. His briefs drag along with his jeans, letting his thick cock spring free.

It's fucking huge. I don't know how it will fit. It's been so long since we have been this way, but I've ached for this moment. I look up at him and lick along the underside of his hard length.

"Fuck baby," he hisses through gritted teeth. I kiss along his entire length and lick the pearl of pre-cum leaking from his crown.

"You taste so good," I moan, with my lips lightly grazing his tip. It's my turn to give him praise. He moves his hand behind my head, molding his hand to my hair.

"Wrap those sexy lips around my cock," he rasps out, licking his lips in hunger.

I smirk and let his dick slide into my mouth. He moans and guides my head up and down as I'm on my knees for my man, sucking him off into oblivion.

My hands grip his strong thighs and I lean forward to give myself more access. "Damn, I love when you take me deep," he mutters out as his cock hits the back of my throat. I hum in pleasure at hearing his moans get louder with every suck.

I make him feel good.

I suck faster, my eyes brimming with tears at how deep he is in my mouth. Both of his hands have a strong grip on the back of my head, but he lifts me off of his cock and looks at me with hungry eyes. His body vibrates with arousal. I'm making a mess of myself between my thighs, and I need him to do something about it.

"I need to be inside you, Audrey," he pants.

Thank god.

He lifts me up off of my knees and gently puts me down on the bed. "Let me see how wet your cunt is for me," he groans out huskily.

I prop myself up on my elbows to watch his reaction as I seduce him, opening myself up one leg at a time. My tits hang hot and heavy as a flush of heat spreads down from my neck to my chest.

His thumb strokes through my wet folds, dipping inside, then back up to circle my clit. I whine at his touch, my body hot like fire. He replaces his thumb with his lips, sensually kissing my sensitive nub.

"You're soaked, baby," he growls, leaving me squirming for more.

"Donovan, please. Make love to me. I need you," I beg, desperate to feel him inside me. He reaches over to his bedside table and opens a drawer to grab a condom, but I stop him.

"No, I want nothing between us. I got tested when I went in for a checkup last week. I'm clean and on the pill. Please," I plead with him, not that it takes much convincing on his end. He flashes his beautiful fucking grin that drives me insane. He closes the drawer and kisses me hard on the lips.

"I haven't been with anyone in years. You want bare? I'll give it to you bare," he groans.

Fuck, that's hot. I'm buzzing with anticipation. Years of wondering. Years of dreaming about what it would be like to be his again.

He hovers on top of me, his forearms settle on either side. He lines up at my wet entrance and slowly enters my heat. My hands grip his firm, muscular ass, urging him to go deeper.

"Damn, Audrey. Your pussy is so tight," he grunts.

I suck in a sharp breath as I adjust to his size. He moves in and out slowly at first, and I move in rhythm underneath him until we find our pace. His thrusts get deeper and faster, my breathing gets heavier.

"Yes, Donovan. God, yes."

He feels so good inside of me. It's nothing like the first time. This time, it's a sure thing. We're more confident. Hungrier. He's here with me, inside me, all around me.

I wrap my legs around him and dig my heels into the hard muscle of his ass to get even deeper. The sound of our panting fills the quiet room. His tongue finds mine as we moan into each other's mouths, the pleasure electrifying our bodies.

"You feel so good on my cock. You were fucking made for me, Audrey."

His voice is low and raspy. He gets on his knees and moves my legs over his shoulders, hitting the spot that I need him to.

God, he feels so good.

I meet him thrust for thrust and feel my orgasm building in my core. Seeing my pleasure, he takes my ankles into his hands, spreading my legs as far as they can go. I moan, loud and indulgent.

My palms lay flat on the headboard above me, banging against the wall with each piston of his hips driving into me. My tits bounce in his view as I arch my back, driving me closer and closer to my release. A sheen of sweat covers us both, our bodies sliding wet against each other.

"Yes. Yes. Yes," I chant out my desire, surrendering my mind, body, and soul to Donovan. The fuse of my arousal is lit inside every part of me, seconds away from my explosion.

"Come for me. Come on my cock, baby," he pants, our breaths ragged and short.

He's pounding me with force, the sound of his balls slapping my pussy echoes around us. His hand slips down and rubs my clit with his thumb, giving me exactly what I need. I'm done for.

"Donovan, I'm gonna…oh, fuck!" I scream out.

Stars explode behind my eyes, and I come into oblivion. My toes curl as the most guttural moans escape my lips. My pussy pulses violently around his throbbing cock. He doesn't let up. He's like a fucking machine. His pants get louder as he chases his own release. He pumps into me once, twice, three times, and I get hit with a second wave of pleasure before I can even recover from the first one.

"Donovan!" I scream his name as another orgasm rips through me like dynamite, exploding throughout my sex.

He closes my thighs together and puts both of my legs on one side of his shoulders, making my pussy tighter for him as he fucks me hard into the headboard.

"Fuck, I'm coming," he grunts as his cock shoots his release into me, and it's my name on his lips when he comes apart. His body glistens with a thin layer of sweat, shining over his taut muscles that flex with every thrust.

He leans down and kisses my tits, trailing his tongue up my neck and to my mouth. I feel his cock throbbing inside me as I squeeze out every bit of his arousal. My back sinks into the mattress, boneless.

He slowly pulls out and lies on his side, facing me. He tucks a strand of my hair behind my ear and our foreheads press together. We lie breathless, our chests rising and falling together from euphoria.

"After ten years, that's all I get?" I tease. He grabs my hips and flips me on top of him, and I giggle in response. My legs straddle his waist.

"Watch your mouth, Mouse, or I'll fuck the tease right out of it," he warns, squeezing my ass in his large hands.

I love his filthy mouth. My heat pools with wetness again, and I make a mess of myself on his torso. He leans his head slightly back, exposing his Adam's apple and the desirable column of his throat.

"You want more, baby?" he hums. His eyebrow arches up. He has one hand behind his head and the other tweaks my nipple. I slide my wet pussy against his cock and feel him grow beneath me.

"At least ten years' worth more," I purr, giving him a playful smirk.

"I'll give you that and forever, baby," he replies, sealing his promise with a deep kiss. His hands grab my ass and he slips a finger into my dripping heat.

I moan into his mouth, my hands grasping his hair. He pumps three more times, then adds two more fingers.

"Yes," I hiss out. I swear, this man can make me come by just breathing on me. I'm *soaked* for him.

He takes his fingers out and lifts my hips, sliding me down on his thick cock in one delicious move. He sits up and guides me up and down on his shaft. His hands grip my ass and his mouth sucks and nips my tits. I roll my head back and ride him hard, moaning his name into the night.

"Look how fucking beautiful you are, Audrey. Look at me," he growls. My eyes snap back to his, and I watch him as he fucks me into another galaxy.

Everything with Donovan is intense. It's passion. It's love. I want to give him everything, all at once. Our breathing is in sync, just like our bodies.

I'm in love with every part of him, and tonight, we make up for all the lost time and the years apart. Donovan reminds me of just what I've been missing.

Six more times.

Chapter Twenty

DONOVAN

I stand in my kitchen and chug a glass of cold water to quench my thirst. My wild woman had me working overtime tonight, and I wasn't mad about it. I look at the digital clock glowing from the oven. 3:00 a.m.

Jesus, we really went at it all night.

I could go twenty-four hours straight if it meant Audrey coming over and over with my name on her lips.

A grin flashes across my face as I think about Audrey's beautiful face and her perfect body coming apart beneath me, on top of me, all over me. The wait was worth it.

"No…please…stop! Get off of me! Get away from me!"

My ears perk up as I hear Audrey yelling. My feet respond before I can even think. No. Not again. This can't happen again. My heart thuds rapidly out of my chest. I gotta get to her.

I swing the door open to see her arms flailing and her legs kicking through the sheets. With a quick scan of the room, my mind expects me to see a man standing over her. But there's not. It's just a nightmare. Not an intruder. Not Kellan. The air empties from my lungs, my hand gripping the door handle so tight I'm afraid it will snap off. I struggle to catch my breath, like I've just run a marathon. Who knew ten feet could feel like ten thousand? The room closes in on me as the image of Kellan strangling Audrey comes rushing in like an unwanted parasite, feeding off of my fear.

It's not real, Donovan. She's having a bad dream.

My legs finally get unstuck and I rush to her side, slipping in bed beside her. I'm careful not to startle her awake too quickly, gently stroking her hair out of her face.

"Shhh, baby. Hey, it's okay, you're okay. Baby, it's me," I whisper, keeping my voice low so I don't freak her out more than she already is. Her eyes flutter open, already wet with tears. She nuzzles into my neck and wraps her body around me. I feel her heart thumping rapidly against my chest. Whatever nightmare she just had really got her spooked.

"Oh my god, I'm so sorry," she whispers. I help her sit up, our backs resting on the headboard. She laces her fingers with mine and I place a soft kiss on her temple.

"You don't need to apologize. What happened? You're trembling, Mouse." My eyes fill with concern. The color in her face has drained and her lips are pale. She looks down at our hands, fidgeting with her thumb on mine.

"It was Kellan. He was on top of me and I couldn't move. My arms and legs felt like a dead weight. I couldn't fight him. I—" her voice cracks and she cups her face in her hands as quiet sobs shake her shoulders.

"Shh…you're safe, Audrey. He can't hurt you anymore," I reassure her. A deep anger boils in the depth of my stomach. I grind my molars, thinking about smashing Kellan's face in for ever laying a finger on my girl.

She puts her head in my lap and cries. I stroke her hair and let her feel what she's feeling. It's difficult to watch someone you love go through shit. I wish I could take all the pain away. Everything she endured and suffered at his hands, I'd take it all.

I recall watching my mom laying in James's bed after he passed, clutching his t-shirts and crying on his bed. It was like the beast of trauma was so big, we didn't think it would ever leave us alone. I wanted to take the pain away from my family and destroy it, so that we could be happy and whole again. It's the thief of joy, and it's doing its worst on Audrey. And there's nothing I can do to help.

Audrey picks her head up and looks at me, her eyes fill with fear. "Donovan, I have to tell you something," she mutters. My heart drops. I silently nod, urging her to go on.

"When I went to get my number changed, I felt someone watching me from outside the store," she whispers. My breath halts. "He was wearing all black with a cap and sunglasses. And um." A pause. "I followed him," she confesses. My eyelids fly open.

"You *what?* Why did you do that?" My tone comes out harsher than intended. I'm trying to stay calm, but her safety is my first concern. She notices my agitation and strokes my forearm, instantly settling me with just her touch.

"I don't know why, but I felt like I needed to. He turned down an alley and the last I saw, he got into a black SUV and drove through some back roads off of Main," she utters, clearly spooked by the entire ordeal. She shakes her head, and a tear falls past her chin. I wipe it away with the pad of my thumb and caress her soft jawline.

"Donovan, what if he comes after me? What if it's him? I couldn't live with myself if he came after you, too," she chokes out a sob. I shake my head and hold her face in my hands, bringing her gaze to mine.

"He won't come after me, baby. You don't need to worry about me. He didn't even see my face," I say with confidence. Her expression turns from worry to fear. Her eyes dart back and forth between me and off into nothing while her hands tremble in her lap.

"He knows about you, Donovan. I fucked up," she whimpers shakily, crossing her arms over her chest. I subtly raise my brow in shock, my breathing becomes shorter. She sits inches from me, but feels a hundred feet away. I start to say something until she puts her hand up to me, shaking her head at me in frustration.

"No, Donovan. Listen to me. I wrote you a letter when I was back in New York. I never meant to send it, and I definitely never meant for Kellan to find it," she confesses, her voice getting more frantic and shrill.

I attempt to say multiple things, my mouth opening and closing, but the words aren't forming. She's crying, holding herself as the fear overtakes her body. I take a deep breath and reach for her hands, knowing that I made her a promise that day in the hospital to keep her safe. I'm not breaking that promise.

"Baby, he can't get to us. He won't," I reassure her again, squeezing her hands in mine. The feeling of defeat creeps over me as she pulls her hands back. Doesn't she believe me?

"He will. You don't know him, Donovan. He is a powerful man. He *knows* your name. He read it, written in my ink. He knows where you *live*. He won't stop until he gets what he wants." She stabs each sentence with urgency, her eyes wild. "And I left him! With no warning!" she cries.

I flinch at her tone, my eyes wide as I see her slipping. I try to keep my voice even, not wanting to upset her more, but a deep red edges my vision.

"He almost killed you, Audrey! What did you expect me to do?! Let him strangle you to death?!" I fume in frustration. Her expression remains cold. I can feel the ice on my skin from her distance. The warmth and love in the room escapes, the gears in my brain work overtime to figure out how to bring it back. I'm losing her to the fear that has her in a death grip. She refuses to look into my eyes. Tears are coming out, but no sound escapes her mouth.

"He wouldn't have killed me," she mutters under her breath.

What the fuck?

"He would've stopped. He would've snapped out of it. You shouldn't have come back for me!" she shouts, her voice so shrill it sends shivers down my spine. I angrily grip the sheets beneath me, feeling the urge to punch a wall. I grind my molars and bite my tongue to keep myself from saying something I'll regret.

"And now I've put you in danger, Donovan! I can't do this," she chokes out a sob that shatters my heart.

She gets off the bed and finds her dress on the floor, rushing to put it on her body. My heart beats wildly, watching her panic and put all of her clothes on. I get up and she puts a hand up to me, motioning me to stop.

"No! Don't come any closer. I'm not safe to be around. I need to go," she snaps. I look into the eyes of the woman I love and don't see her there. She's slipping further away. I reach out for her wrist to keep her from walking away, but she yanks it out of my grasp.

"Audrey, please. Don't leave. It's three in the morning. Let's go back to bed and we can figure this out in the morning. Please," I plead with her. My voice is desperate, and my hope is failing as I watch her grab her things. Her purse strap tangles around her arm and she flails it around wildly, trying to get it loose.

"Ugh! God damn it!" she screams out, slamming her purse on the floor, sobbing as she falls to her knees. I take a beat, then walk toward her. I kneel in front of her, taking her delicate wrist and unwrapping the strap from it. It's red and agitated from her flailing. I gently rub it with my hand and press a soft kiss onto her wrist.

I sit on the floor and gently pull her into my embrace. Her body melts into my chest, sobs racking her small frame as I hold her close.

Her sobs slow down and her breathing evens out. She sits in my lap and wipes her tears off on my chest. "Donovan, I'm so scared," she whimpers softly into my neck. I gently cup my hands around her face.

"Listen to me. He won't hurt you anymore. I won't let him. I won't let anyone hurt you. He doesn't control you anymore, baby. You're so strong, you know that? The strongest woman I know," I stress to her. I need her to know this. I know she believes it deep down, but when doubt and fear take over, she slips. Fuck, I would too if I were in her position.

She chokes out a sob and presses her forehead against mine. My thumbs wipe her tears that fall from either side of her face.

She leans in and kisses me hard, stealing the breath out of my lungs. The kiss is desperate. Her fingers thread my hair as she pulls her body closer to me. I taste the saltiness on her lips from the tears I didn't catch. She straddles me and my hands gently hold her nape. I can't get enough. I need her kiss to breathe. I need her taste to live.

She slowly pulls back and I see her eyes come out of their darkness.

"There you are. I thought I lost you there for a second, Mouse," I say quietly, my fingers grazing her delicate jawline. A faint smile plays on her lips, and a rush of intense relief rushes through me.

"I'm so sorry. I lost my mind for a sec…" she murmurs. Her voice is small, with a hint of regret.

"You don't need to apologize, Mouse. I'm not goin' anywhere," I say. And I mean it. I'd never leave her. I won't let fear or Kellan come between us. I won't lose her again.

I help her up off the floor and she slowly lifts her arms over her head, urging me to undress her. I press my lips into her shoulder and bunch her dress from the hem, slowly lifting it over her head. The moonlight reflects off of her milky skin. Her glow intoxicates me. My eyes move to her perfect full breasts and her pale pink nipples.

The room fills with warmth and love again, no longer cold and gray. It burns with our love for each other—no one can take that away from us.

Her lips are swollen from our kiss, her eyes slightly puffy from crying, but I've never seen her so beautiful. She's choosing to let me see her stripped down. To show me the good, the bad, and the ugly. The pain she's endured in her life is my cross to bear, too.

Nothing about it scares me.

"Take me back to bed, Donovan," she whispers, her arms wrap around my neck. I lift her up and hold her in a cradle, her lips dotting kisses along my collarbone. I gently put her down on the bed, and she grabs my nape and pulls me down on top of her.

We don't talk. I know what she's telling me by the way her body writhes beneath me. She tugs on the band of my briefs, slowly pulling them down. I help her take them off, tossing them on the foot of the bed.

Our hands move in a delicate dance, memorizing every crevice and curve of each other's bodies. When our lips meet, passion and fire ignite within us, burning away any doubt or fear from earlier. I taste her with my tongue as her fingers grip my back. Our kiss grows deeper and desperate, like if our lips part, we won't survive.

Her hips tilt toward my length, signaling me to make a move. I respond, slowly inching my way in, savoring every second as I listen to her sweet mewling noises that escape from the base of her throat. My hands gently cradle the back of her head while my fingers fist her hair. She takes me in to the hilt, and our lips finally part.

We breathe in unison, our bodies becoming one. I tremble above her as I lose myself in her eyes, my heart thumping so loud it drowns out our ragged breaths.

"You're shaking," she whispers as she presses her forehead to mine. Just hours ago, I had no hesitations about being inside her and letting my body ravage her after years of being apart. We fucked—hard. And I loved every second.

But this? This is different. This is deeper. This is the second chance I've longed for. It's a chance for me to show her how much I love her, and that from this moment on, she's mine forever.

She rolls her hips slightly as she stares deep into my eyes. I groan at the movement. Lightning strikes through my bones.

"I'm never letting you go, Audrey," I breathe, my hips meeting her every move now. Her lips crash into mine again as our bodies sync in rhythm, friction building with every thrust.

I capture every moan she slips with my mouth, our bodies pressed so tightly together that I never want to break contact. Her body shapes perfectly into mine, moving as one unit as we chase our climax together.

I feel her walls tightening around me, her fingernails digging into the hard flesh of my back as her tongue swirls with mine. I roll my hips deep into her, pushing all the way in and all the way out as I teeter on the edge, ready for the lights to explode behind my eyes. I coax out every moan from her mouth, fueling into me as I thrust into her heat with a hungry desire.

When our lips finally part, I watch her come undone beneath me, breathing out my name like it's her last words. She's breathtaking when she comes for me. Her back arches off the bed and her hips buck wildly, pulsing around my cock to take me over with her.

She swallows my grunts and groans with her mouth, needy and desperate as I spill myself into her. My body twitches with every pulse of my climax, goosebumps erupting all over my body. She takes every drop, clutching to my body fervently as she kisses me with the force of a thousand suns.

God, I'll do anything for her. I'll give her the world. I'll do whatever it takes to make every dream she has come true, no longer letting her hide behind fear.

Her gaze is dreamy and heavy as she breaks our kiss, her face full of color from her climax. I slowly pull out of her, dragging the tip of my nose along her jaw, down to the column of her throat, placing a delicate kiss in the center. It's a reminder that no matter what, I'll never hurt her the way Kellan did.

"I love you, Donovan," she murmurs. I bring my eyes back to hers, a grin forming on my lips. She traces my dimples with her fingers and smiles at me, making my insides flip.

"Yeah?" I whisper.

"Yeah." She bites down on her bottom lip and nods eagerly, not being able to contain her smile.

"Mouse, you have no idea how much I love you back," I reply, sealing my admission with a kiss.

Whatever fear or doubt she had earlier stays at bay. We know that this fight isn't over, but now she knows that I'm in it with her. I shift beside her, and she lifts her head for me to slip my arm beneath it. She settles into the crook of my arm, splaying her leg across my torso. I kiss her hair and stroke the outside of her arm. Her breathing is slow and even, and I tip my chin down to see her eyes closed, sleeping soundly against my heart.

I let sleep take me, praying that her dreams are kind to her until morning.

Chapter Twenty-One

DONOVAN

Cinnamon and freshly baked bread fill my nostrils as I wake slowly from a deep sleep. Muted bass thumps rhythmically in the distance. I pick my head up off my pillow and squint into a sun flare peeking through my window.

What time is it?

Audrey isn't next to me. Her side of the bed is cool to the touch. She must've woken up way before me. I sit up and swing my legs over the edge, checking my phone on the nightstand. 11:00 a.m. Damn. I haven't slept past 6:30 since high school. I scrub a hand over my face, pausing for a moment to note a faint melody floating in from the kitchen.

I find my briefs at the end of the bed and slip them on. The sound of Audrey's singing becomes more clear the closer I inch toward the door. I press my ear against the frame and grin at the thought that I'm about to walk into something *very* entertaining.

Not wanting to draw her attention, I slowly open the door and peer through the crack, giving me a perfect view of Audrey bending over to take something out of the oven.

Her hair is down and undone from sex and sleep. The sunlight reflects off her silky strawberry locks. She's wearing my t-shirt that rides up as she's bent over, exposing her delectable peach-shaped ass. Her hot pink panties contrast against her fair skin, making my dick to stand to attention. I adjust it in my briefs as I open the door all the way and tiptoe into the living room.

She hasn't noticed me yet. Music is blaring from a bluetooth speaker. She's icing cinnamon rolls on a tray with a butter knife and singing at the top of her lungs to some pop song. Her hips sway back and forth to the beat. Light radiates from every part of her body, as if she were plugged into the sun itself.

I'm happy to see her in a better mood after last night. When we made love, I swallowed every doubt she had and took on her burdens as my own. We were so deeply connected that I felt every emotion as our bodies moved together in sync. But her fear was real, and we could be facing something dangerous.

I knew Kellan was out there on the loose. If someone truly had been following her in Oakwood Valley, then we have a huge problem. We can't avoid the topic forever.

I stalk toward her, trying to stay out of her line of sight while she seductively ices the cinnamon rolls. Is that even possible? Every movement she does turns me on. I duck behind her and wrap my arms around her waist, kissing her neck as she jolts and drops the knife on the kitchen island.

"Oh, my god! Baby! You scared the shit out of me!" she squeals. I chuckle into her neck, the smell of sugar and cinnamon dusted on her skin. Her arms rest on top of mine as she turns her head. I reach over and turn down the music.

"Morning, Mouse. Mmm, it smells amazing. Did you make these from scratch?" I arch my eyebrow. My eyes scan the kitchen; flour, sugar, and dirtied-up mixing bowls covering every surface. She continues icing while I hold her, pressing my erection into her lower back.

"Mmm, well hello there," she says playfully, backing her ass into me. "And yes, I made them from scratch. Sorry for the mess." She uses the butter knife to motion into the entire kitchen. I'll happily wash the dishes every morning if it meant that she would cook for me looking like this.

For a long time, I was content coming home to no one. I had my solitude, other than the odd nights my brothers would stay over when they'd be too drunk to move. But having Audrey here, covered in sugar and flour while singing and dancing in my kitchen, was something—I realize, holding her in my arms as if she'd been there every day for the last ten years—I can't live without.

This house feels like a home with her warmth. The sun shines brighter through the windows. The kitchen appliances have purpose. Her lipstick stains the wine glasses, reminding me I'm not alone anymore.

"You seem happy this morning, Mouse."

The corner of her mouth perks up as she mixes. "I feel better. I think middle-of-the-night orgasms will do that for ya," she teases. There's a hint of worry in her eyes, and I instinctively hold her tighter, my chin resting in the crook of her neck.

"Do you wanna talk about it?" I say softly. She stops mixing and takes a beat to set the knife down on the counter. She turns around to face me, her hands rest on my chest and the worry in her gaze deepens.

"I guess we should, huh?" she says, unsure, shrugging her shoulders.

"Only if you want to, Mouse. But if you're sure that you were being followed, we need to make a plan," I say, stern but soft. Her eyes dart around the room, settling everywhere but in my gaze. Her jaw ticks as she grinds her molars, her chest heaving with breaths that deepen with every inhale. Feeling her discomfort, I chime in to break the silence.

"You're not alone in this. If you want, I can talk to Logan's dad and—"

Her head shakes back and forth as she puts her hand on my mouth to keep me from talking further. "Donovan, we don't need the chief of police getting involved. I *just* got home. I don't want the whole town to know about my past," she sighs, crossing her arms over her chest. "*Please* don't talk to Chief Harper. Promise me?" she pleads in desperation, eyes wide and beseeching.

I want to tell her she's wrong. That this town will have her back, no matter what. That the people who love her will protect her. But I don't. She doesn't need to hear this from me right now. I pull her into an embrace, hoping my actions can speak where my words fail.

"I promise," I whisper, holding her close.

"I'm just paranoid," she mumbles into my chest. "It's probably nothing. I know I'm safe with you." She looks up at me with a smile that makes my knees weak.

"I'll always keep you safe," I murmur. My voice is low, our lips barely touching.

Her hands slip behind my briefs and she grabs a handful of my ass. I waggle my brows and attack her neck with kisses. I nip her earlobe and playfully growl in her ear, ready to devour her right here in the kitchen.

She giggles and tries to shrug me off, and in one quick swoop I lift her up on the counter, settling myself between her legs. Before I can react, she scoops a dollop of icing with her fingers and spreads it across my face.

My mouth gapes open as she continues to spread sticky icing all over my nose and cheeks. Her mouth forms an O shape, her laugh is hearty and loud. Music to my ears. A sort of laugh-type scoff escapes me as I narrow my eyes at her. She has *no idea* the beast she's about to unleash within me.

"Ohhh, Mouse. You better run," I growl. She pushes more icing into my face as she ducks out from under my arms, sprinting into the living room. I've never seen her move so fast—it throws me off guard. "Shit!" I stammer, laughing as I grab a handful of icing myself, playfully chasing after her.

The couch separates us, her eyes wild and smiling.

"This seems familiar, doesn't it, baby?" she teases.

My heart squeezes at the memory of us playing cat and mouse all those years ago. The adrenaline of the chase, of getting just close enough, only for her to run in the opposite direction. I loved every second. Just like I do now.

Her chest rises and falls with excitement. I look at the woman across from me and see the same girl I've always known. That glint in her eye that makes her eyes smile. The playfulness that emerges from her, challenging me unabashedly. The way I desire her, always wanting to get into the pretty head of hers to safeguard her dreams. The heat that builds in my loins just by looking at her. That's my Audrey.

"Don't you remember who won that night, Mouse?" I tease, running around in circles in the living room, chasing her laughter. She grabs a pillow from the couch, thinking it's enough of a barrier between us.

"I *let* you win," she taunts me while I calculate my next move.

"This isn't the only sticky white stuff that I can paint your body with," I growl. Her eyes widen at my comment and a devilish grin appears on her face.

"And I'm pretty sure I remember you liking the way I taste more than your icing," I taunt her back to even the score. My cock twitches thinking about Audrey swallowing my cum. I'm fully hard now, my entire length poking through my briefs.

"You see what you do to me?" I stalk toward her, stroking my cock with my free hand while she watches. Her eyes are catlike as she licks her delicious lips, backing away from me slowly. She tosses the pillow to the side and pulls her shirt off over her head, rubbing her breasts with leftover icing in her hand.

I lick my lips and close the distance between us. I take the icing in my hand and gently rub it on her face. Our game turns playful into something else. I swipe her bottom lip with icing, slowly sticking my fingers in her mouth. Her eyes stay locked on mine as she slowly sucks.

"Tell me baby, whose sticky white stuff do you like better?" I grumble. She smiles and groans while sucking my fingers and kissing my fingertips.

"Mine," she whispers, running past me into the kitchen.

I groan and huff out a chuckle, leaving me dumbfounded with my hands on my hips.

Her head falls back into a fit of laughter as she hides behind the kitchen island. I run after her, and to no surprise, she lets me catch her. Once again, she lets me win.

This woman, I swear.

I lift her back up on the kitchen island and suck the icing off of her nipples. She whimpers and holds my head to her chest, allowing me to devour each taut peak. I look up through half-mast eyes and kiss her on the mouth, tasting the sweetness of sugar that lingers deliciously on her tongue.

"I win," I whisper against her lips.

"You win."

We spend the morning sticky, standing around the kitchen island eating cinnamon rolls half naked. I wouldn't want anything else than what we have right here.

"Baby, you gotta make these for the B&B. I've already eaten half the pan." She beams at my praise. It's true though. These cinnamon rolls are the best I've ever tasted. Sip & Savor makes some good ones, but Audrey's are to die for. She'll be booked solid just for the cinnamon rolls alone.

"That's the plan. I've been perfecting this recipe for years," she says with pride.

Just as I'm about to take another bite, my cell phone text tone pings from my room. "Be right back, I'm gonna check that," I say, kissing Audrey's sweet icing coated lips. "Mmm, I want more when I come back," I growl, Audrey giggling at my advances.

I enter my room and swipe my phone from the bedside table to see my mother texting.

MOM

Hi sweetheart. How are you?

DONOVAN

> Hey mom. I'm fine, just had breakfast with Audrey.
> What's up?

MOM

> Oh how lovely. Well, I know it's been a while since
> you've come home for Sunday dinner....

Ah, this is a Sunday dinner text. My family has been doing Sunday dinner for as long as I can remember. Dad is pretty killer on the grill, whipping out perfect medium rare steaks like it's his job. Mom would make this amazing spread of mouth-watering sides with fresh vegetables from her garden to round out the meal. And it was always a community affair. Logan and his family would join us most weeks growing up; the backyard football with my brothers and our dads was the stuff of legends. Those Sundays are some of the best memories I have.

But then James died, and Sunday dinners haven't really been the same since. Grief took a seat at the table, replacing James's bright smile and contagious energy.

My fingers hover over the keyboard, taking entirely too long to reply. Long enough where the three little dots appear on my screen from my mom.

MOM

> Donovan, I promise your father will be on his best
> behavior.

I let out a half-hearted chuckle and shake my head, not surprised that my mom, once again, can read my mind.

My dad and I haven't exactly addressed things between us yet since the funeral reception. I know I promised Wyatt I'd talk with him, but since Audrey came home, I haven't had the chance. I don't even know where to start. My heart feels blocked up at the thought. I've skipped out on more Sunday dinners than I'm proud of, and I know it hurts my mom and my brothers. I haven't been wanting to be around my dad since he makes things so damn awkward.

We don't talk, we don't connect. It's just...nothing. I can't remember the last time my dad and I had a real conversation that wasn't about work. Having a sit-down dinner with my him while bringing Audrey around for the first time doesn't sound at all entertaining.

Another three dots.

MOM

> Besides, we want to spend time with Audrey. It would be nice if you could share her instead of keeping her locked in your cabin for weeks on end.

DONOVAN

> Alright, alright. You don't have to guilt trip me, mom. We'll go.

MOM

> Really?! Wonderful. See you at 6 then. Love you, hun.

DONOVAN

> Love you too, mom.

I place my phone back down on the side table, contemplating on the edge of the bed. Of course, I want my family to be around Audrey. I already know they're gonna fall in love with her. Maybe this is the push I need to make things right with my dad. Turning my head slightly, I see Audrey's petite frame through the door, elbows propped on the island, bending one of her knees. Sexy without even trying. If I'm gonna brave tonight with anyone, I'm glad it's with her.

I head back into the kitchen and stand across from Audrey at the island, her face still smothered with icing.

"Who was that? Everything okay?" she asks, licking her fingers.

"It was my mom. Everything's fine. Do you think you can make another batch of cinnamon rolls before six tonight, though?" I ask, resting my forearms on the counter while I watch Audrey's tongue slide across her bottom lip. I don't think there's anything this woman can do that doesn't turn me on.

Her shoulders shrug up and down as she tears off another piece and stuffs it into her mouth. "Yeah, I can. Why?" she mumbles, her mouth full of cinnamon roll. I huff out a chuckle at her puffy cheeks.

"Make a batch for Sunday dinner tonight," I suggest. She arches her eyebrow in confusion. She looks cute with that perplexed look on her face and her cheeks full of food, like the most adorable chipmunk who got caught stealing cookies from the cookie jar. She swallows the rest of her cinnamon roll and tilts her head.

"What's Sunday dinner?" she asks, downing a glass of water.

"My parents have hosted dinner every Sunday since I was a kid. My mom wants us to come." Her eyes widen at my request. I chuckle, swiping the icing from the corner of her lip with my thumb and popping it in my mouth.

"Us?" she stammers, knitting her brows together.

"Yeah, us. My mom thinks I'm keeping you all to myself in here," I tease, stalking slowly toward her. She stands her ground, not giving into my antics.

"Well, you kinda are, baby," she retorts, wrapping her arms around my neck once I get close enough.

"Well, I don't wanna share you with anyone," I whisper huskily against her lips, getting a taste of sugar and cinnamon.

"Then don't," she whispers back, pulling me into a deep kiss. Jesus, this woman drives me crazy. Her tongue teases mine, giving me just enough and then pulling away, leaving me wanting more.

"So you'll come?" I pant, restraining myself from taking her on this counter from that kiss. She waggles her brows, nibbling down on her bottom lip.

"I'll come as much as you want me to," she purrs, biting back a smile. I can't resist the gleam in her eye when she teases me. A low groan rumbles within my chest.

"Mouse, careful what you ask for," I warn, my hands raking over her tits. She moans into my touch, pushing herself against me, a light giggle on her lips.

"Yes, I'll come tonight. To Sunday dinner, and on your face," she whispers in my ear. I groan into her neck as her hands snake around my middle. She really knows how to rev my engine.

"Good. On *both* accounts." I growl.

I stare into her sparkling green eyes and smile. Jokes and teasing aside, I love her. Maybe tonight won't be so bad after all. Having Audrey with me can ease any tension in the room. Although, despite all the battles she's won these last few weeks, she's yet to face off with the man who put us here in the first place.

Chapter Twenty-Two

AUDREY

The King Estate looms on the horizon as Donovan and I pull into the large circular driveway. Jesus, this place is huge. Extravagant iron work details the front door, glinting gold in the afternoon sun—reflective of the wealth of this estate, no doubt. The landscaping alone is ripped straight from the pages of a *Better Homes and Gardens* magazine with a fragrant array of marigolds, dahlias, and poppies packed neatly in the soil. My lack of a green thumb could never.

My fingers fidget with the foil-topped Pyrex that holds my, hopefully, show-stopping cinnamon rolls. Donovan insists they're the best he's ever had, but I'm a nervous wreck.

When I saw his family last, it was at Gran's funeral reception. His mother has always been so kind and his brothers were nice enough. His dad, however...I'm not so sure. Donovan never mentions his father, but I guess we have that in common.

I always had an inkling that his dad held this weird grudge against me because of what my father did. Or attempted to do. It doesn't make a difference, though—I am fully aware of how fucked up it was. But the past is the past. I'm nothing like my father. I don't need to prove that to anyone, including Caleb King.

It's surreal showing up at Donovan's parent's house after all these years. I remember standing in this driveway, my heart jumping through my chest, anticipating my night with Donovan. *Would he even acknowledge I showed up? Would I be pushed aside while everyone else fought for his attention?* The warmth I feel in my chest when I look back and think about how our lives turned out—overcomes everything from the past.

The tape, the blackmail, Kellan, my father…none of it matters. I have today.

Take a deep breath, count backward from five.

"You ready, Mouse?" he asks, taking a deep breath. He clenches his jaw and twitches his fingers around the steering wheel. I cock up my eyebrow, attempting to read his expression.

"Are *you* ready?" I retort, his knee bouncing up and down impatiently.

"I'm ready. It's just been a while for me, that's all," he mutters, forcing a smile. I grasp his hands in mine and give them a tight squeeze.

"We can be nervous together," I tease, a grin forming on my lips. He chuckles, kissing my knuckles.

"No, baby. You have nothing to be nervous about. They're gonna love you. I know it," he whispers, flashing me a wink that makes me weak at the knees.

On my slow inhale, Donovan rounds the hood and opens my door, extending his hand to mine. I exhale my nerves as he kisses my cheek, guiding me up to the front steps of the door.

My heart quickens when I hear hushed footsteps on the pavement approaching from behind us. Before I can fully turn to see who it is, a hooded figure wraps his arms around Donovan from behind and covers his eyes, dragging him backward off the step.

"Donovan!" I scream out, dropping the cinnamon rolls on the steps. The man has his large hands covering Donovan's face as they wrestle each other, trying to bring the other down to the ground. Tears prick my eyes as I yell out for help, pleading with the distant patter of footsteps inside the house to hurry. Save him like he saved me.

My vision blurs, my heart works overtime. I struggle to breathe, watching him grapple with this man, my feet dragging through molasses as I try to get closer to him. A wave of nausea courses through me as bile makes it halfway up my chest before I swallow it back down.

The man has Donovan in a chokehold. I'm frozen in place. Not another soul appears while Donovan is immobilized, choking. I think I scream, but I can't hear anything. My ears have a damp filter over them. Everything is muted.

"Did you miss me, baby?" the man grits in Donovan's ear. They both stop in an instant. I whip my head around to the sound of the front door swinging open, my feet rooted to the ground. Donovan's brothers step out front, his mother and father close behind. I'm bewildered to see Kerry and Wyatt grinning.

What the fuck is going on?

The man releases his hold on Donovan. Sandy blonde hair and a wicked smile emerge from under the hood of his sweater. Donovan turns around to face him, his mouth gaping. "Logan?! Holy shit!" Donovan yells out, his arms wrap around Logan's neck with force.

Logan fucking Harper.

Grace hurries down the steps when she sees the discomfort on my face. It's a mix of relief and absolute embarrassment. My hands tremble as I try to regain composure before Donovan sees me upset. Grace's hand comes to my side, rubbing over my arm like a warm blanket. She gives me an apologetic smile as my hand drags to my chest, feeling my heart thump wildly. So this is what it feels like to have a mother's comfort.

"Surprise, motherfucker!" Logan kisses Donovan on the forehead, prompting an elaborate bro sequence of aggressive hugs and back pats.

Logan and I make eye contact as I struggle to shake the remnants of fear from my expression. "Awww, I'm sorry, Winthrop. I didn't mean to spook you," he says apologetically. I half-heartedly chuckle as he pulls me in for a tight bear hug that lifts me off the ground.

He's as tall as Donovan with a similar build, but more square and angular. The afternoon light flickers off his sandy blonde hair, highlighting the wavy locks tousled on top and shaved trim on the sides. The man's cheekbones must be the envy of every girl in Texas. He beams his signature crooked grin, accentuated by one boyish dimple.

"Watch your hands, Harper," Donovan scowls. Logan sets me down gently, squeezing my shoulder before giving Donovan the finger and going up to greet the rest of the Kings.

Donovan pulls me aside from the commotion, his hands cupping my face. "Are you okay, Mouse? I'm so sorry about that. I had no idea he would do that," he whispers, the pads of his thumbs stroking my cheeks.

"Yeah, I'm okay. I thought...I thought—" I fight back tears, instantly upset with myself that I'm about to cry in front of his entire family. He pulls me into his chest, immediately breathing in his scent laced with clean laundry. God, he always smells so good.

"Shh, it's okay. I'm so sorry, baby," he murmurs into my hair. I pull back from the hug, proud of the fact that I didn't let a single tear slip.

"It's alright, Donovan. Let's go inside," I say, eyeing my cinnamon rolls at the bottom of the steps. Fortunately, the goods are still secure.

Donovan guides me up the steps with his hand on the small of my back. Grace extends her arms and gives me a proper greeting.

"Audrey, sweetheart, thank you so much for coming. We are so glad you are home," she croons. Grace kisses both of my cheeks and leads me up the remaining steps, taking me from Donovan. Bergamot and floral perfume flood my nose. It's a comforting scent—I wonder if my mom would smell the same way. Do all moms smell like a warm hug?

Kerry and Wyatt pull me into their arms and squeeze me in a group hug, coercing an earnest giggle from my lips. "Welcome back, Audrey. Happy you're here," Wyatt says with a tight-lipped grin. "It's about time!" Kerry beams. My eyes dart between their faces. I see so much of Donovan in them. The thick chocolate locks, the olive skin that's kissed by the sun, the piercing deep blue eyes they've inherited from their mother.

I can see the tight bond of brothers as Donovan pulls them into a raucous group hug, kissing the tops of their heads. The affection between them is heartwarming. I'm hit in the chest with the teeniest pang of unexpected envy, wishing I had a sibling bond like that. Being an only child is lonesome, but I dealt with it. I had Gran and Pop, and that was enough for me.

I round the doorway, landing me face to face with Caleb King. It takes a second, but his stoic expression morphs into a tight-lipped smile as he reaches his hand out to shake mine. I hesitate, but I clasp my hand in his, giving him the most awkward hand shake of my life.

"Thank you for coming, Audrey. We are happy to have you here with us," he says flatly.

"Thank you, Mr. King," I reply politely. He puts his hand up to me and shakes his head. "Please, call me Caleb," he insists, and I match his tight-lipped smile with a nod.

Donovan's hand finds mine as he locks eyes with his dad. There's a tension in the air that you can cut with a knife. I can see why Donovan doesn't talk much about his dad. This vibe is *weird*.

They stand there, staring at each other, mirroring each other's expressions. It's like a calculated chess game, waiting for your opponent's move to counter attack. I nudge Donovan subtly with my hip, shaking him out of this weird stand off.

"Son, good to see you," Caleb utters, keeping his hands by his side. "Sir," Donovan replies curtly, quickly ushering us past him through the front door. Once inside the foyer, I look at Donovan, surveying the scowl carved on his face.

"Donovan, what was that?" I ask, curiously. He grumbles, continuing to lead me further into the house. I take that as a sign to drop it.

Chapter Twenty-Three

AUDREY

My eyes feast on the King's grand kitchen, seamlessly flowing into the living room. Rustic exposed wooden beams crisscross the lofty ceiling, while a soft ember glows from the brick fireplace, establishing it as the heart of the entire first floor. I can imagine the King brothers gathered in front of it as kids on Christmas morning, laughing and smiling as they open gifts from Santa.

Intricate hallways and doors weave through the space like a labyrinth. Every wall is adorned with family photos, landscape paintings, and travel souvenirs. It's like stepping into a warm embrace at every turn, with gentle lines and curves creating a welcoming atmosphere. The home exudes affluence without a hint of pretension.

My gaze draws to a charming set of French doors, flanked by towering arched windows leading to the backyard—a place I hold dear. The corner of my lip tugs as I sip my Sauvignon Blanc, imagining a teenage Donovan pulling me through a sea of people, eager to get me alone and away from the chaos.

My eyes flit to Caleb and Grace through the window, grilling steaks and vegetables with Wyatt. I insisted on helping with dinner, but Grace politely declined and told me to just enjoy myself. So here I am, soaking it all in as Logan and Donovan drink wine and laugh loudly on the couch in the living room.

I love seeing their dynamic together. His best friend, his brother from another mother. After losing James, Logan was there for Donovan every day that passed. When Donovan missed a week of school after James died, Logan did, too. Everyone knew them as brothers.

My heart tugs, thinking about my best friend Tia. Logan and Tia ended up at the University of Texas together—they've been thick as thieves since freshman orientation. Small town kids stick together. I would hear of their adventures and shenanigans, secretly envious of their freedom.

I'm quietly sipping my wine when a bouncing ball of sunshine plops beside me on a bar stool. "My brother shouldn't be leaving you here all alone. That makes him a bad host." Kerry flashes his bright white teeth and nudges his elbow into mine. My eyes flit to Donovan and Logan, talking wildly with their hands. They throw their heads back into hysteria. Kerry turns back to look at them, his eyes rolling at the sight, but not a hint of jealousy when his lips turn up at the corners.

"I swear, those two could crack each other up watching water boil," Kerry huffs. I snicker into my drink.

"I think it's cute. They clearly missed each other," I reply, shrugging my shoulder while taking another sip of wine.

Kerry's eyes soften when he meets my gaze. "Sure, but not the way he missed you," he croons.

My cheeks flush with heat, completely enamored by his sweet comment. The Kings wear their emotions on their sleeves. They are fiercely loyal and love hard. It would be a dream to be a part of this family. The more I sit with it, the more I want it to happen. Is it too soon to say that? I wouldn't mind having Kerry King as my little brother.

"Oh! Wait here," Kerry says, disappearing down a hallway. He's back before I have a chance to take another sip of wine, jogging over to me with his tongue sticking out like a golden retriever, holding a black book. I tilt my head curiously as he settles back in on the stool next to me. His smile is contagious, just like Donovan's. I suddenly realize that I'm beaming like Kerry. Maybe this is the King effect.

He slides the black book in front of me, and my fingers trace the stitching on the bottom.

For our favorite girl, Violet Winthrop.

"I wanted to give it to you sooner, but now that you're home for good, I thought this was a good time," he pauses. "You *are* home for good, right?" he asks sweetly. I glance at Donovan in the living room, his eyes crinkled, dimples on full display. Our eyes meet for a moment, giving me a wink before continuing his conversation with Logan.

I sip my wine, my smile widening against the brim of my glass. "Yeah. I'm home for good," I reply, my heart squeezing the moment the words leave my lips. Kerry smiles like Donovan, minus the dimples. "Good. Open it," he beams, leaning on his elbow with his eyes glued to mine.

I place my wineglass down and rake my fingers along the edges of the book. I open the book to see Gran's sweet smile beaming up at me. It's the photo that Kerry took of her at Siren's Flask. Her smile instantly fills my heart. I wish more than anything that she was here with us right now.

Kerry watches me intently, anticipating my reaction. I smile at his expression before pinching the corner of the page to turn.

"Oh my gosh, Kerry," I gasp, my eyes glistening as I flip through the disposable camera photos from Gran's happy hour at Sip & Savor. Mr. Frommling taking a selfie with Mrs. Dickson. Josie and Wyatt rolling their eyes at each other. Kerry and Jackson posing like it's their senior prom. Pop making his speech with his arm slung around my shoulder, our eyes wet with tears.

I slip a teary chuckle as I flip through every page, Kerry laughing alongside me. "I love this one," Kerry says, pointing to a candid picture of Donovan and me staring at each other in passing. My finger traces along our faces.

When I see this picture of us, I see the way my eyes gleam when I look at Donovan. Even when I felt like I was drowning, he was my lighthouse in the middle of a violent storm.

Always was. Always is.

I feel a familiar pair of strong arms wrap around my waist, and the comforting scent of fresh linen floods my senses. I close my eyes and melt into Donovan's chest, leaning my head back.

"You see, Mouse? I've only ever had eyes for you," he whispers in my ear. Happy tears form when I open my eyes, overwhelmed by his words and this generous gift. I swivel on my stool, pressing a light kiss on Donovan's lips. I turn my torso toward Kerry, my throat bobbing to keep from crying.

"Kerry, I don't know what to say. This…This is—" I struggle to find the words. I look at Donovan, who stands by his brother with his hands in his pockets, showing me an irresistible half grin.

"Thank you," I choke out, the only words I can muster at the gesture. I hop off the stool and wrap my arms around Kerry's neck, hugging him like the brother I never had. I feel his grief for Gran, too. They loved her like I did. They saw her as I did. Good and pure. Light and love.

"You're welcome, Audrey," he whispers.

"Boys, set the table," Caleb calls out, holding a large tray of sizzling steaks. The smell wafts in my direction, prompting loud grumbles from my stomach. All I've eaten today was cinnamon rolls. *And Donovan.* My arousal grows thinking about the quickie we had just before we left that had me on my knees on his front porch.

"On it, captain!" Kerry shouts, breaking my dirty thoughts.

"I get plates!" Kerry and Donovan shout in unison, running into the kitchen and shoving each other as they race to the plate cabinet. Scattered laughter echoes in the kitchen, and Grace's eyes widen with concern as she trails behind Caleb.

I can imagine her back in the day, wrangling four rambunctious boys around, delegating who does what and no one listening. But these boys love their mama something fierce. I can see it when they look at her.

"Boys, if either of you breaks my new set, you're both on dish duty every Sunday!" she shouts, rolling her eyes in annoyance. "Kerry, you do napkins. Donovan gets plates." Clearly, mama bear gets the last word in this house. Kerry groans loud enough for his mom to glare daggers at him.

Logan and I snicker under our breath, watching Kerry reluctantly grab the napkins from a drawer, trying to slap Donovan in the nuts.

"You would think that my adult children would act more adult," she teases. I offer to take the grilled vegetables out of her hands and place it on the table.

"Thank you, dear," she says to me as I relieve her of the plate. "Logan, silverware, please?" she asks. Her eyes flick to the kitchen, and Logan gives her a salute and dives in to help Donovan and Kerry set the table.

"Is there anything else I can do to help?" I ask Grace, feeling totally useless. I know she insisted I just relax, but everyone is putting in their helping hand and I feel like I'm in the way. She opens her mouth to say something when I feel Wyatt's hand touch my elbow.

"Audrey, help me fill up the water glasses?" he asks with a smirk. I give him a relieving smile as I nod my head. He's not so grumpy after all.

"Sorry I'm late!" A comforting voice floats in the foyer. My grandfather strides in giving a small wave.

"Noah! You made it. Let me get you a drink." Caleb gently places the steaks in the middle of the dining table and saunters into the kitchen, pouring Pop a glass of wine.

Pop opens his arms wide and I find myself in his warm embrace. I've hugged my grandfather more in the past month than I have in a long time. Each time we hold each other, it's a promise that no matter what, we won't let anything come between us. We are all each other has, and I want to make sure he knows I am here to stay.

"Hey, kid. You look great. Beautiful, like your mother," he coos. His eyes soften as he touches a lock of my hair. I clutch my chest, thinking about my mom and Gran, and how much I wish they could be here with all of us.

"Thanks, Pop." I say softly, resting my head on his chest. The steady thump of his heart washing over me with peace.

With the table set, everyone settles into their seats, Caleb and Grace at opposite ends. Donovan intertwines his fingers through mine under the table, kissing my shoulder.

"I'm so happy you're here. It feels complete with you," he whispers into my ear. I give him a wink and my eyes scan around the table. I notice that there's an extra placemat next to Logan, and a confused expression splashes across my face. Donovan follows my eyes and sees it too, mirroring me.

"Are we expecting someone else?" Donovan asks, pointing toward the empty placemat. I look at Caleb and Grace, and they keep a tight-lipped expression. Kerry and Wyatt look just as confused as Donovan and I. Logan grins across from me, his eyes fixed on his phone in his lap.

"Logan, you look suspicious," I grumble, crossing my arms over my chest, tilting my head. He dodges my gaze and puffs out his cheeks to stifle a smile. Pop puts his hand on my back and gives me a reassuring pat.

Am I missing something *again*?

I jump in my seat when I hear the doorbell ring, and I look at Donovan with lost eyes. Caleb gets up from his chair when Donovan puts a hand up to him. "I'll get it," Donovan answers, kissing my hair before turning the corner to the front door.

Logan pinches his brow and starts chuckling, finally meeting my gaze.

"What are you laughing at, Harper?" I scowl, my tone comes out harsher than intended. I don't enjoy being out of the loop, and with that stunt Logan pulled earlier, I've been on edge.

"You didn't think I'd come back from Austin *alone*, did you Winthrop?" he drawls. I raise my eyebrow and hear the front door close. Wait.

No way.

I turn in my chair toward the front entrance when Donovan and a familiar face round the corner, both of them smiling from ear to ear.

"Tia?!" I scream, dragging my chair back as I race towards her. I crash into her chest, burying my face into her thick black hair. I peek out behind her and see Donovan's adoring grin. My heart squeezes realizing that the people I love most are in the same room.

"Did you know about this?!" My voice is high pitched, piercing my own ears. "Mouse, I swear I had no idea!" Donovan puts his hands up in a surrender and shakes his head.

Tia pulls back from our embrace and twirls under my extended arm. Our smiles are too bright to contain. The sun might as well be shining in this house. "Surprise, bitch!" she squeaks, our obnoxious laughter echoing in the foyer.

I prod her playfully in the ribs. "You know I hate surprises! Why would you do this to me?!" She puts her arm around me as we walk toward the table.

"I tried texting and calling, but your number was out of service! I was going to tell you that Logan and I were on our way home, but Logan wanted to surprise D, so here we are."

I fucked up twice now. First, I forget to tell Tia that I'm home for good, and second, I forget to text her my new number. But Tia never holds a grudge, and she deserves a better friend than the one I've been the last couple of years. Now that she's home, I want there to be no secrets between us. No more time apart and memories wasted.

"Oh my god! How long do I have you for?" I ask, breathless.

"You have me for a whole week! Logan and I head back Saturday morning." My mouth gapes open, soaking in the reality that my best friend is actually here.

Logan gets up from his chair, lifting Tia off the ground while he shakes her up and down. "Harper and Young, back in Oakwood Valley to fuck shit up!" he jests. Tia slaps Logan's chest and scolds him. "Language! We are guests here. Jesus, Logan. I'm so sorry, Mr. and Mrs. King," she mutters, giving them an apologetic smile on behalf of Logan's sailor mouth.

"Can we please fucking eat because I'm fucking hungry," Kerry interjects, earning howls of laughter from everyone at the table. Tia rolls her eyes at Kerry and ruffles the top of his head before properly greeting the rest of the family and settling into the seat across from mine.

"Before we dig in, I would like to make a toast," Caleb announces. Kerry groans while throwing his head back. Wyatt slaps the back of his head, and everyone snorts out a chuckle. Caleb rolls his eyes before continuing.

"It's been a long time since this table has had almost every seat taken. I look around here, and I'm thankful for every person sitting in this room." He glances at every person around the table briefly until his eyes land on Donovan. Donovan avoids his father's eye contact, staring at the plate in front of him. I look back toward Caleb and see his throat constrict, clearing it before finishing his toast.

"Uh, anyway. To family," he toasts, raising his wineglass in the air.

"To family." Everyone but Donovan says in unison, raising their glasses and clinking them with one another. His fingers twist the stem of his wineglass before raising it up to cheer those sitting closest to him. I know a real Donovan grin, the kind that makes my insides melt. The grin he's wearing is not it. It's forced. Fake.

"Cheers, babe," I whisper, nudging him lightly with my elbow in hopes of snapping him out of his funk. He looks at me and his grin comes back. Just for me. There goes my insides.

"Cheers, Mouse," he whispers back, kissing me on the lips before clinking our glasses together.

"Well, aren't you two just the cutest thing?" Logan teases, flashing his crooked grin while cutting into his steak. Tia quirks her brow as she forks a piece of asparagus into her mouth, stifling a smile. Grace glances at Donovan and me with a smirk on her face. My cheeks can't get any more red than they already are with all of this attention on us.

"He's right, you two are adorable," Grace croons, pointing her wineglass towards us before taking a sip.

Pop finishes chewing a piece of steak before he chimes in. "You know, Audrey used to just blush over Donovan in high school, and—"

"Pop! Can we not, please?" I interrupt, my face flaming hotter than before. Pop heaves a hearty chuckle, wiping his mouth with his napkin. Scattered giggles erupt around the table as I playfully poke my comedian of a grandfather in his rib. Donovan quirks his eyebrow up at me, those damn dimples making it hard for me to feel embarrassed. He winks before kissing me on the cheek.

Everyone I love is here. If you told me a month ago this would be my reality, I never would have believed it.

Donovan rescuing me from that frigid, loveless prison was the best thing that ever happened to me. He helped me break the chains that clung to every part of me. Day by day, the weight of it all is less and less. And now? I'm free, surrounded by warmth and light and so much love I don't know where to put it all.

I'll probably put it in, on, and under Donovan...later tonight.

$$Chapter\ Twenty-Four$$

DONOVAN

The sun sets just beyond the hill as we all sit around a fire pit in my parents' backyard. The vines stretch for miles, contrasting against the pink and orange hues that paint the sky. Audrey's pallid skin softly glows against the embers, a ring of gold forming around her irises. Her moonbeam smile holds my attention, completely blocking out everything and everyone around me.

"Donovan? Earth to D?" Logan's elbow nudges my arm, knocking me out of my love trance.

"Yeah? What's up?" I answer back, my eyes locked on Audrey as she and Tia laugh across the fire pit. This is the very place where we almost kissed for the first time. Our faces were so close I could feel the shudder in her breath when it brushed across my lips. Now, I get to kiss those lips anytime I want to.

"Damn, brother. You've got it so bad. What's it like?" he teases me, putting his hands under his chin and batting his lashes. I snort under my breath and shove him by the shoulder. "Shut the fuck up, man," I retort, shaking my head.

Logan knows how long I've had it bad for Audrey. He's the first person I ever told about how I felt about her.

We were ten. I went to work with my dad one day that summer, and there she was—reading a book on the Juliet balcony outside her room, hair in a single braid draped over one shoulder.

She must've read something endearing in the way her mouth curved upward, striking a direct arrow into my heart. Her eyes glowed with wonder, like whatever words she read on the page were better than whatever else was happening around her in reality. The sparkle in her gaze drew me in, experiencing her undeniable pull for the first time.

I decided right then and there that Audrey Winthrop was the most intriguing girl I'd ever laid eyes on. She didn't once look up at me, but man, she was the prettiest girl I'd ever seen. Logan came over to play video games that night and I said very matter-of-fact, "I think I'm in love."

"Seriously though, D. I'm happy for you. You finally got your dream girl," he smiles. She really was just a dream for so long. Out of reach, out of touch. Just a movie in my head when I'd close my eyes at night, seeing her face before I'd drift off. It still feels like a dream, only better. It's real. It's concrete. Now when I drift off, it's her face in front of me, not just in my head. And when I wake up, there she is. My dream girl.

"Thanks, brother. Now what about you? You seeing anyone?" I ask, sipping on my beer. He leans back in his chair and stretches his arms behind his head. Logan was known as quite the playboy back in the day, and he definitely carried that reputation all the way to Texas.

"Ah, you know I love my horseshoe honeys," he chuckles. "But nah. No one serious at the moment," he replies, his eyes focused on the fire.

I'd gone to visit a handful of times over the years. Logan insisted I'd come during rodeo season to meet the "horseshoe honeys," his infamous moniker for the never-ending roster of girls he met there. Now, those Texas girls were attractive, but none held a candle to Audrey. Not even close.

"We're pushing thirty, Harper. Don't you wanna find someone and settle?" I ask, grinning against the opening of my bottle. He scoffs and takes a long pull from his beer. Logan? Settling? I'm stupid to ask. "I'll leave the settling to you, baby boy," he teases. We wink in unison and cheers the necks of our beers.

"So when are you gonna put a ring on it?" he asks, glancing at Audrey. Ah, there it is. The marriage talk. If I wasn't so drop dead in love with her, I'd probably get annoyed. But the thought of marriage with Audrey only makes my insides flutter. I wanted to make her my wife the second I saw her at Sip & Savor.

"Honestly? I want to soon, man," I admit. I like the sound of it once it leaves my mouth. Mrs. Audrey King? Yeah, that's it.

He blows out a whistle, taking another pull from his beer. I knew I'd marry her the minute she kneed me in the groin—the pain was blinding, but our future was clear. For every hope she shared, I'd be there to support her, no matter what. Every tear she'd shed, I'd be the one to catch it. Every kiss we'd had, I'd savor it. There's not a doubt in my mind that the woman sitting across the flames with those shining green eyes is my wife. There never was.

"That's crazy, D. But fucking awesome. Can I be your best man?" he jests, flashing me a cheeky grin.

I point my beer toward Wyatt, who's deep in conversation with Noah. Logan's eyes follow, and when he turns back to face me, he pats my shoulder and cups the side of my face.

"He would love that, brother," he beams, playfully pinching my cheek. I look over at Wyatt and my chest squeezes with adoration for my little brother. Despite his broody, grumpy nature, he's my best friend through and through. I love both of my brothers the same, but Wyatt keeps me steady. When the going gets rough, it's Wyatt who holds me together.

My eyes flit to my dad, who's listening intently to Audrey and Tia telling a story to my mom. We haven't exchanged many words tonight—clearly, neither of us is making an effort to talk. But at least he's not being an ass toward Audrey. That's all I care about.

I watch her giggle, her cheeks flushed from the wine. Would she want this type of life with me? Married, kids, Sunday dinners? I know one thing for sure. She's the only girl I'm ever bringing home to my family.

"Oh my god! The cinnamon rolls!" Audrey gasps, scrunching her hands in her hair. She stands up, looking at me over the fire.

"Donovan, can you help me, please?" I put my beer down and give her a nod, standing from my chair.

"Please excuse us. I made dessert for you all," she chirps. Appreciative cheers echo around the firepit. Audrey plays coy, covering her cheeks with her hands.

She walks toward me and holds out her hand. I can tell she's tipsy by her giggles and the way she stumbles on her way to me.

Once her hand is in mine, I realize that I've been missing her touch all night. Our fingers lace together and I pull her closer to bask in her intoxicating scent. It's wildflowers and white wine, packed together like a drug I can't get enough of.

The hem of her baby blue cotton dress flips up in the breeze, exposing her lean legs. I want those legs wrapped around me. My dick strains against my jeans when I see her nipples bud through her dress, knowing full well she isn't wearing a bra.

Why does she do this to me?

As soon as we cross the threshold into the house, my lips are on her so fast she doesn't have a second to think. Her hands rake through my hair and she tugs hard, earning a groan from deep inside my chest.

We stumble through the furniture to get to the kitchen as our tongues wrestle, our hands hungry for each other's skin. I move my hands down below her dress and grab a handful of her ass, claiming her as mine. She moans into my mouth and breaks the kiss, playfully shoving me off of her.

"We aren't done, Mouse," I rumble, crowding her space and caging her against the kitchen island.

I've shared her all night, and I'm done sharing.

"Donovan, what about dessert?" she breathes, unable to control her tipsy giggles.

I lean in, pressing my arousal against her hip.

"I'm looking at it," I growl, my lips hungry for her.

Her breath hitches as she traces her finger down the front of my shirt, torturously trailing down to my waist. She opens her hand and strokes her palm over my jeans, where my throbbing cock is eagerly waiting for her. My eyes roll back and I moan in her ear. It's more than the wine and beer that has me drunk. I'm wasted on the way she touches me. Light-headed, room-spinning, seeing-double type of love drunk for her.

"Hey lovebirds, get a room!"

We both flinch back as Kerry drunkenly announces his presence. Thankfully, my back is to him, so he can't see the bulge straining through my jeans that Audrey was just groping.

She buries her face in my shoulder, giggling uncontrollably with embarrassment. I give in and join her while Kerry stands by the French doors, crossing his arms and smirking. The little shit.

"Fuck off, Ker!" I turn my head out and yell, waiting for my dick to deflate. He flips the bird and stumbles outside to join everyone else. Audrey can't stop laughing, her face beet red.

"Fuck, he's drunk," I say, scrubbing my hand over my face. "I'm sorry, Mouse. I didn't notice he was in the house." I laugh under my breath.

"Let's just get these cinnamon rolls out to everyone before Kerry tells everyone I was giving you a hand job in your parents' kitchen," she teases.

I follow her lead and set the oven to its warm setting. She lifts the foil from the Pyrex. The aroma of cinnamon and sugar floods my nostrils. A secret grin plays on my lips thinking of licking the icing off of her tits this morning.

"By the way, I'm gonna go into town tomorrow with Tia to go shopping. I need new clothes," she chirps, sliding the cinnamon rolls into the oven.

I noticed she didn't bring much from New York. Briggs only packed as much as he could before Kellan woke up. The hairs on the back of my neck stand up thinking back to that day, holding her in my arms while she was black and blue. I shake it away quickly before it festers.

"Of course, baby. I've got some errands to run in the morning and a busy day at the winery. You and Tia should come by for a tasting," I suggest. Selfishly, I would love to see her while I'm helping Frank with the wine tasting room tomorrow. But I'm glad she has Tia in town. I know she missed her.

"Okay, that sounds fun," she winks, and I press a kiss into her cheek.

"Call me if you need me, okay?" My expression marks with concern, remembering what happened to her last time she went into town. She gives me a weak smile and rubs my back for reassurance.

"I'll be alright, baby. I've got Tia. Don't worry, okay?" she replies. She's right. Tia can be terrifying.

On a visit to Austin for me and Logan's 21st birthdays, Logan and Tia took me out to their local hole in the wall. When some guy started getting handsy with her on the way to the bathroom, she grabbed him right by the balls and slammed him down hard on the floor, showing off every bit of of that third-degree black belt in jiu-jitsu. She seems chill on the surface, but you definitely don't wanna fuck with her.

"You're right. But still, *please* call if you need me. I'll be there," I murmur, my hands resting on her waist. Her arms wrap around my middle as she tilts her head up, giving me a good look at those freckles I love so much.

"I will. Thank you," she whispers. I kiss the tip of her nose and help her with her cinnamon rolls once they're out of the oven, placing them on one of my mom's serving plates. Once we have everything in order, we make our way back out to the firepit to join my family.

"God, I hope they love them," she nervously whispers, wearing the cutest expression on her face. She doesn't need to impress my family. She already enamored them with no effort at all.

The moment she approaches everyone with dessert in hand, the ensuing claps and cheers prompt a soft shade of pink to spread across her cheeks. She bows in a sweet, adorable curtsy.

Okay, that was fucking cute.

"Oh wow, Audrey. These look amazing, sweetheart. Thank you so much," my mom gushes, staring at a cinnamon roll as big as her face.

Satisfying groans break out from everyone around the firepit. Audrey's smile shines brighter than the moon, watching everyone's delighted expressions.

"Damn, Audrey. These are better than Sip & Savor's, hands down," Wyatt beams, while Kerry stuffs his face without taking a breath.

"Jesus, Ker, slow down. You're gonna choke, son," my dad chimes in, scolding Kerry with his eyes. Everyone but Noah and my parents are a little drunk at this point, further explaining why Kerry is inhaling his food like a vacuum instead of properly chewing.

Kerry snorts with the cinnamon roll stuffed in his mouth, sparking a chain reaction of snickers from everyone. It starts with Tia, who nearly spits out her food, causing Logan to double over as drool escapes his mouth. Audrey's cheeks puff out like a chipmunk hoarding nuts in its mouth, which makes me spit out my cinnamon roll. It lands in the center of the fire, punctuated by a glow in the center of the flames.

We're laughing so hard that no sound is being made except wheezing and ragged inhales, and someone—I think Tia—sounds like a tea kettle going off. Wyatt slumps deep in his chair, casually eating his dessert with his eyes bloodshot and glazed over, shaking his head at everyone on the floor.

"Oh my Lord, kids! Caleb, we should've cut them off a long time ago," my mom shouts over us, half laughing, half in disbelief that her grown adult children can't handle their alcohol.

"Grace, I can't help that your sons have your alcohol tolerance," my dad retorts, earning a playful slap on the shoulder from mom.

"These are not my sons right now. They're *yours*," my mom counters, pushing her index finger into Dad's chest.

My dad and Noah glance over at each other, both with sly grins on their faces, sitting back in their chairs enjoying dessert. More so, enjoying the shit show unfolding before them.

"I'm sorry, mommy!" Kerry squeaks out, his stomach cramping

from eating too fast and laughing too hard. That sets us off into another wave of silent laughter as we fight for our lives.

Audrey and I slide out of our chairs. Her head buries in my shoulder as tears trickle down her face.

Damn, I haven't laughed like this with my family since...well, before James. We used to laugh like this all the time. My eyes scan around the firepit and an overwhelming sense of joy overcomes my whole body. Even my dad is chuckling—and I realize with a jolt, I miss him.

This is what Sunday dinners are about.

I look down at Audrey and lift her chin up to meet my eyes. Her giggles have settled, and her irises glow with the embers of the flame before us. Absolutely beautiful without even trying.

"Can I have forever with you?" she whispers, creating a bubble around us to live in, just us two.

I press a gentle kiss into her soft pout and whisper back, "Forever with you is only the start."

Chapter Twenty-Five

AUDREY

AUDREY

I'm leaving in 10, T.

TIA

omg make it 20. i'm so fucking hungover.

AUDREY

honestly, same. lol

TIA

why didn't you stop me after the 6th glass?!

AUDREY

no no, don't blame me. i couldn't even keep track!

TIA

this is YOUR fault.

AUDREY

lol. Donovan invited us to the winery for a tasting.
you up for some hair of the dog after we shop?

TIA

fuck yeah lol.

AUDREY

be there in 30 then.

TIA

I woke up with Donovan deliciously between my legs, devouring what he couldn't have last night. I got embarrassingly drunk with his family after dinner and blacked out. The two orgasms he gave me this morning helped get rid of my throbbing hangover headache, and I made it up to him with a blowjob in the shower. I squeeze my thighs together, licking the faint taste of him on my lips, thinking about his gorgeous face coming apart for me.

Before I passed my limit, last night was amazing. Donovan's family, including Caleb, were so gracious and kind, welcoming me and Pop with open arms. I laughed harder than I have in a long time. I realized last night that this could be my life. My life with Pop, Donovan, and his family. Tia and Logan too. I didn't think it was possible, considering where I was going a month ago.

Kellan was all I had known since I was nineteen. I shut out everyone who loved me, because it was clear I didn't love myself—Kellan made sure of that. I closed my heart off to the possibility that it could get better. That I wanted it to get better. I convinced myself I'd already had my chance of love that night with Donovan in the gazebo; I wasn't worthy of more. I believed Kellan's lies, wrote my own narrative around them. These last few months with Donovan have taught me how to rewrite my story. The man gives me his love in capital letters. Unabashedly. And I relish in every syllable.

And now, with Tia home, I'm going to tell her everything. I'd been so deprived of friendship for so long. I admit, I was nervous if Tia and I would connect like we used to. It'd been ages since I had seen her in person. I wondered if we both had changed too much.

But all of that doubt evaporated into thin air the moment we embraced. Everything was as it had always been. And now, I was really looking forward to our girl's day.

I opt for a pair of light-wash flared jeans and a lavender razorback tank top. I've had to get used to seeing myself in colors again since I moved back.

I zhuzh my hair a bit, smiling at my natural color that I've always loved. I lean closer into my reflection, inspecting the freckles sprinkled across my nose. All my life I had been insecure about these dots that pepper my face—until Donovan. The wide grin pulling at my lips is too big to hide. I'm able to look at myself and love who's staring back. My fingers trail along the column of my neck, down to my collarbone. The bruises that used to live there vanished with every gentle kiss from Donovan's heavenly lips. He's healed me from within, and the beaming smile in my reflection is proof that I'm going to be okay.

I give myself a reassuring nod in the mirror and head into the living room. I swipe the keys from the hook by the front door and step onto the porch, getting hit with a wave of dry heat. A cool breeze brushes against my cheeks as I make my way down the steps, thankful for some relief from the sweltering air.

Donovan left me his truck and took the quad to work so I could go pick up my Jeep from Pop's house. As I settle into the driver's seat, I reach forward to turn the ignition when I see a folded note perched on the dashboard.

I grab the note, reading "Mouse" written across the top. Just like the note he left for me with my dress. Damn, I'm down bad for this man.

Hey baby,

Have fun with Tia today. Can't wait to see you at the winery. Maybe I can steal you away so we can finish what we started this morning.

I love you,

D

Can your heart smile? If it can, it's doing it right now. A big, fat, cheesy smile. I place the note in my purse and fire up the engine, making the quick ten-minute drive to Pop's.

I approach the garage to swap cars and put the truck in park, sliding out of the driver's seat and walk toward Jules. It's a perfect day to cruise in the Jeep with no roof, no windows, and no worries. Just me and my best friend.

I open the door and find another neatly folded note sitting in my seat.

"Aww, Donovan," I giggle quietly to myself, overwhelmed by his affection.

> *Mouse,*
> *"My feelings will not be repressed. You must allow me to tell you how ardently I admire and love you."*
> *I really do,*
> *D*

Jane Austen. My copy of *Pride & Prejudice* is beaten and tattered from the amount of times I've read it. The apples of my cheeks are sore from smiling. I'm like a love-sick teenager around him, squealing and giggling, kissing his picture on my wall, scribbling "Mrs. Audrey King" in my diary.

AUDREY

Don't ever stop writing me love notes.

DONOVAN

Never.

AUDREY

I want one every day for the rest of my life.

DONOVAN

Done.

AUDREY

Promise?

DONOVAN

I promise.

"Holy shit, I can't believe we are riding in fucking Jules!" Tia yells out into the open air with her hands above her head as we cruise through the country roads with nothing but grapevines as far as the eye can see.

"I know. It's so surreal. I feel sixteen again!" I lift one arm in the air and let the cool breeze kiss my fingertips. Our smiles beam so brightly, they outshine the sunrays stretching over the sky.

We scream the lyrics to "C'est La Vie," our favorite song to drive around to back in the day. Tia balls her fist like a microphone, her face scrunching up as she sings at the top of her lungs. I glimpse at the picture of us on my dash. Just two best friends ecstatic to have some freedom after getting a new car. Looking at Tia giving the performance of her life in my passenger seat right now, I know we're still the same teenage girls, deep down.

Tia turns her whole body to face me, tucking her legs beneath her. "I'm so happy we're together again, Auds. I missed you so much."

I glance toward Tia, my gaze instantly softening at her affirmation. Her hazel eyes shimmer beneath the sun, looking at me like she's piecing the memories together from our childhood.

"I really missed you, T. I can't believe you flew out here to surprise me." But really, I'm not surprised she did this. That's Tia. A fierce and loyal friend, through and through.

"The second you told me you were home, I told Logan—naturally. Then he told me that Donovan told him that…" she rambles. My eyes flit back and forth toward her and the road, balancing the dual tasks of trying not to crash while following her mind map. Tia has always been a spitfire. You gotta keep up. "And so, yeah! We booked tickets and got our asses here. I mean, our parents were happy to see us too, I guess," she chuckles. Tia's parents moved back to Oakwood Valley two years ago, but she stayed behind in Austin working as an interior designer. I shake my head and giggle, softening my gaze as I look out toward the road.

Tia and Logan coming home is a reminder of how I never want to shut anyone out again. That's just the thing with small town friendships: they're hard to shake, no matter how hard you try.

Main Street is alive and buzzing today. Tourists flood the side-walks, drifting from shop to shop. A twinge of anxiety bubbles in my chest at the amount of people out, considering what happened last time I was here. But that was just paranoia, a lapse of letting Kellan get under my skin, just for a second. I won't have another freak out moment like I did the other night in front of Donovan. The look in his eyes wrecked me.

"You okay, Auds?" Tia's voice cuts through my negative thoughts, and I quickly push them away.

"What? Yeah, of course. It's just a lot of people out today. No parking anywhere, Jesus," I reply, breathless. Our eyes scan up and down the street. My hands grip the steering wheel a little tighter as I try to push the rest of the anxiety out of my chest.

Chill out, Audrey.

"Oh! Car's backing out, get it get it get it!" Tia squeals, frantically pointing at a black SUV backing out. I slam hard against my brakes, causing us to lunge forward rapidly.

"Jesus, Audrey! Are you good?" Tia rubs her collarbone, her eyes stunned. I hold my breath as I watch the SUV drive off before slowly pressing the gas and taking its spot. I try to catch the license plate, but it's gone too far. Either my mind is playing tricks on me, or that was the same SUV the man from the other day got into when I'd followed him out of the store. Please let it be mind tricks. I break into a cold sweat, my breaths uneven.

I put the car in park, and I feel Tia's eyes on me like a hawk. I stare blankly at the black SUV pulling further away, turning into a tiny black speck in the distance. So much for trying to chill out.

"Hey, what's wrong? You look flushed. Are you feeling okay?" Tia asks, her voice laced with concern. She quickly unbuckles herself and leans over the center console, pressing the back of her hand into my clammy forehead. I really need to get my shit together.

"Hmm, no fever," she mutters. Her hand rests on my shoulder, tension forming in her brows. I bury my face in my hands and shake my head, unable to stop the stinging in my eyes.

"I'm sorry T. It's just...fuck," I whimper into my hands. Tia's hand gently strokes my back, trying to calm my breathing.

Take a deep breath, count backward from five.

"Auds, talk to me. What's going on?" Her voice is full of worry as she watches me fall apart. Heat forms behind my eyes and the stinging gets stronger, tears almost forming.

Don't you fucking cry right now.

I lift my gaze and face her. I guess shopping can wait. After all, I did say no more secrets. We sit in silence for a moment before Tia cuts the tension.

"How about we grab a coffee and then talk?" she suggests, and I'm thankful she can read my mind right now. Coffee sounds great. After shutting her door, she rounds the front of Jules and loops her arm through mine, her free hand rubbing my forearm. We don't talk the whole way, but the silence is deafening.

Will she judge me for staying with Kellan for so long? Will she think I'm stupid for thinking that he's out to get me? So many questions thunder inside my brain, I want the noise to come to a halt.

Tia leads us into Sip & Savor, and Josie pops her head out from behind the espresso machine. "Hey Audrey! Good to see you! I'll be with you in just a sec!" she shouts out over the machine, preparing a coffee order for a woman standing by the pickup counter with a little girl.

"Hey Josie. No problem at all," I reply, not being able to take my eyes away from the mother and her daughter. She looks about three or four, her little chubby fingers tightly wrap around her mother's hand. They both share the same ice-blonde hair, the little girl a mirror image of her mom. *Just like me.* A rush of envy and sadness seeps out of my heart, wondering if my mom would have taken me into town while she picked up coffee, holding my hand.

"Ugh, she's so cute," Tia sings, giving the little girl a tiny finger wave. The little girl smiles back at her shyly, burying her face in her mom's skirt. The woman looks down at her daughter, smiling and stroking her hair.

I wish my mom were here.

Josie hands the woman her coffee before greeting us with her bright smile and pink-streaked hair at the register. My eyes follow the little girl as she passes me, giving me a tiny finger wave like Tia had given her earlier. I give her a wink, a soft grin forming on my face as I turn my attention back to Josie.

"Sorry about the wait. We've been busy today," she sighs, wiping her brow with the back of her hand. I glimpse a music note tattoo on the underside of her wrist.

"Hi! I'm Tia. Cool hair," Tia gushes while Josie runs a hand through her hair. Tia's arm stays linked in mine as she scans Josie up and down.

"Thanks! I'm Josie. Nice to meet you. What can I get you guys?" she asks.

"I'll have a cappuccino with oat milk, please. Auds?" Tia asks. "I'll have a caramel macchiato upside down non-fat, please," I reply. Tia gives me the side-eye and I slip my arm from her, squaring my shoulders toward her as I cock up an eyebrow.

"I see you haven't changed your coffee order since we were old enough to drink it," she teases. I roll my eyes and give Josie some cash, and we snag a table in the far corner of the shop. There's a busy chatter all around, but no one looks familiar. I scan my eyes around the room one last time before looking back at Tia, her arms crossed in front of her, leaning on the table.

"Okay, enough stalling. Talk to me, Auds. What the hell was that out there?"

Take a deep breath, count backward from five.

"Listen, what if we just like, shop and go to the winery and laugh and drink? This conver—" Her hand covers mine and her eyes are stern on me. She's not letting me get away with this. I let out a heavy sigh and rub my temples, trying to figure out where to even start.

"Okay, okay. I'll talk," I sigh. "Well, you know about Kellan and how we were together for a really long time." I place my hands under my thighs to keep them from shaking.

This is Tia for Christ's sake. Just be honest, Audrey. Let it go.

We spend the next hour sitting at the table, sipping our coffee while I lay out every painful detail of my last nine years with Kellan, Donovan's trip to New York, and the black SUV. She never interrupts, she just holds my hands and her eyes go wide from time to time when I share graphic details of everything that has gone down.

"So, he would hit me, call me a whore, and tell me I was a piece of shit," I say dryly. She winces and closes her eyes, like she can't bear to see me in that kind of pain. "And then the next day, he would bring me roses, tell me how sorry he was and how much he loved me," I utter, keeping my eyes down. I hear Tia sniffle. As much as it hurts me to share the gory details, it feels like a huge weight lifted.

Once I had told Pop, it felt like the last person who needed to know what I had suffered was Tia. I kept her in the dark for years, claiming I was living a lavish, happy life in the city. Seeing her cry for me breaks me into a million pieces but brings me so much peace knowing that the secrets are out.

"Fuck, Auds. I'll fucking kill that guy, I swear," she seethes. That gets a laugh out of me. The situation is not funny by any means, but knowing that Tia would burn the world for me makes me happy.

"No wonder I love you. Donovan said the same thing," I reply, giggling. She smiles at me, her eyes red from crying. She leans in closer on the table, gripping my hands. "First, thank you for telling me. Second, I'm so fucking sorry that was what you were going through all this time," she murmurs. I shake my head to deny her.

"Audrey, you haven't had an easy life. I don't want to dwell on the past anymore, but let's focus on today. Look at you now, babe. You are glowing, and beautiful, and..." Her eyes shimmer as she looks at me, tilting her head like she needs to find the right words.

"In love?" I whisper, a genuine smile forming on my lips.

"Yeah, Auds. In love," she beams. "And damn, does he love you right back."

My heart squeezes knowing that my best friend can see that radiating from me. It's validation that I didn't ask for, didn't know I needed. Tia's eyes suddenly shift to concern, pursing her lips tight together.

"But don't you think we should talk to Chief Harper? I mean, if you think you're being followed—"

"No, Tia. No police. I know Logan is your best friend, but please promise me you won't say anything," I plead. She looks at me with worry, nibbling her bottom lip as if she wants to tell me something that I won't like. But she doesn't. Her sigh is loud and clear, telling me she doesn't approve, but she nods in agreement, anyway.

"You're my best friend, by the way," she teases, squeezing my hands tightly.

"You're mine, too. Always," I reply.

She rounds the table and reaches her arms out, motioning me into her embrace. I slowly get up and wrap my arms around her, inhaling a deep breath of citrus that lingers from her shampoo. We pull away and she kisses my cheek, looping her arm in mine.

"Let's shop our worries away. We can maybe find you a hot little number for Donovan, hm?" she purrs, waggling her brows. I bite my lip and entertain the thought that I wouldn't mind getting a little lingerie for Donovan. I'd love to see the look on his face when he sees me wearing bits of lace that barely cover my intimate parts.

"I know just the place, and you won't believe who owns it," I chirp, waving goodbye to Josie as we walk out the door.

We walk arm in arm down the sidewalk, throwing our heads back in laughter at every inside joke that surfaces. Lavender Lane is just a few strides ahead, when an elderly couple abruptly exits the store next door. I see them in my peripheral vision, but I'm not quick enough to avoid my shoulder ramming into the old man's.

"Oh my gosh! I'm so sorry, are you alright, sir?" I ask, my voice shrill and panicked. I knocked his glasses off of him, and I bend down to pick them up before he has a chance to. His wife keeps her arm linked in his and gives Tia and me an apologetic smile.

I hand the man his glasses as he adjusts them back on his face, eyes squinting at me. He gives me a wide grin and gently touches my elbow.

"It's quite alright. Thank you, little bird."

My body freezes, turning my bones to pure ice. I'm sure Tia can feel the temperature in my body drop. I stop breathing. The only sound I hear is my heartbeat in my ears. The pain in my chest tightens, the panic growing inside me gets bigger. So big that I'm on the cusp of a full-blown anxiety attack.

That was just a coincidence. A sick, twisted coincidence.

The man and his wife move past us, but I don't miss the puzzled look on their faces before walking away. Tia squeezes my arm as soon as she notices my distress. I can't move. I can't think.

"Audrey? Jesus, you're ghost white. Audrey?" Tia waves her hand in front of me, but I'm not here. I'm with Kellan. In the penthouse. Under his hold. Tia moves in front of me, gripping my shoulders and physically shaking me.

"Audrey? You're scaring me! What happened?!" she cries, desperate to help. She pulls me in close to her, hugging me so tightly that it snaps me out of it. I exhale a painful breath that I'd been holding. My body stays cold and rigid. She holds me in the middle of the sidewalk, helping me slow down my breaths as she breathes against my chest. I blink rapidly over her shoulder, but no tears come out.

"It's okay, Auds. I got you. You're okay," she whispers, burying her face in my neck. It's not until I hear those words that I melt into her embrace and squeeze her back. As Tia holds me, I couldn't be more thankful that she is here right now. In this moment.

I'm okay.

She pulls back and leads me to a nearby bench. We sit side by side for a minute, no words exchanged. Just her hand in mine, my head resting on her shoulder.

"Auds, don't take this the wrong way…but you need some *serious* therapy."

I lift my head so quickly off of her shoulder and look right at her. We stare at each other for a beat until we are laughing so hard my stomach cramps up and I can't breathe.

She's not wrong, though. I need help, and it's a harsh reality to accept. I can't freeze up and fall back into Kellan's grip every time I'm triggered. I need help to work through this.

"It's not funny, but you're right. I do. You think you could help me find someone to talk to?" I ask breathlessly, our giggles subsiding.

"Of course, babe. I got you. But first, shopping therapy. No more distractions!" she replies, poking me in the ribs.

"Yes, shopping therapy is *definitely* what I need right now," I retort, smiling at Tia as we get up from the bench.

No more distractions.

Little bird. Go to hell.

Chapter Twenty-Six

DONOVAN

"So Donovan, are you single?" a leggy blonde from the group I'm hosting asks, her friends giggling around us. She bats her long lashes, biting her bottom lip, which looks swollen. Almost unnatural. Before Audrey, I may have entertained this. I would've flirted back, let my charm do the talking.

But not today. Today, I've got Audrey.

I smile politely, pouring another flight of wine. "I am not. I've got a girlfriend."

Damn, I love saying that.

She dramatizes her puppy eyes, her friends echoing a collective disappointment in my answer. I've been getting ogled all day by the girls trip groups and the bachelorette parties. Frank takes the groups with the older ladies, trying to find himself a good time since his divorce last year. Damn him. I get the occasional group dates and married couples, which is what I prefer these days.

"Well, that's too bad. You got any single brothers?" she teases as her friends lean in closer, curious for an answer. I clear my throat and start introducing the flight, ignoring her question. I'm doing my brothers a favor.

"So this one here is a 2021 Pinot Grigio that has hints of green apple and white peach with high acidity for a crisp and refreshing flavor. It's light body and—"

"Donovan, you didn't answer my question," she purrs, using her arms to squeeze her cleavage together. I glance at the door when an angel walks through it.

Thank god.

"Excuse me, ladies. I'll be back to bring you your food pairings." I politely nod and make a beeline toward Audrey. We lock eyes and she does a cute little hop and waves, skipping in my direction. My heart flutters when she smiles, already craving her touch.

"Baby!" she squeals out, leaping into my arms. Strawberries and fresh flowers fill my nostrils as I breathe in her scent. I lift her off the ground and kiss her deeply.

"Hey, Mouse. Damn, I missed you. Did you have fun with Tia?" I cup her face in my hands, wanting to sneak away and have my way with her.

"I missed you, too," she whispers, smiling as she places a peck on my lips. "And yes, we had so much fun." I look her up and down, appreciating her body.

Her tank top contrasts against her milky skin, pushing the swell of her breasts up. It takes everything in me not to bite them. Her jeans hug every curve of her ass, tight around her toned thighs and flared at the bottom. Fuck, she looks delicious.

"Baby, you're making me hard by just standing there. I'm at work," I tease huskily, getting turned on that she's making me feral in public. I love seeing her cheeks turn pink when I tell her what she does to me.

"What are you gonna do about it?" she counters, arching her eyebrow at me in challenge. I groan against her neck and kiss it lightly, pulling back from her to adjust my erection.

"I have a group I'm taking care of right now, but after, *you're mine,*" I growl, lacing her fingers through mine.

I glance over her shoulder and see Tia walking in. I nod my chin in her direction and she waves, skipping her way toward us.

"Hey, D! We are ready to get our flight on," Tia sings. She leans in to give me a hug, and I make sure I shift my hips back so she doesn't feel my dick that's still hard for Audrey.

"Hey, T. Alright, I have you girls set up right over there," I say, pointing to a section across the room. I lead them to their table, taking Audrey's hand in mine. We pass the group of women that I'm serving, earning a glare from Ms. Flirt and whispers from her friends. A grin flashes on my face, knowing that I have the most beautiful girl on my arm.

And she's all mine.

"Okay, ladies. I'll have Jake bring you a flight. I gotta finish up this group and I'll be with you later. Enjoy." I lean down and kiss Audrey, heading into the kitchen to grab the pairings.

"Jake, my girl is at table four. Can you bring out the summer white tasting for her and her friend, please?" I ask as my eyes scan the kitchen for everything I need. Jake is one of our youngest sommeliers. He started with us this summer and has amazing potential. He's Kerry's age, so it's nice having him around like a little brother.

"On it, sir," he salutes, and I chuckle at his formality. "Please, it's Donovan," I reply as he grabs the freshly washed glasses from the rack above him. "Okay, Donovan. I'll make sure I take care of your lady and her friend." I walk past him and clap his shoulder, grabbing the food pairings I need for my table before loading them on a tray. As I'm about to walk out, my phone vibrates in my pocket.

CHIEF HARPER

Hey Donovan. Can you stop by the station early tomorrow morning?

DONOVAN

Sure thing, Chief. Thanks.

Guilt rises from my stomach as I push my phone back down in my pocket. I know she told me not to reach out to Logan's dad, but we have to be one-hundred percent sure that Kellan is going to stay out of her life.

I may not understand what Audrey is going through or has gone through, but my only instinct is to protect her. Protecting her means guaranteeing her safety, so that's what I'm doing.

I push through the double doors and walk to my table, placing the food pairings with their respective wines. The girls at the table sear me with their eyes, flirtatiously giving me their full attention. A slight discomfort settles in my stomach at the eye contact, but it eases when I glance at Audrey and her bright green eyes across the way.

"Okay, ladies. Here are your pairings. We have candied orange dark-chocolate for the—"

"Donovan, is that your girlfriend over there?" Once again, I am interrupted. The leader of the group points her manicured finger right at Audrey, who is sipping her wine, listening to Tia ramble about something. Her lips wrap around the glass and I'm turned on again, imagining those lips on my cock.

I shake my head and reply, "Yes. That's her. Now, back to the pairings. I have a goat cheese from a local farm—"

"She's very pretty. Right, girls?" Okay, now I'm annoyed.

They nod in unison while staring at Audrey, and she turns her head to see the entire table looking at her. Her eyebrow quirks up as she makes eye contact with me. I give her a wink and bring my attention back to my table that I desperately want to pass off to another employee.

"Ladies, I'm here to make your wine tasting experience great. I'd appreciate it if you would let me do my job," I say. My tone stays professional but stern. I feel Audrey's eyes on me as Ms. Flirt stares daggers at her.

What is happening?

Next thing I know, Audrey's delicate fingers graze my back, instantly shooting goosebumps up my neck. She wraps her arm around my waist and stands confidently in front of the group of girls whose mouths are gaping. She stares down the leader, claiming me in front of her.

"Are you ladies enjoying my winery?" she says boldly. My eyes widen in shock, not expecting those words to come out of her mouth. There's my girl, full of sass and fire.

"*Your* winery?" Ms. Flirt replies while she swirls the wine in her wineglass.

"Yes, mine. Audrey Winthrop, nice to meet you." Audrey reaches her hand across the table while Ms. Flirt hesitantly shakes it. I love this feisty side of her, and it's driving me crazy. I'm about two seconds away from whisking her away and fucking her in the back.

"Ladies, have another round on me. I'm gonna have Jake take care of you for the rest of your tasting. Enjoy now," she croons, plastering the fakest of smiles on her face. I snort under my breath as Audrey takes her hand in mine and pulls me away, leading me toward the exit. I look back and Jake approaches their table, while Tia salutes me, a playful grin across her face.

Audrey leads me out of the wine tasting room into the open air, dragging me across the gravel. I don't ask questions, I just follow. Clearly, this woman is on a mission and I'm here for it.

We get to her Jeep, parked in the corner of the lot, and she slams my back against the car door, crashing her lips onto me. Her tongue searches for mine, and I gladly meet it, our kiss languid and deep. We've memorized each other, moving in a perfect dance.

She moans into my mouth as I cup my hands over her tits, squeezing them together. My thumbs brush over her nipples, pebbled underneath her tank top. She grinds herself over my rock hard arousal, her hands scratching my nape.

"Fuck, you drive me crazy, baby," I groan into her mouth. We stand in front of each other breathless as she bites my bottom lip.

"I need you to fuck me. Right now," she begs, her hand stroking my cock through my jeans. I look around to make sure the coast is clear.

"You want me to fuck you?" I rasp in her ear, desire oozing from every pore of my body. Her eyes are dark. She bites her bottom lip and nods.

"Beg for it," I growl against her swollen lips from my kiss.

"Please," she whimpers, her hand stroking me harder.

"Please, what?" I grunt, my body feeling heavy with arousal the more pressure she puts on my cock.

"Please, fuck me. Hard." Her voice is desperate. She bites my lip harder and a pleasurable pain shocks my body.

"Good girl," I praise, my thumbs grazing her nipples. She rolls her head back and whimpers. I need a taste of her right this second and I don't give a fuck that someone could walk around her car and see us.

I grip the top of her tank top and pull it down, her tits spilling out. Her pretty pink nipples are hard, begging me to suck them. I squeeze them together, claiming her in my mouth and flicking her hard peaks with my tongue.

"Yes, Donovan. Please. More," she moans. I love hearing her beg. I pop one of her tits out of my mouth and look around again, rubbing them with my thumbs as I scan my eyes around the parking lot.

I pull her tank top back over her chest and grab her hand, seeing a pile of wooden crates stacked up on the side of the wine tasting room.

"Over here, let's go," I say with urgency, running behind the crates. I gently push her back against the wall once we are out of sight.

"I'm gonna fuck you hard, right here. Don't make a sound," I whisper huskily, trailing my tongue down her neck, across her collarbone, into the dip at the base of her throat.

Her hand reaches down in between the front of my jeans and she grabs a handful of my cock. My mouth gapes open as she strokes it with her hand, my pre-cum coating her fingers.

"This? *This is mine*," she growls, gripping my heavy cock in her hand, setting a wild fire inside of me I can't contain.

I won't hold it in. Not with her. The world can burn for all I care. Let it burn.

Chapter Twenty-Seven

AUDREY

I've never had sex in public before. Not like this. We are out in the open, blocked by the wooden wine crates right outside the tasting room. It gives us just enough coverage, but anyone could pop around the corner and catch us in the act. It's something I never thought would turn me on, but I have Donovan's thick cock in my hand and there's nothing more that I want right now than to suck it. Let them watch.

I spin him around and push him against the brick wall. Claiming him in front of that group of girls was the most exhilarating feeling. It got me hot and bothered, and I'm about ready to implode. My panties are completely soaked in my jeans—I'm eager for Donovan to pull them off me and have his way with me in the alley.

I quickly unbutton his jeans and pull them down along with his briefs, freeing his cock, glistening with arousal. I get on my knees, thankful I wore jeans to help cushion the gravel. The sharp little rocks sting, but I don't mind with his steel rod staring me down. I eagerly lick the bead of pre-cum dripping from the tip.

He grips my chin and strokes his thumb across my bottom lip. He sticks his thumb into my mouth and I suck, giving him a preview of what I'm about to do to him. His mouth slightly parts, desire completely taken over his body. Even though I'm on my knees, I have the power.

He pulls his thumb out of my mouth and I swirl my tongue around his tip, running it down the length of him and back up. His hands fist into my hair as I hungrily take his whole cock into my mouth. My eyes roll upward at the fullness, letting the salty taste coat my tongue as I lap up every bit of his arousal.

"Suck my cock just like that," he moans. His eyes are hooded and hungry. His hands slowly guide me as he pumps himself into my mouth. I flatten my tongue against the underside of his dick, taking him deeper down into my throat. I gag as my lips press all the way against his hilt.

"Fuck, you like deep throating me, baby?" he hisses through gritted teeth. I hum in pleasure as I suck him off as deep as I can go.

He pops me off of him, tears pricking at the corners of my eyes. I wipe my mouth with the back of my hand and he stands me up, crashing his lips onto mine.

He turns my back against the wall and pulls down my top again, my tits on display for him. He sucks my nipples as his fingers work to unbutton my jeans. I hear a snap and zip, and cool air hits my thighs. My panties come down with my jeans, and I shimmy them off completely.

Donovan's large fingers run through my wet slit as I try to stifle a moan. Fuck, it's gonna be really hard to be quiet. I'm a screamer. Or so I've discovered. Only Donovan makes me scream.

"Look at you. Always so wet for me," he rasps, his fingers finding my clit.

"Always, baby," I whimper back, his fingers stroking me until I go cross-eyed.

"Lift your leg. Give me more of this pretty pink cunt," he groans. I do as he says, lifting my leg from my jeans that are in a pile on the ground. I turn to putty in his hands when he talks to me with that filthy mouth.

My leg drapes over his arm as he holds me up, and with one quick move, he enters me, filling me instantly. I gasp, and he takes his free hand and covers my mouth.

"Shh, quiet baby," he whisper moans, slowly thrusting into me, pulling all the way out and all the way in. It drives me fucking crazy, and I grind into him, needing more.

We find our pace, and I moan into his hand. I wrap my leg tighter around his waist as he pistons his hips into me harder, my tits bouncing with every pump. It's dirty, raw, and unfiltered. I let Donovan take every part of me. Every thrust and moan he earns from me, it's all for him.

"Take it, baby. Take it all," he grunts, keeping his voice low. Our breathing gets heavier and out of control. I whimper into his hand as I feel my climax approaching, building like a fire deep inside my core. My pussy walls tighten around his cock, and he thrusts harder, never letting up, knowing exactly what I need to take me over the edge.

I've never felt this type of desire until Donovan. He drives me wild, letting me be free and untamed for him. It's liberating to be so fiercely loved by someone who takes you for who you are, no questions asked. I'll give this man every inch of my body and soul for as long as I live.

"Come for me, Audrey." His hand stays over my mouth and I bite down on the fleshy edge of his palm to keep myself from screaming as I come full force. I hear voices in the distance of people walking in and out of the building, only turning me on more.

"Good girl. I want you to come again," he grunts, his thrusts never letting up. He takes his hand from my mouth and kisses me hard, our tongues fighting for attention. Then he pulls out, and turns me around. My ass is pressed against his dick, and his hands come around to rub my nipples.

"Put your foot on that crate there. I wanna fuck you from behind." A devious grin plays on my lips and a low chuckle emerges from my throat. "Fuck, you look so sexy like this baby," he whispers, his hands still knead my tits as he grinds his thick cock against my ass. I prop my foot up on the crate, showing off the cowgirl boots I wore with my jeans.

"I want you to wear those boots next time you ride me, cowgirl," he teases. I giggle as he kisses the length of my spine. His large hands cup my tits as he slides easily back into me. A loud moan escapes my mouth and his hand clamps back down to keep me quiet. This angle drives me nuts, and he wastes no time as he pumps into me hard and fast.

"I love the way you look from behind. You were made for me," he moans, driving into me harder. One hand grips one globe of my ass while the other twists into my hair, tugging it back just enough to tip up my chin.

"Harder, Donovan. Fuck me harder," I moan out, not caring that I'm not as quiet as I should be. I'm completely bent over, both of my hands gripping the brick wall in front of me. He's fucking me into another wave of a climax as I feel his cock getting thicker in my walls.

"Donovan, make me come," I cry out, doing my best to keep my voice hushed. It's not working. It feels too good.

"Fuck, Audrey. I'm coming," he groans out, both of his hands gripping my ass for dear life. My orgasm rips through me like dynamite, lighting every part of me. Donovan grunts my name through his release, pouring into me as he draws out his thrusts. We ride our high together, sweat coating our bodies in the summer heat.

I lean back against his chest as we try to catch our breath. He stays inside me, throbbing and thick. He grasps my chin, turning my head to claim my mouth.

"I love you," he pants, resting his head in the crook of my shoulder.

"I love you, too." We both let out a breathless chuckle, in shock that we just fucked with people fifty yards away. He slowly pulls out of me, kissing my shoulder as I pull my tank top back over my chest.

We slip our jeans back on and gather ourselves before stepping out into the parking lot. Donovan laces his fingers through mine and checks first, craning his head out past the alley to make sure the coast is clear.

"Okay, we're good, Mouse." he says, pulling me toward my Jeep. I step in front of my side-view mirror to assess the damage.

"Holy shit, Donovan. I look like I've been properly fucked," I gasp, my hair in tangles and my mascara smudged. He lets out a hearty laugh and hugs me from behind, bending his head down to look at our reflection.

"You begged me to 'fuck you hard,' baby. Your words, remember?" he jests, kissing my cheek. There's no hiding the smirk on my face. I sure as hell asked for it. And damn, I'm glad I did.

"Tia is a real one. She could sense that I needed to pounce on you when those girls weren't leaving you alone," I purr. His eyes crinkle as his lips lightly graze the edge of my ear.

"That was hot. You getting all possessive over me. You need to come visit me more often at work," he teases. I turn to face him and wrap my arms around his middle.

"I've told Pop about the bed-and-breakfast. He's all for it. We'll get to see each other at work everyday soon," I beam. I want him to know that I include him in my plans. In my future. It begins and ends with him.

His eyes light up bright, his hands cupping my face. My heart flutters seeing his expression, like I've hung the moon. "That's amazing, baby. No one deserves it more than you," he praises, showing me that dimple grin that makes me want to drag him back into the alley for round two. "Now, let's get you back to Tia before she cuts my balls off," he clips, narrowing his brow. I chuckle at his fear of Tia's wrath.

"It's okay. Logan came to keep her company, so we're in the clear," I reassure him, tugging on the collar of his shirt. I bury my nose in it, reminding myself of his smell that's now soaked into my skin. A scent that grounds me.

"Oh, good thinking, Mouse." He slings his arm around me as we make our way toward the wine tasting room. As soon as he opens the door, Logan and Tia look up from their table, giving us a slow clap and cheers as we shamelessly walk toward them. The table of flirty girls stare with bug eyes, the blonde one crossing her arms over her chest.

Yup. That's my man.

"Wow, well done, you two. I mean, that was record time, King. What was it, two minutes?" Logan jokes. I slap him on the shoulder and scold him with my eyes. Donovan rolls his eyes and clings me closer to his hip.

"More like ten minutes and two orgasms," I counter. Tia's mouth gapes open and earns a hearty laugh from Donovan. I cock up my eyebrow at Logan, satisfied at the way his lips form an O shape at my quip.

"Holy shit, Logan. Have you ever made a girl do that?" she teases. He throws his hands up in surrender and settles back in his chair. "Alright, alright. Touché, Winthrop." Logan glares at Tia and replies, "And yeah, Tia. If you must know, I've made plenty of girls do that."

She rolls her eyes. "Yeah, *okay*," she mocks his voice and he flips the bird in response.

"Alright everyone, simmer down. I need to get back to work, but I'll come bring more wine," Donovan chuckles, giving me a chaste kiss before retreating to the back.

I join them at the table, and Tia waggles her eyebrows. "So, how was your quickie?" she croons. I look at her with a glint in my eye, biting down on my lip. Heat flares in my cheeks *and* between my legs.

I'll be replaying Donovan taking me in that alley for a long time.

Maybe I'll steal him away in half an hour.

I'm a wild woman now.

Chapter Twenty-Eight

DONOVAN

I left Audrey sleeping peacefully this morning, placing a handwritten note on my pillow for her to find when she wakes up. The sun is on the verge of rising, enveloping me in the blue morning hue as I make the drive to the police station.

Yesterday morning, when I knew Logan would still be asleep, I stopped by his parent's house to talk with the chief on his day off. I told Chief Harper I believed Audrey could have been followed and asked if he could look into the situation.

I know Audrey didn't want me to, but I needed to guarantee that Kellan wouldn't fuck with her. I'm not naïve. He has power. His resources are so endless, who knows what strings he's able to pull to skirt the law. I had to make sure this didn't follow us here—because I swear, if he still has her in his grip, I'll be the one to break his fucking hands.

After I got the text back from Chief Harper yesterday at the winery, I'd been eager to find out what he knew. I hardly slept—not even our marathon love-making session last night could knock me out cold. My mind ran through every possibility that Chief Harper might tell me. If he has any valuable information to share that would get us closer to closure, I'll take it.

I pull into the parking lot, squad cars lined up in front of the station. Not much crime happens in our small town outside of the odd belligerent drunken bar fight at Siren's Flask or petty theft offenses. The last time anything newsworthy happened was with the Ted Winthrop and Duke Taylor scandals, and sadly, James's death.

I slide out of the driver's seat and breathe in the fresh morning dew. It's 6:00 a.m., and the sun is making its way over the horizon, turning the sky the color of Audrey's hair. I place my hands in my hoodie pocket and stride up the steps, pulling on the iron door handle.

It's a quiet, still morning at the station. I see Ms. Lisa behind the glass, typing away on her computer. I tap the glass with my finger to get her attention. She looks at me with stunned eyes, squinting through her thick-framed glasses. "Donovan? Is that you? Oh, my goodness, aren't you just the most handsome young man I've ever seen!" She smiles wide, her red lipstick smudged on one of her front teeth.

"Hi, Ms. Lisa! Thank you. Um, you got a little..." I flash my teeth and use my finger to rub my front tooth, gesturing for her to do the same.

"Oh! Oh my, I'm sorry about that," she stammers, covering her mouth with one hand and rubbing her tooth with the other. "You don't let a lady walk around with lipstick on her teeth, do you? What a nice boy you are," she coos, keeping her mouth closed as she smiles at me.

"No, ma'am. It's the chivalrous thing to do," I wink, causing her already flushed cheeks to deepen in color.

"What can I help you with, dear?"

"I'm here to meet with Chief Harper. He asked me to come in this morning." She holds a finger up to me and picks up the phone, dialing a couple of numbers. I hear a faint beeping from the receiver and a hearty voice on the other end.

"Chief, Donovan King is here to see you." She nods and hangs up the call.

"Donovan, you can go to his office. Walk through the bullpen and his is in the very back. Can't miss it." She points toward the door and

I nod a thank you in her direction. I hear a buzz and a door click, and I make my way into the inner station.

Only a couple of officers are in this morning, probably going home soon from the night shift. I see the glass windows ahead with "Chief Randall Harper" plastered across the door. He sits behind his desk, shuffling through the stack of paperwork scattered in front of him.

I knock, and his head whips up, giving me a warm smile and motioning with his hand for me to come in.

"Donovan! Good morning, son. Great to see you," he bellows, his voice a low timbre. He bends around his desk and pulls me in for a hug, getting a whiff of aftershave and black coffee.

"Hey, Chief. Great to see you too." He pats my shoulder and points to the seat in front of his desk.

"Please, sit. Let's talk." He plops in his chair, the air whooshing out of the cushion below him. He's fit for an older man, definitely where Logan gets his build from. You don't wanna fuck with the chief. He's intimidating to others, but he's like a father to me.

"So, what have you found out?" I ask, eager to hear his response. I sit up straight, discreetly tapping my heel into the carpet.

"I had my guys check the CCTV footage from T-Mobile and Lavender Lane. We weren't able to catch the plates on the black SUV." He slides a series of pictures from the footage across the desk.

My heart beats faster, feeling the pulse on my neck thud. The man stands outside of T-Mobile, staring into the glass. Another picture shows Audrey walking out of the store, following him. The next picture is the man driving off in the black SUV with Audrey in the corner staring in his direction.

Chills run through my body as I think about how terrified she must've been. I should've been there with her.

"Damn. So none of the cameras in this area caught the plates?" Chief Harper slowly shakes his head no, pursing his lips into a thin line.

"The only thing we can see in the footage is that this SUV has a slightly dented bumper. You see? Right there." He points to the dent in the photo. At least there's something to go off of.

"Okay…what about Kellan? Anything on him?" I ask desperately, feeling like I'm grasping at straws. He shuffles through his papers, his gaze narrows.

"He's in New York. Looks like he laid low for a couple weeks after the arrest, but he was at a fundraiser for Teach for America just a few nights ago," he says, sliding the paper in front of me.

It's the first time I've seen his face since that night. A fresh scar slashed on his eyebrow that Audrey left. I smirk at the thought of her fighting back and making her mark on him.

"How can we guarantee her safety then, Chief?" A hint of regret sits like a rock in my stomach, knowing I shouldn't have come here without Audrey's permission. He leans back in his chair, crossing his arms behind his head.

"As far as the SUV goes, we can't prove that she was being followed. It looks coincidental from the tapes," he states. I clasp my hands together under the desk, squeezing them so tight that I lose feeling in the tips of my fingers.

"And Kellan seems to be out of the picture. There's no restraining order filed against him, but he seems too deep in the public eye to do anything spontaneous. There's no connection between him and Oakwood Valley." His tone is stern given his position, but soft because I'm like a son to him. He didn't have to look into this for me, but he did because I love Audrey.

"Well, alright then. Thanks, Chief. Do I have your discretion?" I sigh, a mixture of emotions swirling in my chest. It's relief and defeat fighting one another. I should feel relieved nothing is wrong, but the defeated feeling is what's eating at me. Why is it I *want* something to be wrong? Or is that even the right term to use? It's more like my instinct is screaming something's not *right*.

He stands from his chair and comes around his desk, opening his arms to me. I stand to meet him and give him a hug, taking in his black coffee and aftershave scent one last time.

"Of course, son. You have my word. I'll have my boys look out for the SUV if it comes rolling back into town. But you got nothing to worry about."

I hope you're right.

"Thank you, Chief. I appreciate your help," I say gratefully, although my smile doesn't quite reach my eyes.

"Anytime. Tell your mother I want an invitation to the next Sunday dinner," he chuckles, placing a firm grip on my shoulder.

"Yes, sir. I will."

He leads me out of his office and waves me off as I walk back through the bullpen. I push through the door and wave goodbye to Ms. Lisa.

I walk to my truck, kicking a pebble along the way. That unsettling feeling tugs at me again as soon as I touch the door handle. I freeze, taking a second before I hop in.

"It's fine. She's fine," I mutter to myself.

Once I'm in the front seat with the engine running, getting to Audrey is the only thing on my mind. I need to see her, hold her, kiss her, and tell her we're gonna be okay. I wrestle with the fact that I have to tell her I went to the chief behind her back, but she'll understand.

She's not being followed, and Kellan is gone.

Right?

Chapter Twenty-Nine

AUDREY

I clutch the note from Donovan to my heart, smiling at the ceiling as I lay in bed. He promised me a love note every day for the rest of our lives, and so far, he's not breaking that promise.

I place the note on the bedside table and flop on my back, stretching my arms high over my head to release the morning stiffness that lingers in my muscles. I close my eyes and grip the edge of the cotton sheets, pulling it up to my chin.

My memory takes me back to the night before, when Donovan and I made love too many times to count. His hands know exactly what to do and where to touch. His mouth memorizes my entire body, licking and sucking every curve and line. Our bodies fit so perfectly together as we move in sync, coaxing out every bit of pleasure we each have to offer. Our orgasms are mind-blowing, exploding like TNT—nothing but fire and hot sparks.

A door shutting shoves me out of my memory as I shoot up from the bed. My heart flutters hearing the familiar gait of footsteps come closer to the bedroom. My mouth goes dry as Donovan opens the door, his sexy grin instantly aching my core. He looks handsome in a plain black hoodie and sweatpants. So casual, so fucking hot anyway.

"Morning, Mouse," he rasps, diving into the bed and crashing his lips onto mine. I wrap my arms around his neck, giggling when his stubble tickles my neck as he nips and bites under my ear.

"Hey, baby. Thank you for the note," I whisper in his ear. He pulls his head back and looks at me, kissing my lips tenderly. He rests his head on my chest and wraps his arms around my lower back as I hold him close to me, breathing in his signature musk and teak scent.

"What time do you work today?" I ask, my nails scratching along his back through his sweatshirt.

"Not for a couple of hours," he replies. His cheek stays resting against my heartbeat. I bring one hand to the back of his head, lightly scratching his nape and through his thick chocolate locks.

"I thought we could take the quad out and go for a ride? Maybe head down to the river for a bit. Weather is supposed to be nice today," I murmur, placing a kiss onto his head. He turns his head and presses a gentle kiss at the dip of my throat, deliciously working his way up my neck. I mewl at the contact, instinctually wrapping my legs tight around his torso.

"I have to tell you something," he mumbles, removing his lips from my neck to meet my gaze. His eyes look sad, immediately filling me with concern. I sit up taller, pulling him up with me.

"What is it? Are you okay?" I ask, trying to stay calm. He tears his gaze away for a moment and swallows hard before giving me his full attention again.

"Um. Well. I just came back from the police station," he mutters. His expression is stoic, unmoving. My breath slightly hitches, and the tips of my ears get hot. "I talked to Chief Harper," he blurts out.

"You *what?*" I reply tersely. I adjust myself to sit up completely, pulling my legs under me to move Donovan out of the way. He sits across from me, his shoulders slump when we're no longer touching.

"I'm sorry, Mouse. I know th—"

"Donovan. I specifically asked you not to. You promised me," I interrupt, pulling the sheet up higher over my body to cover my breasts. I feel too exposed, wanting to hide myself from him. My chest flames with heat. The unwanted feelings of betrayal creep in.

He scrubs his hand along his stubble and sighs, knowing he fucked up. Before he can say anything, I interject once more.

"I trusted you. I told you I didn't want the chief to know. Logan is home, for Christ's sake!" My voice escalates, clutching the sheet tighter to myself, as if I could meld it into my skin.

"Audrey, I'm so sorry. Logan won't find out. And even if he did, he'd never say anything. I wanted to ensure your safety. I needed to know that we were gonna be okay," he stammers. His tone is desperate, like he's trying to justify that what he did was okay. I wrestle with myself and the emotions that surface. He's betrayed me before, and all was forgiven. I thought we were past this. I thought we promised each other that we would never go back there.

"Donovan, it's not about you! It's my fear and my shit that I have to deal with! You had no right to go behind my back and do this," I cry out. He pinches the bridge of his nose and keeps his gaze on the sheets.

"So what did you end up finding out, huh? Did you get the information you wanted?" I spit out the words with poison behind them. My skin is hot and itchy and the frustration that is bubbling inside me is trying to find a way out.

He pauses before answering, my breaths ragged and short. "The chief ruled everything out. No one is following you, and Kellan is not in the picture anymore," he states curtly. When he looks at me, his eyes break my heart. The navy hue is dull, full of regret and sorrow.

I want to shout "I told you so," but I bite my tongue. The familiar ache of betrayal and mistrust flood my brain. I want to cry, but no tears form. No sting brimming the edges of my eyes. I forgave Donovan for everything in the past. I fell madly in love with him. And now, it hurts so much more.

"Donovan, you betrayed my trust," I whisper, clenching my jaw while staring into those ocean blue eyes I can't resist. "I love you, but I need space," I say, swiftly moving out of bed to find clothes to put on.

He doesn't get up, just watches me as I dart around the room, gathering my things to put them in a duffle bag from the closet. Once I'm fully dressed, he stands to meet me at the foot of the bed.

"Mouse, I'm sorry. You were right. I betrayed your trust. I fucked up. But I will never be sorry for wanting to protect you." He pauses, cupping my face in his hands. "I know that this is something that only *you* have to overcome, but don't you think this hurts me too? Seeing you hurt? Seeing you fall apart because of *him?*" he murmurs, holding my face so gently, afraid I might crumble to dust beneath his hold.

"You're right," I admit with a sigh. "But you could've talked to me first. You *should've* talked to me. I went ten years without knowing what happened between us. You shut me out once—" I choke, tears forming quickly now. "You shut me out and now, after everything, after I asked you not to go to the police...you did it anyway," I whisper with a crack in my voice. I shift my cheek out of his hold and use my shoulder to wipe the tears from the corners of my eyes.

I pick up the duffle bag and sling it over my shoulder. "I'm gonna go stay at my gran's cottage tonight. I need some space and time to think. Okay?"

He slowly nods, wrapping his arms around my waist and pulling me close. My stomach flutters at the gesture, loving how I feel when we are close like this. He presses his forehead to mine, his breaths are deep. In through the nose, out through the nose.

"Take all the time you need. I'm sorry, Mouse. I love you so much, you know that, right?" he murmurs. His breath skates along my skin, flooding me with love and warmth. God, I love him so much it hurts. But I need to step away for a second. I need to process alone.

"I know," I whisper, placing a tender kiss on the corner of his mouth. I leave Donovan standing in the bedroom, his head hung low in defeat. In sadness. Probably in regret.

I swipe my keys and hastily make my way to Jules, tossing my bag into the backseat. As soon as I start the engine, I look in the rearview mirror and see Donovan leaning against the door frame.

My eyes well up and his image blurs as I blink away the tears and drive off, his image getting smaller and smaller in my mirror. I choke back sobs as the morning air stings my skin, checking my rearview until Donovan is no longer there.

Chapter Thirty

DONOVAN

I approach the black iron gate, gravel crunching beneath my tires. My muscle memory kicks in as I make the familiar turns around the cemetery. A right at the big willow, a left at the water fountain with an angel perched on top, another left at the gold-roofed mausoleum, a right at the wooden bench.

I used to come here almost every day after James passed. I'd sit for hours talking to him about school, sports, and girls. Well, one girl in particular.

I pull off to the side of the gravel road and park my truck, grabbing the bottle of Coke from the cupholder. I take a quick glance around and notice I'm alone today. Usually there are one or two people nearby sitting by their loved one's headstones having quiet, one-sided conversations. Today, it's just me and James.

I wish Audrey were with me. We should be together right now. This is the longest we've gone without talking. I watched her drive away yesterday morning and haven't heard from her since.

Work was a blur. My mind and heart weren't in it. It took everything in me not to drive up to her cottage, knock on her door, and sweep her off her feet, begging for her to come home to me. She needed space, and I promised I'd give her that. I also promised not to go behind her back, but I did anyway. How could she trust me again after that? I take a deep breath and trek my way to James, hoping my big brother can bring me solace.

I spot his headstone in the distance and tread carefully around the other graves, making sure I don't step on any. Approaching his headstone gives me pause—it always does. I'm not sure I'll ever get used to seeing my brother's name inscribed with a glossy finish on a cold, hard stone. I squat down in front of it, gently running my hands across the text.

In Loving Memory of James Caleb King
Loving Son, Brother, and Friend
June 4th, 1994 – August 8th, 2012

"Hey, big bear. Happy thirtieth birthday," I whisper, carefully picking the overgrown grass gathering at the base of his grave.

"Here you go, old man. I brought your favorite. It was the last one, too. I had to bribe some kid for it. Lost ten bucks," I chuckle, placing the glass bottle on his grave, like an offering.

Mom rarely let us drink soda growing up, but when she did, James insisted that he only drink Coke from a glass bottle. He said it tasted better, that it was the only way to drink it. We used to sit at the edge of the river after a long day of fishing and drink our Cokes from the bottle. It was just us two, sitting in silence, enjoying the sound of flowing water and each other's company.

I lower myself onto my bottom, picking my knees up and looping my arms around them. I take a moment and read his name over and over, like if I read it enough times, I can will him back into existence.

"Sorry I haven't visited in a while. The winery has been doing really well, the vineyard too." I look up at the sky and squint when I catch a sun ray in my eye. A few clouds float along, and I try to stare long enough to see if I can spot James in them.

"I went to Sunday dinner. It was...nice. Dad wasn't a total prick, and we all got too drunk, which made Mom kind of mad," I chuckle, quickly clenching my jaw when a wave of grief hits me. I stare hard at his death date. "Wish you were there..." I take a long pause between my conversations with him, imagining what his words would be if he were here to reply. I play his dialogue in my head and mask his voice over my thoughts.

"What is it with you and Dad?" "You're both stubborn as hell." "You need to shave." "What are you benching these days?" "Find yourself a nice woman yet?"

"So, I wanted to talk to you about someone. Well, not just someone. It's Audrey Winthrop." I fidget with my thumbs, feeling a little embarrassed for getting nervous in front of my brother's tombstone. The corners of my lips tug upward when I imagine James hitting my shoulder and giving me shit about being in love.

"I know I've talked to you about her before. I mean, she's the only girl I've ever really told you about." I wish he could see us now and really get to know Audrey. He would absolutely love her. I swallow the lump in my throat and sit up straighter.

"I love her, big bear. She's the one. Always has been. And I don't know how or why or what I did to deserve it, but somehow, she loves me too." I close my eyes and imagine him and me sitting at the riverbank, his arm draped across my shoulder.

It's been twelve years, and I still see his face so clearly in my mind. The scar across his eyebrow from when a fishing hook got caught in it when we were kids, his chocolate brown hair matching mine, and the dimples that only he and I share.

"She's had it rough for a long time." My fists clench when a flash of Kellan pops into my mind. I shove it away quickly, not wanting to bring his face into this place. "And she was hurt. He fucking hurt her, James. He fucking tried to kill h—" My voice breaks, angry tears brim my eyes. I rub my eyes on my sleeve, staring off into the rolling valleys ahead. For a place so beautiful, a part of its beauty will never be whole since James died.

"But I fucked up, James. I betrayed her trust *again*. I thought I was doing the right thing, but I did the one thing that she asked me not to do..." I murmur, resting my chin on top of my knee.

"Now, she won't talk to me. She left my place to go stay at her cottage. She said she needs space, but how the fuck am I supposed to protect her if she pushes me away?" I stare harder at his tombstone, begging him to speak to me. I'd do anything to hear his voice.

"I'm not giving up on her. On us. I won't lose her a second time. I'll do whatever it takes."

Even though she doesn't want to see me right now, I'm not letting her go. Audrey is fire and lightning, hot to the touch and hard to catch. But somehow, I was the lucky bastard to catch her. Hell, I've been burned in the process, but it's worth it.

Every. Fucking. Time.

"I'm gonna ask her to marry me. Maybe not today or tomorrow. But one day, I'm gonna make her my wife."

I pull the ring box out of my pocket and flip open the top. It's a simple oval cut diamond with a rose gold band. The afternoon sun glimmers against its facets, my heart aflutter imagining Audrey's delicate ring finger marked with my promise.

I bring back my gaze to his name, taking a deep inhale of fresh-cut grass. "We have a long way to go, but I want forever with her. If you were here, I'd want you to be my best man." My voice cracks as I let the tears fall. I grieve for my big brother. We should be celebrating with beers at Siren's Flask, a barbecue at Mom and Dad's, fishing with Wyatt and Kerry. Instead, I sit here while he's six feet under, wondering if he can even hear me.

I close the ring box and shove it back into my pocket. "I miss you. We all miss you," I whisper, pushing myself up to stand. I brush the grass off my jeans and kiss the top of his tombstone. I look up at the sky, imagining his face in the clouds.

"I love you, big bear. Until I see you again. Happy birthday." I graze my fingers one last time across his name, and turn on my heel toward my truck. I halt in my tracks when I see a familiar car parked behind mine.

"Dad?"

I see my dad round the hood of his car, his eyes lock on mine. I move toward him and meet him at the edge of the grass.

"Hey, son."

"Hey, Dad. I thought you would have come this morning..." I trail off, surprised to see him here without the rest of my family.

"Uh, no. Your mother and brothers did, but I wanted to come alone. I'm sorry, I can leave and let you—" I shake my head and wave my hand in the air.

"No, it's okay. Stay. I was just leaving," I reply curtly, reaching into my pocket to grab my keys.

"Donovan, wait. Can we talk?" he asks, his jaw clenching as his hard eyes stare at me. I guess we're doing this.

James, you sly bastard.

I nod and motion at the bench nearby for us to sit. We sit a foot apart, staring at the giant oak tree that stands before us.

"You know, when your brother was five, he climbed so high in a tree just like that one." He points in front of us, squinting his eyes as the sun peeks through the leaves. "We almost had to call the fire department because he refused to come down," he chuckles under his breath. A smile tugs at my lips, thinking of a five-year-old James giving my parents hell. His hands clasp together in his lap, admiring the giant oak that probably has many stories to tell.

"Really? I don't remember that," I murmur, willing my memory to jumpstart.

"You were with Logan's family that day getting ice cream while your mother and I bribed James with a new toy." A sad smile forms, his eyes sad too. We both sit in silence for a moment. The only sounds that surround us are songbirds in the trees and the breeze weaving through a set of chimes hanging nearby.

"Donovan, I'm sorry," he whispers, his gaze finally meeting mine. I don't know what to say. The words get stuck in my throat as I try to talk. I grind my molars, looking out toward the oak tree. Before I can speak, he holds his hand up to continue. My eyes flit back to his.

"Son, I'm sorry. I'm sorry about everything. After we lost your brother, I..." His eyes well up and his voice shakes. He composes himself before finishing his thought. "I didn't know how to handle my grief. I took it out on you, and I couldn't look at you for months because you look just like him. It killed me, son," he cries softly. His eyes shimmer in the late afternoon sun. When I look in his gaze, I see a brokenness that mirrors mine. Two sides of the same coin. Two people fighting grief who took it out on each other.

"I should've been there for you. I should've fought harder for you and for our family when Duke started threatening blackmail," he chokes out. Now I'm the one who puts my hand up to say my piece.

"Dad, you were trying to protect me, and now that I'm older, I get it. After being with Audrey, I realized everything that happened... happened. Nothing can change the past." I pause and glance toward James's tombstone. "I was angry with you for so long, but not because you took a deal with Duke and made me break it off with Audrey..." My voice is shaky and I feel the sting under my eyes of unexpected tears. What does Audrey always say?

Take a deep breath, count backward from five.

"I was angry with you because I needed you. I needed my dad, and you shut me out. When all that shit happened with the tape, I knew you were trying to protect me and our image. But I didn't care about any of those things, Dad," I cry out, my tears flowing faster, letting the years of anger fade with each confession.

"All I cared about was *you*. I only ever wanted to make you proud. You seemed so ashamed of me, and after James died, I only wanted my dad." My hands cover my face and I let the rest of the anger fall away, being closer to forgiveness than I have ever been. My dad walks in front of me and grabs my shoulders to stand me up, pulling me into the warm embrace I've needed for a long time. The moment our arms wrap around each other, I swear I feel James hugging us, too.

"I'm so sorry, son. You're right. I wasn't there for you. I was selfish, and I was wrong to put so much on you. Please, forgive me, Donovan," he pleads, holding my collar so tight it crinkles my shirt.

"Of course I forgive you, Dad. Do you forgive me?" I ask, squeezing my eyes shut to coax out the last of my tears. He pulls me back from the hug and smiles.

"Yes, son. I love you."

"Love you too."

We step back and chuckle, wiping our eyes. A huge weight lifts off of my shoulders. I'm ready to move on and start over with him, rebuild the relationship that we never got to have.

My phone vibrates in my pocket, and I hold a finger up to my dad to check it. My heart squeezes the second I see a text from Audrey on my screen.

AUDREY

Donovan, I'm so sorry. Please come to the cottage. Something's not right.

The air exits my lungs all at once. Every muscle in my body tenses to attention. My dad's eyes draw wide in response to my impeding panic.

"Donovan? What's wrong?" he asks, his eyes frantically scanning me up and down.

"Audrey needs me. Something is wrong. I need to go." He looks over my shoulder at James's tombstone and back at me. He nods, his brows furrowing with determination.

"I'll go with you." He grips my shoulder, his gaze softening for just a moment.

"What about James?" I ask, looking back at his tombstone.

"You're here, son. Right now. I'm coming with you," he reassures me, pulling my shoulders in for another hug. I gotta get used to this affection from him, but I'll admit...it's nice. We pull back and he kisses my cheek.

"Thanks, Dad. Follow me, okay?"

"Okay, Son."

We hastily jog to the front of our vehicles, and before I slide in, I give James's grave a final glance and a nod. I fire up the engine, seeing my dad in the rearview mirror. He gives me a thumbs up and I speed my way out of the cemetery with my dad in tow. I whip out my phone to send Audrey a text.

DONOVAN

I'm on my way, Mouse. Hang tight. I love you.

Before I can hit send, my screen lights up with Chief Harper's name. My heart beats faster, anticipating whatever I'm about to hear on the other line. I silently pray before picking up his call.

Please don't tell me it's Audrey. Please don't tell me it's Audrey.

"Hey Chief, what's going on?" I answer, steely.

"Donovan, we've got an ID on the black SUV. One of my patrol cars clocked it on the way out of town not yet an hour ago, matching the same description from the footage. Ran its plates."

My stomach feels like it's in my throat, my body tingling with adrenaline. A cold sweat forms on my brow, and I briefly take my hand off the wheel to wipe it away. I pause before answering, glancing back at my dad, who is still following close behind.

"And?" I ask, bracing myself for what I'm about to hear.

Please don't be Kellan. Please don't be Kellan.

"It's Ted Winthrop."

Chapter Thirty-One

AUDREY

Over the last six weeks, Donovan and I hadn't gone more than an hour without speaking, seeing, or touching each other. He would text me at work. He would leave notes for me to find. We'd laugh. Touch. Play. Make love. Constant communication. And now, it's been over twenty-four hours since I left him in the doorway outside of his cabin without so much as a word since.

I spent most of that first morning crying in Gran's cottage. My cottage. The space isn't large by any means, but it's perfect. It offers me solace and the space I need to breathe. Think. Process. Cry.

The windows let in the natural light, casting romantic little spotlights throughout the square panes. The rustic birch wood countertops in the quaint kitchen adds a warmth to the space. I imagine Gran making her pie crust from scratch, coating the well-worn apron that now hangs lifeless on the hook, dusted with flour. When I close my eyes and breathe deeply, I can still catch the scent of lemons and berries lingering in the air. Being here has felt like a warm hug from Gran, a comfort I needed after Donovan's decision to go to the police.

Tia came over and held me while I cried. A lot. We baked cookies, painted each other's nails, and talked about Donovan. Being in love with him only made the betrayal hurt more. Tia helped me understand his sole purpose after what happened with Kellan was to protect me. But protection requires trust. And that trust was broken.

All night I held the keys to Jules, twisting them around my fingers, contemplating getting in my car and going back to the cabin. Back in his arms. Back *home*. Because that's what it was, wasn't it? My home? My clothes hang in the closet. My toothbrush sits in the cup by the sink. My recipes are tucked away in the kitchen drawers. Donovan's cabin—*our cabin*—has been home the moment I came back to Oakwood Valley.

Tia stayed the night, lightly snoring on the futon in the small living space with the television on. I laid on my back all night, clutching those keys to my chest until I was too tired to think anymore. I missed Donovan.

He hasn't tried to text or call. I asked for space, and he was giving it to me. I woke up this morning after a horrendous sleep with Tia brewing coffee on the stove. She had plans with her mom but asked if she wanted me to stay. If my mom were here, I'd spend the day with her, no hesitations. So, I told her to go and that I'd be okay.

Today is a big day for me—a day that I was supposed to share with Donovan. I hold the paperwork close to my chest as I stride down the sidewalk in town, just leaving the Oakwood Valley Planning Division office. The afternoon sun is warm as my face naturally tips up towards it, like a cat that always finds the rays through a window.

I got permission for the estate to be converted to a bed-and-breakfast and submitted all of my paperwork into the city. Now we wait for the review process and fingers crossed, approval. I'm one step closer to my dream. One step closer than I thought I'd ever be. A ghost of a smile appears on my face, but doesn't quite reach my eyes.

Donovan should be here with me.

I push my sunglasses back up the brim of my nose, unlocking Jules and sliding into the front seat. Shoving the papers into the glove compartment, I grip the steering wheel and sit quietly, my thumbs picking over the frayed stitching with anxious energy.

"Today is a good day, Audrey. I'm proud of you," I whisper to myself. My chin quivers and my jaw ticks as an unexpected wave of tears form behind my eyes. I'm tired of crying. I find my phone out of my purse and unlock it, pulling up Donovan's name. My thumb trembles over the call and text buttons, darting back and forth between the two. I opt for text and type a message.

AUDREY

Hey... I have some good news to share?

delete

AUDREY

Hi... I miss you...

delete

AUDREY

I'm not mad anymore. I love you. I need to see you now. I'm going crazy without you.

delete

"God damn it," I mutter, tossing my phone back in my purse, massaging my temples with one hand.

To keep from sulking, I fire up the engine and back out of the parking spot with an itch to bake something. Maybe I'll bake Donovan a pie. A mixed berry pie that says, *"I love you, don't give me space anymore."*

I hum to myself as the music blares from the speakers, making the familiar turns back to the cottage. My hair whips around my sunglasses when my eyes catch something in my rearview. Pushing my glasses over my head, I squint into the mirror.

What the hell?

My heart races immediately, the heavy thud pounding against my chest cavity as my eyes fix on a very familiar black SUV. No. Donovan said that I'm not being followed. The police ruled everything out. Kellan is in New York—he's forgotten me. This is a silly coincidence.

My eyes nervously flit back and forth from the road to the mirror, the SUV trailing behind. The windows are heavily tinted, making this so much fucking worse. It's fine. *You're fine.* There's plenty of people in Oakwood Valley who drive a black SUV. It stays a good distance behind me, but my turn into the winery is only a mile up the road. What if I *am* being followed? I don't want to lead them to my house.

I nibble my bottom lip, sinking my teeth in so deep I make myself bleed. I make the split-second decision to make a random turn off, away from the winery to ease my suspicion. Or confirm it.

I turn right onto a dirt path that leads to what used to be the Taylor's vineyard. My hands slip on the wheel, damp and clammy from the nerves that have taken over my body. Stay. Calm.

Please don't turn right.

My eyes lock onto the rearview mirror as I mumble a silent prayer to myself. The thumping moves from my chest to my ears, pulsing so violently that it makes my temples throb. I grind my molars so tight that my jaw clicks, a sharp pain shooting through my neck.

No.

The SUV turns right, just yards behind me.

"Fuck fuck fuck," I stammer, about ten seconds away from full-blown panic mode.

Stay. Calm.

Suddenly, the SUV picks up speed and zooms past me, my head following it as a cloud of dust engulfs my vision. My throat burns from the dirt, coughing as the SUV cuts in front of me. Its red brake lights flash, and my eyes bulge out in fear as I slam both feet hard into my brake pedal.

"Shit!" I scream, the dust swirling around me, covering the man who steps out of the driver's side. I frantically try to put the car in reverse, but my hands tremble so badly that I can't get my bearings.

Audrey, focus.

He approaches my car hastily, his hands up in surrender. His cough is gravelly and dry. His black shirt drapes off him like it's three times too big, his build fragile and weak. He's tall, more skeleton than human.

Pepper spray. I fumble with the center console and grip the aerosol can with haste, flipping the top around to point it at the man quickly closing in on me.

As the dust settles, he is standing at the hood of my car with eyes sunken and cheekbones jutting out like he's malnourished. I point the pepper spray at him, hands shaking, heart beating so hard that I'm breathless.

"Audrey, please don't! It's me," he rasps. His dark brown eyes resemble the color of whiskey. Eyes that I know. Eyes that haunt me in a different way than the ocean blues I wish I were staring at instead. I keep the pepper spray held to his face, not realizing that I'm already crying.

"Dad?" I whimper, not believing what I'm seeing. I blink incessantly, like if I do it enough times, he'll vanish. Like he did for most of my life.

"I'm sorry I scared you. I need to talk to you," he pleads, his hands still up in surrender. He looks so different. Sickly. Not at all the man I remember. His hands are smeared in grease and dirt. His face is covered in messy stubble, unkempt and dirty.

"What are you doing here? Wh…h-how?" The questions speed through my mind too fast for me to comprehend. It's just words flying out of my mouth, incoherent thoughts.

"I'll explain. Could you just…?" He motions for me to take the pepper spray out of his face. Maybe it's a moment of weakness, or that I'm in shock that my father stands before me. But I comply and lower the spray from his direction.

"So it was you that followed me the other day? Outside of the store?" I ask, my voice shaky. I will myself to be strong. I clear my throat and steel my spine. I'm not letting this man take another ounce of control in my life.

"Yes," he admits, his gaze softening, like a father that misses his daughter. That pisses me off.

"Don't fucking look at me like that. You don't get to look at me like that. Like you feel sorry for me!" I shout with unshed tears. He doesn't once wince at the punch in my words, so I give him more. "You don't get to come here and look at me like you love me!"

I stay glued to my seat, hand on the gearshift, in case I need a quick escape. My car stays running, a gentle hum underneath the heaviness and grit of my words. His expression remains soft, fueling me with more rage. Where the hell was this when I needed him? My whole life?

"You're right. I'm not here to ask for your forgiveness, Audrey," he says, his voice just above the hum of my engine. "I'm here to warn you." His tone is hard and harsh, Warn me? My eyes go wide, the aching throb returning to my temples. I ignore it.

"I was contacted by a man named Kellan Vanguard about a month ago."

No. No, that can't be right.

I hold my breath, feeling a familiar pain in my lungs as I stifle my breathing.

"He told me he'd send me fifty thousand dollars to let him know your whereabouts," he chokes. His eyes are wet, reflecting as the sun falls deeper into the horizon. My entire body is cold, veins frozen at the sounds of Kellan's name coming from my dad. Another monster in my life.

"I racked up a lot of debt, and when he wired me the money, I couldn't believe it. I couldn't say no," he cries. I scoff, my eyes hardening like metal. Not an ounce of remorse seeps out of me. I once feared this man, begged for his love. Now when I look at him, shriveled up, small, and weak—I'm stronger without him. Always have been.

"He told me he loved you, and that he was trying to reconcile. But the more I talked to him, the less I wanted to hurt you," he says, voice trembling. "In no way do I deserve to be a father. *Your* father. But you're still my kid, and I refused to keep in contact with him." He stands a little straighter, jutting his chin out. He never moves, keeping our distance from each other like two strangers in passing.

"That made him angry. He snapped, and now the money is gone. I don't care. I just...I want to make it right. For once," he stammers, scrubbing a bony hand over his face. There's that soft gaze again. It doesn't make me as angry as before, but my walls are up and I don't plan on bringing them down.

"Please be careful. That's all I wanted to say. Well, that and…I'm sorry. For everything," he mutters, a single tear streaking down his face. I grip the gearshift a little tighter as I watch him turn around.

Just as I'm about to shift into reverse, he glances back at me one last time and murmurs, "You're so beautiful. Just like your mother."

Dusk is sweeping quickly across the sky as I sit on the futon at the cottage, staring into space. Seeing my dad shook me to my core. I hadn't expected him to be linked to Kellan at all. The fear that I'd worked so hard to keep away? It's barging at me with full force and no signs of stopping. The warning my father gave me struck a chord. If he was afraid, he had reason to be. I know Kellan better than anyone. Suddenly, I don't feel so safe anymore.

I texted Donovan about ten minutes ago, but no response. I lean back with the phone between my legs, checking it over and over for his name to pop up. When I tried calling, it went straight to voicemail.

I pick up and call again.

"*Hi, you've reached Donovan Ki—*" I hang up, grunting in frustration.

To pass the time, I scrounge for my laptop and find it stuffed in my duffle bag. I set it on my lap, pull up the web browser, and type into the search bar: "Kellan Vanguard Events."

An article from two days ago shows a picture of Kellan with his parents at a gala. In all the years we were together, I've only spoken to his parents a handful of times. Looking at his picture seems like a distant dream—or nightmare, rather. My insides twist when I see a scar above his eyebrow where I smashed a vase on him.

I find nothing more about him other than this picture. He's smiling, putting on a show for everyone, per usual. He'd mingle, turn on the charm, caress my cheek in front of the important New York elite, then leave a bruise on it later that same night.

I shudder at the thought. How I lived my life like that for so long. How I loved him and trusted that he'd take care of me. I shut the computer with a bang, tossing it off of my lap. I pick up the phone again and check Donovan's text thread. Delivered.

"Ugh," I grunt, quickly standing to my feet, pacing the length of the living room. I think back to my dad's words.

"The more I talked to him, the less I wanted to hurt you."

"That made him angry."

"He snapped."

What could Kellan have possibly said to my dad for him to halt his plan? My mind is spiraling, and I find it more difficult to gain control. I lean back against the wall, gripping my hair like I want to rip it out of my head. Why does Kellan have this hold on me still? Why can't he let me go?

Goddamn it, let me go!

The grief I feel is not from my years wasted with Kellan or being betrayed by Donovan. It's grief for my spirit. I'm losing myself piece by piece until eventually, I fade into nothing. Just when I think I'm ten steps ahead, life takes its whip and lashes me twenty steps back.

My head snaps toward the door when I hear footsteps approaching.

Donovan.

My heart practically leaps out of my chest, and all of my fear vanishes, knowing that the moment I step into his arms, I'm safe. I stride hastily toward the door, not able to bite back the beaming smile on my face. God, I missed him so much.

I grab the handle and fling the door open, breathless and yearning.

"Donov—"

"Hello, little bird."

Chapter Thirty-Two

DONOVAN/AUDREY

DONOVAN

My tires skid against the gravel in front of Audrey's cottage. An unfamiliar sedan is parked outside next to her Jeep with California license plates. Not Tia. Ted? Chief said they identified his car leaving town. Can't be him. I throw the gear into park, swinging my car door open as my dad pulls in behind me.

I jog to his side as he rolls his window down. "Dad, stay here. I'm gonna make sure Audrey's okay." His brows knit together, giving me a curt nod before I clap his shoulder and hastily move up her porch steps.

I push open the door, not bothering to knock. I've missed her too damn much. I immediately see Audrey leaning against the wall across from me, her eyes full of panic, breathing erratically, the color entirely drained from her face.

"Mouse, what's wrong?" She's in my grasp within seconds, our hands clutching one another, her head buried in my chest.

"Donovan, please. Leave. Go. Now!" she begs, pushing me off of her. I stumble back, eyes bewildered. There is a terror in her eyes that I've never seen. Worse than the nightmare. This fear is evil, and it has its sharp claws buried so deep in her that she's hysterically crying, shoving me toward the door.

"Please, you need to leave. Now! Go!" she cries out, her sobs frantic and piercing. I steady myself and root my feet into the ground.

"Mouse, I'm not going anywhere. Tell me what's wrong? You told me to come. I'm not leaving," I mutter, her body slumps against mine.

"Mouse? Huh. That's real cute."

A low timbre vibrates in front of me, sending an ominous chill down the length of my spine. I pull Audrey close, clutching her to my chest as Kellan emerges from the shadows. The blanket of dusk casts a sinister light behind him, darkening every feature.

He wears a wicked smirk, propping himself against the wall. The dark circles under his bloodshot eyes tell me he hasn't slept in days. His dress shirt is unbuttoned at the top, tucked into a wrinkled pair of suit pants. He rests his hands in the pockets as he tilts his head at us. Our eyes lock as mine blaze with fire. I gently maneuver Audrey behind me, pushing her back against the door.

"So, you must be the famous Donovan?" he teases. My jaw ticks and every muscle in my body flexes to keep me from murdering this guy with my bare hands, like he tried to do with Audrey.

"What the hell do you want, Kellan?" I seethe, narrowing my eyes. Audrey's forehead rests on my back with one hand linked in mine. Her touch is kerosene, lighting me up for her.

"Well, my buddy Ted let me know that you and the little bird weren't together last night," he utters, jutting his chin as he talks. So Ted was involved in all this. Fucking hell.

"I came to bring Audrey home," he growls, his head leaning to search for Audrey behind me. "You took her from me, after all. Didn't anyone ever teach you manners?" he teases. The rage in my chest boils over as I spit my hellish anger straight at him.

"*Manners?* You were fucking killing her. You're the last person on this earth to know anything about manners," I hiss through my teeth. "I won't let you fucking touch her again, you hear me? You stay the fuck away from us."

If Audrey wasn't holding onto me, I would've already had this asshole in a choke-hold, escorting him myself to the police. But her grip on me is desperate, mirroring the expression in her eyes. Kellan's face remains unamused until the slightest of smirks tugs the corner of his lip, pissing me the hell off.

"Little bird, we're leaving," he demands, raising his voice. Audrey moves out from my hold. I try to move her back, but she puts her hand on my chest and gives me a reassuring nod.

She squares her shoulders to Kellan, eyes like steel. She's no longer hiding. She's standing strong, facing the demon of a man who beat her. Who trapped her in a loveless life for nearly a decade.

"I will *never* go back with you. I don't love you. 'Cause you know what, Kellan?" She pauses, taking one more step forward. "I fucking *hate* you. Now get the fuck out of my house," she spews every word with confidence. Strength. Conviction. I watch her stare him down— her stance never wavers and neither does her voice.

That's my girl.

My eyes flicker back to Kellan, whose expression morphs from unbothered to fuming. Something shifts in his eyes. They go completely black. Dark and empty.

"Now, now, little bird. I gave you everything. What does he give you?"

"Everything you never could," she spits back boldly. No hesitations.

He throws his head back and laughs. It's menacing, undone and unhinged. I grab Audrey by the wrist, pulling her back to my side. Kellan moves his body in an animalistic fashion, cracking his neck like he's morphing into a snake. It's unnerving, but I stand my ground. I'm not letting this fucker get away.

He stares hard into Audrey's eyes and lets out an exasperated exhale, thinning his lips. His eyes well up unexpectedly, grinding his molars, creating a flex in his jaw.

"Audrey, my dad is outside. Go to him. Now," I mutter under my breath. Her eyes fix on Kellan as she slowly shakes her head, pursing her lips.

Jesus, this stubborn woman.

Kellan's shoulders shake up and down as quiet sobs escape him. This guy is losing his goddamn mind.

"Audrey, I love you. I'm sorry for hurting you. Please. I need you. Just come home," he cries, his voice trembling. Audrey shows no weakness. Her body is tense, wound up so tight that if you touched her, she'd snap. Her anger fumes, vibrating from her body and off the walls.

"I. Am. Home." Every word she spits comes on a growl, rumbling deep in her chest. My eyes flick back and forth between them. "I won't say it again, Kellan. Leave or I call the cops," she seethes, not a tear falls from her face. I'm on edge seeing Kellan's expression shift unstably. One minute he's angry, the next he's crying. This guy is off his rocker and I need to get Audrey out of here.

"Mouse, he's not right in the head. Leave and let me deal with him," I plead, grabbing her wrist while I reach for the front doorknob to usher her out.

"Fine. You leave me no choice, little bird," he chokes. I snap my eyes to Kellan, my grip tightening on Audrey's wrist. "If I can't have you, *neither can he.*"

Kellan's hand emerges from his pocket, exposing a shiny silver pistol pointing straight at Audrey. The world stops spinning. All I see is Audrey. My girl. The love of my life. Seconds go by, but it seems like hours. Days even. I twist and maneuver my body in front of her. Time moves slowly. The only sound I hear is a faint ticking that echoes from a clock that hangs nearby.

Tick.

Tick.

Boom.

A sharp pain. A searing burn. My eyes lock onto the green irises that hold so much love. So many memories of us. The light in her eyes instantly warms my chest until I realize that warmth is seeping out of me quickly. Blood. Audrey's eyes widen, an incoherent sound leaves her lips.

"Donovan?! Oh, god! Baby?!" Her arms clutch mine, gripping my forearms so tight that her nails dig into them.

"Audrey, are you hurt? Are yo—" I utter breathlessly.

I fall to my knees, taking Audrey down with me. Her mouth is moving, but nothing comes out. I home in on the freckles that dance across her nose, mustering all of my strength to trace them. To touch her. I open my mouth to say something, but I can't.

Blood spreads all throughout my back and chest, warm, wet, and sticky. I can't hold myself up. I need to lie down. Audrey catches my head, putting it in her lap. I want to hear her voice.

Mouse?

God, she's gorgeous. How did I ever get so lucky? My vision blurs and I will myself to focus just a little longer. Let me see that beautiful face. I see a rush of movement blur past Audrey above me, but I keep my eyes on her. My Audrey. My ears dampen, unable to hear my girl. Her voice is muffled as her hands touch my face and over my chest. I love the way her touch feels against my skin, like reading a favorite book for the first time. That's how she feels. Like it's the first time.

Searing hot pain rips through me like a scorched branding iron for a moment, then leaves me. There's that ticking again, mixed with my heartbeat.

Tick.

Thump.

Boom.

Please let me hear her voice. She's trying to say something to me, but I'm fading too fast.

I gotta tell her I love her.

Focus, Donovan.

But I can't. Audrey, I'm so sorry.

I hold on just long enough to see her strawberry hair frame her delicate face. Her lips full, eyes so green I want to explore the forests inside them.

Maybe that's where I'll go.

Maybe I'll find her there.

And maybe I'll wake up.

But I don't.

AUDREY

Caleb comes crashing in, sprinting past me. I don't look up. My eyes stay on Donovan. There's so much blood. Too much blood. I press my hands against his chest, trying to stop it from seeping out.

Guttural grunts and struggle fill the room, but all I care about is Donovan's labored breathing.

Boom.

My body reacts, jolting to a second gunshot, only to see Caleb rushing to my side moments later. I don't look behind me. I know Kellan is dead.

"Son? Donovan? Oh, god. No, please!" Caleb wails, his hands grasping Donovan's. I apply firm pressure on his wound, my tears falling on their own accord. Caleb's screams are raw, emitted from the deepest parts of his soul. I close my eyes for a moment, feeling my breath shudder as my hands tremble over Donovan's chest.

"Caleb, call 911. He's okay," I say calmly, staring deep into those ocean blues. "Come on, baby. Stay with me."

"My son! I can't lose another son! God, please!" Caleb sobs, heavy and heartbreaking. The walls surrounding me threaten to close in, but I don't let it. As badly as I want to take Donovan and sink beneath the ground, erasing what just happened—I can't. I need to save him. Like he saved me.

Twice. God damn it, Donovan.

I can't keep my hands from shaking as they push on Donovan's chest. His eyes stay locked on mine as he struggles to breathe. I turn to Caleb as his gut-wrenching wails vibrate off the walls.

"Caleb, call 911 right now. He's alright," I reassure, my eyes darting back to Donovan. The blood pools around his body rapidly. My eyes bulge at the sight. His breaths are shallow, and he's fading quickly. Caleb frantically dials 911 and screams into the phone, pleading with the operator to get someone here quickly.

I push one hand firmly on his wound and the other through his chocolate locks. His head rests peacefully in my lap as I stroke his hair. I love threading my fingers through his hair, like the very first night he kissed me in the gazebo. The first night we touched.

"Hey baby, you're okay. You're gonna be okay. Help is on the way," I whisper, kissing him on the forehead.

"He's dying, Audrey. There's too much blood. I'm going to lose my son, aren't I?" Caleb cries out, faint sirens blaring in the distance. Donovan's eyes are half lidded, but his gaze never leaves mine. Caleb holds his hand and cries into his palm, a visceral roar that will haunt my dreams.

"He's gonna be alright. Caleb, it's okay," I tell him, the sirens getting closer. I lean closer to Donovan, his breaths getting more and more shallow.

Please get here faster.

"Stay with me, baby. Don't sleep. Stay awake for me. Stay with me," I whisper. I press my lips against his, my tears fall on his face. "I love you. Don't leave me."

He stops moving. His body goes limp. The slam of a door. The hurried footsteps up the porch. EMTs work around me, carefully moving Donovan off of my lap. His face is lifeless, the color completely drained. I glance behind me and see another set of first responders on Kellan.

A puddle of blood pools around Kellan's body, a gunshot wound to the chest. His dirty blonde hair is speckled with blood. The sharp features on his face droop as his limp body is examined by a first responder. He's dead. Kellan's whiskey brown eyes stare back lifelessly, and I feel his hooks unclasp and release me.

I'm free from Kellan forever. For good.

Caleb is in hysterics in the corner of the room, hands covered in blood, screaming at the EMTs to save his son.

I look down and assess myself. My hands are warm and sticky, my clothes drenched. "Ma'am, are you hurt? Do you need help?" A first responder asks. I shake my head no and rise to my feet as they lift Donovan on a stretcher. Everyone moves so quickly, but my world is in slow motion. I silently beg for Donovan to turn his head toward me and grin that beautiful grin.

"I'm okay, Mouse," he'd say. But he doesn't.

"I'm going with him in the ambulance," I demand as I watch them strap an oxygen mask around Donovan's face. I look at Caleb, whose hands are above his head, trying to gain control of his breath. His eyes follow Donovan as they whisk him away.

"Caleb," I clip, getting his attention. "I'm going in the ambulance. I'm not leaving him," I choke, my voice finally breaking as the emotions flood back into me.

First responders cut through Donovan's shirt to dress the wound as I step up into the back of the ambulance. It's chaos as hurried voices float in the small space. I'm not in my body. I'm more like an obscure fly on the wall, bug-eyed and vision blurry.

They hook him up to an AED, strategically placing the pads on his chest. I jerk at the first shock, Donovan's chest arching off of the stretcher. A man with large hands administers CPR, trying to pump life back into him. I'm frozen in time. I study Donovan's features, following the perfect slope of his nose with my eyes. His lips are full, but the reddish pink hue is gone. He's still so beautiful.

Another shock.

My shoulders jerk at the sound. Suddenly, everything moves in real time. It feels out of control, the world spinning chaotically off its axis. My hands shake as I hold them up to my face, the blood drying, but still wet against my clothes. This can't be real. This isn't happening.

Another shock.

I reach for his hand, lacing my fingers through his, but he doesn't grip back.

Please, hold my hand. Just let me know you're still here with me.

"Donovan, baby, wake up. Come on. Wake *up!*" I grit, my voice cracking as the hot tears streak down my cheeks.

My world begins with Donovan King. It always has. And as I look up at the heart monitor, all I see is a flat green line, like the horizon of a world now devoid of sun. A long torturous beep, piercing the deepest part of my soul. The part that belongs to Donovan. A part of me gone forever.

My world now, as I know it, ends with Donovan King.

Chapter Thirty-Three

DONOVAN

I wake up lying in a soft bed of grass. My eyes slowly flutter open—the sun is warm, shining bright above me. I squint at the sky, raising a hand to shield the rays. Not one cloud in sight, a bluebird day. My fingers brush through the soft blades as I slowly bring myself into a sitting position. My toes wiggle, stretching across the grass beneath me. The air is clean, like a spring morning laced with dew and earthy soil. The faint chirping of songbirds floats on the air. My hands clutch the white cotton fabric of my shirt. I look down and see no blood.

But I thought I'd been shot…

I slink my hand behind me, gripping where the bullet entered my back and through my chest. Nothing.

Had I fallen asleep out here and dreamed it all?

I whip my head around in a panic, surrounded by nothing but lush green rolling hills. It takes a second for me to realize that I know this place. As I turn around, I see a white gazebo in the distance. A flicker of strawberry blonde hair blowing in the breeze. Her back is to me, looking ahead.

Audrey.

I quickly get to my feet and jog down the hill, needing to get close to her. I need to feel her. I need to breathe her in.

"Audrey!" I call out, but she doesn't move. She remains seated on the bench inside the gazebo, no reaction. I get to the steps and see her beautiful fair skin and signature sunset hair. She's wearing a flowy ivory dress that reminds me of the night I fell in love with her. I walk toward her and reach for her hand. But when she turns around, I look closer. The freckles on her nose are there, but her eyes are not my Audrey's. They're green, but a different shade. The gold flecks that dance in the sun's rays are missing. I take a step back, confusion and panic rise in my throat.

She stands up, slightly taller than my Audrey. She reaches for my hand and I flinch, snapping it back.

"Donovan, sweetheart. It's okay. Don't be afraid," she coos. That's not Audrey's voice. She looks similar, with the same dainty, feminine features. But it's not my girl. Not my Mouse.

"Where's Audrey? Who are you?" I ask, with pain lacing my voice. She smiles and sits back down, patting the open space beside her.

"It's okay. I'm not going to hurt you. Let's just talk," she says. I don't know why, but a wave of peace washes over me. Like someone tapped into my body and shifted my emotions. Suddenly, I'm not afraid. I take the seat next to her and look into her eyes.

"So, you're wondering who I am and how I know you," she says, the corner of her lips curling. I swallow a lump in my throat and nod. She chuckles, her laugh resembling Audrey's, and I wonder if I am in a dream. I must be dreaming.

"My name is Wren."

Wren? Like Audrey's middle name Wren?

"Wait…you're…y—?" I stutter. The words fail me, unable to articulate my thoughts.

"Yes. I'm Wren Winthrop. Audrey's mother." I stand up too fast and stumble back, my hands flying to the back of my head in utter disbelief. Audrey's mother? That explains the similarities. But Audrey's mother is…

Dead.

Tears brim the edges of my eyes. She reaches out and holds my hands, standing before me like she's the most real thing. She's real, isn't she? If I can see her, does this mean that I'm...dead? She responds, answering the questions in my head as if I've said them out loud. "Donovan, it's hard to explain. You're tethered between worlds. You're in what we call half heaven."

My eyes dart back and forth, suddenly feeling lightheaded. I will myself not to faint. She squeezes my hands. Her fingers are long and dainty, palms so soft and comforting.

"Breathe, honey. I know you because I've always known you. I've known that you have loved my little girl with your whole heart for a long time. And she loves you, too. So much, Donovan."

I let the tears fall, unable to keep them in any longer. I lean into her, and she holds me against her lean frame while sobs rack my body.

Half heaven.

Did that mean I was...half dead? Dying? Dead but not ready to go? She pulls away from me, putting both of her hands on my cheeks, holding me there to meet her gaze.

I pause, letting myself saturate in Wren's calming energy. The eyes that stare back are comforting and familiar, as if I've known them my whole life. I need to get back to my girl, but the sobs continue at the thought that I don't think I'll see her again.

"Donovan, half heaven is an in between place. Your soul hasn't crossed over yet," she murmurs. I shake my head, not wanting to believe her. "No, NO. I can't be gone. I can't leave her. We didn't have enough time. There wasn't enough ti—" I sob, falling to my knees as my hands cover my face. I failed her. I failed to protect her. I promised her I'd keep her safe, and now I'm here.

Not down there.

I feel a hand squeeze my shoulder and I look up, expecting to see Wren, but it's not her. My voice shakes and I struggle to stand as my body trembles.

"Violet?" I whimper. Her kind eyes smile at me as she pulls me into her arms.

"Hi there, my sweet boy," she croons, holding me like she did so many times that summer when my heart was broken. I missed her so much. I tower over her, my eyes flitting back and forth between Wren and Violet. Two beautiful pieces of my Audrey. I pull them both into an embrace as the half-heaven sun peeks through the wooden frame of the gazebo.

"I was shot. Kellan shot me. He tried to kill Audrey, and I jumped in front of her. I—I tried to protect her," I choke out. They hold my hands as I let the tears fall in defeat.

"Donovan, you *did* protect her. You saved her life, honey. You saved our girl," Violet says with a softness to her tone. The tears stop, but the heaviness in my chest lingers. A weight that I don't know I'll ever be able to lift. The three of us sit back down on the bench and hold each other's hands without speaking. Quiet. Stillness. Violet and Wren have their eyes closed, breathing in the pure air around us.

A buzzing energy builds in the atmosphere, when suddenly my eyes close and my mind travels to a memory of Wren, pregnant with Audrey. She is sitting in a rocking chair, her pointer finger poking different parts of her swollen belly.

"Where are you, my honey tulip?" A tiny kick hits her hand. She smiles. *"There you are, baby. I love you so much, Audrey Wren. You are my legacy. I will love you forever, my honey tulip."*

My eyes fly open, my breath rides on a shudder. Wren and Violet still hold my hands. Their eyes remain closed. Something tells me to close my eyes again, so I do. My vision tunnels behind my eyes; it streaks of neon colors and bright flashes until another memory greets me. This time, it's Audrey looking in the mirror in what I assume is her old room.

There's my beautiful girl.

She groans in frustration and changes out of her clothes into a sleep shirt. She lies on her bed and stares at her ceiling, tears pooling in the corners of her eyes.

I'd kiss them away.

Violet comes into the room, sitting beside a very frustrated Audrey. Violet's voice is warm like a freshly baked batch of cookies. She looks at Audrey with wisdom and knowing eyes, giving her advice about living for today, and that she is beautiful no matter what. The admiration in Audrey's eyes for her gran is bright, giving off the shade of green that sets my soul on fire.

"Wait, Gran. What if I show up and he pays no attention to me?"

The realization hits me. She's talking about *me*. This was the night. Our night. She was nervous about whether I'd pay attention to her? She's always had my attention. Every ounce.

"And don't think I didn't miss him practically running to you after the cere-mony today. A boy with a look in his eyes like that can only mean one thing…"

I grin, thinking about picking up Audrey's graduation cap and how our eyes met, how our fingers touched and the spark was so tangible between us, tethering us together in that moment. I keep my eyes closed—I want to live in this memory a little longer.

"And what's that?" Audrey replies with the cutest expression on her face, like she's hoping for the exact answer she wants to hear.

"That you will be the center of his night. Trust me on this, sweetheart."

And she was the center of my night. She was the center of my *life*.

I open my eyes. Wren and Violet follow as they smile at me, giving me a gentle squeeze around my fingers.

"H-How did you do that?" I breathe. I'm met with silence as they stare at each other, a grin tugging at the corners of their mouths. I give them a breath of a chuckle, grateful for a moment to see Audrey, even just for a moment.

"Thank you for showing me. I don't know what else to say," I murmur. Violet leans over and kisses my temple while Wren pats the top of my hand with hers.

I look toward the vineyard that surrounds us, remembering my night with Audrey.

Her dress flowing in the wind. The sound of her contagious laugh. Her hair flying wild. Her electric touch on my skin. Her heart-stopping smile. Her delectable kiss. Her comforting voice. God, I want to hear her voice again. I let the memories take me to that place. Over and over.

Heat spreads throughout my chest and up my neck. The tips of my ears are hot to the touch, and this overwhelming sense of loss hits me like a devastating tsunami. My throat constricts as I try to gain control, having a visceral realization that the reason I'm able to see Wren and Violet's memories is because I'm in half heaven. My future with Audrey on earth died the moment I got here.

A movement stirs in the distance. There's someone on the hill, but I can't make out who it is. I stand up and walk to the edge of the gazebo, squinting my eyes to focus on whoever is walking toward us. Wren and Violet trail behind me, placing their hands on my shoulders. I look at both of them and their gazes soften.

"Go to him, Donovan." Wren says softly.

Him?

I see the figure coming closer into view, and I step down the stairs, putting my hand over my brows to shade my eyes. As I walk closer, my bare feet wade through the grassy hills, squishing the ground below. A peek of brown hair, tall and lean. He jogs towards me, and I take one step closer to see his face emerging over the hill.

"James?" I whisper.

I turn to face Wren and Violet, who are beaming and holding hands in the gazebo, nodding in my direction. I whip my head back around, my breathing erratic and wild. The flutters in my stomach nearly lift me off the ground as I run.

"James?!" I call out, pumping my legs faster as they thud on the wispy grass.

"James!" I scream, a rawness from my voice as it cracks. His brown hair flows in the breeze, shining under the half-heaven sun. He looks just how I remember him. Forever eighteen. His smile is so bright it leads a clear path to him as we close in on the distance between us. My arms and legs work harder than they ever have. Every stride I take, my heart leaps with it. Adrenaline shoots through my veins, and in ten long strides, I collapse into my big brother's arms.

We fall to our knees and he holds onto me, my head pressed against his chest as violent sobs leave my body. I cling to his shirt, grappling with every part of him to see if he's actually here. He kisses the top of my head and hugs me tight, the years apart crashing down in one giant wave of emotions.

"Hey, little bear. I missed ya," he cries, holding my face in his hands as he laughs and cries at the same time. I mirror him, slamming my head back into his chest as he holds me, falling apart in his arms.

"I missed you too, big bear." I murmur into his chest. He lifts my head to meet his gaze, beaming like the sun, and ruffles my hair. We stand up and sling our arms around each other, walking toward the gazebo.

"So, you got yourself shot, huh?" he teases. I nudge him in the rib as I shake my head. "Oof, okay, okay, too soon?" he chuckles.

"Way too soon," I retort, laughing under my breath. I missed joking around with him. I never thought I'd hear his laugh or feel his embrace again.

"You died for love, little bear?"

I look toward the gazebo, Wren and Violet waiting for us.

"Yeah, I guess I did. I died protecting her," I murmur. He squeezes the outside of my arm and looks down at me. He was always taller than me, which used to make me mad growing up. But now, I love looking up at my brother. He was magic.

Is magic.

"I'm proud of you, little bear. I hope you know how fucking proud I am of you and everything you've done," he beams, tears brimming his eyes. My chest blooms with the affirmation.

"Thank you, big bear. That means everything."

We approach the steps of the gazebo, Wren and Audrey opening their arms to embrace James. He hugs them both and the three of them stand in front of me, with James in the middle, his arms around both of them.

My heart tugs in two directions. The ache of it all winds so tight in my chest that I can't take a deep breath. I look at the three of them, in awe of how lucky I am to be witnessing this. They are pieces of Audrey and me. The best parts. But Audrey has the rest of me. I can't accept that this is where it ends. This can't be where it ends.

"I'm so happy to have you all here with me in half heaven. But is there a reason my soul hasn't crossed over? When does that happen? Why am I here and not on the other side yet?" I ask.

James untangles his arms from Wren and Violet and stands before me. "Donovan, your heart stopped. But a piece of your soul is still down on earth, holding onto Audrey," he says. Oh god, is Audrey with me now? Seeing me like that? I'm supposed to be the one to take her pain away, not give it.

"So, how come you guys are here in half heaven?" I ask. Wren steps forward.

"Donovan, we knew this was going to happen. It was written this way. You were meant to meet us here in half-heaven. It's not something you can comprehend. It's...beyond that," she replies. The wheels in my head work overtime, trying to make sense of it all.

"We knew you'd need us. So we came here to help you."

I look at James, hoping he can help me understand.

"Help me with what? Cross over?" I reply, my brows knit together in uncertainty. The three of them stand in an arch before me, the four of us completing a circle.

"We are here to help you go home. Back to Audrey," James whispers.

My heart flutters, thumping wildly out of my chest. I can see her again?

"I can go home? Back to her?" He nods with a dimple grin. Wren and Violet beam with teary eyes.

"Your tie to Audrey is so strong. It's a soul-deep connection that can bring you back to her. And we are here to do that," Violet says, reaching for my hand.

Audrey's my soulmate. Plain and simple. They say love at first sight isn't real—it only happens in the movies. Well, it happened for me. Our story isn't over, and if I can go home and be with her like they're telling me, I'm giving her the whole damn world.

But I'm hit with a bittersweet pang that booms in my chest as I look at James. My protector. My best friend.

"But what about you guys? I just got here. James...I need you.

How can I go back now that you're here?" I cry. My voice cracks when I look into his eyes. My big brother pulls me in for an embrace, and I don't know how I can let go now that I have him back. He locks onto my gaze with tears in his eyes.

"I love having you here, little bear, but this is how it's supposed to be. You need to get back to Audrey. She is waiting for you. That's your future. *Not here*," he whispers. My chin quivers as he presses his forehead against mine. I clench my jaw tighter, holding back the overwhelming emotions that fill me. James passes me to Wren, who holds me in her arms.

"Donovan, thank you for loving my baby girl. Thank you for protecting her and helping her heal." Her hands tremble as she holds me. "Her life was not an easy one, but know this—*you are a miracle*," she cries, her soft cheek brushing against mine.

She's amazing, Mouse. I can't wait to tell you about her.

"Please tell my honey tulip how much I love her." Her eyes water, but they're full of hope.

"I will. I promise."

Violet opens her arms to me and I hold her against my chest, memorizing how it feels to hug her. "I love you, Violet. Thank you for everything. Noah loves you. Audrey loves you. Everyone loves you," I murmur, kissing her hair. She wipes the corner of my eye and puts her hand on my cheek, her palm soft as silk. "Oh, my sweet boy. I love you too. Thank you," she whispers, pressing a kiss to my cheek.

I turn to face James and crash into his arms. We stay like this for a moment, breathing each other in.

"I just got you back. I can't leave you. I need you, big bear," I plead, begging for a way where he can come back with me. Where they all can come back. But I know they can't.

His chest shakes as we silently cry into each other, not wanting to let each other go. But he finally breaks the embrace, placing his hands on my shoulders.

"Now, you listen to me." His eyes narrow in on mine. Ocean meets ocean. "You have a whole life ahead of you. And as painful and wonderful as it is to have you here, you don't belong here. Not yet. You hear me?" His voice trembles as he ticks his jaw, holding my face between his hands. I nod as I grip his wrists, tears rimming the edges of my eyes. One blink, and they fall. "Say hi to Mom and Dad for me? A kiss for Wyatt and Kerry, too," he murmurs, swallowing the lump in his throat. "Love you boys." He kisses the top of my head and stares hard into my eyes.

"I love you, Donovan. I always will. And I will always be there for you, whether I am here or there. I'm everywhere. Forever, little bear."

I stifle a sob, resting my forehead on his. "I love you, James. *Forever*." I breathe, clutching him to me one last time.

"Say hi to Audrey for us. Tell her we love her," James says, his palm resting on my heart. Wren and Violet follow, with tears in their eyes, stacking their hands on top of my brothers.

My eyes close and I see a tunnel of light. I open them one last time and take in their faces, remembering each feature. Violet's kind smile, Wren's sunset hair, and James.

All of James.

Each of them smiles at me, ready to let me go. "Thank you," I whisper, meeting their gazes. James gives me a nod and I nod back, closing my eyes.

I picture Audrey and run towards her. I run towards her laugh, her smile, her soul, her heart. I run until the last thing I see is her bright green eyes drowning me before a bright flash blinds me.

And I gasp for air.

Chapter Thirty-Four

AUDREY

Donovan died last night. He died right in front of me. I watched in terror on that ambulance ride as his heart stopped beating. For two minutes, my person, my soulmate, my best friend, lay lifeless on the stretcher as hands and bodies frenzied around him in a steady beat, trying to compensate for the absence of rhythm on his heart monitor. That lone piercing beep echoes in my head, reminding me of everything at stake. And for two dreadful minutes, my mind conjured painstaking images of a life without Donovan.

As soon as we arrived at the hospital, the paramedics rushed him in through the double doors to the emergency room—taking my heart and my future with them. That was the last I saw of him.

They left me outside those doors. I begged to go in, wailing and screaming, until Wyatt came up behind me, holding me back. I'll never forget the look in Wyatt's eyes when he saw the amount of blood on my hands and clothes. His pupils dilated, darkened in fear, as if I had taken the blue hues and erased them myself. My heart shattered at his expression, wishing I could take the pain away from this family.

"Please, save him! Please!" My own piercing voice haunts my mind. I fell to my knees, falling victim to the tsunami of emotions I held at bay, only for them to take over and drown me from the inside out.

Wyatt and Kerry mustered the strength to whisk me away into the waiting room, holding on to me like I deserved it. *"It's okay, Audrey. We got you,"* they'd said. Every affirmation might as well have been a bullet straight to my chest.

I sat against a frigid wall instead, unable to get myself into a chair, staring at the dried blood on my hands. Caleb held Grace tightly while she sobbed into his chest. His stare was empty and cold. A lot like how I felt.

Wyatt and Kerry sat incredibly still in their seats, as if any erratic movement would put a final stake into the reality that Donovan's heart stopped. The stillness in them held a glimmer of hope, because I was doing the same thing. Every breath held was a frayed rope to hold on to—just enough to keep the faith that Donovan would make it. But as I watched the silent tears fall from his brothers' faces, I blamed myself. I caused pain for this family. I did this.

When a nurse walked in after what seemed like hours, asking for Donovan King's family, everyone but me shot up out of their seats and rushed over to her. I held my breath, my bottom rooted into the floor. Her back was to me, her voice soft. I clutched onto my heart, expecting the worst.

"He's gone." "We couldn't get him back." "I'm sorry."

But those weren't the words that she uttered. "We were able to reestablish a heartbeat, but we're preparing him for open-heart surgery."

Wyatt and Kerry both let out a devastating breath, one that held fear and hope as they cried, clinging to each other. Caleb's mouth fell agape as Grace embraced him with worry and relief clear on their faces. He was alive. Donovan was alive. My heart stopped the minute I heard his started.

That was sixteen hours ago. Sixteen *grueling* hours. The bullet entered his back, piercing straight through his heart and exiting out his chest, missing me by mere inches.

The doctors said it was a true miracle he survived. They were right. He was a miracle. My miracle.

Donovan had to go through a meticulous open-heart surgery.

Thankfully—god, what a weird thing to say—the bullet that pierced him was a full metal jacket, leaving no fragments in his heart or body. Every hour of surgery went by painfully slow, the hands on the clock moving at a glacial pace. But my miracle boy pulled through after seven hours under the knife.

Since then, he's been asleep and recovering. I sat by his bed and held his hand, sobbing into the sterile hospital sheets. Donovan's family and I took turns throughout the night watching over him, waiting for him to wake up.

Pop, Logan, and Tia came as well, bringing coffee and fresh clothes for me. I stood in the hospital shower while Donovan was in surgery, choking back sobs as I scrubbed the dried blood off of my body. Scrubbing off the memory of Kellan's face before he shot Donovan. Everything after that was a blur.

The only thing I saw was Donovan's gaze, and the light was fading. Caleb told me later that Kellan died instantly of a shot to the chest, following a hand-to-hand wrestle for the gun. Donovan had saved my life twice now, but Caleb King was catching up.

He and I held each other in the waiting room after Donovan's surgery, crying into each other's arms. We had to give police reports when Chief Harper showed up at the hospital, eyes tired and shoulders drooped. Turns out my dad skipped town and was under investigation for accessory to murder. It was all too much. Everything collided and crashed in my brain like an eighteen-car pileup. All I wanted was for Donovan to wake up so I could hear his voice. So I could tell him how sorry I was. Tell him how much I loved him.

Regret ached in my bones, thinking back to the stupid reason I'd left the cabin. Why didn't I forgive him right away? Why couldn't I see he was always trying to protect me? Up until the very end, all he did was try to protect me—and look what it cost.

When Kellan stood in my cottage having a mental breakdown, Donovan begged me to leave. And I didn't. I stayed so that I could face the demon who had sucked the life out of me for nine fucking years. But I should've listened. Maybe he could've disarmed Kellan in time. I should've taken that bullet. Not Donovan.

"Hey, you need anything? You hungry?" Wyatt asks, nudging me out of my dark thoughts with a gentle elbow. We're sitting on a wooden bench in the hospital courtyard. Kerry sits against the trunk of a sturdy oak tree across from us, his forearms propped on his knees, picking at the aglet on his shoelace. It's warm out, the afternoon sun draping our skin like a summer blanket.

"No, that's alright. I'm not hungry," I reply, staring at the rustling leaves that dance in the breeze from the big oak tree.

Wyatt furrows his brow, crossing his arms as he leans back on the bench. He lets out a sigh. "Audrey, it's not your fault," he says, keeping his voice low. I avert my gaze, watching Kerry pick at his laces some more. My jaw ticks as I feel Wyatt's eyes burning into my profile. It is my fault. I brought Kellan here. If it weren't for me, Donovan wouldn't be lying in the hospital bed with a gunshot wound to the heart.

"You can't blame yourself," he sighs, sitting straighter on the bench. I scoff and turn to face him.

"What are you in my head or something?" I retort. He chuckles, scrubbing a hand over his tired face. We're all tired. No one has slept in the past sixteen hours. At least not fully. Kerry stands to his feet and brushes the dirt off the bottom of his jeans as he walks toward us.

"But I *do* blame myself, Wyatt. The pain I've caused your family —" I choke, the words thick in my throat. Kerry places his hand on my shoulder as I look into his blue eyes. Not quite the ocean blue I love, but a comforting blue.

"Hey, don't talk like that. He's alive, Audrey. That's all that matters. We didn't lose him," Kerry says with a softness in his expression. He's right. They're both right. Donovan's alive, but the guilt still gnaws at me. I nod and put my face in my hands while Wyatt gently rubs my back.

"You know, we've never seen our brother happier since he's been with you," Wyatt beams. I look up from my hands to meet his gaze. Also, a comforting blue. Kerry nods in agreement, shoving himself beside me on the small bench. I chuckle as I'm sandwiched between them.

"You're part of the family now. One of us. Noah too. We love you guys," Wyatt says softly. A hint of a smirk tugs on my lips. "I thought you were the grumpy one, and he's the happy sunshine one?" I tease, earning a chuckle from Kerry. A small one from Wyatt, too. "Thanks. I mean it. I love you guys," I reply, my heart squeezing at the thought that I have a family now, more than just Gran and Pop. I have a family that feels *complete*.

"I've always wanted brothers," I murmur, smiling down at my feet. Kerry drapes his arm around my shoulder. "Well, you've got 'em now."

The sweet moment between us breaks as Logan explodes through the doors, stumbling into the courtyard. I jolt in response as his eyes expand in shock, fisting his hair with a subtle upturn curl on his lips.

He's breathless, panting like he had just ran a marathon. The subtle curl of his lips morphs into a full-blown, ear-to-ear smile.

"He's awake," he breathes, his eyes lock on mine.

"And he's asking for *Mouse*."

Grace and Caleb quietly slip out of Donovan's door as I stand ten feet away, shaking like a leaf. Grace gives me a soft smile with her arms wide open. I meet her halfway, letting her hold me in a deep embrace. Caleb joins in after a beat as Grace and I untangle our arms to pull him in. No words exchanged, just relieving breaths that Donovan is awake...and alive.

"Where's Wyatt and Kerry?" Grace asks, touching the ends of my hair.

"They're in the waiting room with everyone else." I swallow a lump in my throat. "Um, I can wait for them to see him first. I don't want to intrude—"

"Audrey," Caleb sighs, softening his gaze. My chin quivers as I look past Caleb's shoulder at Donovan's door.

I don't want to barge in there without his brothers seeing him first. They've already suffered so much, and I don't want to take that moment away from them. But there's nothing I want to do more than burst through that door and see him. My heart aches for it. Caleb and Grace look at each other, then back to me.

"He's asking for you. *Only you.* Go on. We'll be with the others," Caleb says with a soft smile. Grace leans in and kisses my hair, clasping her hand around Caleb's, leading him down the hall. I approach Donovan's door, my steps quiet as I grab the handle with a pause.

Take a deep breath, count backward from five.

I pull down on the handle and a whoosh of cold hospital air blows in my face. Donovan turns his head toward me as I walk in, flashing me his best dimpled grin. His eyes shine the deepest of blue, making me weak in the knees. My lip trembles and the stinging comes full force, just one blink away from the tears escaping.

"Hey, Mouse. Did you miss me?"

The wave of tears is here, flowing out of me unrestrained. He's right in front of me. Breathing. But I'd watched him die. I blink again, praying this isn't a dream.

Donovan is here.

Only Donovan King would smile after getting shot. His grin stays plastered on his beautiful face as he tilts his head slightly, leaning his head back on the pillow.

"Come here, baby," he says, with a low, coarse voice. He pats the open space beside him, beckoning me to come sit. A sob escapes me as I run to his side, gently sitting beside him. He takes my hands in his, pulling them to his lips as he kisses my knuckles. He squeezes my hands and I'm fully revived. The second his lips touch my skin, I let go of my inhibitions. He tugs me closer. I hesitate and stiffen my body for a moment, not wanting to hurt him. He tugs me again.

"Kiss me, Audrey. I need your kiss."

I lean in, pressing the most tender of kisses on his lips. My cries come out harder as he takes his hand and cups my cheek, threading his fingers through my hair. I dot kisses over the entirety of his face. I taste the salt of his tears as I kiss his eyes, wiping them away with my thumb. Our eyes glued to each other. Forest on ocean. The most beautiful pairing.

"I thought I lost you," I croak. The pad of his thumb strokes my cheekbone as I lean into his palm, melting into his touch.

"You could never lose me, Mouse. I promised you—I'm not going anywhere," he murmurs, pressing his forehead into mine.

"I watched you die, Donovan. Your heart stopped." I sigh, shaking my head. The image of the paramedics shocking his body, then hovering over him, pumping into his chest over and over, is a stain behind my eyes. The beep of the flatline plays like a haunting song I can't shake out of my head.

"Shh. Hey, now," he whispers. "I'm alright, baby. I'm here."

"Donovan, I'm so sorry. I'm sorry about everything. I should never have left the cabin that morning." The words slip out of me like an avalanche, big and frantic. "I should've listened to you. I know that now. But goddamn it, Donovan, I love you so much. I love you so much it fucking hurts," I sob. His hands stay steady on my face, holding me in place as I fall apart.

He sighs, kissing me hard. "I love you, Audrey. So much. Don't apologize, it's behind us now."

"You saved me. Again. You…you came back to me," I choke. Donovan pulls his face back from mine, taking me in. His touch is electric, sending shockwaves through my veins. He winces as he leans back, my hands immediately gripping his shoulders to ease him onto his pillow. His hospital gown slightly opens near his chest area, exposing his surgical dressing. He takes my hand and carefully places it over his chest where the bullet pierced through.

"You feel this, Mouse? This scar will forever be a reminder that no matter what, I'll always protect you. I'll take twenty more bullets to the heart if it means saving you. And I'd come back to you. Every. Time."

The overwhelming swell in my heart overtakes me. Our journey together hasn't been easy, but I don't see it happening any other way.

We are tethered to each other, forever connected. I no longer have doubts. As for my fears? They'll come back. But they won't control me anymore. Donovan's love heals me from the innermost part of my soul. His love is so big, it's worked its magic on me, shooting its light through my fingertips.

I feel the steady thud of his heart under my hand, the best feeling in the world. So alive and beating strong. For me. For us. Donovan seems so at peace despite the trauma he's just endured. No lines between his brow, no tension in his face. Maybe it's the pain medication he's on. The oceans in his eyes are calm, not even a hint of a wave. He holds my gaze so intimately, and maybe it's from everything that's happened, but I still have to ask.

"Why are you looking at me like that?" I whisper, gently stroking my thumb against his chest. He smiles at me softly, keeping his hand over mine that rests on his heart.

"Your mom called you her honey tulip, you know?" he murmurs. My breath hitches, bewildered that Donovan knows the name my mother called me while in the womb. Gran had been the one who shared that detail with me when I was a little girl, and from that day on, tulips were my favorite flower.

"How do you know that? Did Pop tell you?" I'm not even sure if Pop knew that was what my mother called me. Gran told me she'd watched my mother sit in a rocking chair, whispering *honey tulip* into her belly, prodding for me to kick her hand.

"Wren told me. And she's amazing, Mouse. She's so beautiful, just like you," he whispers groggily, his eyes slowly drooping.

Wren? My mother told him?

My mind races, trying to piece together what Donovan just said. It must be the pain medication. He's drugged up from surgery and doesn't know what he's saying.

"I promise you, Mouse. She told me..." he drawls, as if to reassure me. Even on medication, this man still reads my mind better than anyone else.

I open my mouth to say something, but stop when I see Donovan drifting off to sleep as the steady beep of the heart monitor lulls him. I push his hair back gently away from his face.

I carefully lay myself down next to him, curling up in a tiny sliver of space. I don't mind the discomfort, because as I drift off with my hand pressed to Donovan's beating heart, it's my mom's beautiful face I see before sleep takes me.

Chapter Thirty-Five

DONOVAN

THREE MONTHS LATER...

"You got everything you need, Mouse?" I ask with my arm around the passenger seat headrest. Audrey nods with a vibrant smile. "Yeah, I'm ready."

She hugs her journal to her chest as she leans in over the center console of my truck, puckering her lips at me. I chuckle and kiss her, tender and sweet. "Go get 'em today. Proud of you," I beam, giving her one more kiss before unlocking the door.

"Thanks, baby. I'll see you after?" She grabs the handle and opens the door, her body halfway out. "You got it. I'll be here," I reply, giving her ass a love tap as she scoots her way off the seat. She yelps and shuts the door, playfully scolding me with her eyes before blowing me a kiss.

"I love you, baby!" she shouts through my open window.

"I love you more!" I shout back, her giggles floating around me like tiny cupids shooting arrows into my heart. I watch her saunter to the building, giving me a wink before walking inside.

God, just watching her walk away gets me hard. After my surgery, the doctors told me I had to refrain from any strenuous activities for at least eight weeks. Eight. Fucking. Weeks. Of course, I tried to woo

Audrey every night since I came home from the hospital, but she blocked my advances—*"Doctor's orders,"* she'd said.

I felt sixteen again, walking around with random boners. Anytime Audrey so much as grazed my arm, I was about ready to blow it in my pants. But with each day, I got stronger. The pain became less and less. And when Audrey is ready, I'll make love to her until my heart stops. Well, not literally anyway.

I drive through Main Street, parking in front of Vintage Blossom. My phone buzzes in my pocket.

KERRY

How are you feeling D?

DONOVAN

Feeling great baby bro.

WYATT

Are you ready?

DONOVAN

I've been ready since I was 18.

WYATT

Damn, such a hopeless romantic. You're like mom.

KERRY

it's cute. I wanna be in love like Donovan :(

WYATT

No you don't.

KERRY

you're gonna be alone forever Wy.

DONOVAN

lol it will be some woman to sweep his grumpy ass off his feet

WYATT

HA. HA.

KERRY

Do you need help with anything D?

DONOVAN

Nope, I'm good thanks. I'm picking up flowers now.

WYATT

Okay. Let us know if you need anything.

DONOVAN

Thanks brothers. Love you boys.

WYATT

Love you boys.

KERRY

Love you boys.

I walk into Vintage Blossom and scan the shop for orange tulips when the owner, Ms. Georgia, chimes in. "Donovan! Sweetheart. It's so nice to see you. How are you doing?" The news of the shooting spread through the town like wildfire, which was expected. I'd done my best to stay out of the media since Kellan's death rocked the world, making international headlines. Folks here at Oakwood Valley protected us, refusing to talk to any press that came into town. And for that, I am grateful.

"I'm feeling one hundred, Ms. Georgia. Thank you," I reply with a smile. I see a bucket of a dozen orange tulips and grab them, shaking the excess water off the stems.

"Is that for Ms. Audrey?" she sings, flashing me a bright white smile that's enhanced by her neon pink lipstick. I dig into the back pocket of my jeans and pull out my wallet, dropping a twenty dollar bill on the counter.

"Yes ma'am. Tulips are her favorite," I reply.

"Just like her mother's," she sighs, swiping the twenty and popping open the register to count my change.

A soft smile forms on my lips when I think about Wren. I never told anyone about what I'd experienced when my heart stopped. Maybe it was doubt that others would tell me I was crazy or that something like that could never happen. So, I'd kept it to myself and safely tucked it away in the part of my heart that the doctors stitched up. A reminder for me that what I went through up there was real.

I attempted to tell Audrey about her mom when I was in the hospital, but she thought I was too drugged up to know what I was saying. But she knows deep down that I know her mom. And her mom knows me.

"Great lady, wasn't she?" I reply, waving off the change Ms. Georgia tries to hand me. "Keep it. Have a nice day, Ms. Georgia."

"You too, Donovan."

I give her a wink and push through the door, tulips in tow. Next stop: the market. I'm surprising Audrey with an evening spent making pasta from scratch together. I learned from my mom, taking every opportunity when Audrey was out of the house to sneak over to my parent's place for lessons.

"Donovan! Good to see you out and about, son. How are you?" Chief Harper booms, holding a coffee and a pastry bag from Sip & Savor. I've accepted that everyone in town will ask me how I'm doing. I did get shot after all. But I don't mind; it's comforting to know that everyone in Oakwood Valley cares and has my back, no matter what.

"I'm feeling great, Chief. Each day gets easier to manage, mostly thanks to Audrey," I add. She's been my saving grace this summer, helping me with my recovery without a single complaint.

"You're lucky to have each other." He gives me a soft smile, then his lips slightly down turn as his gaze softens. "Uh, just so you know, though. Ted Winthrop's court hearing was last week. He's been sentenced."

"Oh," I say, not sure how else to respond.

"Ten-year sentence for accessory to murder and stalking," he states curtly. I nod, shoving my hands in my pockets.

I believe Ted should've gone to jail a long time ago. But despite how I feel about it, it's still Audrey's father. She will still need to face whatever she went through with him, but this time she doesn't have to do it alone. I'll be there to stand by her side in the fight—every day of my life.

"Okay. Thanks for the heads up, Chief."

"No problem, son." He takes a sip of his coffee and raises the pastry bag toward me like a toast. "Take care. See you for Sunday dinner," he calls out, already halfway down the sidewalk.

A quick spin around the market nabs me everything I need for dinner tonight. I grab extra flour for pasta—with recipe testing for the bed-and-breakfast underway, flour doesn't last long in our pantry. I tick off my mental list as I roam the aisles: produce, check. Cheese, check. Violet's Vintage waiting on the counter back at the cabin to be aerated? Check.

I look into my bag and double check I got everything before loading my truck. Another buzz goes off in my pocket as I settle into the driver's seat.

DAD

Hey son. Are you ready for tonight?

DONOVAN

More than ready.

DAD

Good. Your mother told me to tell you not to overcook the pasta and that fresh pasta only takes 2-3 minutes to cook.

DONOVAN

Haha, I know dad. Tell her thanks.

DAD

Does Audrey have any idea?

DONOVAN

About the pasta? No. It's a surprise

DAD

No dummy. The other thing?

DONOVAN

Oh. Uhh, I don't think she does. I hope not.

DAD

Well, I'm happy for you, son.

DONOVAN

Thanks dad.

DAD

Good luck, not that you need it.

and I love you.

DONOVAN

Thanks dad. I love you too.

It's hard for your perspective on life not to shift entirely when you die. Since taking a bullet to the heart, it's only grown bigger and stronger for those I love in my life. My family is at peace for the first time since we lost James. Audrey takes up so much of my heart that sometimes, I don't know what to do with all the love I have for her.

But tonight, I know just how to show her.

Chapter Thirty-Six

AUDREY

"My name is Audrey Winthrop, and I'm on week eight of this program. My last week," I say, a grin stretching across my face. I sit in a rickety plastic chair surrounded by seven other women. Their eyes beam at me but still hold a brokenness that we all share. It never truly goes away. It's a fight to keep the glimmer. But we're in this fight together—I'm not alone.

The last few months have been a ride. It almost didn't seem real. My shoulders would jolt when I'd hear a door shut too hard. I'd lose sleep some nights, pressing my cheek into Donovan's chest to make sure he was still breathing. I saw Kellan in my nightmares; sometimes his hands were around my neck. Other times, I glimpsed the deep terror in his dark gaze in the seconds before he shot Donovan.

Eight weeks ago, I started coming to this support group for domestic violence and trauma at the Oakwood Valley Community Health Center. After the shooting, I knew I needed help to sort through everything I had endured.

Donovan drives me to support group every week, encouraging me to continue my journey of healing. Because that's what this is, isn't it? A journey. There's not just one destination. Trauma isn't linear. It's gray and ugly, push and pull. One minute you're okay, and the next...well, you're not.

But today, I sit tall in my rickety plastic chair, roll my shoulders back, and open the journal in front of me. Heather, our moderator, gives me a soft smile and a wink, allowing me to take the floor. For my last session, we were to write a letter to ourselves. An exercise of self-acceptance, to never settle for the path of least resistance.

I'd crumpled at least a hundred pages before I was satisfied with what I wrote. The thing is, this letter can change tomorrow and the next day. So, I wrote the letter on our front porch this morning before I left. I look at the women in the circle around me and slowly close my eyes. This is for them. This is for me.

Take a deep breath, count backward from five.

Dear Audrey,

Look at you. Do you see yourself? Did you ever think this is where you'd end up? Do you feel the sun kissing your skin? Can you smell the clean air around you, free from smog and cognac? I know back then you felt your life was void of hope. Void of love. Void of happiness. The walls were closing in so fast you couldn't catch your breath. But I'm here to tell you something. I think you've always known deep down this is exactly where you're meant to be. Surrounded by so much love, you don't know what to do with it. You know what you do? You give it back. Take the chances. Take the risks. Don't be afraid to fall, because this time you'll know how to recover. Because you're strong. You're not alone anymore. Everything that has happened to you led you here. You never stopped fighting. You may not have seen it then, but I see it. You never gave up. This journey is not over. Far from it. But I want you to know…I'm so proud of you. Proud of us. You are a survivor. You opened your heart and you let your dreams fly. You're soaring through the air, your wings in full flight, no longer clipped. How does it feel? Does it feel like a dream? Well, guess what? It's not a dream. It's real. You are free. Thank you for never giving up. Thank you for fighting every day. So, Audrey. Look at you. Look at us. I love you.

Audrey

"Donovan? Have you seen my cowgirl boots?" I shout from the bedroom. Donovan stands at the kitchen sink, washing the dishes from the amazing dinner he cooked for me: bolognese with meat sauce. After picking me up from support group, he ushered me into the kitchen, hands over my eyes then lifting to reveal a whole setup for us to make fresh pasta together. My favorite flowers sat pretty in a vase on the counter next to a bottle of Gran's wine. Knowing Donovan, he will never give up his surprises, no matter how much I protest.

I hear the water turn off and he shouts back, "What?"

"My boots! Have you seen my cowgirl boots? I want to wear them tonight!" I shuffle through my shoes in the bedroom, getting on all fours to check under the bed. Nothing.

"Check the closet, baby!" he shouts back, turning the water back on to resume the dishes. Right, the closet. Since moving in with Donovan officially, my stuff was still all over the place. New clothes, new shoes, new everything. I'd donated most, if not all, the clothes that came back with me from New York. I wanted a fresh start.

Tia extended her stay after the shooting. Since her parents moved back, she put her life in Austin on hold to spend more time with me this summer. She took me shopping, helping me with an entire new wardrobe. It's been fun to discover what I like and don't like, adding color back into my life. I don't deserve her, but I'll allow myself to believe that I do. If I learned anything in support group, it's that every day is an opportunity to shift your perspective. Days where you don't feel worthy? Change out the lens. So, I deserve Tia's unwavering friendship, simply because I do.

I stride purposefully into the closet and flip on the light. Donovan's scent lingers on his clothes as I walk through and graze them with my fingers. No tailored suits, no glitzy jewelry or watches. It's faded Levi's, soft cotton t-shirts that hug Donovan's body like a second skin, and the sweaters I slip on at night for reading on the front porch.

And then there's my empty section, brimming with the possibility of everything I might hang there. No more frilly blouses and pencil skirts. I want the rainbow. It may just be clothing, but it's so much more. I'm free to express myself with no repercussions. If I want to wear clashing colors and mixed-matched patterns, I will. My clothing will no longer be a uniform to hide myself or please another man's desires. It's for me. And Donovan loves whatever I put on because, well, it's simple: he loves me.

I bend down to see some shoes of mine that have gone rogue, somehow finding their way to the back of the closet. "Ah! There you are," I say, grunting as I get on my hands and knees to reach for my boots. I grip the toe of one and drag it toward me, a shoebox coming along with it. It's a simple black shoebox and curiosity gets the best of me when I slip off the lid.

I gasp as I lift a picture from the box. It's a picture of Donovan and me from graduation night. My head is pressed against his chest, a subtle smile curved on my lips. I remember this moment. My eyes are closed in the picture. I had my ear right over his heart, swaying to the thud of his heartbeat, as if I knew then just how precious it was. He's kissing my hair, his arms wrapped around me, holding me close. God, we were so young. So in love, we didn't even know it.

I glimpse a second picture in the box, but it's face down. I pick it up to read the smudged ink on the back.

The day I fell in love with Audrey Winthrop
May 31st, 2014

My breath hitches when I turn the picture over, seeing that beautiful dimpled grin I've always loved. I'm laughing into his chest, my cheeks tinted pink. He's leaning his cheek on top of my head, beaming so bright toward the camera. He's always been beautiful. The youth on our faces, the hope of a summer spent every day together, it's all in the picture. I trace his face with my finger as the tears well up in my eyes.

"Mouse, did you find your boots?"

I turn my head around to face Donovan, leaning on the door frame. He's wearing a fitted heather gray t-shirt with sleeves that grip deliciously around his biceps. His faded jeans hug his toned thighs, strong and masculine. He's breathtaking.

"Yeah, I got 'em," I croak, lifting my boot in the air. His face immediately grows in concern when he sees me tearing up, and he rushes to my side, bending down beside me.

He sees me holding the picture and chuckles under his breath. "I see you found the pictures," he murmurs, kissing my temple as he drapes his arm around me. I turn to see his face, his eyes locked on the picture. "Look at us, Mouse," he whispers as I lean my forehead to his temple.

"I am."

Those two in the picture? It's still us. Audrey and Donovan. We're still just two crazy kids in love. I pull back to his face and ask, "Why didn't you tell me about these? We can frame them."

"To be honest, I forgot about them," he blurts, and I playfully hit him on the arm. He chuckles and shakes his head. "You see, these pictures were all I had of you for ten years. You see how the corners are bent and how worn they are? That's because I held onto these pictures and looked at them every night we were apart."

"Every night?"

"Mhmm. Every night. I stopped looking at them the day you came home with me. You know why?" he murmurs, gently lifting my chin. I have an idea, but I shake my head and stifle a grin, selfishly wanting to hear his answer.

"Because you're no longer a dream. You're as real as it gets, Mouse."

He tugs my chin toward him and seals his lips over mine. *"You're no longer a dream."* I imagine Donovan clutching the photos to his chest before drifting off to sleep. All I had during the years apart was my imagination, painting Donovan behind my eyelids as I lay in bed at night. But we're as real as it gets, and right now, his taste makes me dizzy as he tenderly kisses me, dotting a feather-like kiss into the corner of my mouth.

"Get your boots on. We gotta go," he whispers. I nod and tuck the pictures neatly back in their box, closing the lid and sliding it under the clothes that hang above. He helps me to my feet and takes my hand.

"Are you gonna tell me where we're going?" He turns his head, smirking playfully. I roll my eyes because I know the answer. "It's a surprise," I grumble.

"You're finally catching on, Mouse," he says, waggling his brows.

Outside, the sun has already set, lending a crisp chill to the night air. Dusk blankets the sky, granting us just enough light to see across the valley from where we stand on the porch, grapevines in full bloom.

"Wait here," he says, hustling down the steps to round the side of the cabin. Moments later, I hear a sputter and a roar as Donovan swings the ATV around the front.

My eyes light in delight as I scurry down the steps, Donovan greeting me with his signature grin. "Ready to go for a ride?" I nod eagerly as he flicks his chin behind him, beckoning me to hop on. I swing my leg over, scooting all the way up on the seat, firmly pressing my chest into his back. I crane my neck over to his profile and plant a deep kiss on his lips. I trail kisses along his shoulder and back, wrapping my arms around his waist.

The quad takes off on the path as we head into the horizon. He takes an easy pace, slow enough to look out and enjoy the beauty that is this vineyard. The story of us is within these vines, deeply rooted and going through seasonal changes. Once bare and empty. Then growing and sprouting new leaves, needing to be tended to and nurtured. Some vines make it, some don't. But when they do, they bear beautiful tendrils and fruit, ready to be made into something greater. That's us. Donovan and Audrey.

Donovan reaches down and strokes his fingers against the back of my calf, sending shivers throughout my body. My hands creep under his shirt, splaying my palms across his chest. I trace over the raised skin that houses his scar, pressing a kiss into his back.

"This scar will forever be a reminder that no matter what, I'll always protect you."

I squeeze my eyes shut, letting Donovan's words echo in my

mind. At first, it was hard to look at the scar. A constant reminder of the worst night of my life. Until Donovan came out of this alive and gave me a new lens.

This scar is a symbol of his love for me. The great lengths he will go to protect me. Heaven and back. It represents the pain I endured, a testament to the fierce battle I overcame to be with him. We were once growing on two separate vines, but now we're intertwined, crafting a story that's both stronger and more beautiful than we could have ever imagined. That's what we are: forever intertwined, a perfect blend of our individual strengths and shared love. *Soulmates.*

He moves his hand from my calf and snakes his hand up his shirt to clasp my fingers around his. The gesture is simple, but it's like he hears my thoughts and reassures me with his touch.

I see a familiar white structure in the distance. My heart floods with warmth the closer we approach it. The ATV slows, coming to a full stop on the path. Donovan swings his leg over and reaches his hand out to me. "Come on. I wanna show you something."

"Okay," I whisper, letting him guide me through the vines. I had almost forgotten the simple beauty of this gazebo. The moon makes an appearance, just as it did all those years ago. Its light cascades over the dome, like it was plucked from heaven above and placed on earth, just for us. I haven't seen the gazebo since graduation night. Not like this, at least. We've passed it on our quad rides here and there, but it sat in the distance, waiting for us.

Right as I'm about to take the first step on the stair, I halt. "What is it?" Donovan asks, his face glowing from the moonbeams. I look at him and smile, reaching down to take off my boots. I toss them to the side, letting my bare feet sink into the springy ground beneath me, needing to sense this place like I did on that first night. He grins and does the same.

He motions me to go first, and as soon as I take that first step, we're eighteen again. It's like my footprints are imprinted on the wooden planks below, remembering me and welcoming me back. I'm wearing the ivory dress Donovan bought me, the hem rippling softly in the breeze. I trace my fingers along the rails like I did once before, the ridges and divots in the wood molding beneath my fingers as if I'm the one who put them there.

Donovan's quiet gait steps close behind me as I feel the warmth of his body tantalizing me. I search along the railing for the inscription, smiling when it comes alive under my fingertips.

Meet Me in the Vines

Donovan's chest presses against my back as he wraps his arms around my middle, resting his chin in the crook of my shoulder. His lips barely graze my ear as his light breath skates along my skin. "You know, that night when we kissed right here in this very spot? I knew right then and there that I'd found her," he murmurs, squeezing me tighter.

"Found who?" I whisper, twisting around to face him. Those ocean blue eyes wait for me like they always do. Like they always have. He tucks a strand of my hair behind my ear, gently outlining my jaw with the pads of his fingers.

"My wife."

He leans in and kisses me, swallowing the hitch in my breath as he devours my mouth. His tongue glides over my bottom lip, and I eagerly let him in. I rake my fingers through his hair like I've done a thousand times, letting them swim through his thick chocolate locks. Our kiss deepens, laced with hunger and need. A moan escapes me as his tongue works its magic, dizzying me into his enchanting kiss.

When we pull apart, our lips are swollen and wet. My fingers link behind his nape, our breathing tattered with wanting. A playful smirk tugs on his lips as he stares deep into my gaze. "Want to play a game?" he breathes, his eyes glint with challenge.

I quirk a brow and chuckle under my breath. "What game?"

"Cat and mouse," he whispers, untangling his arms from my middle while slowly walking backward. A small whimper slips from my lips at the loss of his touch. I flash him a grin as I push myself off the railing, taking a step in his direction.

"Yeah, we can play. I want revenge for last time," I tease, crossing my arms. I see the memory of Donovan crashing into my back and lifting me off the ground in capture, our laughter filling the atmosphere like our favorite song. Even though I had *let* him win that night.

"But this time, you're cat and I'm mouse," he says with a hearty chuckle. I raise my eyebrow in intrigue, satisfied with the change up. "Deal. And what do I get if I win?" I croon, taking another step toward him. He closes in on the distance and cups his hands around my face.

"Win and you'll find out."

He kisses the corner of my mouth and I groan, leaving me hot and bothered. I've been needy for him since that kiss in the closet. Every touch he leaves on my body is enough to set me off. But I'll play the game and pray my prize leads to more than just kissing.

Donovan strides to the edge of the gazebo as I stand in the center. "Okay, Mouse. Close your eyes and count from ten. No peeking," he teases, flashing his dimpled grin that's just for me. I giggle as I lift my hands over my face, my heart racing from the excitement.

"Ten...nine..."

I smile underneath my hands, imagining Donovan weaving through the vines. Would he let me win like I did that night?

"Eight...seven..."

His steps are so quiet I don't think I hear him. No rustling or frantic thuds against the dirt. He's gonna make this hard for me, huh?

"Six...five..."

His taste lingers on my lips as I lick them, like honey and wine—a sweetness that has me close to calling it quits and begging him to take me home to bed.

"Four...three..."

This is us. This is who we are. We laugh, run, and play. Donovan brings out the best in me, and I'm a better woman because of it.

"Two...one..."

I drop my hands and open my eyes, scanning the vines for signs of him. But I don't have to search far. My breath hitches as my gaze falls down to Donovan on one knee in front of me, displaying a gorgeous oval-cut diamond.

"Oh my god, Donovan…" I whisper as tears prick the corners of my eyes. The moonbeams cast a spotlight on him, the diamond glinting under its reflection. Instinctively, I kneel in front of him, clasping my hands around his wrists.

"Audrey Wren Winthrop, it was in this very spot ten years ago where you came soaring into my life, marking me forever." I let out a quiet sob, gripping onto his wrists like if I let go, I'll sink beneath the planks. "I knew then that I would marry you one day. It took us a while to come back to each other, but deep down, I knew it would happen. We never gave up," he murmurs, smiling so big that it outshines the moon.

"Will you make me the happiest man in the world? Will you marry me?"

"God, yes, yes, yes!" I cry out, throwing my arms around his neck and crashing my lips onto his. The flutter storm swirling inside is enough to lift me off the ground, sending me into the stars. I pull back as I laugh and cry at the same time.

"Give me your hand, baby," he whispers, our fingers trembling together. He slips the diamond on my ring finger, kissing it delicately. He pulls me in for an embrace as we kneel on the floor, his heart thudding rapidly against my chest. I look down and place my left hand on his heart, gazing into his ocean blues.

"Are you okay?" I ask, worried that the rapid thuds are too much for him. He nods his head, resting his hand over mine.

"I'm okay, Mouse. Never better."

"I love you," I breathe.

"I love you, too."

I lay him back gently and settle beside him, splaying my leg over his waist. He lifts my left hand over us, displaying the promise of forever. "It's perfect," I whisper, bringing my hand down to turn his face toward me. I kiss him deep, needing him more with each swipe of his tongue on mine.

He flips on top of me, our lips never parting. I buck my hips into him, urging him to press himself on top of me.

"Tell me what you want, Mrs. King," he rasps, nipping my bottom lip, trailing kisses along my jaw. I hum and wrap my arms around his muscled back, savoring his weight and warmth on top of me. Something about him calling me Mrs. King lights a fire in my core, the heat building through my sex.

"I want you. All of you," I whisper.

Donovan savors me, peeling off my clothes like I'm a long-awaited gift on Christmas morning. He drinks me in, exploring every curve and valley like it's the very first time. His touch is addicting, like the purest drug ever made, just for me. And when he finally takes every inch of my body and soul, rocking me onto the edge of the world, he also gives so much more.

He gives me *everything*. A safe space in his arms. A loyal confidant to lean on. A future to build a family. And when we come apart falling off the earth together, nothing but a mess of tangled limbs and boneless, it's always *my name* on his lips.

Our night goes on with a chase through the vineyard, our laughter drifting in the wind. It's our game of give and take.

But this time, *we both win.*

Epilogue

AUDREY

THREE YEARS LATER...

"You're doing great, Audrey. Deep breaths now, sweetheart. Another contraction is coming." My doula Josephine kneels across from me at the edge of the tub, chanting praises and encouragement as I breathe this baby down. I don't even know what time it is, but it looks like early morning from the window. The sky has that muted blue hue, right before the sun stretches its rays across the sky to wake up the world.

This isn't my first rodeo, but it is at home—in my tub. I was so confident after the birth of our first child at the hospital, who came as a wonderful surprise, that I wanted our next child to be born at home. I sit between Donovan's legs as he uses all of his strength to massage my lower back with each contraction that comes.

"You're doing great, Mouse. You're so beautiful. You got this," he whispers in my ear as very questionable sounds escape my body. My mother-in-law told me before having my first that mooing like a cow really helps with the pain. So here I am, mooing away.

"Okay, Audrey. Big push now. Go, go, go!" Josephine urges. I groan out in excruciating pain as I grit my teeth, giving everything I've got to get this baby out.

"That's it, baby. Keep going." Donovan insisted on being in the tub with me. At first, I was unsure. Not because I didn't want him to be, but because I didn't want him to be grossed out. Well, I was wrong. This man isn't grossed out by anything. During the birth of our first, he was wide-eyed and fascinated by every part of the birthing process, asking the doctors and nurses a million questions like he was the one about to deliver our baby. As if I couldn't fall more in love with the man.

So, I gave in and told him he could be in the tub. And thank god he's in here with me because doing this without an epidural is hard as hell. But every praise from his lips and every reassuring touch gets me through it. How did I get so lucky with Donovan King?

"The head is crowning, Audrey! And so much hair!" Josephine beams. I reach down and feel the baby's head. An explosion of a smile blasts across my face. "Donovan, the baby's almost here! I'm doing it," I whisper as he kisses my temple.

"You're fucking doing it, baby. Such a goddamn rockstar." I take a beat to rest between contractions, leaning my head back into the crook of Donovan's neck. We wanted to be surprised and find out the gender once our baby is out. We restrained ourselves with our first born and it was so worth it. I've come to love surprises over the years, so this is one that I could get behind.

The tightening in my uterus revs up again, prompting another contraction to rip through me. Donovan peppers kisses on my shoulder, whispering praises in my ear as I push. A burning fire flames through me as I yell out in a feral war cry. "That's it, mama! Head is out!" Josephine's eyes meet mine as I gasp for air, nodding my head at her to keep going. "You're almost there. Go, baby. Go!" Donovan cheers, working the pads of his thumbs into my shoulders as I push through another contraction.

I'm so tired I feel like stopping, but I've come so far. I've worked this hard. Every push is a second closer to meeting our baby. A piece of Donovan and me. The best parts of us. As I feel his warmth pressed against my back, I'm reminded of the deep, soul connection that tethers us. I feel his love for our family. The family we've dreamed of creating together. He's the best dad and gives me all the motivation to not give up on myself.

I told myself years ago that giving up was never an option. No matter how hard life got, I'd always push through and overcome because I am a goddamn survivor. Giving birth is the most raw and primal experience I've ever gone through, and with Donovan holding me as I give him another child, I feel like the most powerful woman in the world.

"Gahhh!" I roar in the most guttural way when suddenly—I feel no pain. I reach down instinctively and feel the soft skin of a newborn. "Oh, my god!" I cry out, scooping my baby from underwater, straight onto my chest. Right on my heart.

You did it, Audrey. Go you.

With a few firm back rubs, the most beautiful sound in the world echoes off the walls of our bathroom. Nothing compares to hearing your baby's first cry. And this one's got a set of lungs.

"It's a girl!" Josephine beams with tears in her eyes. I couldn't have done this without her, too. She's become one of my closest friends since she moved to Oakwood Valley three years ago, when I met her at a baby birthing workshop she was hosting. We automatically hit it off and became instant friends.

"It's a girl?! Baby! It's a girl!" I croon, turning my head to face Donovan. He kisses me so tenderly, shooting all the love he has for me through one kiss. "You did it, Mouse. You were amazing," he praises, grazing his fingers through our daughter's hair. "Hey honey tulip, welcome to the world," he murmurs. Donovan and I lock eyes, instantly sending me into the happiest of sobs that shake my whole body.

Our honey tulip.

I look down at our daughter, our dream girl. Her hair is lighter than our first born whose hair came out looking exactly like daddy's. Her sweet, chubby fingers wrap around mine, holding onto me as if she were telling me, *"Hi, mama."* I lean down and kiss her cherub cheek as her cries fade, turning into sweet newborn coos. I take a deep inhale of the top of her head, wishing I could bottle up that smell forever.

"Josephine, can you send him in now, please? I want to see him." Josephine nods with a smile, quietly exiting the bathroom. Donovan wraps his arms around both of his girls, his chin resting on my shoulder. For a moment we breathe each other in, basking in the perfect bliss that is our daughter.

"She's so gorgeous. Exactly like her mama," Donovan murmurs, stroking our daughter's hair. "I love you, Audrey. So much."

"I love you more. Congrats, daddy," I breathe, smiling against Donovan's lips as I prompt him for another kiss. The door clicks open and I hear a patter of precious steps coming to the edge of the tub.

"Mama!"

"Hey big brother," I coo, puckering my lips to get a sloppy kiss from my toddler. His smile lights up the room, showing off the sweetest dimples he inherited from his daddy. "Hey little man, come here," Donovan says, kissing our son's forehead.

His eyes go wide when they land on his newest sibling. "Sistuh?" he asks, pointing his finger at her with the most adorable expression. His big blue eyes stare in curiosity, peeking over the tub at the little wonder.

I smile, nodding my head. "Yes, James. That's your little sister."

Grace strides in, her hands flying to her cheeks with her mouth agape. If my mother were here, she'd have the same expression. But I love Grace like my own mother, and I'm so grateful for her.

"Oh, my goodness gracious. She is so beautiful, Audrey. Great job, mama," she cries, kneeling at the side of the tub, wrapping her arms around James. "Congrats to you too, dad," she teases Donovan, who chuckles. "Thanks Mom, but Audrey was an absolute warrior. I've never seen anything like it." He presses a soft kiss into my shoulder as Josephine comes over, wrapping a baby blanket over us.

"It's true. She was really amazing. I'm so proud of you, Audrey," Josephine says with a sweet smile, settling into a chair at the end of the tub.

"Sistuh name?" James asks, gently rubbing his sister's back. The gesture is so heartwarming, I just know it in my bones that he is going to be the best big brother.

Exactly like his namesake.

Donovan meets my gaze as he flashes me my favorite dimpled grin. We both nod in unison, looking down at our baby. The morning sun greets us, and a sunray shines over our daughter like a greeting from up above. The strawberry flecks in her hair glow as she peacefully sleeps in my arms. I glimpse out the window, as if I know that sunray. I smile.

Hi, mama.

I look at my son, who can't take his eyes off of his new sister. I take a deep breath and count backward from five. Settling in this moment.

"Her name is Wren. Wren Violet King."

Thank you so much for letting Audrey and Donovan into your lives. I hope you love them as much as I do. If you'd like a cheeky bonus scene that takes place one month after their proposal as they get ready for their engagement party, subscribe to my mailing list! You'll get it straight in your inbox. Subscribe here:

I'm not ready to leave Oakwood Valley just yet! Surprise! You don't want to miss Logan and Tia's story, which will be book two of this series—coming at the end of 2024!

What to expect with Logan and Tia's book:
    College best friends to lovers
    Reformed playboy MMC
    Fierce and badass FMC
    Mutual pining
    She falls first, he falls harder

Acknowledgments

If you're reading this, you've just made my dreams come true. It means you've taken the time to read my art, my hard work, my ultimate passion. I can't believe I've finished my first novel! I am in complete awe and extremely humbled by the support and the whole journey. There was no way I could've done any of this alone.

To my editor and friend, Abby. This was truly OUR project. You believed in me and in Audrey and Donovan's story from the very beginning, when they were just scattered thoughts on a Google doc. You've pushed me, challenged my thinking, and stretched my writing brain beyond anything I could've ever expected. You helped me find my voice, my style, and my heart in every word. This book would not be what it is if it weren't for you. Thank you for tolerating my shenanigans, late night thoughts, and love for steak. Thank you for your respect, friendship, and your goddamn genius brain. I am forever grateful for our paths to have crossed, and to call you my friend.

To my beta readers. My girls! Grace, Paige, Kelsey, and Karah. Thank you for being my number one fans and reading my book in its ugliest form. You all helped shape Audrey and Donovan's story into what it is. Your reactions, thoughts, and feedback were nothing short of entertaining and helpful. Hearing your compliments and affirmations kept me motivated throughout my writing process, and really pushed me to keep being the best version of myself that I can be. I love y'all so much! Thank you, thank you, thank you!

To my designers Anya and Morgan. I mean, wow. How lucky am I to have both of your artistic brains in my corner? You both captured this book to a T. From the cover design, the color schemes, to the website and author branding, you two deserve all the flowers. Thank you for sharing your art with me, and now with the world!

To the man, the myth, and the legend formatter extraordinaire, Bob! Man, am I glad Abby connected us. You have been the most helpful and supportive person. Thank you for your wisdom, your advice, and for making my book look like magic! You never made me feel stupid for asking questions, and your guidance through this whole new author thing put me at ease. Thank you so much for your time and generosity.

To my wonderful friend and PR baddie, Jess! You were such a God-send. Working with you has been such a joy, and my book wouldn't be possible without your help. Thank you for believing in my vision and dedicating yourself to indie authors all around. You are a true example of rising tides raises all ships. Thank you for your humility, hard work, and passion for the book community.

To the ARC readers who took a chance on a new author and her debut novel, I owe you everything! Your reviews and thoughts of this story truly warmed my heart. Thank you for spreading the word, and for your respect and honesty. I appreciate you all so, so much.

To the readers and my friends! That's you! Thank you from the bottom of my heart for reading my book. All the texts, DMs, comments, likes, and shares do not go unnoticed! You are the reason this book even has any attention at all. I cherish every conversation with every new person I've connected with through socials. I hope you felt my support for you as much as I felt yours for me. And to my friends outside of the book world—you guys are the best. The book club talks, the hype, the LOVE?! I don't deserve it. But just like Audrey says, I deserve it simply because I just do. Thank you.

To my family, who gave me their unwavering support throughout this journey. I was a mess of nerves to share that I'd be writing a romance novel—especially with the amount of spice in this book! But at the end of the day, you all wanted what was best for me and hyped me up the entire time. Thank you for believing in my dreams. And a special thanks to my mom and dad who unknowingly were buying me romance novels since I was fifteen. You're the reason I am in love with this genre and sparked my ultimate passion for reading! Oops! Love you all so much.

And last, to my real life book boyfriend—my husband, Travis. I wrote Donovan with you in mind. Every good part of him, every bit where people can fall in love with him? That's you, babe. You are my entire world, my motivation, my best friend. I truly could not have gotten through this without you. You took every crazy idea I had and said, "Fuck yeah. Do it, babe." You are our daughter's fiercest protector. We feel so safe with you, and every MMC I write will forever be 'Trav-coded'. I love you, daddy. Thank you for safeguarding my dreams and nurturing them so that they can come true. Damn, I am a lucky woman.

Ginsa Michelle is a romance author who brings her vivid childhood dreams to life through her enchanting stories. Residing in Texas with her husband and daughter, she crafts tales set in quaint small towns where strong and complex heroines navigate love and life, keeping their charming heroes on their toes.

When not immersed in her writing cave, Ginsa can be found exploring new destinations with her family, igniting a passion for reading in children, and indulging in her favorite poke bowls.

Ginsa's passion lies in breathing life into her characters, making them feel like old friends who linger in your thoughts long after you've met them on the page. If you share her love for heartfelt stories and genuine connections, she invites you to join her newsletter for exclusive insights into her latest work. Welcome to her world!

Follow Ginsa on Instagram and TikTok: @authorginsamichelle.

www.ginsamichelle.com

Newsletter signup: